THEY CARVED A CIVILIZATION
OUT OF BLOOD AND STONE . . .

Echata—The fierce Anasazi warrior who embarked with his people on a breathtaking quest—sworn to uncover the ancient mysteries of Mesa Verde . . .

Li-Tia—The Chacoan medicine woman whose visions of a city of silent stone would bring adventure and a dangerous destiny with the leader of a rival tribe . . .

Dasiu—His dreams took him far from Mesa Verde and into a world where fortune beckoned—and where a brother's betrayal would lead to tragedy . . .

Xcinco—The son of a revered master builder, he possessed the secret of the great cliff dwellings. But his gift of prophecy would lead to exile . . . and the end of a civilization and a way of life. . . .

By the acclaimed author of *Yosemite, Grand Canyon* and the forthcoming *Yellowstone, Mesa Verde* is another chapter in the stunning saga of America's magnificent national parks.

WILLIAM W. JOHNSTONE
THE PREACHER SERIES

MESA VERDE

Gary McCarthy

Pinnacle Books
Kensington Publishing Corp.

http://www.pinnaclebooks.com

PINNACLE BOOKS are published by

Kensington Publishing Corp.
850 Third Avenue
New York, NY 10022

Pinnacle and the P logo Reg. U.S. Pat. & TM Off.

First Printing: June, 1997
10 9 8 7 6 5 4 3 2 1

Printed in the United States of America

*For Lonnie Beesley,
and the
"ancient ones" of Mesa Verde*

Preface

Since 1888 when the first pair of lost and nearly snow-blinded Colorado cowboys discovered them, the ancient cliff and mesa-top dwellings have been a source of continuous wonder and fascination. Mesa Verde National Park is the largest archaeological preserve in the United States and contains almost 3,900 sites, 600 of which are cliff dwellings. Archaeologists have determined that this was once the center of the great Northern San Juan Anasazi civilization, a thriving pre-Puebloan culture that existed for more than a thousand years.

So spectacular are these cliff dwellings and the remains of this ancient and highly evolved civilization that, in September of 1978, the World Heritage Convention of the United Nations selected Mesa Verde National Park to be a WORLD HERITAGE CULTURAL SITE—one of the first seven sites selected in the *world* for this esteemed cultural recognition.

I have chosen Cliff Palace, Mesa Verde National Park's grandest cliff dwelling, as the main setting of this Anasazi saga. And while there is still a great deal to learn about those industrious people, enough has been discovered to create realistic characters who would have lived at MESA VERDE across the unfolding of many difficult but triumphant centuries.

One

Southwest corner of Colorado
December 18, 1888

The man from the Mancos River Valley was nearly snow-blind as his pony picked its way across the high, windswept mesa. The animal's head was down, its ears back and its tail tucked tight between its legs as it followed a narrow cattle trail through a heavy stand of piñon and juniper pine that offered scant protection from the hard, biting wind.

"Richard, even cattle aren't stupid enough to be up here in this blizzard!" Charlie Mason yelled from behind. "Dammit, we gotta turn back!"

"Just a little farther," Richard called, steamy breath swirling in the wind.

"We can come back up here when the weather clears! Your pa won't hold us to blame!"

Richard Wetherill's father was a reasonable man but a dozen stray cattle were too important to lose. Furthermore, this wild mesa country still belonged to the Utes and, although they were friends of the pioneering Quaker family, the Indians always were hungry in winter.

"I'm telling you, we've *got* to turn back!"

But Richard ignored the cowboy, vowing instead to press on until he chanced upon the stray cattle or was blocked by the rim of a deep canyon. He pulled his hat down a little tighter, buried his beard deeper into the collar of his fleece-lined coat and let his horse plod onward, trusting that the cows were just up ahead.

They pushed on for another half hour, the wind twisting through the trees, the temperature holding steady as noon came . . . then passed. Richard was not worried about getting bogged down in drifts because the hard wind was sweeping the snow, dry as alkali and cold as starlight, off these high, tabletop mesas.

He'd never ridden into this country before. It was a wild land, said to be haunted by ancient Indian spirits who had left their dwellings high in the canyon cliffs where only eagles could nest. Richard had seen a few of these crumbling cliff houses and had marveled at their impossible placements. The dwellings usually were small, pressed back under the brow of some heavy rock and often difficult to find unless you really were searching for them. Most of the ones he'd come upon were tiny, more like storage sheds than houses. He'd tried unsuccessfully to enter them, on the outside chance that they might yield Indian treasures.

A sudden gust almost tore the hat from Richard's head and then the wind changed direction, slanting under the brim of his hat to plaster his beard and cheeks. Going on was madness.

Richard was just about to rein in when his bay gelding stopped, planted its feet and snorted with alarm. A moment later, Charlie's horse bumped against him and the cowboy's sharp exclamation was lost in the wind.

Magically, the blowing snow again changed direction and swirled upward suddenly to part like a shimmering lace curtain. Richard's jaw dropped as he stared eastward down into a canyon, perhaps a thousand feet deep and at least that far across. This, by itself, was no great surprise. Dozens of major canyons furrowed these mesas where spring snow melted and fed into the great lower river valleys. The astonishing thing was how the sun broke through the storm clouds with a brilliant bolt of shifting sunlight highlighting a cliff dwelling of such magnificence that it hardly seemed of this world.

Richard wasn't expert at guessing distances, but he judged that its protecting cavern was about four hundred feet wide and sixty feet high. Every inch of that immense amphitheater was filled by the ancient city.

Richard blinked twice and then, to make sure that his eyes weren't playing tricks on him, he scrubbed them with the back of his glove. When the sun-washed cliff dwelling remained, he leapt to the ground with such excitement that he would have slipped and tumbled to his death had he not made a desperate grab for the stirrup.

"Hey!" Charlie shouted. "What's going on! Are you all right up there!"

"Charlie," he answered, hauling himself back to his feet and gripping his saddlehorn for support. "Come look at this!"

"Did you finally spot 'em?" Charlie asked, dismounting to hurry forward. "Because . . . oh my God!"

They stood there in the snowstorm, two icicles breathing steam and with tears leaking from their staring eyes. The great cliff dwelling lay well-protected by an immense bowl-shaped cavern formed by a great, smoke-stained wedge of sandstone. And, even through the falling snow, Richard could see that the city was constructed of dozens of imposing buildings, some three and four stories high, many dotted with windows and connected by ramps, stairways and wooden ladders. Every inch of the cavern had been utilized by its builders, who must have labored for centuries to create this lost city of stone. Richard's attention fixed on a castle tower whose upper floors almost touched the smoke-blackened ceiling.

"How could anyone have done it?" Charlie asked.

"I don't know . . . but they did."

"But *why!*"

"I don't know that either," Richard answered, "but maybe we'll be able to find out when we get inside."

"We're going *in* there?"

"That's my intention."

"You go ahead. I'll keep looking for the cows."

Richard smiled to himself, knowing that Charlie wouldn't dream of separating in this foul weather so far from the ranch. He squinted, noting what appeared to be small storage or work areas farther back under the cavern, muddied up tight like a row of swallows' nests. Even more fascinating were the many open pits whose roofs had collapsed during the passing centuries. Though filled with debris, Richard could tell that they were perfectly round and rock-sided. Their function was a complete mystery.

"Do you suppose this is the place Acowitz kept telling us about?"

"It has to be," Richard answered, remembering the Ute's stories about a haunted city suspended in the sky. "It's like . . . a palace!"

"I've never seen a palace, but that must be what they look like," Charlie agreed. "It's a cliff palace, all right."

"And that's what we'll call it," Richard said, jamming his boot back into his stirrup and preparing to circle the canyon and reach the opposite side where they could descend into Cliff Palace.

But Charlie grabbed his boot, looked up and said, "That place has been there nearly forever. It isn't going to disappear on us now. So what about your cattle?"

"They'll bunch up until this storm passes," Richard said, pulling himself up into his saddle. "Charlie, imagine what we'll likely find inside that lost city."

"Maybe more than we want."

Richard looked down at the cowboy. "What do you mean?"

"According to Acowitz, Indians won't go near these old, abandoned places. They believe they're haunted by bad spirits."

"I don't believe in spirits."

"Well, I do! And how do you propose to enter that cavern, especially in this miserable weather."

"There *has* to be a safe trail we can follow down into it."

"Why?"

"Because," Richard said patiently, "obviously it was the home of hundreds of Indians and they had to go in and out every day for food and water. There will be an easy trail nearby and we just need to find it."

"But even if we do, maybe we won't be able to climb out again before dark."

Richard glanced at the sky. "The storm is breaking up and it's only a little past noon. We'll be fine."

Charlie wasn't pleased but he was game, so he followed Richard around the head of the canyon and up the opposite rim, stopping every few hundred yards to dismount and try to get his bearings until they were almost directly over the ancient city.

"We'll leave the horses saddled," Richard decided, returning an hour later after discovering a trail down to the cliff dwelling. "I found their trail and, in the worst places, it looks as if they've cut foot and handholds into the face of the cliff. All I'll have to do is clear away a little ice and snow."

"And while you're doing that, am I supposed to hold you by the ankles?"

Richard ignored the sarcasm. "Let's get our ropes. We'll probably need them in a few of the worst places."

But Charlie wasn't budging. "I signed at your Alamo Ranch to be a *cowboy,* not a mountain goat!"

"We'll take it slow and easy. If I fall, you can go back to the Alamo and tell everyone not to try to find my body until next spring."

"Don't worry, we won't."

Richard looped his lariat over his head and one shoulder and started down a worn but old and badly neglected Indian trail. He wished that he had better footwear than his slick, leather-soled riding boots. Had it been summertime, he would have removed them and gone barefoot. One careless misstep and he'd spiral down into the trees, rocks and heavy underbrush hundreds of feet below. His body would be mangled beyond recognition. Richard struggled to push that terrifying image out of his mind.

"Are you sure we ought to do this!" Charlie cried from above. "Doesn't it make a *lot* more sense to wait until the weather clears and all your brothers can enjoy this fun also?"

"We're the discoverers!" Richard shouted. "That means we've *earned* the privilege of having the first look!"

The cowboy offered a reply, but Richard didn't hear it; he was too focused on the slow, precarious descent. He reminded himself again and again that this trail must have been used by women and children as well as by the men who had hunted and farmed on the mesas.

Here and there, the trail crossed the sheer face of a rock, but the toeholds and handholds were deep and solid. Wherever there were abrupt switchbacks that required some dicey maneuvering, Richard discovered that he had to begin with the correct foot or he'd be stuck and have to make a dangerous adjustment. It occurred to him that enemy raiders, unfamiliar with the intricacies of the footholds and handholds, also would have experienced difficulties. Cliff Palace would have been almost impossible to attack; enemies would have had to resort to a very long siege.

Only once did Richard nearly topple to his death, and that was when he was finally poised at the entrance of the cavern. His boot slipped from the last toehold and, had it not been for a crack in the rock where he plunged his gloved hand, he would have been lost.

"Watch your last few steps and keep your eyes on your footing!" Richard shouted as he jumped onto a well-worn stone platform.

The wind fell silent, the cavern was eerie and hushed. Richard's heart began to race and he felt so unsteady that he slumped to his knees to place his hands into the rippled powder that covered the floor like ocean foam. He closed his eyes, breathed deeply and then concentrated, listening to ancient voices that whispered from the rocks. Time lost all meaning and his head rocked forward. *What were they saying?* Despite the cold, sweat beaded on his skin and his senses whirled like smoke, as voices, joyous but more often sorrowful, called from every stone.

"Richard! Hey, where'd you go? Did you make it?"

He did not wish to be pulled from this frightening but spiritual reverie. *What were the voices saying?*

"Richard! Answer me! Are you all right!"

The voices died, leaving him alone, cheeks damp with cold tears. "I'm all right! Keep coming, Charlie!"

Rising to his feet, Richard forced himself to concentrate on this amazing archaeological discovery. For the first time, he noted how the walls were glazed with pinkish plaster. Much of it had eroded away, leaving exposed sections that demonstrated how the walls were tied together with mortar and thousands of small "chinking" stones to level and balance everything above the foundations. And, while nearly half of the city was a maze of cobble and ruin, what remained was the toil and love of centuries. Everywhere he turned, Richard noted proud and graceful stairways, plazas, houses and towers, all crowded around him, as if to protect the deep, mysterious pits. There were dozens of them! Were they storage bins for food, or holding areas for domesticated animals? Maybe children were raised in these places for their own self-protection. Or perhaps the more than a dozen open pits were constructed for worship . . . and human sacrifice.

He closed his eyes and concentrated, desperate to learn the mysteries that crowded around him, but the spirit voices were silent.

"Wow!" Charlie shouted. "Would you just *look* at what we've found here!"

Richard opened his eyes. The spell was gone. Maybe later, when he was alone, the aura would return.

Charlie placed both hands on his lean hips and pivoted completely around, head thrown back, mouth hanging open. "It's almost like . . . like being in a big church."

"Almost."

Richard felt a powerful, magnetic force pull him to the edge of one of the huge, rock-lined pits. A section of ladder fed down to the bottom and he gripped it, afraid of what he might discover below.

"I wouldn't go down in there, if I were you," Charlie warned.

"Why not?"

"Could be lots of people buried in these big holes."

"I don't think so."

"Well, then, they might be dangerous. Could even be snake pits."

"I don't see any snakes."

Charlie nervously licked his lips; his head swiveled back and forth and he pressed closer. "Do you think the people who built this place were wiped out by other Indians and maybe thrown down in these big holes, then buried alive?"

"That doesn't seem very likely."

"Why not?"

"Well, given the trail leading down—and the fact that enemies would have had to descend in single file—an all-out attack would have been nearly impossible."

"Yeah, I suppose so," Charlie agreed. "But maybe Apache came and starved these people to death by camping up on the mesa. Or else kept whoever lived here from getting water."

"I don't even know if there were Apache in this country that long ago."

"That's how the Apache would have done it. They'd have made camp on the mesa above and just waited these cliff people out, no matter how long it took."

"They also might have died of a great sickness," Richard

said. "I read that white man's sicknesses wiped out a lot of the Eastern Indians."

"Jaysus, Richard! If it was a sickness, maybe it's still around here. Could be that's why the Ute won't come near these cliff dwellings and maybe why we shouldn't either!"

"I'll stay and take my chances. But go on back to the horses, if you want. I'll be along."

"Naw, I'll stick with you. Besides, we're about as likely to find a lost fortune of Indian gold as getting a disease that ain't been fed for a couple of thousand years and probably starved itself to death."

"Yeah," Richard replied, "I suppose that's the best way to look at it."

"Besides, the wind has really picked up and the snow is blowin'. Be a bad time to climb back out alone."

Richard gazed out across the canyon. What a breathtaking panorama these people must have enjoyed every day of their lives. In the summertime, the broad-leafed packed canyon floor would have offered shade when the cliff dwellers tired of this cavern. Along the canyon floor there would be a sweet, icy stream that fed the heavy forest, each tree striving for sunlight. A few months earlier, this canyon would have been ablaze with autumn colors. Then these industrious people would have harvested piñon nuts up on the mesa. And the vista he beheld put to shame any Currier and Ives Christmas print.

Somewhere behind him, Richard heard Charlie bumping around in the ruins. But his eyes were held by the scenery. On the opposite cliff he admired the stubborn, snow-dusted trees which clung to vertical rock asking no quarter in their struggle for survival.

"Wanna start poking around?" Charlie called.

"Go ahead."

"You just gonna keep standing there?"

"Yep."

"You all right?"

"Just fine."

"I bet there's bodies buried all over this place. Spooky as hell, ain't it!"

Richard decided that the storm was heading south. A flicker of movement caught his eye and he watched as a pair of mule deer stepped gingerly out from the trees down in the canyon. Warily, they looked all around, never suspecting they were being observed from several hundred feet overhead. In a moment, ghostlike, they glided into heavy forest.

Richard drew a deep, cold draught of air into his lungs wondering how many people had once stood protected from winter snows to gaze into the canyon. And why, in God's great name, had they even come here when, less than a hundred miles south, there were warm, fertile valleys? An ancient people would not have lived here for the view; they would have been struggling for survival. Richard could not imagine anyone voluntarily entering this harsh country unless fleeing a stronger, warlike civilization.

"Richard, come look at this pot!"

"Be right along."

How many had lived here and for how long? They would have hunted out the mule deer. There also were mountain sheep, cougar, bear and varmints, but not enough to feed a population large enough to build and maintain Cliff Palace.

"I'll bet we could get rich just selling nothing but these old pots!" Charlie called, his voice echoing through the ruins. "They ain't *all* broken."

Richard turned back to the city uneasily. Was it wrong to disturb this place? If he did not, eventually others would. And, while he might be able to disturb, even collect old Indian pots and old weapons, what if they did find bodies or a great treasure? As a boy, he had learned how Cortez and Pizarro had murdered, then plundered ancient civilizations, but this was very different; the people were already long dead.

Nearby was a huge, four-storied house that actually touched the rooftop. Richard decided to begin his exploration there. He climbed slowly up through rooms connected by narrow passageways, stairs and ladders. The passageways were all T-shaped, made for small people. Richard had to duck, in order to pass from room to room.

Some of the windowless rooms were very dark, but when moving through them, Richard could feel that every interior wall had been plastered and the floors worn as smooth as glass. Emerging from a narrow passageway between two high walls, he came face to face with a perfectly symmetrical tower. He found a doorway and entered a spacious first-floor room filled with jars and pots. One corner of the room had crumbled, but the others were intact and painted red above white. The room was decorated by what appeared to be a line of peaks jutting out of a distant horizon. Between the peaks were a series of triangles and dots which must have been very important but whose meaning was now lost. Was this all a map, perhaps of the place where these people had originated . . . or had gone?

The more he pondered the mystery, the more frustrated Richard became. All he really could say for certain was that a talented artist had once inhabited this amazing and beautiful tower compartment. The person who had lived here had been very important, for no other rooms were decorated with these haunting symbols. He noted a row of beautifully decorated pots filled with what appeared to be dyes and paintbrushes made out of what looked to be the fiber of the yucca plant.

He traced his fingertips over the designs, as if that might pass the ancient knowledge along, but it didn't, and he sighed with frustration, feeling the presence of a kind but powerful aura. He leaned back against the cool stone wall, his mind racing. *Who were you? What good was all this if its meaning is forever lost? What are you trying to tell me? If I were smart enough to understand these symbols, would they tell me the story of your life . . . and death? Or were you just adding beauty to your world?*

Confused and strangely elated, Richard retreated from the

studio and scrambled up a stairway leading to the pinnacle
of the tower. Some sixty feet above the cavern floor, he
gripped a broken ledge and beheld all of Cliff Palace, struggling to comprehend an artist's ancient legacy. Failing that,
he returned to the cavern's floor and began to explore other
compartments, gradually working his way deeper under the
overhang of rock. He discovered scattered bones, piles of
pottery shards, and cooking pits filled with ashes . . . but no
human skulls or skeletons. Richard had no psychic powers,
but he felt the presence of women more than men in these
ruins. The evidence of their habitation was abundant in the
form of reed baskets which were scattered everywhere,
mostly in the final stages of deterioration. Their pottery, however, remained in excellent condition. It was gray and molded
into many interesting forms and sizes. There were corrugated
cooking pots fired with a shiny, black glaze. There were any
number of large water and storage jars, elaborately decorated
with simple yet elegant geometric designs. There were mugs,
ladles and small-necked pitchers, sometimes displaying clay
scrolls and animals. These people thought utility should in-
clude beauty. Richard also uncovered awls, scrapers and
fleshers used for scraping skins.

In one room, he discovered piles of corncobs picked clean
by either humans or varmints. *So,* he thought, *these Indians
were primarily farmers. But where did they grow food, and
how did they irrigate during the short growing season?*

Charlie appeared. "Dammit, I haven't seen any gold or
silver. Not a speck!"

Richard collected his thoughts. "Be patient and keep looking."

"If we find gold, will Mr. Wetherill let me keep some of
it?"

"Of course."

Charlie nodded with relief. "It'd be only fair that I get an
equal share. And I'll bet the Indians who lived here hid their

treasures high up in those little rock rooms but I can't figure a way to get up there without wings."

"I doubt they hold anything of value," Richard said, studying the nearly inaccessible ceiling level compartments. "We can worry about them some other time."

Charlie hurried off as Richard entered a tall, graceful tower reaching up almost to the center of the cavern's great, smoke-stained roof. He noted that every stone had been expertly chiseled round so that the column had perfect symmetry. He began to climb stairways and pass through a succession of smaller rooms.

In one, the light from the window chanced upon a storage niche where Richard uncovered an impressive stone axe. When he went over to a window to get better light, he noted how the stone axe head had been grooved to be bound to its thick wooden handle with stretched rawhide. The axe was well-balanced; as he waved it this way and that, it seemed to have its own life. Richard was startled and actually dropped the weapon. Sheepishly, he picked it up, running his fingers over its sharp blade.

How many animals had this axe brought down? How many enemies? What kind of warrior would have had the skill and patience to fashion such a handsome weapon?

Richard replaced the axe and continued his exploration. When he reached the top of the round tower, he recoiled at the sight of a human skeleton. In the dry, cool air of the cavern, the body had not fully decomposed and there were tufts of coarse black hair and fragments of parchment-like skin which had not been completely nibbled away by rodents. The body rested in a sitting position, rib cage pressed into pelvis, skull tilted forward on an outstretched arm. It seemed to be reaching toward him. Fighting down panic, Richard glanced aside to see pots filled with more brushes and chisels.

My God, he thought, *this is the artist!*

As his eyes passed back and forth between the skeleton and the pots with their artist's supplies, he shivered. Backing away, he ducked through the uppermost doorway and hurried down to the cavern floor.

"Somethin' wrong?" Charlie asked, hurrying over.

"No."

"Are you sure? You look like you seen a ghost."

"Not yet," Richard relied, forcing a smile. "Did you find any gold or silver in that upper storage ledge?"

"Nothin'."

"Don't give up. They wouldn't have left it just laying around."

"I suppose not. You think they might have hidden it down in one of those big pits?"

"It's possible."

"I sure don't want to climb down inside one. I'll keep looking around up here," Charlie said, taking off again.

Still shaken by the sight of the skeleton, Richard continued his search. As he meandered in and out of compartments and picked his way through rubble, he realized that many of the structures were inaccessible; their roofs had collapsed and they'd become cluttered with mortar, fallen timbers and building stones. In the courtyards and on the open balconies, he found many grinding as well as cutting and scraping stones. But, most startling, he discovered an exquisite shell necklace.

"Charlie!" he shouted, holding the treasure aloft. "These people must have traded all the way to the Gulf of Mexico or even the Pacific Ocean. Can you imagine!"

Charlie stuck his head out of a window with a downcast expression that told Richard his friend cared only for gold. "I still haven't found any treasures! Just pots, bones and stuff."

Richard nodded and went to stand beside one of the many round pits. Squatting on his heels, he studied the wreckage below. "Charlie, notice how the roof timbers are blackened by soot. It's my guess that these people lived down there in the coldest time of winter. Those rock-sided walls would hold the heat better than anything built above ground."

Charlie wasn't really interested. "I don't think we're going to find any gold or silver. Maybe we'd better be thinking of climbing back out of here before the light fails and we are stuck in this ghost town."

"You know what I'm thinking?"

"Nope."

Richard swung around, eyes reaching back into the canyon. "I think our Cliff Palace was the center of this whole civilization. There probably are other cliff dwellings nearby."

"Really?"

"Yep. And maybe that is where we'll find their real treasures."

"You could be right." Charlie stared out into the canyon. "It's stopped snowing."

"Then why don't we climb back up to the horses and take a ride around before dark?"

"I'm not coming back down here again tonight."

"We'll camp up on the rim," Richard decided. "It just makes sense because we'd be in a terrible fix if a bear or a cougar spooked our horses and stranded us afoot."

Charlie nodded in vigorous agreement.

Overcoming his urge to linger and explore more carefully, Richard retraced their difficult path back up to the rim. Their climb went easier now that they knew what to expect and, when they reached their horses, Richard judged they still had a couple of hours left before nightfall.

"Tell you what," he said, "let's separate and ride in opposite directions. We'll both turn back just before sundown and make camp here."

"Don't get lost," Charlie warned, "or go hikin' down any more Indian trails by your lonesome. If you fell, I'd most likely never find you."

"I won't," Richard promised.

He rode away, shadowing the rim and peering hard across the canyon, trying to detect an old Indian trail that might lead down to another city. The temperature was plunging with the sun but Richard felt only anticipation as he imagined how today's discovery might improve his Quaker family's difficult circumstances. The hundreds, perhaps thousands of Indian artifacts in Cliff Palace could be sold for more money than could be made raising cattle. And now that he wasn't surrounded by spooks and spirits, selling to the highest bidder seemed like the only reasonable thing to do.

Besides rich Eastern collectors, there were big museums that would want everything the Wetherills could scratch and haul out of Cliff Palace. Maybe they could even file claim on this mesa and charge admission! And, if there were more nearby ruins—and he was sure there were—they could all become very wealthy.

The storm was passing, the sky filling in blue around scattering storm clouds. Richard knew there soon would be a spectacular sunset. It all would have been perfect, except, as he rode along searching for new lost cities, he was being nagged by what he could define only as a silly but persistent sense of responsibility. Worst of all, he wasn't even exactly sure *what* responsibility. Artifacts aside, the structures of Cliff Palace themselves deserved protection, didn't they? Otherwise, booty hunters would ransack, trample and desecrate the place. They would turn that ancient city upside down to steal all the pots, even the broken ones. They'd probably even attempt to chip away the art work and collect that artist's old bones.

I can't let that happen, he thought with a rising sense of panic. *Or can I?*

Thoughts ajumble, Richard was nearly swept from his horse by a low-hanging limb that knocked his hat flying and made his ears ring. He dismounted and retrieved the hat, then turned to spot another cliff dwelling.

He led his horse over to the rim, absently fingering a rising knot on his forehead. He stared hard, noting that this cliff dwelling was a miniature of Cliff Palace, its most striking features those same round subterranean cavities. Now Richard was sure that they had been used for winter living quarters because several of these were still covered with ladders protruding from the center of their rooftops. Because of the physical characteristics of this cavern, these ruins were in an excellent state of preservation. As best he could tell from a far distance, many of the structures were completely intact, with the same distinctive T-shaped doors he had squeezed through at Cliff Palace.

The sun was nearly on the horizon and it was too late to explore this new ruin, so Richard had to content himself with counting the structures. There were eight pits and well over a hundred separate rooms with more hidden farther back and veiled in darkness. This ruin was positioned near the head of a canyon where the trees and vegetation were especially thick, a clear indication of abundant water, probably stemming from an underground spring.

Richard's weary horse stomped its front hoof with impatience, twisted its neck around and whinnied pitifully for its companion as the sky melted into a buttery vermillion.

I've got to turn back and make camp with Charlie, he told himself as he slowly remounted his impatient horse, *but I'll remember this day for the rest of my life. Things will never be the same.*

Richard didn't sleep well that night and neither did Charlie, judging from his worn early morning expression. But they both were so excited they had no complaints. Hungry and with exhausted horses, they decided not to return to either of the newly discovered cliff dwellings but instead turned home toward the Alamo Ranch. On the way, they discovered a third cliff dwelling, small but visually dramatic with its square, many-storied tower soaring above a collection of ruined compartments and the now-familiar round pits.

"There's no way up or down from it!" Charlie exclaimed.

"There has to be," Richard argued. "We just can't see it.

There must be toeholds and handholds dug out of the rock all the way up to the rim, just like we found leading down to Cliff Palace."

"We aren't going to explore *that* one, are we?"

"No," Richard said. "Not without help."

Charlie sighed with relief. "*If* you and your brothers ever manage to get down there, you can tell me what you found. *If* you make it back out."

"We'll name this one Square Tower House. It may be small but it's the most beautiful one yet."

Before Charlie could reply, Richard reined his horse toward home.

Two

Denver, 1889

Andrew Cannaday ripped open the letter from his archaeologist friend and mentor at the Smithsonian Institution and devoured the letter's contents. He then rushed back to his modest office on Larimar Street to discover his wife accepting their first commission from the vice president of the Bank of Colorado.

"Have a nice day, Mr. Oberlander!" Lisa called, giving the man a smile warm enough to melt ice. "We look forward to hearing from you soon!"

"Oh, you shall!" the banker called, shaking Andrew's hand as he edged toward the open door. "Fine work, Mr. Cannaday! We're *very* pleased."

"I'm delighted to hear that," Andrew answered.

"Yes indeed," the banker said. "I predict that you and Mrs. Cannaday are going to prosper. I understand that you also assay ore samples and write geological reports for a few of the larger mining companies up in Central City."

"That's right," Andrew said. "We're small, but diversified."

"That's very wise," Oberlander said. "It never pays to depend on any one client, not even the Bank of Colorado. But rest assured that, if you consistently provide this level of expertise and service, you'll have our repeat business."

"And, in return, you'll be our top priority."

Oberlander smiled, tipped his hat to Lisa and passed through the door.

"Three hundred dollars!" Lisa squealed, waving the check overhead and doing a little jig as the door closed. *"Three hundred!"*

"And they got a bargain. I'll take you out to dinner tonight in celebration."

Lisa kissed his cheek. "See, I told you that if we worked hard and were willing to take a few risks, success was assured."

"We haven't made it yet," Andrew reminded her. "To get this business started, we're up to our necks in debt. And this first check is just a drop in the bucket. I'm still not sure that I shouldn't have taken a job for a few years, *then . . ."*

"Shhhh! We'll be fine," she interrupted. "A year from now, we'll have everything paid off and be well on our way. And, in five years, you'll have captured *all* the important geological and assay work within a hundred miles of Denver."

"Oh, really?" he asked, eyebrows rising.

"Yes, really," she said with full assurance. "And *then,* the day will come when you can go back into archaeology and . . ."

"We can go back into it," he said. "Remember, that's what brought us together in the first place. If you hadn't been visiting the Smithsonian, we'd never have met."

"I know. And I'll never give up on the idea of us founding a great museum right here in Denver. You'll be the director and . . ."

"Whoa!" he exclaimed. "Aren't we getting ahead of things?"

Lisa blushed, feeling sheepish. "I suppose you're right. It's just that all my life I've wanted to be a part of something important."

"Did your father understand that before he died?"

"Oh, yes. Without his help, I'd never have been able to

travel to the East and visit my aunt . . . and all the wonderful museums."

"I can't imagine us not meeting and falling in love. My life has not been the same since then."

"And you're not sorry you left the Smithsonian and came out West to marry me?"

"Don't be silly! It's just been very difficult this first year." She again waved the check before his eyes. "Stop fretting so much. This is only the beginning, Andrew. Only the beginning."

Lisa playfully mussed his long, black hair, thinking again how devilishly handsome her husband was and how expert in his survey and geological work. Yes, Andrew worried to excess, but that would change when they began to whittle down their debts and then to prosper. She would see that they both kept their noses to the grindstone, eyes fixed on their dream.

"Maybe we should deposit this check now," Andrew suggested.

"Yes, and I was wondering—do you think it might be wise to visit Denver National Bank tomorrow and drop hints that your work has been well received by their biggest competitor?"

"Too obvious." Andrew took a deep breath. "Lisa, something else quite wonderful just happened."

"Another commission?"

"Well, not exactly," he hedged.

"Then what?"

"I just received a very important letter," he told her, withdrawing it from his pocket. "It's from Dr. Turner."

Lisa's smile faded. Brilliant, handsome and opinionated, Michael Turner had been Andrew's superior at the Smithsonian. She had grown sick and tired of hearing about the man's impressive credentials and revolutionary hypothesis on ancient civilizations. To Lisa's way of thinking, Michael

Turner's conceit was larger than the great pyramids of Egypt. "And what does the exalted Dr. Turner want?"

"The letter is not from him as much as it is from the Smithsonian," Andrew replied. "And it could change the course of our lives."

"What makes you think we ought to change anything?"

"Honey," he said, "I know that you never cared for Michael, but . . ."

"What does he want?"

"Have you ever heard of the Mancos Valley?"

"Yes, it's on the far side of the Rocky Mountains, several hundred difficult miles from here."

Andrew's expression reflected disappointment. "That's too bad. From the tone of Michael's letter, it's clear that he doesn't realize their discovery is that far from Denver."

"What discovery?"

Andrew unfolded the letter. He skipped the salutation and began to read:

> *A rancher named Mr. Richard Wetherill claims to have found the extensive ruins of an ancient culture in a place called Mesa Verde, which is Spanish for "green tabletop." He has described these ruins in great detail and offered their artifacts to us at prices which—if they are authentic and in the condition reported—would be extremely attractive to the Smithsonian or any other reputable museum.*
>
> *Unfortunately, we receive many such claims of discovery; almost all are gross exaggerations. Therefore, we are reluctant to devote the time or the funds to visit Mr. Wetherill and several extensive ruins which he glowingly describes as being built into the faces of immense sandstone cliffs.*
>
> *As you well know, previous modest discoveries of cliff dwellings in New Mexico and Arizona were looted centuries ago, and now yield little of scientific value. Mr.*

Wetherill says his ruins and the hundreds of artifacts they house never have been touched by modern man. Would you be interested in investigating his claims?

The Smithsonian, of course, will reimburse you a modest amount for travel expenses. If the Wetherill discovery is as promised, we will be doing archaeology a great service and enjoy extraordinary scientific opportunities. Please reply immediately by telegraph as to your interest and availability.

Andrew took a deep breath and looked up. "Michael goes on a few more paragraphs."

"I'm sure that he does," Lisa said. "But you must decline."

"Lisa!" he cried. "I can't do that!"

Lisa forced herself to remain calm. "Andrew, I have a check for *three hundred dollars*. You may never be reimbursed by the Smithsonian. We can't walk away from what we've been working so hard to do these past eighteen months, not just when we've finally gotten a whiff of real success."

"But what if these Mesa Verde ruins are as Mr. Wetherill has described? He claims they have never been violated!"

"Of course. And I can imagine how Mr. Oberlander would react if he has another job for us and we are off exploring on the far side of the mountains instead of taking care of business."

"We can stall Mr. Oberlander. We can make up some excuse for a short absence."

"No."

"This could be the opportunity of my lifetime!"

"*This* is your opportunity, Andrew! Can't you see that?"

He started to turn away in anger but she caught his sleeve. "I'm sorry, but we can't do this right now. Maybe next summer, if . . ."

"It *won't* wait! And it would require only a few weeks."

"Andrew, we've just earned our first commission!"

"I know. But what if Richard Wetherill and his family really have discovered enormous cliff dwellings. This could be my big chance to do something really important."

"Surveying and testing commercial downtown building sites is also important. Good heavens, tall buildings could be built upon those sites and one day collapse!"

"Yes, but there are others capable of doing those routine geological studies."

"Name just one."

"Darling," he said, taking her by the shoulders, "my real interest always will be in the field of archaeology. This is my chance to explore a site that has not been pillaged by generations of thieves and grave robbers."

Lisa sighed, knowing there would be no stopping him. And besides, she had once promised Andrew that, if he would agree to settle in Colorado, she would do everything possible to help him remain an archaeologist.

"Lisa," he was saying, "it could be like the honeymoon we couldn't afford. Don't you see that?"

"Yes," she heard herself reply because there was nothing she would rather do than to explore a great new archaeological site. She hadn't enjoyed formal education or scientific training, but she did share Andrew's love of archaeology. After arriving in Denver, when work was unavailable and they had too many hours to brood, they'd kept their sanity by prospecting for arrowheads or other artifacts in the nearby mountains. Those had been their happiest hours. Lisa well remembered Andrew's excitement when he made a discovery left by prehistoric Indian people.

"All right," she agreed, "we ought to be able to finish up things and leave by this weekend."

"Wonderful!" He grabbed and swung her around in a full circle. "Lisa, I swear it will be the opportunity of our lifetime."

"I hope so," she said when he put her down. "But you also have told me that most claims like this prove to be overblown or outright fabrications. I don't want you to be disappointed if Mr. Wetherill turns out to be a crackpot."

"I won't be," he promised. "Now, give me Mr. Oberlander's check and I'll hurry off to cash it before closing time."

"Why don't *I* do that?"

He feigned an injured look. "Don't you trust me?"

"Of course, but I also know you love to spend money almost as much as you worry about the lack of it."

"We'll cash the check together. And then we'll go shopping for provisions. Remind me to keep a record of our expenses for Michael."

"I'll do better than that," she promised. "I'll keep them myself."

"Good idea!"

Lisa knew that he had no intention of keeping records. Left to his own devices, he would have forgotten to keep any records and then have written Dr. Turner with some vague estimate of his real expenses. No, she would keep the record and the Smithsonian would pay for both of them to travel to the Mancos Valley.

Almost a week later, Lisa's dark eyes drank in the picturesque Mancos Valley. Their trip south to meet Richard Wetherill had been beautiful. After a train ride down to Trinidad on the Denver and Rio Grande Western Railroad, they'd boarded a stagecoach the same afternoon to Durango, a mining town that had prospered during the gold and silver strikes. Unlike many other boom and bust mining settlements, Durango had survived to become a trade and ranching center for much of southwestern Colorado.

Next, they'd spent two full days sightseeing and enjoying the hospitality of a quaint little Victorian boarding house before it was time to board the weekly mail coach to Cortez, passing into the fertile Mancos Valley.

The stage driver, a cheerful and talkative old man with big, blue-veined hands and a tobacco-stained gray beard, already had told them about the frontier town of Mancos which had been homesteaded by ranchers drawn by the valley's rich grass and plentiful water.

"About ten years ago, they had an Indian scare and built that there log fortress around the schoolhouse. That's where they figured to rally in case of an attack. But the Utes never returned and that was a damn good thing because these settlers jest never quite got around to putting up a fortress gate!"

Lisa studied the stockade with its missing gate. The fortress already was starting to fall down but she could well imagine the panic that these isolated settlers had felt being so far from an army fort or any other protection. It reminded her of how the West was still wild and largely untamed beyond the boundaries of towns like Denver and Santa Fe.

"Over there is the post office," the driver said, using his whip as a pointer. "And there's the general store and the saloon. Fellow by the name of Mr. George Bauer owns most everything in town . . . and he's gettin' rich."

The stage rolled up to the post office and the driver wasn't gone five minutes exchanging mail before their trip continued. During that time, Lisa was aware of the attention she was attracting from a number of cowboys who lounged up against porch posts. Some smiled shyly, but others puffed up their chests and threw back their shoulders.

"How far is it to the Alamo Ranch?" Andrew asked, trying to ignore all the posturing cowboys.

"About three miles," the driver answered as they rolled on through the little ranching town. "The Alamo Ranch sits on a pretty bench overlooking a bend in the Mancos River. It's a shiny place but it wasn't when they first settled. B. K. Wetherill and his wife Marion started out with less than a section of land but they've sure added to that over the past ten years or so. They're awful hardworking folks."

"So I heard in Durango," Andrew said.

"Yeah," the driver continued, "and you won't find the old

man or his sons hanging out at the saloon like most of the cowboys who work so hard making Mr. Bauer even richer. No sir! The Wetherill men are working fools. Why, they've planted hundreds of acres in oats, wheat and alfalfa. A tighter-fisted bunch you'll never find anywhere, but to hear 'em talk, you'd believe they were all facing starvation."

Lisa had to smile. "Is that right?"

"It is fer a fact," the driver said, spitting a long stream of watery tobacco juice at a clump of already well-stained sage.

When they finally saw the ranch house, it was impressive. Lisa could see that the original log cabin was now just a wing of the long, rambling house which was shaded by tall cottonwood trees and bordered by irrigated pastures. The house faced east toward barns and corrals, all backdropped by a line of majestic, snow-capped mountains beyond a sparkling river.

"My!" Andrew exclaimed, "they really *are* doing well!"

"Like I said, they're like most all Quakers, sober, tight-fisted, hardworking and mighty damned lucky to discover that old Injun stuff up at Mesa Verde that they've been selling to anyone with cash money."

"Have they sold much?" Lisa asked.

"Tons!"

The driver didn't notice the stricken expression on Andrew's face as he hauled his team to a stop beside a rutted road feeding a half mile up to the ranch house. "I'm sorry, folks, but company rules won't allow me to deliver you to the Wetherills' doorstep. Got to stay on this road and on schedule."

"This is fine," Lisa said, squeezing Andrew's arm and then giving him a gentle tug to pull him out of his dark thoughts.

"Are you sure you want to be left out here?" the driver repeated as they gathered their bags and prepared to walk a half mile up to the ranch house.

"We're sure," Andrew said. "It'll feel good to stretch our legs."

"If no one is home, just go inside and make yourself comfortable. It's fall roundup time and they might be driving cattle to market. Also, they travel a bit."

"We'll make do," Andrew said, picking up the heaviest bags.

"Good luck!" the driver shouted, cracking his whip.

They stood rooted, bags in hand, watching the wagon slowly disappear into the vast blue canvas of sky and sage. After a few moments, Andrew said, "This is pretty lonely country, isn't it."

"Very."

"But maybe we could get used to it. I mean, if we really *needed* to."

Lisa could tell by his expression that Andrew wanted a reassurance she couldn't offer. She'd never intended to be a ranch wife or a pioneering woman and doubted that she'd be good at either one, or happy. And yet, the idea of being away from Andrew for any length of time was unthinkable.

"We might as well go and see if anyone is home," Lisa said, taking up a bag in each hand and starting up the long, rutted road.

"Looks vacant," he said, catching up with her. "But I do see horses in the corrals so they can't be away for long. I've heard nothing but good things about this family," Andrew went on, trying to sound cheerful. "Everyone says the Wetherills are hardworking, God-fearing people as well as being outstanding ranchers."

"In addition to becoming grave-robbers and amateur archaeologists," Lisa said.

"You're right. But I'll keep my feelings to myself as long as they haven't completely altered or destroyed the site."

As they trudged up a rutted wagon track toward the ranch house, Lisa was torn by conflict. On the one hand, a big archaeological discovery would offer Andrew the professional opportunity of his lifetime. On the other hand, she loved Denver and had no desire to relocate to this scenic but sparsely populated country. Denver was where she wanted to raise a family. Besides, it offered great potential for Andrew's promising assay and surveying business. Lisa resolved to let God decide what was to be their future. He always knew what was best.

When they were still several hundred yards from the house, a dog appeared from under the front porch, a large, brown animal that barked for several minutes. Lisa wasn't afraid—its tail was wagging. A few minutes later, a middle-aged cowboy wearing chaps, run-over-at-the-heels boots and a Stetson, emerged from one of the barns. When he saw them, he sauntered forward with a smile on his sunburned face.

"Howdy, folks!" he called. "My name is Charlie Mason. What brings you clear out here to the Alamo?"

"We're from Denver," Andrew began, then quickly explained the purpose of their visit.

"Yeah," Charlie said, "Richard told me he was going to write the Smithsonian but none of us believed they'd even get the letter. He just addressed it to Washington, D.C."

"Is Mr. Wetherill around?"

"Nope. He's up at Mesa Verde along with his brother. The rest of the family has all gone over to Cortez to deliver cattle and won't be back for a couple of weeks."

"We can't afford to wait that long," Lisa said. "Is there some way that we could visit Mesa Verde tomorrow?"

"Sure! You could borrow a pair of our saddle horses."

"We'd pay you to be our guide," Andrew offered.

"I could use some extra cash, but I've got a busted axle to fix and some stock to tend."

Andrew's brow furrowed as he scanned the rugged mountains jutting up in all directions. "How far is Mesa Verde?"

"You can make it in a day. And we've been going up there so much since we discovered Cliff Palace last winter that the trail is easy to follow. No way that you could get lost."

"My husband is a fine scientist, but not a good rider," Lisa said, not wanting to offend. "Can you give him a gentle horse?"

"Old Stewy is as gentle as a milk cow."

"All right then?" Lisa asked, glancing up to Andrew.

"Sure. Sounds good. Maybe we need to pack some food."

"You'll need blankets and a few other things as well," Charlie said. "Gets right cool up there at night this early in the fall."

"We'd be grateful for anything you could provide," Lisa told the cowboy.

"Well, we can go inside and I'll brew a fresh pot of coffee," Mason said, "but maybe the first thing you'd like to do is to see the Indian stuff that we've already brought down from Cliff Palace."

Andrew stopped dead in his tracks. "You've actually stored some of it here?"

"That's right. In the barn and the house. We've sold a fair amount to local collectors and folks. I think they are even driving a wagonful over to Denver next spring. But . . ."

"I'd like to see it now," Andrew said, clipping off each word.

"Well then, just drop your bags and come along!" Charlie paused. "There might be one small problem."

"What kind?"

"It's about your wife," the cowboy hedged, looking quite uncomfortable. "I sure wouldn't want to upset her. Ma'am, there's Indian skeletons in there that . . ."

"I'll be fine," Lisa promised. "Don't worry."

"Yeah, but I'd feel plumb awful if you fainted . . . or got sick and chucked up your guts."

"Thank you for your concern, but I assure you that I am not squeamish and am every bit as interested as my husband in what you have to show us."

"Well then," the cowboy said, looking dubious, "come along 'cause we've got some things that will pop your eyes."

Lisa took her husband's hand as they followed the cowboy toward the barn. Andrew was practically walking on air.

"The light is poor in here and we've nailed up some of the things in wooden boxes that we can't open," Charlie was saying as he entered the small barn. "But other stuff we just laid out to appear as we found 'em."

"Oh my God!" Andrew whispered, coming to an abrupt halt in the doorway.

Lisa's jaw nearly dropped. Lined along one wall of the barn were the remains of at least a dozen Indians. Some of the skeletons were fairly intact; others were missing limb bones and major parts of their skulls. In some cases, the leg or arm bones did not even match.

"You found these buried at Mesa Verde?" Andrew asked in a hushed voice as he rushed forward, then dropped to his knees in front of the collection.

"A lot of 'em weren't buried except in the trash heaps we dug through," Charlie explained. "A few were buried and wrapped in skins or something. We learned to tell that because they had possessions."

"Where?"

"What do you mean?"

"I mean, where are their possessions?"

"Mostly in the boxes or we sold 'em or put the better ones in the house."

Lisa heard her husband's low oath.

"Is he gettin' sick?" Charlie asked, studying Andrew with a cocked eyebrow.

"No," Lisa answered, "it's just that he would like to have seen the bodies as they were buried and then matched possessions to their former owners."

"Why?"

Lisa took a deep breath. Her hand was resting on Andrew's shoulder and she could feel him trembling.

"Because," she said, mustering all her patience, "exactly

how things are placed in a burial site is very important to an archaeologist."

Andrew picked up an intact skull and examined it in a block of sunlight streaming through the barn door. Lisa watched her husband's fingers trace the seamed cranial bones, then come to rest on a molar worn down to a nub.

"Lisa," he whispered without looking up, "this skull is very old."

"How old?"

"At least five hundred years. Perhaps as many as a thousand. I can't really say."

"Then who could?" Charlie demanded.

Andrew shook his head, never taking his eyes off the skull. "Mr. Mason," he said in a strange, detached voice, "I think it might take years of study to answer your question."

"Years?"

"That's right."

Andrew had to struggle to pull his eyes from the skull. "Are those the boxes where you've stored other artifacts?"

"Yes."

"Pottery?"

"Sure, lots of it."

"What about weapons?"

"Most of them we sold or stored in the ranch house."

Andrew pushed to his feet and shakily ran his hand across his face. Lisa saw that he had grown pale.

"Are you all right?"

"Yes," he said in a hushed voice as he replaced the skull. "Mr. Mason, I'd like to see the pottery."

"Sure thing! Of course, there was a lot of reed baskets too, but they were so rotted they fell apart when we tried to bring them out."

Lisa heard Andrew's low, despairing moan.

"The best pots are in the house. You want to go in there and look at 'em while I get a fire going and make us that fresh coffee?"

"That would be fine," Andrew managed to say.

Lisa took his arm and they followed the cowboy back to their baggage which they collected before proceeding into the ranch house. The first thing Lisa noticed was the floor, carpeted with blue denim strips sewn over a layer of what must have been straw.

"My, how soft!" Lisa exclaimed, marveling at the feel that was not unlike walking on moss.

"Yeah," Charlie said, looking pleased. "Marion—I mean, Mrs. Wetherill, she has bad feet and this makes it easier on her."

"I see," Lisa replied, studying the room with interest.

The furniture was handmade, sawn or hewed with an axe. The large stove was cast iron and there were good oil paintings on the walls depicting scenes of the local mountains and valleys. Lisa took in all of that with a sweeping glance, before her eyes settled on a big table laden with Anasazi artifacts. She was astonished at the variety of pottery she saw, all of it of the same gray color decorated with intricate black markings.

"Pretty good stuff, huh?" Charlie asked as he tromped over toward the stove and began filling it with firewood. "We sold dozens of things, but we kept the best of it for the big museums."

"Thank you," Andrew breathed, caressing a clay pot decorated with concentric designs.

"I can't say this for sure, but I'd say that the Wetherills and myself would be willing to give you a good price for a package deal. Some of it, of course, we probably wouldn't want to sell."

Andrew turned to stare at the cowboy. "Why would you want to keep *any* of this?"

Charlie didn't glance up as he lit the fire and then filled the coffeepot from a pail of water.

"Why? Well, some of that stuff just has kind of gotten personal, if you know what I mean. That first day in Cliff Palace was like going on a treasure hunt when you was just a little kid. Some things were laying right on the floor, either in a dusty little room, or maybe up on a balcony or spilled on stairs. We really had to scratch and dig for other stuff."

"Are they still scratching and digging?" Andrew asked in a voice so strained that it was hardly recognizable to Lisa.

"Yep! We think we've only scratched the surface. John and Richard have been living up there this summer having all the fun while poor, miserable me has got stuck down here in the valley tending the livestock and doing regular chores."

Charlie's twinkling eyes belied his words as he added, "But we've all found stuff. Some of the ruins are so hard to reach that we haven't bothered with 'em yet."

Andrew blinked. "They're untouched!"

"Sure. We can't even figure out how to reach 'em."

"I . . . I see."

Lisa could read Andrew's thoughts as plain as the words on a page. Anything untouched would be irresistible to an archaeologist. It would lure Andrew as gold would a prospector.

"Tell me," Lisa said quickly, "how big is Cliff Palace?"

"It's huge. A fair amount of it has fallen down and we're always clearing away the rubble. And there's all these deep round pits where roofs have collapsed. We're hoping that they have some gold in 'em or something valuable."

"Describe the pits," Andrew said, gently placing the pot down so that he could examine another.

"Well," the cowboy began, "we haven't excavated any of 'em yet, so I can't rightly tell you exactly how deep they are, but most are at least fifteen feet across."

"Rock-lined with sort of a bench near the bottom and a ventilation shaft rocked in on the floor?"

"How'd you guess?"

"It's typical of the Puebloan peoples," Andrew answered. "How were the roofs constructed?"

"They looked to be flat on the top and supported by heavy spruce timbers."

"Did they have ladders coming out the top?"

"Yep, poking out of a square smoke hole in the middle of the top. It must have been awful durned smoky down in there. Maybe they used 'em to jerk meat."

"The Hopi call them *kivas*. They're ceremonial gathering places for the people."

"What about the smoke?"

"If they're constructed as I expect, they'll have a draft vent and small deflector rock that channels the smoke upward to an exit hole. I've read that the kivas are still used by the Pueblo people. They are warm and comfortable in the wintertime, cool in the summer."

"Huh! Well, there sure is a lot of soot on them collapsed roof bottoms," Charlie said. "Do you think that we'll find gold in them kivas, or just more pots and skeletons?"

"I don't know," Andrew admitted. "I've just read about these kinds of places but I've never really been in one."

"Then you should have a fine time when you get to Cliff Palace. Wish I could come along."

"You both can bed down tonight here on the floor or spread your blankets in the barn. Mrs. Cannaday, I'm sorry, but the family don't have a guest room."

"The floor will be fine," Lisa said.

"Good. I'll make the coffee and put on something to eat for supper. I expect that you are both hungry. Where you come from?"

Lisa took one look at her preoccupied husband then went over to keep the cowboy company. He didn't even notice as Andrew began to examine every artifact in the house and then disappeared for nearly an hour to revisit the barn. Andrew returned after dark with an expression like that of a child on Christmas morning.

Lisa felt in her bones that their lives had been altered in ways not to her liking. Their new, hard-won Denver business was about to vanish like smoke in an Anasazi fire. She would cope because she loved Andrew with all her heart. So he wasn't going to be a businessman with an office full of young, bright engineers and geologists. So they wouldn't have a fine house in the better part of Denver or raise their children to enjoy the cultural activities that a thriving city had to offer. Instead, they would live here, or maybe even, God forbid, at Mesa Verde with a village of Anasazi ghosts. Her skin would grow tough as boot leather and her fingers knotty from digging around in the dirt of an ancient civilization that she would probably come to loathe.

Despite her best effort, tears filled Lisa's eyes and ran down her cheeks. Andrew didn't notice. But Charlie noticed and he almost dropped his coffeepot.

"You all right, ma'am!"

Lisa sniffled, then sleeved her eyes dry. "Yes."

"Damn me, I just *knew* them ugly skeletons would upset you! But just try to believe that those old Indians lived happy lives and so there's no reason to be so sad about 'em. Ain't that right, Mr. Cannaday?"

"Huh?"

"Never mind," Lisa said, struggling to adjust to what the future now held for her and the family she hoped to raise someday.

That evening, Charlie fixed supper and they let him do all the talking about Cliff Palace and the other ruins. Lisa made a bed on the floor with a mound of blankets and fell asleep waiting for the cowboy to run out of talk and go off to wherever he slept.

At dawn the next morning, Charlie awoke them with more coffee and a huge breakfast of bacon and flapjacks.

"You better stuff yourselves," he warned, " 'cause the eatin' isn't so good up on the mesa."

"Food isn't what we're here for," Andrew said, eyes bright with anticipation.

"Has that Smithsonian Museum got a big pot full of money?"

"Not as much as you might think," Andrew replied. "In

fact, they didn't have enough money to send someone out from Washington, which is why they asked me to come inspect your ruins up on Mesa Verde."

"I was afraid that you might say something like that," Charlie said, looking glum. "Well, there are plenty of other museums. Richard even wrote the Mormons over in Salt Lake City 'cause we heard that those folks collect all kinds of stuff. We heard they got a whole building crammed full of records and other archaeology."

"They mostly collect genealogy," Lisa told him.

"Yeah," Charlie said, stuffing a forkful into his mouth, "same thing."

After breakfast, they went out to saddle the horses. Lisa was relieved because Andrew's mount, Stewy, was an old roan gelding, probably pushing twenty years old—with sad, droopy eyes. Her own mount was a younger, spirited sorrel mare named Rose.

"Your mare won't be happy unless she's in the lead," Charlie explained after he finished saddling both horses and tying on their packs and some extra food.

"Then she's like some women I know," Andrew said.

Lisa didn't rise to that bait. Besides, Rose was dancing around and acting up.

"Whoa now!" Charlie shouted, jerking on the mare's reins. "You settle down! What's the matter with you, anyway!"

"I don't want my wife on that wild animal," Andrew protested.

But Lisa stepped forward with as much confidence as she could muster. "I'll be fine. Rose is just excited but I'm sure that she'll settle down once we get underway."

"You might want to point her toward the far mesa and then run the fire outa her belly," Charlie suggested.

Lisa considered herself a very good horsewoman. Her father had always loved animals and some of their best times had been on horseback excursions before he'd died of stomach cancer. As she'd grown, so had her skill and need for more challenging animals to ride. She could handle Rose, once the mare let off a little steam.

"Just let me mount up and then stand back," Lisa told the men.

"Rose don't usually act up so bad," Charlie offered, while looking every bit as worried as Andrew.

Lisa punched a foot into the stirrup and swung into the saddle. She took up her reins, screwed down her hat and, when Charlie released the mare, she booted Rose in the ribs and they shot out of the ranchyard like a Chinese rocket. Lisa could hear both men shouting as the mare raced down to the stage-line road and turned east, running like a demon with her ears laid back flat. Lisa leaned forward over the mare's withers and let her storm for a mile before she steered Rose into a wide, hair-raising turn through the sagebrush and pointed her back toward the Alamo Ranch. By the time they loped back up to the house, Rose was blowing and puffing and covered with soapy lather.

"Wooo-weee! Where did you ever learn to ride like that!" Charlie shouted.

"I always had my own horse," Lisa said proudly. "And I think Rose and I have come to a very good understanding."

"I would say so." Charlie grinned. "You ever need a job, you could probably hire on to this ranch—or one just like it, Mrs. Cannaday."

"Thanks, but no thanks. Andrew, are you ready?"

He hauled himself unsteadily into the saddle, gripped the horn with his right hand and lifted his reins. "I sure am!"

Charlie waved them good-bye. Though winded, Rose stepped out while poor old Stewy plodded along behind. A half mile later, Andrew's confidence reached the point where he dared to shout, "Come on horse! We're about to make the scientific discovery of a lifetime!"

Lisa glanced back over her shoulder. *Dear Lord,* she thought, *Andrew is exhilarated, I'm devastated, and poor old Stewy is just plain worn out.*

Three

Their long horseback journey up to Mesa Verde was spectacular, with vistas that Lisa would have found inspiring had her mind not been in such turmoil and Andrew in such a hurry. The autumn air was cool and, when they gazed back into the Mancos Valley and far beyond toward the La Plata Mountains, Lisa was sure that the visibility exceeded a hundred miles.

In the higher elevation, there were deer everywhere and they even saw a bobcat sunning himself on a flat rock. Most of the trees were piñon and juniper, but they also rode through fine stands of Gambel oak which an early frost had already started to color. They saw a place where a bolt of lightning had started a brush fire that had consumed an entire mountainside, leaving a dark smudge that already was starting to regenerate with vigorous sage.

In every canyon and gorge, Lisa could observe nature at work busily eroding away the mountains. They finally crested a ridge at over eight thousand feet. Poor Stewy was about to call it quits so they dismounted and soon realized that Mesa Verde was really many fingerlike mesas, all with a southward tilt and emptying into the great San Juan River basin of northwestern New Mexico.

"Can you imagine what all this must have seemed like to those first Indian people who climbed up here?" Andrew asked, massaging the sore insides of his knees. "And *why* did they come? Lisa, that's what most puzzles me. After all, in this high desert country, you'd have thought those prehistoric peoples would have stayed by the rivers."

"It's true that they would have had to struggle for water up here," Lisa said. "I don't know how much rain or snowfall Mesa Verde gets, but I'm sure it has at least a few permanent springs."

"Has to have," Andrew agreed, wincing a little from his first saddle sores. "I wonder how much farther it is to this place they named Cliff Palace. Charlie said we could make it easy in a day, but I tell you, Stewy and I are about to call it quits."

"The climbing part is over," Lisa said, tightening her cinch and patting Rose. The mare had proven herself to be an excellent mountain trail horse.

"You know," Andrew said, leaning wearily against his horse and gazing across his saddle. "I think this country is magnificent! Sure, it's hard, but it's probably cool in the summer."

"But colder in the winter."

"Maybe not," Andrew mused. "I've read that these mesas actually can be warmer in winter because warmer air rises off the cold, lower valleys. The ancient Indians might actually have enjoyed a *longer* growing season up here."

Lisa found that difficult to believe but saw no point in saying so. "Well, we'd better mount up and move along."

They arrived at the point overlooking Cliff Palace just before sundown and found that the Wetherills had built a rough little shack and corrals. After unsaddling their weary horses and pitching them some loose hay from an old buckboard wagon, they went into the shack and cooked a quick meal, then bedded down for the night on a rough plank floor.

"Are you sorry we came?" Andrew asked just before Lisa fell asleep.

"Not sorry."

He rolled over to peer at her in the darkness, his handsome face just inches away. "But not glad, either."

"I'm doing the very best that I can, Andrew. I'm just afraid that you might decide we should live up here."

"Ha! Is that what's got you worried?"

"Yes."

He tried to pull her into his arms but Lisa was not in the mood to be cuddled or loved. "Andrew," she said, "we've had a long day and tomorrow is going to come very early. Let's just go to sleep."

He tried not to sound hurt, but utterly failed. "All right, darling. But stop worrying. We'll just spend a few days up here and then we'll return to Denver. I'll write Michael a good scientific report and then it's back to the easy life."

Lisa didn't believe him.

The next morning, they negotiated their way down to Cliff Palace, an adventure they would never forget. Lisa, who had grown up hiking and riding in mountains, was comfortable descending the sheer rock cliff, but Andrew had major problems. He was not athletic and certainly not an outdoorsman despite his love of geology and archaeology. Several times he found himself trapped with the wrong foot in the wrong hole and had to climb back up the rock until he could get straightened out.

When they finally passed under the lip of the great cavern and at last viewed Cliff Palace, all the soreness and difficulties of their journey were forgotten.

"Lisa!" Andrew cried. "Can you believe this!"

Lisa had to blink twice before nodding her head. *No question about it now,* she thought, *we're doomed to live up here forever.*

A few minutes later, Richard Wetherill and his brother John hurried over to greet them. The Wetherills were of average height, sturdy and obviously pleased to have company and the chance to show off their discovery. John was younger and shy. Richard could not have been much past thirty but his hair was prematurely gray. He had penetrating eyes that rarely blinked when they looked at you. In contrast to his slouching younger brother, Richard stood ramrod straight and had the rough, battered hands of a very large man.

When the brothers learned that Andrew had been sent by the Smithsonian, they became even more animated. Soon, they were rushing around, eager to show off all of Cliff Palace at once. Lisa stood quietly by the lip of the cavern, still trying to comprehend everything she saw. She had not been prepared for anything approaching the size of these ruins. She began to meander, and when she came to a place with grinding stones and scattered shards of old pottery, she sat down in the cool, dry dust and let her mind drift back across time, trying to imagine the women who had once lived, struggled and loved here centuries ago. It wasn't as hard as she had thought. Something about Cliff Palace evoked spirits more powerfully than any place Lisa had known before. To brush her fingertips across a rough metate where corn had been ground to flour, to roll a piece of pottery between the palms of her hands, created almost mystical images.

Later, when she rejoined her husband, Richard was attempting to explain what they had excavated. Lisa saw that it was all Andrew could do to keep from expressing outrage as the brothers boasted that they had excavated enough artifacts to earn them over three thousand dollars.

In fairness, the Wetherills had not been reckless or unnecessarily destructive. They had labored to clear away fallen rubble and actually attempted to shore up a few of the crumbling walls. Despite all that, Lisa knew that much of what any serious archaeologist would have hoped to find had already been destroyed.

The amazing thing to Lisa was that, despite the ravages of time, elements, and the Wetherills, Cliff Palace retained a powerful but indefinable aura of mystery and majesty. Lisa had only to brush the cool adobe walls with her fingertips to sense a communion with its builders. And, a few hours earlier, when John Wetherill had escorted them up into the tower to see the wall paintings and then had shown them the artist's bones and brushes, Lisa had felt a chill pass through the length of her own fragile bones.

This is wrong, she thought, only half listening while the brothers related their adventures and discoveries. *We should NOT disturb this place. It is like a great tomb and I do feel spirits, especially those of the women and children.*

Andrew squeezed her arm. "Lisa, are you all right?"

Startled, she nodded.

"I want to see the mummies," Andrew said, glancing toward the back of the cave. "Darling, perhaps you would rather remain here and relax."

"No, I'll come, too."

"Mrs. Cannaday," John Wetherill said, speaking as if to a child, "I'm not sure that is such a good idea. The mummies look so real that you can read their expressions—and some of them look like they died of fright—or in screaming agony."

"I'll be . . ."

"They've got hair and everything," Richard added. "They're pretty spooky, ma'am."

It took all of Lisa's will not to scold them for being so condescending. Yet, how could these cowboys know that she had seen her own mother killed by a runaway freight wagon and her father wasted by a terrible cancer?

"Mr. Wetherill, I've already seen the skeletons in your father's barn and I will be just fine."

"Yes, ma'am," Richard said, looking doubtful as he led the way toward the rear of the cave. When he reached it, he pointed and said, "This was their major trash heap."

"By far the largest we've found," John added. "A real gold mine. And it's where we've been digging hard for the past few weeks."

The "trash heap" was huge and Lisa could see that the brothers had done a tremendous amount of excavation aided by a wheelbarrow which she supposed they must have lowered from the mesa top by ropes.

"Where have you been dumping the excavation dirt?" Andrew asked.

"Over the side of the cliff into the canyon below," John answered. "You can't imagine all the stuff we've found in it—most of which I wouldn't mention in the lady's company."

Lisa glanced away, lips tightly compressed. It was then that she spied the mummies resting back in the shadows. Andrew must have seen her expression change because he practically jumped to block her view. The brothers made the same move but Lisa flanked all three of them.

Richard finally said, "Like I told you, Mrs. Cannaday, we've dug up fourteen so far."

Andrew dropped to his knees beside the mummies. "Lisa," he whispered, "they're almost perfectly preserved!"

"We told you," John said. "It's a miracle to find 'em in such prime condition."

Andrew expelled a deep breath. "You say they were buried deep within this trash pit?"

"That's right. Seems pretty . . . well, disrespectful, don't you think?"

"Not if it was wintertime when they died and the ground outside was frozen," Andrew replied as he squatted down on his heels and reached out to touch the dry, black parchment that once had been flesh.

"Why are they still so perfect after all this time?" Lisa asked.

"I can't be sure," Andrew replied. "But my guess is that, buried way back here under the cavern, untouched by snow or rain for centuries, this accumulated trash was dry enough to quickly dehydrate the corpses and prevent normal tissue decay."

"They wore their hair long," Richard said. "Some wore braids, but most just let it hang to their shoulders. I think they look just like our local Ute Indians."

Andrew shook his head, then gently separated the hair of one of the mummies to reveal tiny seed-like objects. He looked up at them and said, "Do you want to guess what these are?"

No one said anything so Andrew said, "What we have here are ancient, mummified lice."

"Lice!" Richard exclaimed, staring hard at the pale little capsules.

"That's right," Andrew said, picking and then placing several in his shirt pocket to examine under his microscope when they returned to Denver. "This proves that body lice were very common."

Andrew returned his full attention to the mummies, then brushed his fingers across the dried flesh. "I'm amazed that they didn't disintegrate when you moved them out of that trash pit."

"We were real careful," John explained with obvious pride. "We laid each one on a horse blanket and carried it out gentle as a newborn baby. Those things are going to be worth a lot of money."

"You *can't* sell them!" Lisa startled even herself by the outburst. "I mean, they're *people.*"

The Wetherills exchanged glances and then Richard said, "They're just old mummies, Mrs. Cannaday. It's not like they are going to be offended, or anything. And besides, we expect them to sell for a small fortune."

"Please don't do that," Andrew said, trying to keep his composure. "I mean, it would be like selling the body of one of *our* ancestors."

The brothers began to look very uncomfortable and Richard finally said, "We don't want to do anything wrong. Maybe, if we just sold them to museums, then it would be all right."

"It would *not* be all right!" Lisa cried.

"Ma'am, no disrespect intended. These mummies are just as lifeless as a pot or a stone axe. And, to be real honest, we want the cash."

Andrew came to his feet and, in a strained voice, said,

"Lisa, I'll see if the Smithsonian can resolve this so that everyone is satisfied. This is not the time to get angry or disagreeable. We've come a long way and Dr. Turner will be expecting results for his travel money. Furthermore, our hosts have done a lot of work here and it is clear that they have treated these bodies with respect."

Lisa turned away for a moment, choking down anger and outrage. Andrew was right. She would be a fool to say anything more that might result in their being expelled from Cliff Palace. Better, she realized, to spend the rest of her days living on this wild mesa than to forfeit Andrew's love and respect.

"Excuse us," Richard said in a terse voice as he took his brother by the arm and led him back down to the front of Cliff Palace.

"What's the matter with you?" Andrew demanded in a low, urgent voice. "Are you trying to ruin everything we've come so far to achieve!"

"I'm sorry."

His voice softened. "Lisa, for what it's worth, I'm also having a difficult time. These ruins do not *belong* to them. Yet, they act as if they alone have some kind of special claim to everything they've discovered."

"They've found a gold mine. In the West, whoever discovers gold, keeps it . . . or dies trying."

"But they really don't *own* this cavern, or this canyon, or Mesa Verde. I'm going to try to convince them that this is all public land and these ruins belong to everyone."

"They'll never agree to that."

"They might."

"No." Her mind was clear and focused on the objectives. "The more you talk, the more stubborn they will become until we are banished. And then what can we do?"

"I suppose we could return to Durango and locate a . . . a United States Marshal."

"We could. But he'd refer us to a local judge who wouldn't dare rule against this popular ranching family."

"I find that unbelievable!"

"Because you're from the East and have a very different frame of reference. The Wetherills would win control of these ruins in a local court of law."

"Then we would be forced to take the matter to the Supreme Court," Andrew said, throwing his hands up in a gesture of utter exasperation. "I know that's what Michael would want for the Smithsonian."

"And by the time the case arrived there, years would have passed and this family—in spite or anger—might destroy everything." Lisa realized she and Andrew had completely switched stances. "My dear, like it or not, we have to accept *their* thinking and terms."

His hands fell limp at his sides. "You're right, as usual. And I'm sure that I can deal with the artifacts, but to *sell* the bodies . . ."

"Convince Dr. Turner to buy them and everything else at Mesa Verde," Lisa urged. "That's the only possible solution. I'll tell them that the Smithsonian is sure to purchase everything. That will get us back in their good graces."

"Thank you. Just make whatever excuses are necessary."

Lisa kissed his cheek and went to make amends. She resolved not to lose her temper again with these cowboys because, at least for the time being, the Wetherills owned the mummies and everything else in Cliff Palace.

The following week was spent excavating and exploring not only Cliff Palace but also Square Tower and Spruce Tree House. There was no further mention of selling mummies or artifacts, and it seemed that the Wetherills were satisfied that the Smithsonian would make everything right. Furthermore, Andrew began to show how to minimize the excavation damage and handle newly recovered bones, archaeological evidence, and a treasure trove of Anasazi artifacts.

One afternoon he discovered near the back of the cave a

secret compartment that had been concealed by rocks and a
thick layer of plaster. As he opened the compartment, which
was about the size of a man's torso, everyone gathered
around. The Wetherills were hoping that at last they might
have unearthed a cache of gold or silver. Lisa, too, felt her
pulse quicken as Andrew reached far back into the compartment and groped about.

"You feel anything!" John asked.

"Yes."

"Treasure, I'll bet!"

"I'm afraid not," Andrew replied, drawing out a handsome
stone axe and a very unusual wooden device that was perhaps
two feet long. Its upper surface was flat with a projecting
spur on one end and a double looped leather thong on the
other. Accompanying the flat stick was a shaft about four feet
long with a feathered end much like an arrow, into which
slipped a six-inch stone-tipped dart.

"Look," Andrew said, pulling the stone point and dart out
of the hollowed end of the longer shaft, "this spear point is
detachable. After it penetrates flesh, the longer shaft fell away
and could be fitted with another dart and hurled again to
insure the kill."

Lisa felt an urge to reach out and grip the weapon. Glancing up at the expressions of her companions, she realized that
they were seized by the same compulsion.

"What kind of weapon is that?" John asked.

Andrew cradled the wooden device in hands that trembled.
"These are very, very old," he told them in a reverent voice.
"Probably the oldest I've yet seen in Cliff Palace. Lisa, you
know the name for this," Andrew said, grinning at Lisa. "You
saw one at the Smithsonian, remember?"

"It must be an atlatl."

"Yes!"

"A what?" John asked.

"Watch this," Richard said, fitting the three pieces together, then slipping his fingers through the leather thongs

and cocking his arm back over his shoulder. "Can you see how, if I made a strong throwing motion, it would propel the spear with far more velocity than I could generate with my arm?"

"Yeah!" John said, grasping the concept. "You'd have more leverage. And that flat piece would stay in your hand while the shaft and dart were launched, right?"

"Exactly. This weapon has been found throughout Europe," Andrew told them. "Archaeologists are sure that it preceded bows and arrows by thousands of years."

"So how old do you suppose this one is?" Richard asked.

"It was probably made around the time of Christ. We believe these weapons were obsolete by 500 A.D."

"If they worked so well, then why?" John asked.

"They are less accurate than the bow and arrow. Also, their range was shorter."

"I think it would be a superior weapon facing big, dangerous animals," Richard argued.

"You may be right. A skillful hunter could hurl a spear off an atlatl with tremendous force—much greater than that of an arrow. But the short distance and inaccuracy were limitations. Only a very powerful man could use this atlatl well."

"So," Lisa ventured, "after the invention of the bow and arrow, you're saying that this might only have been used against a bear, or mountain lion?"

"That's right," Andrew replied. "From the bones of wild game that we have found up to this point, I would say that almost all of the hunting on the mesa was done with bow and arrow to bring down rabbit, deer and even a few bighorn sheep. And, of course, we've found a lot of evidence that these people raised turkeys, both for food and to make feathered robes and blankets."

He looked at each of them, as his hands were caressing the atlatl. "However, *if* these people were threatened by grizzlies, mountain lions or perhaps even some extinct species of predator we haven't even discovered, the Anasazi would have required someone expert and courageous enough to use this older, but far more powerful, weapon."

"What if they were attacked by other tribes?" John asked. "Wouldn't these weapons be real handy?"

"I don't think so. An arrow could fell raiders beyond the range of this heavier and cumbersome atlatl. I'm sure that a wary enemy easily could have dodged spears near the end of their flight."

"And then maybe used them against the thrower," Lisa suggested.

"Yes, possibly. But an arrow is too swift to be dodged, especially during a major battle when the air might be as full of them as a sky full of hornets."

Richard picked up the atlatl and balanced it in his hand. "I could whittle up one of these without much trouble."

"You might find them a little deceptive," Andrew warned. "Balance is crucial. The fit has to be perfect or else the shaft will inhibit the flight or alter the trajectory of the spear."

"Huh." John reached for the weapon, saying, "I'd like to give this one a try."

"Please don't," Andrew said. "The atlatl is not rare, but neither is it commonplace, especially in the American Southwest. In fact, I'm sure that the Smithsonian will want this artifact."

"How much do you think they would pay us?"

"It's cracked," Lisa said before her husband put his foot in his mouth with a too generous figure. "Why, just look at the shaft! And the spear tip has also been damaged."

"It *has* been cracked and the tip looks like it's been coated with tar or something," John said, leaning forward to examine the weapon.

"Blood," Andrew said as he scratched a flake away with his thumbnail. "It's coated with dried blood."

John's eyes bugged. "Maybe the blood of a monster grizzly."

"Or a mountain lion, or even a man."

"But it's still cracked and I'm not sure that the Smithsonian would want something that's unsound," Lisa interjected. "Or, if they did, they wouldn't want to pay much. A hundred dollars tops."

"I'm sure we'll find better ones," John said, looking eager and excited. "Either here or in one of the other ruins. And a hundred dollars sounds fair, huh, Richard?"

"You bet it does!"

Andrew counted a hundred dollars saying, "Then let's consider it sold. I'm confident that the museum will pay me back."

"I'll find a better one before winter," John promised. "And, if I can't, then I'll whittle one just like it."

Lisa watched her husband run his hands over the weapon and she noted something near to ecstasy buried deep in his eyes. Later, when they were alone, she said, "I guess we shouldn't have spent so much of our money, but . . ."

"Don't say that. Cracked or not, this is a magnificent artifact. And did you notice that whoever made it even left his own personal signature!"

Lisa had to lean close to see the faint mark of ownership almost worn away by a hunter's callused hand. But there it was, a neat design which, upon closer inspection, appeared to be a large bird . . . perhaps an eagle, or hawk or raven.

"Close your eyes," Andrew breathed, closing his own. "Darling, just imagine who made and used this fearful weapon. Try to picture whose blood coats the flint tip and why it was hidden in that compartment and then plastered over so carefully that it was not discovered by future generations of Anasazi."

Lisa's eyes popped open. "All right, but first, how did *you* happen to see it?"

"I would have missed it as well a few centuries ago," Andrew confessed. "But the plaster cover had corroded and my eye just happened to settle on the right place when the light was brightest in the rear of this cavern."

Gary McCarthy

"I see." Lisa leaned her head on his shoulder. Her hand dropped to rest upon his, which in turn rested on the atlatl.

"Now, *really* close your eyes," he urged. "And listen for the story of the atlatl."

"As told by you, or the spirits?"

"The spirits. Listen and you will hear them as I hear them now."

They were resting near the front of Cliff Palace and the sun was warm on their faces as Lisa's eyelids grew heavy. And then, she drifted off to sleep, captured by the spirit of a very strong and ancient hunter, the one who had made and fought with this atlatl.

Four

THE ATLATL

circa 400 A.D.
Animus River Valley
Northwestern New Mexico

The leader of the Raven Clan sat alone in the high desert moonglow, his powerful legs drawn up close to his chest, chin resting on his knees. At five foot six, Echata was taller than most of the hunters in his clan and considerably more muscular. His straight black hair was separated in three thick braids, each tied with a leather thong and bearing a shiny raven's wing feather. Echata's oft-broken nose was flat and crooked. The back of his head was flattened on account of his first years spent strapped tightly to the cradleboard. A long, puckering scar emerged from his scalp above the right eye and crossed jaggedly down to twist the corner of his lip, giving the clan leader a perpetual half smile.

Echata's people were starving. Every night, hungry children cried themselves to sleep and the old ones grew weaker. All this summer and deep into the fall, the Raven Clan had scoured the vast recesses of the Great Basin in a vain search for enough food to keep themselves strong and healthy. But this was the third year of a great drought and springs that had flowed cool and sweet for as long as Echata could recall were now reduced to stinking seeps. Even the nearby river that had always nourished this land and its game was dying. Rain God had turned his back on the People and gone north, leaving only buzzards to circle endlessly across a pale, blistered blue sky.

What had the People done to deserve hunger and death? Even their protector, Raven, had deserted them. Echata had last seen Raven flying northwest, away from the river and into the high mesa country where the People did not go for fear of great bears and evil spirits. But, Echata wondered, had Raven flown to the mesas expecting the People to follow? The mesa country was at least ten days' walk, much too far for the weakest members of his already small clan. What should he do? Abandon the old and young to certain death? Echata was not sure if he could do such a terrible thing but perhaps there was no longer a choice. Only yesterday, he had attempted to speak to the clan elders and learn their thoughts about this terrible dilemma. But they had not spoken from their hearts. His brother, Oomat, had spoken truth and made it clear that the clan must never be divided. That they must all stay together even into the spirit world. But Oomat was crazed by grief, for he had lost both of his wives and all of his children except the one that he loved more than his own life. Oomat would never follow Raven north but would stay in this place to die. But Oomat was not a leader.

Echata's bleak thoughts were interrupted by the mournful howl of Coyote. Like the People, Coyote sounded very weak and hungry.

"Echata?"

It was his wife, Tizu. Echata did not have the heart to answer; he was filled with confusion and despair. He remained still, gazing at a full moon pinned against a cursed and cloudless sky.

"Echata! Where are you, my husband!"

Noting the anxiety in her gentle voice, Echata came to his feet to see Tizu silhouetted in the glow of the campfire. She was as thin as a boy but her head was up and Echata knew that his wife remained strong. He waved, glad that she had come to be with him. The presence of Tizu always raised his spirits because she was still beautiful. She had given him four children and two of them yet lived, but one was a daughter.

"I have brought you food," Tizu announced, coming to stand close before him. "A little."

Echata accepted her offering of seeds mixed with the precious fat of rabbit. The mixture had been rolled into a ball no larger than a small bird's egg. Echata popped it into his mouth and took his time chewing so that he could savor the taste.

"May I speak openly with you?"

"Yes," he replied, knowing that she would anyway.

Tizu glanced back over her bare shoulder toward the clan's cooking fire. She wore a rabbit-skin skirt and tightly woven yucca sandals. Her hair was cut short and bore no decoration although, as wife of a clan leader, it was her privilege to wear Raven's feathers.

"Your brother has spoken again of the need to follow this river south to the place of the shallow canyon and big trees."

"I have been there," Echata said. "It is no good."

"Oomat says there is always water in that canyon. He says we could all go and live in that place."

"It is the hunting ground of our enemies, the Chacoans. Oomat should know that we would all be killed or enslaved."

"Oomat says that we could become their friends, if you would agree to teach them how to make and use the throwing stick and spear."

"Never!"

"And," she continued, ignoring his indignant outburst, "if our women would teach their women how to weave *good* baskets."

"I tell you this, Tizu. The Chacoans would steal our secrets and *then* they would kill us. And that is why I cannot lead our people south to that valley, where we would be at the mercy of our enemies."

"But we cannot stay here! My husband, our time is passing into darkness and death will soon claim us."

Echata looked away. When he felt his wife's hand touch his shoulder, he knew he had to offer her some hope. "I . . . I will pray again to Raven and to the other gods," he said, trying to sound hopeful. "I am *sure* that I will have a true vision. One that will tell us to follow Raven north, to the mesas."

Tizu drew her hand away and looked through his eyes. "And, if there is no vision?"

"I will offer blood."

"No," she shook her head back and forth. "Let *my* blood flow instead. You must stay strong in order to save our children and all of our people. I want to stay here with you."

Echata gave this request serious consideration. Tizu was agreeable in all ways. He could not imagine why the spirits would object to her presence but, then again, he could not be sure. Deciding he could not take the risk, Echata was about to order Tizu back to their camp when he glimpsed, out of the corner of his eye, a fiery star flash across the face of the moon and disappear.

"Tizu," he cried, "did you see that!"

"Yes!"

Echata traced the flight of the burning star to make sure that he remembered it correctly. His heart began to beat fast because there was no doubt about it—the star had vanished north—like Raven.

"My prayers are answered," he told his wife. "Raven chased the star north so that I would know that we *must* climb the mesas."

"But how can you be so sure? I saw the star but . . . not Raven."

"That is because he is blacker than night."

Tizu was quiet for a moment, then said, "It is high where the Raven goes. Too high for the People. Up there, winter kills."

"Do you forget that we have many rabbit-skin blankets?"

"Not enough."

"Tizu," he said, aware of her deep fear of the cold season, "Raven has given us yet *another* sign. We have already angered him and that is why some have died in this place."

He heard Tizu expel a deep breath and then she said, "And what of those who are too weak to go so far?"

"Would you have the strong die so that the weak would live a few days longer?"

"No, but . . ."

Echata was now sure of himself. "North," he repeated. "It is our only hope."

"And what of our food?"

This was the time to demonstrate his confidence. "We will leave all the food with those who cannot follow Raven. Once we begin the journey, Raven will feed and protect us."

Tizu nodded. "What about Oomat? He will never go to the mesas and leave the weak behind."

"But he *must!*"

"He would rather fight you to the death," Tizu whispered. "But if you kill him, we will all be cursed. None will survive."

"Then he can stay and die," Echata decided. "And one day, I will return to find and bury his bones."

Tizu sat and so did Echata as they began to pray. Echata began by thanking Raven for the burning star. He was also thankful that Tizu had been at his side so that, now, she could tell the other women who would in turn tell the children and all the People would be filled with hope. When this happened, even Oomat would realize that Raven had not forsaken them and was making their new home on the northern mesas, far from their enemies. Echata believed that the power of Raven was so great that he might even spread his wings across the top of the world and shield his children from the cold and falling snow.

They sat late together in the moonlight and, although he

would not have admitted it to anyone, Echata refused to look up at the heavens again for fear of seeing another star traveling other than to the north. Instead, he thought about this land that was all his ancestors had ever known. His father had been a great hunter and, when Echata was very young, had fashioned him the two-part spear and throwing stick. They had gone off alone every day to practice and, by the time Echata was fourteen, he was a skilled and valued hunter. Oomat, however, had never been interested in hunting. Perhaps he had wanted to find something he could do very well without the competition of his father and older brother. So he had gone among the elders and listened to their stories. Oomat, for all his stubbornness, was wise in important ways. He could remember everything the elders said and, early in his life, had won their respect for his knowledge and intelligence.

By the time Oomat was fifteen, he was the favored healer among the Raven Clan and many believed he had special powers to see far into the past and the future. People listened when Oomat spoke, even the most revered of the clan's elders.

"Echata?" Tizu asked, "how many are strong enough to reach the mesas?"

"All but a few."

"Without food?"

"Raven will protect."

"Are our children strong enough to come?"

"Yes."

He heard the low sob of relief in his wife's throat and took her hand. "You must have faith, Tizu."

"I have faith in you," she said.

"And Raven."

"Yes," she finally added. "He will protect."

Echata twisted around to glance back at their camp. The fire was almost dead, just a faint orange glow around which he could detect the silhouettes of the last of the Raven Clan. There were so few now. No more than fifty. And how many would or could follow him to the mesas? Half, at best, and less than half that again were strong enough to hunt or fight.

"What are you thinking?" Tizu whispered.

"That we will be so few among so much. That there is much darkness in the mountains."

"In darkness dwells the most evil."

"But here dwells our death," Echata told her as he turned his gaze north to the great upthrust of mountains and mesas.

From his earliest years, Echata had been told that the higher country to the north was the home of evil creatures and spirits, that death was watching like a mountain lion from on high. No wonder Oomat and the others had fiercely resisted his pleas to follow Raven. But now, with death edging closer to each member of the clan, perhaps they would listen and believe this new sign of the fiery star.

"I believe," Tizu whispered, "that you are the greatest of all hunters and fighters. You know how to make and use the throwing stick better than all others. Raven will give you the strength to protect and feed us up there."

Echata was humbled by her faith but her words also swelled his chest, for they gave him power. He held Tizu close, feeling his passion stir like the warmth of summer wind. It had been a long time since they had joined. It had been a long time since Echata felt so whole and confident. Tizu and Raven were *his* strength and, when they reached the high mesas, then he would again become one with them both.

Echata did not sleep that long night. Instead, he worried about Oomat who was quick to anger and very stubborn. Since losing his wives and all but one of his children to hunger because of his poor hunting skills, Oomat had succumbed to bad spirits. Echata often had seen his brother sneak away. Curious, he had followed Oomat and was shocked to watch his brother throw himself to the earth and twist around like a headless snake, snarling and flailing at everything within his crazed reach. This Oomat did for hours until he lapsed into a fitful sleep broken by yip-yips not unlike the frenzied cries of a coyote. Shamed and distressed by his brother's behavior, Echata had always returned to the clan saying nothing about what he had witnessed. If the elders knew of Oomat's strange behavior, he would be banished or stoned.

It was only when Oomat was with his last child, Gejo, a frail boy of ten winters, that he seemed completely of this world. But Gejo was very weak now and Echata was certain that the child's death would plunge his brother into a dark world from which he would never return. Echata knew that he must convince Oomat and Gejo to stay under his protection.

When the sun rose above the eastern horizon to burnish the world, Echata got up quietly and went off to be alone. The early morning was sacred time for it held the deepest silence. Sun was still half asleep and not yet angry. Coyote was already sleeping; Snake and Owl, hiding, feeding on their night kill. The air was still, the earth hushed and heavy with the fragrance of sweet sage.

Jumping onto a flat rock, Echata spread his arms above his bowed head and began to chant the old prayers. Soon, all doubt and worry slipped from his mind as it drifted in the company of spirits. After an hour, he shook himself back into this world and returned to the People, feeling confident and untroubled. By then, Tizu had already told everyone in the camp of the blazing star and how it was Raven's sign to go live upon the wild, uninhabited northern mesas.

"*I* also saw that sign," old Miuta, the stone chipper said, offering them his nearly toothless grin, as he pointed north.

Echata was encouraged to hear several others say that they too had seen the flaming star, though none had realized that it was being chased by Raven who was too black to be seen at night. "How do you *know* this was Raven's sign?" Oomat challenged.

"I have prayed on it," Echata replied. "And the vision is true because I was the last to see Raven. He too went north."

"But surely you know that the dark mountains are death to the People!"

"No longer is that so," Echata argued. "For Raven is there now and he waits to protect us."

"He is dead!" Oomat snapped.

The People gasped in horror. Even Echata felt his bones shiver with dread. "No!"

"Sun killed Raven and he fell from the sky."

"Where?"

"To the north," Oomat said, now looking very sure of himself. "When Raven flew over the high country, evil spirits came out of the earth and drove him into Sun where he burned. His black feathers litter the mesas and everything about them is dead!"

Out of the corner of his eye, Echata caught a glimpse of Tizu gathering their two children into her arms. Her face was stricken with terror and the People were almost too frightened to speak.

"That is why," Oomat continued, "we must go *south* to the wide, shallow canyon called Chaco, with deep grass and trees where we can hide from Sun until he is no longer angry. Only then will we find deer, rabbit and other foods to fill our empty bellies. This I see in a true vision."

Echata felt as if his bones were leaking out of his legs like a river of hot sand. His head swirled and he clapped both hands to his ears, stilling the world. How could his vision have been so wrong? How could Raven be dead!

"That is untrue!" he cried. "Raven is *not* dead. He has gone to wait for us on the mesas!"

"He has *fallen* from the sky and his bones and feathers litter the mesas!"

"No!" Echata went over to grab his atlatl. He fit his spear and pointed it at Oomat's chest, then drew back his arm and screamed, "You lie!"

Oomat's lips twisted downward. "You are the one who lies. You saw *no* vision. Only a star and a black bird!"

"If you go south, the Chacoans will cut out your hearts," Echata warned, drawing back his throwing stick even farther.

"We can make them our friends!"

"How, by letting them cut our throats and mount our women?"

Tizu threw herself forward and grabbed the upraised spear an instant before Echata would have buried it in Oomat's lying heart. She cried, "Echata, you cannot do this!"

He collected himself and pushed her away, knowing she had saved him from a terrible mistake. "I *will* go north!"

Tizu's entire body shook and sweat burst out on her face before she grabbed the hands of their children and nodded. *"We* go north to find Raven together!"

Echata lowered the atlatl and started to leave, but Oomat's threat stopped him in his tracks. "If you go, I am the new leader of the Sun Clan."

"There is no Sun Clan! You will find nothing but death at the hands of our enemies!"

Oomat dismissed him and turned to face the People, many of whom were crying or shivering with fear.

"You have heard my brother," Oomat began. "Echata claims that he has had a vision. But I am the one who can foretell the future and see into the past. Raven *is* dead. He is no longer our protector!"

Oomat threw his head back and raised his arms to the hot morning sun. "Sun is master of all things now and he has told me that we should flee south to the canyon of the big trees and grass. There, and only there, the People will be protected from the death winds and snows. There we will find that the grass is always deep, the many deer fat . . . and as stupid as my brother."

"Echata, no!" Tizu whispered as he started to raise the atlatl again.

Oomat didn't notice the threat. He clapped the palms of

his hands together, then wiped one hard against the other, showing the People that one was smeared with ashes, the other clean. He turned the blackened one north saying, "This one, black as Raven, leads to death."

With a flair for the dramatic, he turned the clean palm to the south and proclaimed, "This one, white as sun, leads to life! I alone know all and have suffered as much as any. I alone know that Sun is punishing his children by chasing away Rain. Why? Because we forget that, in the earlier world, there was only cold and darkness. That it was Sun who opened the sky and brought the People up to the Fourth World and onto the Rainbow Path. But now the People pray only for Rain and Sun is very angry. I alone have gone away to speak to him."

Oomat raised his hands toward the giant orb of rising Sun. His voice grew shrill. "I alone have been praying to Sun! I alone have been told to follow this river to the wide canyon of the deep grass and tall trees. To please Sun, I gave him the spirits of my wives and all but the last of my children. And now, I am your leader and you must follow me!"

"No!" Echata shouted. "I *have* spoken the truth. The mesa has no enemies and Raven still lives and waits for us there! Only Oomat has spoken with Sun, but you have all seen the flaming star that went to the mesas."

Tizu took his arm and led Echata away. "You have spoken. He has spoken. Now, the People must decide who speaks the truth."

"But what if *we* are the only people who believe Raven is waiting on the mesas?" Echata choked.

"Others will follow you," she said, dashing away for a moment to gather the family's meager belongings. When she rejoined Echata, she said, "Be strong, my husband, for I know others who also believe that Raven still lives and that you are the true leader of his clan and alone know truth."

Echata was desperate to turn and look back to see if anyone was going to follow him instead of Oomat. But pride would not allow this so he fixed his eyes ahead and began to walk north. Within a single hour, Sun grew very hot and seemed to turn all of his searing anger on those who still believed in Raven. Tizu walked on Echata's right hand while their children and whoever else believed in the sign of Raven followed. Not once would Echata allow himself to look back but instead marched through lung-searing heat until even Sun grew weary and slipped behind Earth to rest for the night.

It was at that time, when Sun could no longer burn their flesh and stew their minds, that Echata finally allowed himself to know how many had followed him instead of Oomat. There were many more than he had expected. Twenty at least, five of them good hunters, the rest women and children.

"Raven will give us food," he said, his suffering red eyes studying the baking land.

"Where?" one of the hunters asked.

Echata did not know where, but he did know that, without food, some of his faithful would die tonight and others would be too weak to continue in the morning. He said nothing but instead began to walk about in widening circles. He was searching for something, seeds, bugs, a snake coming out to swallow a rat. Anything! The sun sank into the earth but left its heat. The moon floated above a barren ridge and Owl swept soundlessly overhead as the hunters walked on and on into the night, sandaled feet dragging against earth until Echata saw something moving slowly through the low sage.

With a yip of joy, he jolted forward and landed squarely on the back of Tortoise.

"He is so big!" a gaunt hunter named Denio cried.

"Yes," Echata shouted, drawing from a leather sheath his stone axe and slamming it down on Tortoise's neck before it vanished under the thick, checkered shell.

Tortoise made a sharp, choking sound as Echata chopped off its head with the jaws still opening and closing. The last hunters of the Raven Clan offered quick prayers to the departing spirit of Tortoise before they each collapsed to their knees and gulped the spurting blood until it ceased to flow. With faces smeared crimson like the sunset that burned the western skies, they grabbed the legs of heavy Tortoise and carried him back to the People, singing praises only to Raven.

Five

After the gift of Tortoise, the People discovered ample food and water as they trudged north toward the high mesa country, but Rema, a girl of six winters, continued to weaken. One especially hot afternoon, she grew dizzy and then her frail body began to spasm as she cried words that must have been the voices of demons. Rema vomited stinking green bile and died, her face quickly turning black. The clan became frightened and many decided to return to Oomat and the others of their clan. Echata refused them.

"I promise you," he told his fearful people, "after we reach the mesa and survive our first winter, we will return south to find Oomat and reunite the Raven Clan."

"But what if they do not want to come with us?" one of the older women demanded.

"They *will* join us. By then they will have suffered much at the hands of our Chacoan enemies."

Echata's words brought no comfort, only confusion. Why, the People asked—if they survived—should they return to this place of death?

There was much argument. Finally, when Utaal, the strongest of the hunters threatened to take his family away, Echata warned, "If you try to leave the Raven Clan, I will kill you."

Utaal stood his ground, his spear poised lightly in his fist. "I am not easy to kill. It is *my* choice to turn back with my family."

"No! We must stay together. You are needed to feed the

Raven Clan and to fight the great bears which are said to live
on the mesa. Besides, we are already too few in numbers."

"Look at Rema!" Utaal exclaimed, pointing to the child
who had died in such agony. "This girl was made to suffer!
Sun has spoken—Raven has not!"

"He has given us Tortoise, other food and water. That is
the way he speaks to his people."

Utaal thought about this but, when his wife tried to pull
him back south, he said, "Echata, would you spill *my* blood?
We have been friends since birth."

"I am leader. I would spill your blood to save this clan."

Utaal was brave but no fool. He dropped his spear saying,
"No good will come to us on the mesa."

"*All* good will come to us on the mesa." Echata countered,
lowering his atlatl, the most feared weapon among all the
Raven Clan.

They spent the rest of that day preparing for Rema's burial.
At dusk, the body was placed in a small cave undercutting
the banks of a dry arroyo. Rema's thin legs were drawn up
to her chest and she received a basket of precious seeds and
nuts to transport her into the spirit world. Her grieving father
carved her a spirit stick about six inches long. One end of
the stick was shaped like the head of Raven while the center
was decorated with soft leather streamers bound up with bird
feathers.

That night, the clan was fervent with prayers. Some, including Tizu, believed it important to pray to Sun also, asking
forgiveness, but Echata and those bitter from the loss of their
relatives and friends refused. At midnight, they gathered their
few belongings and continued up a narrowing canyon, following a sandy river bottom choked with sagebrush.

Being a hunter, Echata noted evidence of wild game even
in moonlight. Even a child could not have missed seeing that
these canyons teemed with rabbit and mule deer, sage hen
and wild turkeys. And, despite grieving for Rema, he was
encouraged by the abundance of game and the variety of

birds. Circling above he saw a red-tailed hawk. Around him, the strident calls of blue jays lapped against the high canyon walls. The thick brush and trees were a haven for thousands of hummingbirds, quail, nuthatches and warblers.

The People were excellent rock throwers and they were able to kill several birds, one huge rattlesnake and a strange green lizard with yellow banding its plump body. Nothing was wasted. The birds were prized for their feathers which would be used for decoration, while roasted lizard and rattlesnake proved to be as delicious as quail.

Being accustomed to the flat, southern deserts, the People grew apprehensive as the canyon walls hemmed them in ever tighter until they could see only a thin wedge of indigo sky.

"If we reach the end of this canyon and cannot find a way up to the mesa," Aeeok, the best spear-point maker among the hunters said, "we will die in this place."

"I know," Echata replied, eyes scouring the imposing sandstone cliffs pocked with caves that they regarded as likely hiding places for evil spirits to rest in the daytime.

"Maybe Bear lives in those caves instead of evil spirits," Utaal wondered aloud.

"No," Echata said. "Bear could not reach those high caves."

"Then maybe your brother Oomat really did have a true vision and Sun has already burned Raven from the sky."

"My brother was sick in his heart and had no vision. You shall see this tomorrow when I find a way to the top of the mesa."

That night Echata had a vivid dream of Raven swooping down to catch Snake. The viper squirmed and tried to strike Raven's breast but could not as the embattled pair floated higher and higher, growing ever larger until they completely shadowed Sun. Snake's blood began to pour like the rain until Sun turned dark.

Echata sat up in terror, reaching for his axe.

"What is wrong?" Tizu whispered.

"Nothing. I had . . . a bad dream vision."

"Of Raven?"

"Yes, killing Snake over Sun."

"Did Raven burn in the sky like Oomat said?"

"No. Raven was above all. He humbled Sun who will rise drenched in blood, then grow warm. Sun is again our friend."

Tizu pressed her body close. "And what about Oomat's vision?"

"He had no vision," Echata said, slipping his arm around her shoulders.

Neither of them slept for what remained of the night until Sun peeked over the edge of their deep canyon, very red, as if blushing with embarrassment. Afterward, Tizu recounted her husband's prophecy again and again, giving the People new hope.

The last few miles of climbing up to the mesa were made easier by a game trail that weaved back and forth until it brought them over the lip of the canyon. The first thing they saw was a huge bear feeding on the flesh of a rotting deer. When it saw them, the creature rose up on its hind legs and roared. Echata had never seen anything so terrible and he gathered his people close until the animal swung away and lumbered into the trees.

The size of the bear left all of them shaken but, after awhile, they began to look around at this land so close to the clouds. It was a very green land, thick with forest. Nearby, a spring-fed creek flowed across pitted capstone to empty into an oval-shaped basin. From there, water seeped over the rim to smudge the brow of the cliff, then fall across the mouth of what appeared to be an enormous cavern. That was when everyone saw Raven sailing over the canyon, sun flashing on his black wings. Then he swooped down to settle in the cavern below.

Echata clapped his hands together with joy and the People

began to sing high prayers again. It was time for a feast. Throwing both hands up to the sky and parading back and forth along the rim of the canyon, Echata shouted, "We will gather pine nuts and offer thanks to Raven."

The trees were heavy with nuts. Very soon, baskets were filled to overflowing. By nightfall the Raven Clan had feasted until they could feast no more.

It rained that night. Thunder boomed across the mesa and rumbled through the canyons. Under cover of a low, spreading juniper, Tizu clasped her children and shouted, "Husband, is this a *good* sign?"

"Yes!" Echata cried. "And very soon, Raven will come dancing on the Rainbow and the sun will warm his wings until they shine. Our time of death and sorrow finally have passed."

"How do you know this?"

"After seeing Raven chase the burning star to his place, how could it not be so?"

Echata was serene with confidence, even when lightning struck a nearby tree, flaming it like a torch. And in the morning, the storm was gone so that the earth smelled rich as it steamed under a warm sun.

Echata returned to the rim of the gorge to peer across the abyss toward the immense canyon where he had seen Raven. Almost immediately, his keen hunter's eye spotted two mountain goats almost half a mile away as they moved from some trees along the canyon's floor. Echata wondered about the taste of the flesh. He vowed to know that taste before he passed into the next world.

"Echata," Tizu said when he returned to their camp. "Will you and the men hunt today?"

"Yes."

"We will soon need many new skins for winter," she told him. "And the People are still weak."

"Then they should eat pine nut cakes while they scrape hides. Tell the children to set snares."

"We have already done this while you were resting," she said, pointing to the children just now returning to camp. "Did you see Raven today?"

"No."

"What about Bear?" Tizu asked, trying not to look afraid.

"No."

Tizu managed to nod as he gathered his atlatl and selected his finest spear points. Echata slipped them into a long, leather pouch sewn by Tizu. He had never required more than two spear points on a hunt but, now that he had seen the great size of Bear, he was taking extras.

When Echata began to call his hunters together, Tizu said, "I fear Bear. I beg you not to take your hunters far from this camp."

Echata nodded in agreement. Perhaps there was only the one bear and it had run away at the sight of the clan. As they left the camp, Echata was aware that their numbers were few but each hunter was seasoned and they all knew what was expected. At the sight of deer, the hunters would form a V with the purpose of stampeding game into the atlatl's killing range. Echata would then leap from cover and hurl his spear points with deadly accuracy. The other hunters would soon have their chance as the panicked quarry darted, blindly attempting to escape but often bolting directly into the path of a waiting spear-thrower.

With so few hunters, it would be difficult. Echata knew that he must be at his very best. He said a quick prayer that his arm and his eye would not fail. It seemed vital that this first mesa hunt be successful. The people needed to regain their strength before the onslaught of winter and, to do that, they required fresh meat.

Niako was the oldest and craftiest of Echata's remaining loyal hunters but also the weakest. His teeth were either missing or badly worn away and he had a pronounced limp because of a poisonous cactus spine which had lanced his foot while he was chasing a rabbit. The spine had broken off inside the foot, the wound had abscessed and never healed properly. Niako suffered greatly despite his thick sandals. But Echata had faith in the old hunter.

A short time passed before they came upon a small meadow. The grass was brown but still tasty enough to attract the hungry mule deer. Echata counted six does, three young bucks and one exceptional stag. Fitting his atlatl with a spear point, he slipped his fingers through the leather thongs and carefully balanced the weapon. Using hand signals, Echata sent his hunters around the meadow. When his men were in place, he raised the atlatl and stepped boldly forward. The stag saw danger first, and tossed his fine antlers in defiance. It occurred to Echata that the stag had probably never before encountered man and therefore had no fear.

It was going to be almost too easy to hunt deer for a few seasons. Echata walked boldly out toward the stag and, when it pawed the earth with its front hooves, he drew back the atlatl and hurled the spear point at very close range. The stag's front legs broke at the knees and it fell, then somehow climbed back to its feet and attempted to run in spite of its mortal wound. Echata's second spear point sent it tumbling across the coarse brown grass.

The deer broke for the trees, running directly toward the Raven Clan hunters. Spears filled the air and, for a moment, everything was blood, shouts and confusion. But when the surviving animals were gone, the hunters counted four kills, including the stag.

The hunters offered thanks to the dying animals. After that, they were bled and quickly gutted. Old Niako was so hungry he began to devour the slippery entrails and organs as soon as they were removed. Echata and the other hunters joined him and they fed until their bellies were near bursting.

"Thank you, Raven!" Echata called to the sky, the lower part of his face a crimson mask as he gorged on a handful of dripping liver.

When Echata and his hunters could eat no more, they began to quarter their prey and make preparations for carrying it back to camp. Afterward, they would break tradition and return to this meadow to help the women and children prepare meat and hides. Because the autumn hunting season was now very short, their need was great to accumulate winter stores.

The hunters were so busy that they did not at first see Bear as he broke from the trees like a dark flash covering ground with amazing quickness. The animal grabbed Niako by the back of his neck. Niako threw up his arms and shrieked. His gore-streaked face was now a crimson mask of horror. Echata lunged for his weapon, but his hands were slick with viscera and blood. Twice he tried to fit his only remaining spear on the atlatl but his hands failed. Echata could not take his eyes off the ghastly scene nor scarcely comprehend the size and viciousness of the huge beast that was now dragging a dying old Niako into the trees.

A small voice within him screamed, *You are leader! Save poor Niako and kill Bear!*

But he could not. And, as Niako's screams faded, Echata realized his entire body was quaking and that he could do nothing except listen as the mesa became still with death.

Six

Echata recovered old Niako's body, or what was left of it after Bear had his fill. Rather than bring the remains back to the shaken clan, Echata covered the old man's bones in a shallow grave while offering a prayer for Niako's spirit.

Knowing that he had to do something to protect the clan, Echata then tracked Bear to a small cave. He vowed that, in the season of deep snows, he would sneak inside and cut sleeping Bear's throat. But even as he swore to avenge Niako's death, Echata realized that other bears also would prey upon the clan. Women and children gathering seeds or setting rabbit snares were especially at risk. Echata could never kill so many bears.

"It is not that I am afraid," he said to Tizu that night while they kept watch over the Raven Clan's camp, "for I can kill a sleeping bear before he kills me."

"But, if he awakens and kills you instead, then we are lost."

"What else can I do?"

Tizu was careful not to answer too soon. After a suitable deliberation, she said, "Wait for Raven and his sign."

Echata wondered how long it would be before Raven appeared. He would not admit it to Tizu, much less to any of the others, but he worried that Raven might have flown right over this mesa country without even stopping. If that were true, then Echata had made a terrible mistake by bringing the People to this place.

"Do you think Bear will attack our camp?" Tizu asked,

voicing the same question that Echata had heard every day since the savage death of Niako.

"I do not know," Echata admitted. "But if Bear smells meat, he will come."

Tizu drew her knees up to her chin and frowned. "My husband, we *must* hide the meat away from our camp."

"Then other animals will find and eat it."

"There might be *one* place where they would never find it."

Echata reflected very hard about this because, as leader, he felt he should be the wisest among The People. Finally, he thought he knew the place that Tizu was suggesting. "Bear can climb into the trees. I have seen his marks."

"I was not thinking of the trees."

Echata felt a stir of impatience. "Not in the rocks, either," he said, "because Bear is so strong he could tear them away."

"You are right, but I was not thinking of hiding our food in the rocks."

"Then where?"

"In Great Cave—under the cliff beside our camp."

Echata almost laughed. "How could we do this? We have no wings!"

"Would you like me to show you?"

"Now?" he scoffed. "In this darkness?"

"There is moonlight and the way is not so hard." Tizu came to her feet. "Even your son and daughter have been there. Have you not heard them talk of Great Cave just below the rim?"

"No."

"That is because your thoughts are dark and troubled. Come! There is enough moonlight."

Echata thought this a bad idea. "If we go, then the People will have no eyes. Bear could come and kill them in their sleep."

"Then awaken a hunter." Tizu cocked her head a little to the side. "You are leader."

"You should not tell me what to do," Echata said in his sternest voice as he also came to his feet.

"I am sorry. But I have a great need to show you this place where the People can be safe from all enemies, even Bear."

Echata did not understand. Why would Tizu insist that they see this place in the night? And how could they possibly reach it without tumbling to their deaths?

He almost told his wife that she was being foolish and needed sleep, but Tizu tugged on his arm and then ran her hand down his leg so lightly that Echata felt himself stir with arousal. And when she started toward the rim of the deep canyon of caves, he awakened young He-tok to watch over the camp and then followed his wife.

"You must come slowly," Tizu's voice called from the shadowy darkness somewhere below the rim.

"And will you catch Echata when he falls?"

"He will *not* fall because he is strong and nimble—like Goat."

Echata would have appreciated Tizu's humor if he had not been so worried. And, when he started to follow her into the canyon, he saw that he must descend with care, making full use of every niche and cranny.

"This is madness!" he called down to Tizu.

"Come on, my fine goat! It is not so hard!"

Echata could not turn back but, had it not been for Tizu's laughing taunts, he never would have climbed down this cliff—not even in the day. Now he had little choice but to follow, knowing that even one misstep would send him plunging to his death far below.

The air was cold, the moon a wan crescent of gold as Echata inched his way down, sometimes squeezing through narrow defiles, or ducking under an imposing outcropping. He soon grew furious with himself for being baited into this madness.

"Tizu, enough! Come back!"

"Just a few more steps!"

Echata bit back an angry response, then at last rounded a

boulder to stand at the mouth of Great Cave. Darkness enveloped him. His flesh turned clammy and cold. Echata crouched, tingling with dread. It was as if he suddenly dropped into Middle Earth to find it now haunted by evil spirits. Echata's heart pounded and he strained, peering deeper into the cave.

Tizu appeared not to notice. "I told you that this was a place where even Bear could not enter."

"You speak the truth!" Echata finally hissed. "But what *is* back there in the darkness?"

"Nothing but rocks and dust. All is safe here."

As if to prove her point, Tizu picked up a rock and hurled it into the black void. Echata heard the ricochets and then the cave lapsed back into a deep, brooding silence.

"See," Tizu said, bending to take handfuls of the powdery dust which she then let sift through her fingers. "My husband, we could safely store our meat and seeds in the back of this great cave and *all* live here without fear of Bear. Rain and snow would never touch us, nor would cold winter Wind."

"It is *very* cold here."

"We could stay close to the fire. It would be easy to lower wood down from the mesa. And the bottom of this canyon is thick with trees and bushes."

"You have been down there, too?"

"Only once. It is easier than the other way, but a little farther."

"And what of water to drink?"

"A spring bubbles softly from the head of this canyon. It is not so far away. And when the snow melts or Rain falls, we would only need to hold out our pots to catch dripping water."

"You have been thinking much about this," Echata said, craning his neck around and wondering at the size of Great Cave.

"Yes," Tizu admitted, "because only I understand how you sorrow at the death of Niako. Only I know how your heart yearns to avenge him and how you would even give your life to take the life of Bear."

"I was afraid and I shamed myself."

"Everyone was afraid! We have never seen such terrible animals in our desert lands."

Echata squatted on his heels, still unwilling to turn his back on the cave's deepest darkness. "Tizu, since you are wise, you must know that Bear will return. I *must* kill him."

"Or be killed. And, if you die, the People will have no strong leader. Then we would *all* die and Bear would have had his true victory over the last of Raven Clan."

"And so the clan must always live surrounded by this darkness, existing like frightened mice?"

"Not always," Tizu replied. "Raven will show us how to live in canyon sunlight, or up on the mesa among the clouds."

Echata's heart and mind turned one way, then the other. In truth, he had no desire to face Bear again. But neither was he willing to allow the People to become Bear's favorite prey.

"We *must* listen to Raven," Tizu continued, "for he will tell us how to protect ourselves from Bear. We *must* be patient."

As much as he hated to admit it, Tizu was right. "How did you become so wise?" he finally asked, pulling her very close.

"By coupling with you."

Echata doubted that this was true but was more than willing to accept the explanation and eager to give his wife fresh wisdom. And he might have done so then had Tizu not begun to collect wads of sticks and feathers from birds' nests. Soon, they had enough tinder for a good fire which Echata created with his sparking stones. Warm at last and with Echata finally at ease, they made love in the soft dust of Great Cave as if they were young.

In the morning, when climbing back to the mesa, Tizu stepped a few feet above Echata and cried, "Look, Raven watches us!"

Echata twisted around, his toes and fingers fitted into a tight niche in the rock. He craned his head upward and there *was* Raven, circling above the canyon. With a loud call of greeting, Raven floated on the updrafting currents and then swooped to disappear into the heavy growth of trees far below. Moments later, Raven emerged with Mouse in his claws and landed in Great Cave to feed.

"He *does* tell us to live here!" Echata shouted. "This is *very* good!"

A dozen feet above, Tizu allowed herself a faint smile. The evening before, she alone had spotted Raven soaring over this very canyon, but she had kept this secret, knowing it was good for her husband to see Truth first—at least sometimes.

With the appearance of Raven, the clan was infused with fresh hope. Fearful of Bear, they needed little urging to move down into Great Cave, despite the climb which, to Echata's way of thinking, was all the more terrifying in daytime. The children were the least intimidated. With their nimble hands and feet, they made their way down the cliff as if playing.

Their relocation was well-timed for, only a few days later, the first winter snow dusted the mesa although the sun quickly melted it away. With Raven ever-watchful, the clan worked harder than ever. The last of the fall harvest of piñon nuts was gathered. Deer were hunted, then lowered on long yucca fiber ropes, butchered and their hides tanned for warm winter clothing. Just as important was the insatiable demand for firewood. As Tizu had suspected, most of this first winter's supply was gathered down in the canyon and hauled up to the cave. By the time of deep snows, the People were well-prepared. The most troubling problem was that the difficult trail separating them from the mesa became treacherous when covered with snow and ice. Several of the People nearly tumbled to their deaths until Echata and his hunters spent many cold hours chipping hand and footholds into the rock wherever they were needed.

But, most of the time, life was better than it had been on the desert. The clan offered daily prayers to Raven and even to Sun who sometimes touched the mouth of Great Cave so that the People could bask on the warm rocks, away from smoke and fire. During those first anxious weeks of winter, Echata began to hear laughter. For some reason, however, their newfound happiness brought back memories of starvation and of Oomat and the other members of the Raven Clan. Echata wondered if they had all died or been captured and enslaved by enemies.

If *only* Oomat had listened and believed enough to follow him to this high country! If he had, they would all be together now, a whole people living without fear in a land where game was plentiful and their only threat was Bear. Whenever his restless mind returned to Bear, Echata felt a stirring of shame and renewed his vow to warm his family with Bear's thick robe. But when he confided this to the other hunters one snowy day, they became very anxious, arguing that Raven might even help them by casting a spell over Bear so that he would never again awaken.

"And besides," Utaal argued, "we are safe in Great Cave."

But Echata disagreed. "In the spring, when the snow melts and the days grow warm, Bear will awaken hungry. He finally will kill us because we are easier to catch on the mesa than Deer."

"Then we would fight," the quiet hunter named Sanja promised.

"But," Echata persisted, "if we kill Bear in his *sleep,* there is less danger."

"How will this be done?"

Echata looked around to make sure his wife and children were not listening. Satisfied, he whispered, "I will cut his throat while he sleeps."

"No!" Mawi, their best tracker protested. "Bear would awaken and kill you in the darkness."

"Then I will take a torch into the cave and set him on fire!"

The hunters of the Raven Clan exchanged worried glances but Echata's mind was set. "If you do not wish to come," he said, "then stay here with the women and children. I will kill Bear alone."

Shamed, the hunters agreed to the plan. Preparations were made that evening and prayers were offered. It began to snow but the People were dry and protected in Great Cave. When they lay in their blankets by the fire, they watched orange shadow-demons dance on the ceiling high above. Families slept, the wind blew, and snowflakes veiled the cold moon.

Echata fed the fire until dawn when Tizu finally awakened, studied his face and said, "I still do not think this is such a good idea, my husband. It is not good to kill Bear while he sleeps."

"Would you rather I awaken him so that he can kill *me?*"

"Of course not!"

"Then what else can I do?"

"Light a fire outside his cave. Let the wind blow smoke inside. When Bear awakens, he will not be able to see—he will choke and feel very bad. If he tries to come outside and kill you, the fire will singe his hair and he will be easy prey for your spears."

This same idea had occurred to Echata but he had rejected it as being unnecessarily risky. And yet, he also knew the thickness of Bear's coat and how it would dull the thrust of his stone knife. To open the throat of fallen Deer was one thing, to creep into a cave and kill Bear, quite another.

"My husband," his wife was saying, "do not go inside with Bear. Poison him with smoke—burn him with fire."

"But it would ruin his coat!"

"Maybe it will only burn his *feet,*" she reasoned. "Will you do this?"

"I will decide when we get to Bear's cave."

Tizu knew better than to press her husband. He blamed himself for Niako's death and needed to redeem his honor. She handed him his atlatl and a lighted torch. By now, everyone was awake and the hunters were ready to leave.

"The sky is clear but the wind yet blows strong," Utaal growled. "Echata, we should wait for a better day."

"No. Bear sleeps near."

Utaal looked to the others for help but no one said anything and so they all left, shouldering out of Great Cave into the swirling wind, trying hard to shield their sputtering pine torches.

The climb to the top of the mesa was difficult and dangerous because of the footing, the weather and their extra spears, but they managed it without a fall. As soon as he was on the mesa, Echata ducked into the heavy stands of piñon and juniper pine for protection. It was freezing and Echata felt numb and afraid but he kept pushing until they arrived at Bear's den.

"There," he said, coming to rest.

"If you go, you will be killed," He-tok warned.

In reply, Echata drew his stone axe and took a hard swing at a low-hanging branch. Hacking it free, he said, "All right, then we will build a fire before the cave and smoke Bear out, *then* kill him with our spears."

Echata began to chop more branches and drag them over to the mouth of the cave. Because the wood was damp and the wind gusting, it was almost impossible to light the branches. Echata finally lost his patience.

"I will go inside," he announced, tossing his sputtering torch away and unsheathing his knife.

"No!" Mawi, their best tracker cried. "We must push the branches deeper into the cave and out of this wind. That way, they might burn."

Shoving the pile of wet branches farther into Bear's cave, they soon had a smoky fire lit. They fell back to wait.

Long minutes passed without a sound from the cave. Utaal finally whispered, "What if Bear has already gone away?"

"No," Echata said, "he is . . ."

A great roar swallowed Echata's words. He and the others recoiled in terror, then collected their wills and readied their weapons. Bear roared again, but now he sounded confused. Soon the great animal would be forced to charge outside.

But Bear retreated deeper into his cave, still roaring with anger and confusion. The hunters chopped more limbs to toss into the cave's entrance, but Bear refused to appear.

"We should run away," He-tok urged. "This goes badly!"

Echata shook his head believing that, if they ran, Bear would gain enough courage to finally charge through the smoke and fire, then chase down his tormentors and slaughter them one by one. Emboldened, Bear might even manage to descend into Great Cave to slaughter all the clan women and children.

Echata went up to the boiling smoke, drew back his atlatl and sent a dart whistling through the fire into the cave, resulting in a fearful bellow of pain. He jumped back, fitted another dart on his throwing stick, and hurled it into the blackness.

Bear charged through the flames, hair smoking, eyes rolling, mouth open and drooling. Confused, making a strange sound in its throat, the monstrous beast reared back on his haunches and batted at his singed and smoking coat, roaring and snarling like Cougar.

"Kill him!" Echata screamed.

Each hunter launched his spear with all his strength. Bear was knocked down. Echata fit another dart and jumped forward to bury it in Bear's chest. The animal collapsed, fur smoldering.

Echata drew his knife, cut Bear's throat, then threw back his head and howled like a wolf at the moon. It was over! They had defeated their enemy.

The hunters fell upon Bear with their knives, laughing and

slashing. Soon, they carried his flesh down into Great Cave where they celebrated with feasting and stories, telling and retelling Bear's death, each time with more imagination. The meat was rich with fat. Echata knew that it would strengthen the People all this winter.

Echata was, of course, the center of admiration and had no modesty as he demonstrated how dart after dart from his atlatl found Bear's strong heart.

"I know where other bear go for winter sleep," he announced later that night while sitting close beside Tizu. "And one by one, we will kill them."

"No!" Utaal protested. "It is wrong to kill unless we need the strength and food of Bear. To do that would anger the spirits."

"Utaal is right," Sanja agreed.

When everyone began to nod in agreement, Echata decided to remain silent. There was no point in ruining this celebration with another argument. But he *would* kill more bear this winter and every winter of his life. He would kill them until all of them were gone from this mesa, as they were gone from the hot desert. Afterward, the Raven Clan would forever be warm in winter and strong with Bear's meat. And next spring, they would go south to find Oomat and the rest of the People so that—all together—they would multiply to become a great nation, fearing *nothing*.

Seven

After surviving that winter in Great Cave, Echata carved his son's first atlatl and they practiced using the weapon until young Kitka became almost as skilled as his proud father. Six years afterward, Echata's daughter married and delivered her first child, a boy who would not be named until his fifth birthday.

During those early years living in Great Cave and hunting on the mesa top, the Raven Clan had existed in peace and without hunger. Every winter, they tracked and killed more of the terrible grizzly bears by lighting fires before their sleeping dens and then spearing them as they burst through the flames. The People now had many warm bearskin blankets.

In spite of their blessings and the constant protection of Raven, Echata remained restless and dissatisfied. Every spring, he urged the hunters to join him in a dangerous journey south to find Oomat and the rest of their clan and bring them to live in Great Cave, but always the mesa people were afraid of the south. The Raven Clan hunters and their wives argued that the desert still must be suffering a drought, its few rivers and springs parched dry. And they were certain that they no longer would be content with the meat of snakes, birds, lizards, bugs and an occasional stringy and wormy jackrabbit.

To leave this beautiful mesa was madness. Here, the mule deer were as trusting as pet dogs and slow to recognize danger. The hunters now donned antlered deer masks and hides so that they could enter a band without arousing suspicion. Killing deer was easy and they were all big and fat. The only danger now was Bear, and even that threat was decreasing as Echata and his hunters killed more of them each winter. Now, they were rarely seen on the mesa above Great Cave.

If the Raven Clan hunters refused to go south to find the rest of the People, what could Echata do? As leader of the clan, it was his responsibility to reunite his people, but they seemed to be losing their spirit and toughness. There were times when he felt almost sickened by the ease of a deer hunt. He would stand in a meadow of fallen animals and notice that the hunters chose only the best parts of the carcasses and left the rest to rot or be eaten by scavenging animals. The hunters' prayers for the spirits of their dying prey often were spoken without feeling, no more than a hurried afterthought. No doubt about it, his band of survivors was becoming soft. Raven had made their lives too easy.

Early one June morning when Echata was lamenting these developments to his wife, she grew irritable and snapped, "My husband, you should forget about your brother and those people. They are probably dead anyway."

Her words shocked and angered him. "But what if they are not? What if they are still hungry or . . . worse yet . . . enslaved by our enemies? I think that is what happened, Tizu. I cannot live so well when my brother and the Raven Clan suffer!"

"They are *not* the Raven Clan anymore," Tizu said in a very firm tone of voice. "We both remember how you pleaded with Oomat and the others to follow us to this mesa. But Oomat had his own vision and would not listen. Remember how you almost killed your own brother and how I cried out to stop you?"

Echata's chin dipped. His anger was replaced by shame and remorse. "I remember. Why do you remind me?"

Tizu slipped her arms around her husband's waist, feeling a thick belt of scar tissue. Last winter, when killing another bear, there had been a mistake by one of the hunters and Echata had suffered the consequences. He had not yet fully recovered from a terrible mauling and was still weak; his throwing arm no longer had the power to hurl the atlatl. And yet, Tizu was proud because Echata remained fearless and good, a true leader of his people.

"Echata, dear Goat," she said, knowing he was amused and pleased by that endearment, "has it occurred to you that Raven might read your heart and think you ungrateful? That he might punish all of the clan for these thoughts?"

"Yes," Echata said. "Whenever I see Raven, I say a prayer of thanksgiving and speak to him about my brother."

"And what does he tell you?"

"I think he wants me to go find Oomat and the others so that his clan can live here and grow in strength and numbers."

Tizu had not been expecting this answer and she was saddened by it. Thinking quickly, she said, "If Raven wanted you to go south, then he would lead you in that direction."

"I have seen him flying south."

"You have?"

"Yes! Only three days ago, he flew across the sky and down the mesa to disappear in that direction."

"But I saw him yesterday!"

"He always returns, but then flies south. I think Raven is trying to tell us to go find our people."

Tizu had no more to say. The thought of leaving this cool, beautiful world by the clouds and returning to the searing harshness of the desert filled her with dread.

"Maybe I should go alone," Echata said after a long, thoughtful silence.

"No!"

He touched her cheek. "Kitka is almost grown and would take my place as leader. I have been teaching him all the ways. In a year, or two, he will be ready."

But Tizu shook her head and then hugged her husband

with every bit of her strength. "I would *never* let you go alone. I would go with you."

Echata felt his throat knot and his heart swell with pride. "Kitka has said the same. Even when I refused to allow him to come, he said that he would follow me."

"We would *both* follow you into the spirit world."

"I must go south," Echata declared. "I cannot grow old and die in this place without knowing the sad fate of my brother and his followers. I must try to save them. I turned my back on old Niako, I will *not* do the same with my lost people!"

"When will you leave?"

"As soon as I am strong, Tizu."

She took some comfort in that and, when she gazed into his troubled eyes, Tizu knew that she and their son would travel at his side.

In midsummer, Echata announced his intention to return to the desert country. When he spoke, the other men lowered their eyes and looked away. Kitka moved to his father's side, atlatl in hand, head held high and eyes flashing with pride. Tizu joined them and they waited to see who else would find the courage to follow their true leader.

It was a surprise when young He-tok and the quiet, thoughtful Sanja finally stepped forward, leaving Mawi and Utaal who refused to leave their families and friends without protection.

"This is good," Echata said, looking first to his wife and son and then to the two loyal young hunters. "We leave to-day."

Nothing more was said but everyone, even Utaal and Mawi's families, went to work collecting food and provisions for the expedition. Each hunter carried his two best spears, as well as skin bags for water and plenty of food.

They would take no blankets or extra clothing, for the desert would be on fire.

"Utaal! Mawi!" Echata shouted to the pair of hunters who were to remain behind and had shrunk back into the shadows.

They finally came forward and appeared so ashamed that Echata placed a hand on their shoulders, saying, "If we never return, Utaal, you are leader of the Raven Clan. I leave an atlatl behind. You must learn to use it to protect the People. Mawi, always do as Utaal says and do not try to kill Bear next winter. Take care of the women and children, breed many babies and never forget that Raven watches and protects this clan."

The two hunters nodded in acquiescence and then each of the clan's women and children said good-bye. The last to do so was Wo-tu-am, their daughter, with her child and young husband who was no older than Kitka.

Tizu almost cried and had to bite her lower lip to keep the tears from flowing. But very quickly they were climbing out of Great Cave and up the face of the cliff. No longer did height hold any terror for them and they scrambled up to the mesa without a thought of falling. Echata led the way across the open space, following the little creek that stained the brow of the cliff. Soon, they were on a well-traveled and familiar path through the heavy piñon and juniper forest. Echata first, then He-tok, Mawi and Tizu, with graceful young Kitka following with his atlatl lightly balanced in his right hand.

Tizu trembled with excitement and fear. She wished she were back at Great Cave with her daughter, her grandson and all the other women and children. They would be working on skins, grinding seeds between smooth stones or gathering wood and telling stories. Great Cave would ring with their laughter and there would be no worry about hunger or death.

Tizu glanced over her shoulder at Kitka and gave her fine son a broad smile. He also looked very worried until he realized that his mother was watching. Then, he too smiled and Tizu was very glad. Her husband was leader, her son also would be leader. Already, he was wise and strong beyond his years. Echata had taught him the ways of a man, a hunter and a leader; but Tizu had taught him the clan stories and given him wisdom.

In the days that followed, Tizu said little as she kept up with the men. They always had told her that they were much better walkers. Now, she knew better. The men might be stronger of arm and leg, but they tired just as quickly as the women who were accustomed to the hard work of gathering food and firewood. And it was the women who, in late summer, had to carry all the water into Great Cave from the spring at the head of the canyon.

Only age slowed Tizu down. He-tok and Sanja were young men and Kitka still half boy. They were tireless. She was grateful that her husband was setting a reasonable pace, for he too was growing old, although it would have been foolish to remind him of this.

The trail they followed was better than the one to the mesa. It took only two days to reach the desert but then the difficulty began. Sun grew very hot and the land was even more blistered than Tizu remembered. No longer accustomed, they suffered in a heat so intense that it radiated through their sandals to burn their feet.

Echata remembered the way back to their old hunting grounds. He found the springs, or what remained of them and ordered rest in the middle of the day. Remembering their flight from this scorched land, they searched for Tortoise, but he was hiding like Rabbit so they tried to throw stones and spears at the birds. Sadly, they had lost that gift and had to be content with eating lizards and snakes, bugs and roots, in addition to their own food supply which they knew would not last until their return to Great Cave.

"How much farther?" Sanja asked through cracked lips at the end of the second week of desert. "How many more days until we come to this wide canyon where water flows and our enemies live?"

Echata was not sure, but thought it only a few more days. His eyes, weeping from the glare of the sun, strained to penetrate the grayness veiled by undulating heat waves. His lips, too, were cracked and bleeding, his mind almost in a fever of worry over his ability to reach the place of their enemies and find Oomat. And, even if they did reach this place, what would they do against so many? They were already weakened and just three grown men, a fine boy and a great woman. Not enough to put up much of a fight. What if they were captured and tortured to death?

The very thought that he might be leading his wife and son to their deaths was worse than a spear twisting in Echata's brain and in his belly.

When they finally reached the river, it had become but a stream which, as if seeking relief from Sun, often plunged into the fourth world only to reappear many miles farther to the south. But it was easy enough to follow the river, even when it disappeared, for its meandering underworld path was marked by a steady line of trees whose roots also must drop into the lower world.

"Look!" exclaimed young Kitka, whose eyes were nearly as sharp as those of Eagle. He pointed toward the southern horizon.

Echata did not see what his son was pointing at but there was no mistaking the excitement in his young voice.

"What is it?"

"Smoke," Kitka said, looking to Mawi for confirmation. When he received it from the young hunter, Kitka said, "The campfire of our enemies, Father."

Echata took his son at his word. Lightning-caused fires were unusual in the summertime, but not rare. However, they produced far more smoke and often burned across the face of the dry, brush covered land. The smoke of a campfire had a very distinct shape and appearance.

Echata sought the shade of a cottonwood tree and sat down on his haunches, his mind searching for answers.

"What do you know about these people and how can we trick them?" Tizu asked.

"I don't know," Echata admitted. "I think they are called Chacoans and that word means nothing to me. But they are very bad people and kill strangers."

"Have you seen them?" Sanja asked, his young face shiny with perspiration and tight with anxiety.

"Once I killed two of them," Echata admitted. "I was no more than your age and hunting alone. I came upon them and they attacked me without warning. I had my atlatl, a gift of my father, and they were easy to kill."

"I have not heard you speak of this in a long time," Tizu said.

"The memory is a sadness for me," Echata confessed. "The two Chacoans were not much older than Kitka and they died slowly. One spoke our language. He put a curse on me and I was afraid. Raven alone saved me."

"Did they speak of the numbers of their people?"

"Yes," Echata replied. "They had heard of the Raven Clan and said that we were weak. I reminded this man that my father was leader of the Raven Clan and, as his son, I had proven my strength."

"And what did he say?"

"He wanted me to show him my atlatl. I did this and he smiled before his spirit passed to the other world."

Even Tizu had never heard so much of this story. She had known that her husband had fought and killed two of the Chacoans but, whenever she asked about this fight, he had become so sad that she stopped thinking about it . . . until now.

"Did Oomat know of this story when he took the People to this place?" He-tok asked.

"He knew but would say nothing. Oomat is no fool."

"So what do we do now?" Mawi asked, licking his cracked lips. "I do not want to throw my life away for nothing."

"Nor I," He-tok said.

Young Kitka's normal calm broke and he said angrily. "Do you think our leader is a fool! Do you think my father will just run into their camp to die!"

"Shhh," Echata said, calming his son and then adding, "we will stay here until darkness and then we will sneak down to their valley and watch. If Oomat and our people are not to be seen by tomorrow, we will steal away and return to Great Cave. But, if they are in the Chacoan village, we *must* help them."

"But what if they don't *want* our help?" He-tok said.

"What do you mean!" Echata snapped.

"I mean, what if they have become Chacoans?"

"Don't be a fool! My brother would never allow this to happen."

Echata looked to his wife for confirmation but she was studying their son. Her face was a mask which not even he could read. "Now," he said, "we should sleep until darkness."

Everyone nodded and began to scrape little hollows in the sand where they could rest more comfortably. Tizu scraped a pair for herself and Echata and lay down in the shade, motioning her husband to come and join her. Echata did, but he could not sleep. When he was sure that the others were asleep, he turned to Tizu and whispered, "Do *you* have a plan?"

"No," she said. "But we will think of something. I will not allow the Chacoans to kill my son and his father."

"I wish you would stay here and wait for us, Tizu. You cannot run fast and . . ."

She placed her hand over his dry lips. "You cannot run so fast either. So let us not speak of that. Instead, let us rest and think."

"I cannot do both at once."

"I can," Tizu said, closing her eyes.

Echata knew this to be true, so he went to sleep, comforted knowing Tizu was working on their problem in her mind. Just as she had great faith in his ability to lead the People and to keep them safe from all danger, so he had great faith in her ability to think of a way to save Oomat and most of the Raven Clan.

They awoke well after dark, parched and still weary. Two miles along the trail of the trees, they found where the river came back up to this world and they spent time drinking and washing their bodies. The change that water brought to them was profound. It refreshed them all and they were in much better spirits when they began to skirt the broad canyon called Chaco. It was well past midnight when, on the rim of the low canyon, they found a good vantage point.

"There are *many* campfires!" Mawi said in awe. "More than I have ever seen in one place."

"Yes," Echata said, looking first to his son and then to his wife. "But the real question is, if they yet live, which fire belongs to Oomat and our people?"

Tizu had no answer. Neither did anyone else, so they settled down to wait for Sun to show them truth.

Eight

Echata had never seen Chaco Canyon before, but he'd heard stories about it. And now, with dawn peeking over the eastern horizon, he saw that the canyon was just as it had been described. It resembled a valley, wide and shallow with crumbling rock walls that ascended like broken steps to a huge expanse of high desert, a nearly treeless tabletop that ran as far as the eye could see.

But, down in the canyon itself, as the light slowly strengthened and washed clean the dark shadows, Echata saw a confusing sight. Rows of plants ran neatly along the banks of the river, all fed by little streams. Echata had never seen anything so strange.

"What are they?" he asked, squinting hard. "Tizu?"

"I do not know, my husband. Perhaps, if we wait and watch, the truth will become clear."

"Yes," Echata said, "that was what I was about to say."

So they waited and watched, eyes on the many campfires and the strange villages with little pointed houses. As the sun struggled higher, the Chacoans began to emerge. They had many barking dogs. Echata watched men and women go out into the brush to squat. This camp awakened slowly. Fires were fed; people, too. Then, before the sun was very high, both the men and the women walked to the green rows along the river and began to do work that Echata could not understand.

"What are they *doing?*" Kitka asked, looking to his mother.

"They are digging . . . and moving the streams. Look! See how the water runs down between the rows."

"But *why?*" Sanja asked.

"These are very strange people," Echata said. "No wonder they are enemies."

"But so many!" He-tok said, shaking his head in wonder. "How could this land *feed* so many?"

"They are weak," Echata said with contempt. "They cannot fight well because they are so hungry and weak."

"They do not look weak."

"But they are."

Everyone settled down to wait. Tizu was fascinated by the great villages that dotted the canyon floor. She saw women not unlike herself carrying babies on cradleboards and tending campfires just as her own clan women would do on such a fine morning. She watched them grind seeds on stones and, when the breeze shifted in just the right direction, Tizu thought she could hear the comforting laughter of women and children, no different than the laughter that echoed inside Great Cave. It was strange; Tizu had always heard that the Chacoans were demons who appeared nothing like the People.

She had been wrong.

"Does anyone see Oomat!" Echata wanted to know. "My eyes are not so young anymore."

"I would not know his face," Kitka admitted.

"I would," Sanja said, gaze sweeping from one collection of huts to the next.

"Do you see . . ."

"There!" Sanja cried. "I see Oomat . . . and his son, Gejo. Gejo is a man now, but I recognize him! And I see others of the Raven Clan. They all live together!"

"Where!" Echata exclaimed, straining to pick out the familiar faces.

"Right there," Sanja said, pointing. "That big village off by itself. See?"

"I *cannot* see," Echata said with exasperation. "They are too far away."

"I see them!" He-tok whispered with excitement. "Yes! Those are our people."

Echata twisted around to stare at his wife. "Can you see them?"

"No," she confessed. "I also am growing old."

"He-tok, what are our people doing?"

"They are doing the same things that the Chacoans are doing. The women are fixing a meal, taking care of children and some of them are walking out to the green rows to work."

Echata muttered to himself, then added, "And my brother?"

"He and Gejo are doing . . . nothing. They sit and eat. Your brother has grown very fat."

"No!"

"It is true," He-tok swore. "Mawi, Kitka, see that big man, the one who wears silver sitting beside a younger man with his hair braided?"

"Yes," Kitka said. "Is *that* my uncle?"

"It is. And your cousin Gejo."

"He also wears silver."

Echata could not bear this. He had dreamed of this moment for years and had expected to find his people suffering so that he could save them. But now . . . now he was hearing that they were acting just like the enemy! And his brother was fat and wearing silver.

Echata turned away from Chaco Canyon in disgust. He stomped across the tabletop, confused and filled with anger.

"Echata!"

"Go away, Tizu, I . . . I feel bad."

But she did not go away. Instead, Tizu came to his side. They walked until the sun grew hot and Tizu was panting and covered with perspiration.

"My husband," she pleaded, "we cannot go on. There is no water here and, besides, you are leader and must lead!"

Tizu was right. Echata came to an abrupt halt and slowly pivoted. He had not realized how far they had marched and this land was baking. Tizu looked so exhausted that Echata was ashamed of his behavior.

"I am sorry. We can go back now."

"To Great Cave?" she asked hopefully.

"No. To find a way to reach Oomat, Gejo and the others."

Echata was not sure what he would or even could say to them now that he had to admit that they were not only alive, but living like the Chacoans. And Oomat had become fat! None of the Raven Clan had ever had this gift of fatness. Echata could hardly imagine such a disgusting thing.

Tizu trudged wearily beside him, trying to voice her own agitated thoughts. "My husband, it is clear that we have come far for a good and noble purpose. But it is also clear that your brother and our people are neither dead nor enslaved. Instead, they have their own village in this canyon and are living like Chacoans."

"They would rather live at Great Cave under the protection of Raven!"

"We do not know this. And, if we try to find out, we could all be killed."

"I have no choice but to find out."

"How?"

"I will sneak into their village after darkness and speak with my brother. I will tell Oomat of the mesa country and how it is good and we live very well. How we do not have to work and the hunting is easy. How we miss our people and want them to come back with us to Great Cave."

Tizu's head bobbed up and down as she tried to match her husband's stride. For the first time in a very long time, she was fearful of speaking her mind.

"What?" Echata said, glancing sideways at her and noting a troubled expression.

"I do not think that they will want to come with us."

"They will! When they see us and learn of what we have found on the mesa, they will be grateful."

"And we might all be killed if we are caught."

Echata made a face to show his contempt. "We are *hunters,* Tizu. These people are . . . I do not know what they are but they are *not* hunters. They are weak. I have told you how I killed two of them long ago."

"You were all boys then. It is different now. And there are so many in this canyon."

"Then they will not care if a few are missing tomorrow morning. And they will be too lazy to follow."

When Echata announced his intention to sneak into Oomat's village that very night, the reaction of his hunters was not to his liking.

Sanja, almost always agreeable, said, "We should go back to our mesa and leave Oomat and the others here. This land is no good for us."

"Then," Echata asked, "why is it good for them? Are they not also us? Is their blood not *our* blood, their spirits, *our* spirits?"

"Yes," Mawi said, "but it has been many winters since they belonged to the Raven Clan. They are Chacoans now."

Echata's face darkened with anger and he gazed up toward the sun. "If Sun tells Raven what you have said, we will be punished! These are still Raven's people."

"But what if they refuse to come?" Kitka dared to ask.

Echata could not imagine such a thing, even though Tizu had already voiced the same fear. Grabbing his atlatl, Echata prepared to leave the group, saying, "By darkness, I will be on the canyon floor, close to Oomat's village. Soon after, I will be among the Raven People again. When I tell them of Great Cave, they will follow and we will all join at the north end of this canyon. By morning, we will be far away."

No one dared to voice an objection, not even Tizu. But when her husband started to leave, she and Kitka followed.

"Go back!" Echata ordered in his harshest voice. "Go with Mawi and Sanja and wait for me to the north."

"No, my husband."

"Kitka! Go!"

But the boy would not leave. Instead, he took Tizu's hand and they came forward.

Echata was not in the habit of striking his wife or his son, but he very nearly did this time. He *would* have, if he thought that hitting them would send them away. But Echata knew Tizu too well, so he turned and began hiking along the rim of the canyon, seeking a downward path on which the Chacoans would not be able to see his approach and that would bring him close to Oomat's village. What kind of sickness had entered the People's minds that they would live this way and move water around fields? Echata was really worried, not about being caught and killed but about the state of mind of Oomat and Gejo.

They found a way to the bottom of the canyon, and there was so much broken rock and rubble that it was easy to hide close to Oomat's village. The day was very hot, though, and they suffered, wishing they could cool themselves in the shallow stream where Chacoan children played beside mothers who once had belonged to the Raven Clan.

Echata was patient. He had waited years for this night and now he was close enough to recognize Oomat. He never would have recognized Gejo. The boy was fat also, but not nearly as fat as his father. Small wonder. The two of them did nothing all day but eat and smoke pipes while being waited upon by girls and women. The sight of them filled Echata with repugnance. How could this pair descend from his mesa down into Great Cave? And, should they manage that, how would they ever climb out again to hunt and to gather piñon nuts, wood and water? Would they expect always to be waited upon like this? Echata thought much about these questions but could arrive at no clear answers.

"My husband?"

"Yes?"

"It is nearly dark and I ask you once more, for the sake of your people and for Kitka, do not do this."

"Why?"

Tizu was slow to answer.

"Why?" Echata repeated with a hard edge to his voice.

"Because," Kitka interrupted, "my mother does not like . . . or trust . . . Oomat."

Echata swung toward his son, then back to Tizu who lowered her eyes. "Tizu, is this true?"

"He always wanted to be leader. He spoke behind your back when the Raven Clan divided and I never believed he saw true visions. Oomat is evil and this evil has passed to his son."

"Gejo was only a boy."

"His father's boy," Tizu argued. "They are the same, only of different ages."

"Father," Kitka added, "if it is your wish, we will speak no more of these troubling things. But we would be happy to leave this bad place now."

"I cannot leave after waiting so long," Echata said, thinking not only of his brother and of Gejo, but also of the other members of the People. "As soon as it is full darkness, I will go and speak to Oomat. But this time, you *will* remain here to wait."

Tizu and Kitka nodded but looked so upset that they made Echata feel guilty. "It will be all right," he said, trying to sound confident, "I am still leader of Raven Clan. The People here will listen."

When a half-moon floated over Chaco Canyon, and bats began to feed on insects as they flickered through the warm, rising air down along the columns of cottonwood trees, Echata stood up and, without a word, left the cover of boulders and walked toward Oomat's hut. He could see the bloated figure of his brother but Gejo had disappeared. Oomat was resting beside a fire, surrounded by three slender women. When Echata entered the light of the campfire, the women came to their feet, then retreated into the darkest shadows.

Oomat was lost in thought. His many chins were folded on his chest and his eyes were fixed on the firelight.

"My brother!" Echata said in greeting. "It is I, Echata!"

Oomat's head snapped up. Fire danced in his dark eyes. He stared for a moment. Without moving, he asked, "What brings you to my village?"

Echata hid his disappointment well. He had expected some joy from Oomat, or at least a civil greeting, and had gotten neither. "I have come a long way . . . from high in the mountains," he explained, motioning to the north. "We now live happily on the mesa and in Great Cave. Raven led us there, just as I saw in the vision."

"Vision?" Oomat's lip curled. "You have *never* had a vision!"

"This is not true," Echata objected, squatting beside his brother. "I have dreams."

"You have petty ambitions."

Echata struggled to silence his anger and pain. His fist tightened on his atlatl and he pushed ahead with the words that he had rehearsed so long. "My brother, hear me well. Up on the mesa, the air is clean and cool. The water is sweet and the deer very fat and stupid. There are so many piñon nuts that we cannot harvest them all, even the ones very near Great Cave."

"Then go back to the mountains. This is my home and that of my people."

"Your people?"

Oomat wagged his chins. "Yes. I have three wives now and I eat very well. I have no wish to go with you and neither do my people."

"But they are not your people! They are still Raven Clan

people and I have come to take them away from this bad place."

"They will not go," Oomat said, for the first time really studying his brother. "They will see that you are thin and that you look old and tired. They will not give up this life."

"You are wrong!" Echata hissed, jumping to his feet.

"And you are a fool," Oomat said with yawning contempt. "Go away! We are Chacoans now and you are not even worthy of being called Enemy."

Echata drew his stone knife and grabbed his brother by the throat. "Do you wish to die!"

Oomat's eyes widened in fear. "No!"

Echata pushed his brother over backward. Oomat made the sound of a frightened rabbit and had to struggle like Tortoise on its back in order to right himself.

"You are as soft as a woman! *Softer* than a woman!" Echata said with contempt and loathing.

"Gejo! Gejo! Help me!"

Oomat's son appeared. He was taller than Echata and far heavier but looked weak and harmless, even with a long silver knife clenched in his fist.

"Father! Who is this!"

"It is Echata," Oomat gasped. "He has come to take us with him. To leave this canyon and go climb mountains and live in a cave like rats! Drive him away!"

Gejo boldly advanced. He was sweating and wore only a breech clout but there was silver on his wrists and fingers. There were feathers in his hair, brighter than any Echata had ever seen before, and the silver knife in his hand was long. It glittered in the moonlight, mocking Echata's crude stone weapon.

"Go!" Gejo ordered in a high-pitched voice. "Or we will kill you!"

Echata retreated from the firelight. "Gejo, you were a boy when I last saw you, but you must know that I am the true leader of the Raven Clan."

"We are Chacoans!" the young man said proudly, tossing his long braided hair like a young girl. "My father saw in a dream that one day you would come back. And he saw that you would die."

Echata held his atlatl lightly balanced in one hand, his knife in the other. "I *will* speak to my people! Summon them now!"

Oomat's nervous laughter was obscene. It sent chills up Echata's spine and, when he turned back to the fire, Oomat began to shout for help as if he were under attack.

Echata took a step toward his brother. "Why . . ."

Gejo's blade plunged into his back. Echata groaned. His atlatl slipped from his hand as he tried to reach around and yank the knife free. He could feel Gejo's flabby body as the younger, heavier man began to rip the knife upward through his ribs.

"Tizu!" Echata screamed as his knees buckled. "Tizu!"

Kitka's stone-tipped spear point entered Gejo's right side with such force that it exited the left as he and Echata collapsed. Tizu snatched up Echata's stone knife and drove it up into Oomat's great, soft belly. Echata heard his brother shriek like a panther. He looked up to see Tizu tear his knife from Oomat and slash his throat. Oomat batted her away, then attempted to crawl toward his hut, but Tizu landed on his back like a cat and finished her bloody work while Oomat's arms and legs beat helplessly at the Earth and he made watery death sounds.

Echata's hand clasped his atlatl because it always had been his strength. He felt himself being lifted and then he and Kitka were struggling back toward the rocks.

"Run!" Echata pleaded. "Get Tizu and run!"

But Kitka would not leave him. They made it across the canyon floor and back into the rocks. Tizu joined them a few minutes later.

"My husband!" she sobbed. "We must leave this canyon and go back to the mesa! These people will find us soon and . . ."

"I am dying," he said, reaching to caress her face. "You must leave and join Mawi and Sanja. Then hurry back to Great Cave and prepare the People to fight."

Tizu shook her head. In a voice ragged with grief, she cried, "I am *not* leaving! I am old and cannot run so far. I stay to die with you."

"Obey me!"

Instead, she collapsed across Echata and hugged his neck, weeping so hard that he used the last of his strength trying to comfort her.

"Kitka, you must go *now*," Echata whispered. "You are leader. Save the People. Never come back to this place!"

Kitka covered his face with both hands and his slender body convulsed with grief. He started to leave but his father's voice held him for a moment.

"Take my atlatl!" he begged. "The Chacoans must never learn my secret. Take it!"

"I will," Kitka vowed as he hugged them and took both his own and his father's great weapon.

When their son was gone, Tizu and Echata listened to wails of grief from Oomat's young wives. Men began to shout in alarm, then anger. Tizu's heart trembled when she saw torches being lighted and men coming to find and kill them.

"My husband," she whispered. "What shall we do!"

But Echata could not answer. Wishing to join him, Tizu cut her own throat just as she had cut Oomat's. She did not shriek in terror as the warm blood coursed down her chest. Her dying thought was that her blood and that of her husband now flowed together, just as perfectly as had their lives.

Kitka held his father's blood-slickened atlatl in his right hand while, in his left, he clutched his own throwing weapon. Chaco Canyon was filled with shouts of anger and confusion. He was unable to run. Dazed and numb with grief, it took all of his will just to move toward the path that would lead him out of this place of wailing demons.

He missed the path that had brought him down with Echata and Tizu and began to thread his way up through a jumble of huge boulders before he came face to face with a sixty-foot cliff. Slinging both throwing weapons over his shoulder to free his hands, Kitka scaled its impossibly steep and crumbly walls swiftly and with ease, for they were nothing compared to those he and his people climbed almost every day in order to leave Great Cave for their high hunting mesa.

Grief so overwhelmed Kitka that he continued to sob as he crested the canyon's rim, then pivoted to glare back down at the frenzied madness far below.

"Ahhheiiii!" Kitka shrieked into the starlit night, raising and shaking both throwing weapons. "Ahhheeeiiii!"

His high, eerie howling echoed across the canyon walls and the village below was suddenly cloaked by an eerie silence.

"Ahhheeeiiii!"

"Kitka!" Sanja yelled, racing ahead of He-tok to grab and pull him around and away from the precipice. "Are you mad! What happened down there! Where . . . ?"

Kitka threw off the man's arms. "Echata and Tizu are *dead!*"

He swayed on the very lip of the rim and lifted his outstretched arms so that his silhouette would appear to the Chacoans as terrible as Raven pinned against an indigo sky. Below, enemy torches massed and then flowed toward him like the earth's belly fire.

"We *must* go!" Sanja cried, trying to pull him into a run.

"Go then," Kitka said, digging in his heels and throwing aside his friend's grip. "I will catch up soon."

"But . . ."

"Go!"

The two hunters tried to grab and haul Kitka back from the rim, thinking that he was going to hurl himself to his death, but Kitka fought free. "I *will* catch you . . . and well before dawn."

"This is your promise!" He-tok exclaimed.

"Yes. It is my word as *true leader* of Raven Clan."

The pair left on the run. Kitka watched as their shadows faded into the northern horizon and then he carefully placed his weapons down and waited as the torches began to float upward like fiery embers in smoke. Kitka didn't know . . . or even care . . . how many of the enemy were gathering below—perhaps fifty, maybe hundreds. It didn't matter. Their wild impassioned curses were music to his ears. He laughed aloud at them as he savored a deadly vision. When he finally opened his eyes, Moon smiled. Kitka smiled back, then knelt beside a large boulder. With all the power in his hard, young body and with Raven and the great spirits of his parents breathing power into his being, the huge boulder began to move and finally to slide over the rim. Kitka rested on hands and knees, chest heaving from the exertion. A smile formed on his cracked lips as the tenor of furious Chacoan voices was transformed into terrified shrieks and then muffled under the ominous rumble of rocks and oceans of sliding shale as a huge cloud of billowing dust bearded grinning Moon. Kitka knew that all the enemy would not die—that the very quickest and strongest would survive to use their many well-known paths to the top of this canyon. When the first Chacoan crested the rim, bruised, gasping and already half-dead, Kitka easily kicked his body back over the rim to tumble into the hated canyon. He killed three more in the same fashion and would not have stopped at all if the Chacoans had not begun to come at him like an army of warring ants.

"Ahhheeiiii!" Kitka howled at happy Moon again as he gathered both his own and Echata's atlatls and began to jog to the east to greet a rising, blood red Sun.

As he ran on and on through what remained of the night, Kitka had never felt so exhilarated or powerful. He floated like Raven on canyon winds. Unhurried, he bounded over obstacles and laughed often. This was better than any vision he could imagine. And the best part was yet to come. When Sun peeked over the eastern horizon, Kitka would stop to rest and wait for the strongest of the pursuing Chacoans. With these weary enemies stumbling into his trap, he would teach them that only death awaited those foolish enough to attack the true Raven People ever again.

Kitka vividly remembered that long, victorious night across the years and especially on the day when he announced that his first son would be named Echata, in memory of the Raven Clan's greatest leader. Kitka's wife, La-ati, was over-joyed. The legend of Echata and Tizu would live forever in the memory of the People. The fact that not even Kitka had been present at the moment of their gallant deaths was all for the better. It allowed endless interpretations . . . more val-iant with every succeeding generation.

Kitka himself, having been the last to see his parents, had the greatest vision. He told and retold the People how he had slain Gejo and then how his mother had leapt on fat Oomat and opened his throat. And he always added a few Chacoans to the number that he had killed with the great rolling rock.

Because of their losses and their fear of Raven's protection, the Chacoans never tried to invade the high mesa country and Kitka felt confident that they never would. The Chacoans were many, but as Echata had foretold, they were a weak and lazy people—even those who once had belonged to the Raven Clan. Better, much better, that they had been expelled for choosing to follow Oomat.

As for Echata and Tizu, they were gods now, almost as revered as Raven and Sun. Kitka ordered his father's atlatl to be sealed in a stone. The People always bowed their heads and whispered a prayer of thanksgiving when they passed that simple rock shrine.

Nine

April 27, 1890

Dr. Michael Turner, Director
Smithsonian Museum of Anthropology
Washington, D.C.

Dear Dr. Turner:

Several months ago, we received your letter demanding that my husband tender an explanation as to why we have not kept in contact regarding our findings at Mesa Verde. It is with deep sorrow that I inform you that Andrew has just passed away due to severe injuries sustained from a fall at Cliff Palace last winter while in your employ. I should have written you earlier but I have been in a very depressed frame of mind, as even you can imagine.

Our research expenses for the Smithsonian total $193.66 and I am enclosing a detailed accounting. In addition to this sum, I request that you send me enough money to pay for Andrew's medical and funeral expenses for which I also have enclosed a full accounting.

The Mesa Verde ruins are a major archaeological find. I'm sure that you will be upset to learn that much of the collection has already been sold. I admit no small part in urging the

Denver Chamber of Commerce and Historical Society to authorize the purchase of many Anasazi artifacts.

As of this date, it is my understanding that the Wetherill family has excavated 182 separate Mesa Verde ruins, mapped the entire area, and even agreed to sell a collection to a Swedish baron for export to that country.

The Wetherill family has every intention of continuing to excavate and profit from Mesa Verde until they run out of artifacts. My only consolation is that Andrew never knew to what extent this great archaeological site is being commercially exploited.

Please forward compensation as requested. I apologize for the delay and hold you personally blameless, but the Smithsonian must fully accept its financial responsibility for the loss of my husband's life while working in its service.

> *Sincerely,*
> *Mrs. Lisa Cannaday*

Lisa posted the letter that very day and then returned to finish clearing out her husband's office which held, among other things, several artifacts from Cliff Palace, in addition to the prized atlatl. An intricately woven reed basket was filled with the seeds of corn, squash and beans . . . all staples of an agricultural society that had replaced the earlier and much simpler hunter and gatherer society.

Andrew had named this artifact the "Treasure Basket" because it contained what he believed were sacred seeds, probably blessed during an important Anasazi religious ceremony.

Lisa drifted back to the happy moment of this surprising discovery—with her beloved Andrew—at Cliff Palace. Then, she bowed her head and let warm tears wash the precious seeds.

* * *

THE TREASURE BASKET

circa 650 A.D.
An Anasazi Pit House
Chaco Canyon, New Mexico

Araba was fourteen years old and the youngest and most prized wife of the next great Chacoan leader, Matezi. But Araba had lain panting against the hard earth of the pit house, struggling to give birth until the ordeal finally robbed her of all but the last of her strength. Araba was sure she was dying, and the baby with her. To compound the tragedy, if this was a boy child, he would have been blessed, since his father was the true leader of the ancient and venerated Sun Clan.

"Unless this ends soon, both Araba and her baby will die," Li-tia, the medicine woman said as the women prepared for yet another long night in Araba's large pit house. "We must pray and use stronger medicines."

"If she dies then you would have to answer to Matezi," a toothless woman warned. "And, if the baby is a boy, he might kill you also."

Li-tia had already considered this. Araba's husband had gained too much power already over every person in the Sun Clan. He also was possessed of a vicious temper that some-times erupted into a murderous rage.

"I have one last medicine," Li-tia told the other women. "But it will take a little time to prepare."

"Hurry, or she will die first!" the irritable Puatu snapped.

Araba was certain that her death was very near. Her strength and even the worst of her pain were ebbing away like her spirit. Only sorrow remained. Why had the gods so turned against her when this should have been the time of her greatest happiness? Matezi had as much as promised that, if she bore him a son, the child would be his likely successor.

Oh, how happy that had made Araba! From the day she first had known she was with child until only a few hours ago, her life had been fulfilled and she had been treated by all the People with great reverence and honor.

But now . . . now she was going to die and the brave infant still struggling in her womb would die, too. Matezi, in his disappointment and bitter rage, would have *both* their bodies dragged out of Chaco Canyon. They would be set upon by wild animals and devoured by dawn. Their disgraced and banished souls would howl in darkness eternally.

That fear gave Araba fresh resolve. *I must not give up! I must keep on trying!* Her dark eyes searched the room, trying to gain strength from the familiar and usually happy surroundings. Her rock-bound hearth provided fire and warmth and, in its flickering yellow light, Araba recognized comforting and familiar faces. But when an unexpectedly powerful contraction tore a scream from her throat, Araba closed her eyes and struggled to preserve the final shreds of her unraveling reason. Her splayed fingers dug into the dirt floor and, as if she were floating above the others, Araba could visualize everything.

Because of her station as the favored wife of the Chacoan's next leader, her pit house was large. Araba rested on soft rabbit-skin blankets piled high on the five-foot deep subterranean floor. Four strong timbers supported the roof while off to her left was the familiar anteroom where Araba stored her husband's best grain, tools, weapons and furs. That room was now filled with smoke. Prayers for it had been taken over by Li-tia whose voice was joined by those of the other women in her attendance. One of the women was humming Death Song. They would sing all night, even after Araba died. She didn't care. The harder she tried to push the baby out, the faster her spirit departed her body, like smoke through the hole in the roof and nothing—not even Li-tia's strongest medicine—could ever bring back old smoke.

"Araba! Araba, awaken!"

Araba felt her jaw being forced open and then a scorching fire burned her throat as her stomach heaved and lights flashed before her eyes. An icy sweat erupted across her aching body.

"More!" Li-tia insisted. "Drink more!"

"Poison," an old woman said, shaking her head. "She kills Araba in the hope of saving the baby."

Li-tia did not waste even a glance at the fool. "I will save them *both!*"

"But Araba is lost!"

Li-tia was not so sure. The girl's pulse remained strong, Li-tia knew that because she could see the swollen vein throbbing in her neck. And the medicine woman knew that Araba had a great will to live. In all her years, Li-tia had never seen anyone fight so hard.

"Araba, you *must* drink more!"

Li-tia watched the girl's eyelid's flutter. Had she understood? Did she even have the strength to swallow? And would this final, desperate concoction rekindle her will to live?

When Araba did not respond to her commands, Li-tia again pried the girl's jaws apart, aware that they still held enough power to crush her fingers. She poured the vile medicine down Araba's throat, massaging it with both thumbs.

"Swallow!" she pleaded. "Araba, swallow!"

The pale throat convulsed as Li-tia emptied the small, gray medicine jar. She used the softest of doeskin to pat Araba's face, neck and chest dry.

"Li-tia, what . . . ?"

"Ssssh!" Li-tia hissed.

Araba's body arched with a powerful contraction. Gasping and spitting, the girl tried to curl up in a fetal ball but Li-tia shouted for her friends to pin Araba's legs flat and wide apart while she held her arms down, feeling noxious vomit and her medicine wash over her body.

"It's coming!" a watcher screamed. "I see the *baby* coming!"

Li-tia could hardly believe her ears. "Is it alive!"

An eternity seemed to pass before several women cried in unison, "Yes!"

Joy flooded Li-tia until she glanced at the women and saw them recoil in shock. The baby, covered with blood but already breathing, was deformed. All the joy and relief died in Li-tia's heart. Her hands began to shake and she tried but could not reach out and take the quivering infant and do the thing that had to be done to insure its life.

"Don't touch it!" one of the women cried, leaping to her feet. "The thing is *cursed!*"

Li-tia's hands began to shake uncontrollably. The women were leaving, frantic to climb the ladder and get away from the bloody abomination. She heard them screeching like turkeys scattering before coyotes under the moon.

"Li-tia," Araba whispered. "What is wrong?"

"Nothing."

But the stampeding women made Li-tia's words a lie and the deformed infant still lay between the girl's legs, fighting and choking.

Araba tried to lift her head but had not the strength. "Li-tia, what is *wrong!*"

Li-tia used the soft doeskin to take up the baby. She tied the umbilical cord with a leather thong and then bit through it as her mind tried to comprehend the full extent of this cruel tragedy. Like the terrified women who even now were still fighting to leave this place, she realized that this infant would be considered cursed. Not only that, but the curse was compounded because it had been sired by the next leader of the Sun Clan!

Li-tia was afraid to touch the deformity but neither could she tear her eyes away from it. Only the arm was so awful. It was a stunted twisted limb whose hand was . . . yes, webbed like the foot of Swimming Turtle. Between the ridges that must have tried to become fingers there was a thin blue membrane.

Li-tia felt a cold shiver pass the length of her body. Poor

child! Poor mother! Poor *me!* Matezi would explain this
shocking disgrace by declaring that he was not the abomination's father, that Araba was weak and had been seduced by
evil spirits who had impregnated her as an inhuman joke and
that, in order to spare the Sun Clan from being cursed also,
Araba, her evil abomination and Li-tia who had brought it
into the world must *all* be destroyed.

Of course. What else could he do?

Li-tia was not afraid of death, but neither was she willing
to die in order to spare Matezi this shame. And besides, in
all other respects, this boy-child was normal. In fact, he was
quite large and already greeting his unforgiving world with
a lusty squall.

There was not much time. *I must run away,* Li-tia thought
with a sense of doom. *I must gather what precious things I
can carry and run for my life before Matezi and the elders
arrive with their proclamation of death!*

Li-tia placed the infant in Araba's arms but not before
wrapping it tightly with the doeskin so that the poor girl could
not see the deformity and realize their fates.

"A boy?" Araba whispered, tears of happiness streaming
down her cheeks.

"Yes. A . . . a boy."

"And he is still strong!" she breathed, now finding the
strength to hold the infant up before her eyes. "Listen to him,
Li-tia! Someday his voice will be the one that leads our people!"

"Don't think of what is to come, think only of what you
have *now.*"

Araba nodded, eyes shiny with happiness. "His name will
be Quaeto. It is a name worthy of a great leader, yes, Li-tia?"

"Yes, very worthy."

"I owe you everything," Araba whispered. "I love you with
all my heart. You never shall be without my friendship. Someday I . . . I will consider it an honor when you pass into the
spirit world as I have almost done."

"Please, save your strength."

Li-tia already was stuffing her largest and strongest gathering basket with everything that she could carry and would need in the wilderness. She had no idea where she would go or how she would survive, but at least she would try to live.

She would need weapons. She would fill her basket with Matezi's finest bow and arrows, although she had no experience using them. And sharp knives and food. Yes, and her mano and metate, even though they were heavy, and warm rabbit skin blankets and . . . turkeys. No, she could not dare to steal a pair from the People's flock. It would be far too risky. Whatever she took, it must come from this house and it must be taken fast.

"Li-tia, I am so happy," Araba said almost dreamily as she held her infant to her breast. "I was sure that I was dying. Your medicine is great indeed."

"Hush!"

Araba opened her eyes. "What are you doing with my husband's bow and arrow?"

"I . . . I am just moving things."

"Ah, I see. Be careful."

"Yes, very careful."

"Are you taking food?"

"Some."

"Take as much as you want. I owe you everything."

Li-tia was thirty-two, old for an Anasazi woman, yet she felt young, strong and very determined to live. She had never suffered the agony of bearing children and, without a family to feed, had lived very easily compared to the other women. She had learned to survive alone and not to become too attached to anyone, but now Araba's naïveté and praise were breaking her heart. Araba had been one of the very first babies that Li-tia had helped bring into this world and so she had always been a favorite. Now, Li-tia realized that she must abandon Araba and her baby to a horrible death by fang and claw.

Li-tia bit her lip and tasted blood. The pain kept her mind off the girl and she hurriedly collected several smaller reed baskets containing medicines and seeds. The harvests of the Chacoans were legendary in comparison to those of other Anasazi peoples and Matezi always had kept the finest seeds for his own households. It was likely that these corn, bean and squash seeds could be bartered for things of vital importance. They also could be soaked and cooked to fight off starvation in desperate times.

"Li-tia?"

"Yes?"

"How soon should we bind Quaeto to the cradleboard?"

She finished packing and slung the heavy basket over her shoulder. "In a few days."

"Must we wait that long?" Araba closed her eyes, fingers stroking little Quaeto into silence. "I want his head to be perfect."

It was the custom of Li-tia's people to bind the heads of newborns and infants tightly to a cradleboard so that the backs of their skulls would become flat. The higher the station of the newborn, the more flattening was expected.

"Do not talk so much," Li-tia said. "You must be still."

"When can I feed Quaeto?"

"Soon!"

Li-tia had fine things of her own, but it was already too late to return to her house for them. She must flee Chaco Canyon with her basket full of Matezi's finest goods, though her heart was full of guilt and sorrow.

Li-tia knew that she would stand little chance in a deadly contest of words against Matezi. But before she was forever silenced, she would mortally wound that man's pride and damage his standing among the Chacoans.

"Li-tia," the girl whispered.

She *must* leave. Basket bulging, heart racing, Li-tia placed her hand on the ladder to climb out of this sorrowful place.

"Li-tia!"

She turned and let the heavy basket slip from her shoulder to the floor. Kneeling beside the girl, Li-tia leaned very close and wished with all her heart that Araba and her baby had died in labor. It would have been a mercy. "Yes, my beautiful daughter?"

"Where are you *going?*"

"I . . . must . . . go," Li-tia replied in a voice even she did not recognize.

"Please, hurry back!" Araba rolled her head around, finally noticing that they were alone. "Where did all the watchers go?"

Li-tia grabbed up her bag. Scrambling up the ladder, she ran for the canyon wall . . . hating herself for running away without even having the courage to tell Araba and little Quaeto that their lives were about to come to a vicious end.

The moon was thin and rising as Li-tia climbed out of Chaco Canyon. She had no fear of heights but the basket made this climb difficult. She could have taken the usual trails, all well-marked and easy, but Matezi already might be sending out runners to intercept her at those places. And while Li-tia was strong and surefooted, she knew that she stood no chance of outdistancing young men. Furthermore, once her trail was discovered, Matezi's best runners and trackers would quickly overtake and kill her before she could use the power of words against their next leader.

As she approached the rim of the canyon, out of breath and with fear feeding her strength, Li-tia thanked Moon for being shy this night. Over and over, she told herself that it was really in Matezi's best interests to let her escape. *I would, if I were he. Matezi is no fool. It will be enough to have poor Araba and Quaeto dragged to the place of abandonment and death where they soon would be attacked and eaten. Yes, that is all that Matezi need do to save face.*

When Li-tia crawled over the rim, she sat down to rest for

a few minutes and to gather her wits. If she were to escape and to somehow survive, she must think clearly instead of running through the brush like a frightened rabbit.

So, where do I go? What do I do now? If I go south, east or west, I go to the friends of my people who dare not protect me. If I go north, to the high mountains, I go to unknown enemies—the Raven Clan.

Then Li-tia remembered Araba's great fighting spirit and her indomitable courage. Araba, whom she had abandoned in order to save her own life. Araba, who thought of her as a friend and who loved her completely. These thoughts caused Li-tia, the most important and respected of all Chacoan medicine women, to collapse and weep. Time lost all meaning and the moon floated up to the highest stars before she forced herself to stand, and turn her tear-stained face toward the northwest. As she began to walk away from the only world she had ever known, Li-tia wondered if she could somehow survive this desert and then find happiness, in spite of the memory of Araba and little Quaeto.

Without looking back to see if she was being pursued, Li-tia decided to set her course by the North Star. And she would have, except that the howl of a coyote froze her in trembling motion. Li-tia glanced back toward Chaco Canyon and saw the high place where, even now, Matezi and his followers would be leaving poor Araba and Quaeto to the terrors of wild beasts. What was Araba thinking by now? Did she realize what was about to happen?

The lone coyote's howl turned into full chorus. Li-tia knew that coyotes hunted and roamed in packs. She pressed her hands to her ears but the howls would not go away and instead grew louder than Thunder. Li-tia reeled and fell, cutting both knees.

Stop this! Stop this!

Li-tia beat her fists against the soft, caked soil until, at last, her screams died. But the gleeful howls would not because the wild dogs of the desert were gathering to feed on the most pure and innocent of human flesh.

If you do not try to save them, evil spirits will eat your soul and you will finally go mad. Li-tia don't you know that it is better to die fighting than to be driven mad?

Li-tia picked herself up and brushed stinging nettles from her knees. Madness was worse than any physical death. Li-tia had no choice but to try to save poor Araba and little Quaeto. Even if she could, what would that gain? They all were almost sure to perish, either among enemies or in this great unforgiving wilderness.

Ten

When Li-tia had crept up near the place of abandonment and death, she could watch the silhouettes of a great many Chacoan men who were gathered all around Matezi as he stood over his sobbing wife and banished son.

Matezi's words rang with anger and conviction as he told the gathering that his wife had been weak so that the evil spirits had entered her womb and left their inhuman mark on this cursed child.

"It is only by leaving them here to be eaten by wild dogs that the Chacoans will be rid of this curse!" Matezi shouted, raising his fists to Moon. "Tomorrow, we *all* will begin fasting and prayers to Sun so that he will protect us from this evil. And *I*, the great Matezi, will offer a sacrifice beyond all others!"

Li-tia slipped the gathering basket from her shoulder and hid it in the underbrush. Oh, how she hated Matezi and ached to jump to her feet and race forward, denouncing all his foul lies. And Li-tia knew that, at least for a few moments, she would be heard, because she too was an important person. But then, as quick as the strike of Snake, Matezi would have her slain.

It would almost be worth death to speak out against this terrible man, to tell everyone at the very top of her voice that it was Matezi, not poor Araba or little Quaeto, who deserved this awful death, and that, with regard to the baby, nothing created by man or woman ever was perfect but that did not mean it should be sacrificed. Perhaps most of all, Li-tia wanted to shout that Matezi even lacked the courage to do his own evil leaving it instead to the wild beasts.

But Li-tia did nothing. To announce her presence would have sealed her doom as well as that of Araba and Quaeto. She hid like a frightened rabbit, waiting for the Chacoan men to leave so that she could dash forward and learn if life yet remained in the banished mother and her innocent child. And, if not, then at least this small act of bravery would put her guilty mind at ease.

As the night passed, Li-tia was again reminded that Matezi was a gifted orator. Now, he was using this sacrilege as an excuse to urge the Chacoans to become ever more on guard against evil. Had it not been the law for the abandoned to be left in *darkness,* Matezi might have talked all night.

Even Moon and the stars had grown weak and weary by the time Matezi finally turned to glare at poor Araba and her baby. He said something harsh and guttural. For a moment, Li-tia feared that Matezi might plunge a knife into his wife and then his son, but he did not. Instead, he spat on them, turned and led the others back to Chaco Canyon with head held high and imitating the manner of a good man, wronged but unbowed.

Li-tia rushed forward, very close behind her people, because there was no time to spare. The smell of the birth-blood of little Quaeto floated on the night wind, drawing in the wild dogs. Li-tia could hear them snapping and whining in the thick underbrush as they worked themselves into a frenzy. Matezi was not yet out of sight when Li-tia dropped beside Araba and her baby; both lying on a crude stretcher.

"My daughter, you must awaken!" she hissed.

When Araba did not answer, Li-tia pinched her arm—hard. "Araba!"

The baby's eyes opened and it stared up at Li-tia, mouth working in hunger.

"Araba!"

The girl stirred at last. She opened her eyes but seemed unable to focus. "Araba, we *must* find shelter from the coyotes!"

"Go away, it is time that I must die."

"If you die, then your baby dies, too," Li-tia said coldly. "It will die of hunger or be eaten by the coyotes who are already very close."

Araba came fully awake. And when she pushed herself up into a sitting position with Quaeto clutched to her naked breast, the little one began to suckle. A strange and wondrous thing happened, for each drew life from the other, back and forth, mother and child. Li-tia might have kept on watching this mystery except that Araba suddenly yelled in fear. Li-tia twisted around to see a pair of coyotes, yellow eyes shining, fangs long and as white as sunbleached bone.

Li-tia's hand stabbed into her basket and rummaged frantically until it closed on one of Matezi's best knives, an obsidian blade attached to a deer-antler handle. Jumping to her feet, Li-tia rose to her full height.

"You are slinking cowards!" she hissed, showing her own white teeth.

The coyotes were not afraid and their sharp fangs seemed to grow longer and whiter.

"Araba! We have to find a hiding place in the rocks or we are dead!"

Somehow, Araba gained her feet. Li-tia saw her sway but remain erect, pale thighs dark with crusted birth blood. To witness such strength where there should be no strength gave Li-tia fresh courage. She scooped up her gathering basket and slipped her left arm around Araba's narrow waist. She could hear Quaeto suckling as they began a slow, cautious retreat toward a jumble of boulders.

Sniffing and snapping, the hungry coyotes followed. More of the beasts appeared and several began to quarrel over the blood-stained litter. Li-tia never took her eyes off the wild dogs. Once, she tripped over a clump of sagebrush and almost fell. At that instant, one of the largest coyotes, jaws open wide, leapt for Quaeto. Its fangs bit into the infant's doeskin wrapping but not before Li-tia's knife plunged deep into its muscular neck. The dog howled and fell back, hissing like Snake and trying to close its terrible wound. The rest of the pack, already crazed by blood, fell upon the wounded one and tore it apart. It was then that Li-tia saw her best chance to escape.

"Hurry!" she cried, grabbing Araba and pushing her into a stumbling run.

There was no time to hunt for a good hiding and fighting place where their backs could be protected. Just before reaching the rocks, Li-tia saw at least four of the coyotes break from the pack and come running low and fast toward them, eager for another kill.

Li-tia did not wait or retreat but instead attacked, slashing at the coyote who bit her arm. She screamed in pain, stabbing until the beast fell away. Another coyote bit her on the leg, fangs sinking deep into her exposed calf muscle. Li-tia did not feel pain but her heart was cold with a mixture of rage and terror as the beast tried to drag her down so that the others could rip open her soft throat.

Somehow, Li-tia got her knife wedged into Coyote's mouth and she opened it wide. Blood gushed and the coyotes went into a second killing frenzy. Li-tia grabbed Araba and Quaeto, propelling them into a tight, rocky fissure and shoving them back as far as they could go. The coyotes were swirling and battling like demons. Li-tia could see fights going on everywhere as the pack lost its sanity to blood lust.

She realized that she was breathing hard. Her knife was warm and slick while her chest heaved and her heartbeat was out of control. She never had been more frightened but also never more determined.

The coyotes finally stopped fighting, howled at Moon as if to gain new strength, then crept forward, ears back and teeth bared. Li-tia reached back into her basket and found a

second knife. Araba and Quaeto were safe as long as she
could stab and strike.

But Coyote was very wise and now was growing cautious.
When Li-tia also snarled and then slashed one across its long,
narrow snout, Coyote lost the will to fight.

With Sun came light and with light the coyotes vanished
although Li-tia knew that they would not go far. As day grew
bolder, she saw them quarreling over the scattered remains
of their fallen pack and Li-tia knew that their hunger would
be satisfied only long enough to give her time to find better
protection from the dogs. They were wounded and unable to
travel.

Li-tia's leg and arm were already swelling and throbbing
with fire. But the fight might still be won, Li-tia reminded
herself, because she had medicines in her gathering basket
and plenty of food and water. Enough for herself for seven
days. Enough for all of them for five days . . . if they escaped
Coyote.

As Sun grew warm and bright, Li-tia dragged Araba out
of their little sanctuary and, together, they struggled to a distant collection of boulders. In the full sunlight, they discovered an ideal hiding place whose entrance could be blocked
so that even Coyote could not slip inside with his snapping
jaws.

"Araba, you must take one of your husband's knives and
wait while I go away for a short time," Li-tia instructed. "I
do not think Coyote will come while I am gone, but he
might."

The girl's hand locked on her arm. "Don't leave us."

"I must," Li-tia said in a firm but gentle voice. "But only
long enough to trick Matezi or any others into thinking you
and Quaeto were eaten last night. For that, I must have the
doeskin and . . . and some of your hair."

Araba understood. Without more words, Li-tia cut her hair
with Matezi's sharp knife, then did her best to hurry back to
the place of abandonment and death. Her progress was both

painful and slow. Every step was in agony and there was no time to use her good medicines.

Li-tia discovered the litter ripped to shreds and drenched with blood. She dropped Quaeto's little doeskin blanket and scrubbed it around and around with Araba's shiny black hair. Then, she cut a branch and wiped out all traces of their retreat. Every few moments, she looked up, expecting to see Matezi or one of his followers arriving to inspect the night's savagery. But no one came. When Li-tia returned to Araba, she could gaze back a mile to the place of death and feel sure that no Chacoan would ever guess her secret. For the first time, Li-tia felt really confident and hopeful.

If not for her medicines, Li-tia was sure that her leg would have become terribly infected, but the power of her prayers and medicines were very great. On the second morning, Li-tia, Araba and her baby journeyed north into a strange and inhospitable land. Fortunately, the weather was mild and it even rained one afternoon, which filled all the stone basins and caused the dry washes and creeks to race with foamy brown water.

"The gods favor us," Araba said, trying her best to smile as they trudged along, still picking meat off the bones of a pair of rabbits that Li-tia had trapped using yucca fiber snares. "But where can we go now? And how can we live alone?"

"We cannot," Li-tia answered. "I have been thinking much about this and we *must* find . . . Raven Clan."

"Our enemies!" Araba was so aghast that she almost dropped poor Quaeto.

"At first I thought that we should slip between enemy and friend," Li-tia explained. "By myself I could have done this and lived alone. But you and Quaeto change everything. The pair of you could never live alone."

"We would not be alone if we all lived together!"

Li-tia scoffed. "What kind of happiness would there be for us then? Who would teach Quaeto to hunt and to fight?"

"You," Araba said, unable to keep from grinning. "No man could have fought Coyote better."

Despite her modest character, Li-tia swelled with pride at these words . . . for they were true.

"Araba," she continued, bringing her mind back to the issue at hand, "listen to me well so that if something should happen, you will understand what must be done."

"I understand that if you die—we die."

"No! Not after you are strong again. If we are found by friends of our people, they will return us to Matezi for favors. And, when we are back in his grasp, he will smash our skulls."

At the mention of her husband, tears slid down Araba's cheeks. "Not so long ago my son was going to be leader one day, now . . . now poor Quaeto is . . . nothing!"

"Don't be foolish," Li-tia scolded. "Of course he is something."

"But with his arm and the turtle hand, what can he do?"

"What can he *not* do?"

"He cannot use bow and arrow!"

"All right," Li-tia conceded, "then he will use a spear with his good hand. And look how strong he is despite everything! Quaeto almost never cries. He will be a fine son and then a strong and wise man who will feed and protect you when you are old and even sillier than now."

"I am *not* silly!"

When Li-tia turned to go without deigning to respond, Araba cried, "And who will protect you?"

Li-tia stopped and turned, carefully thinking out her answer, "I will die when I am ready. But in my *own* time, not Matezi's."

Just saying that made Li-tia feel better. And, after what they had been through, she believed they were destined for a happy end to this journey. As for the Raven Clan, Li-tia knew nothing other than they were said to be a mesa people who lived among the clouds, had no gods, and believed in nothing other than themselves, and that they were fierce and possessed the power to kill with ease and even laughter.

Well, Li-tia thought, *we have no choice but to see if this is true.*

It was not difficult to find the mountains. They stood tall, rugged and purple on the northern horizon. To Araba, they appeared dark and foreboding but they posed no threat to Li-tia for she had heard that things near clouds were softer, sweeter of smell and far greener. Her wounds still troubled her and the fang marks always would be red and angry.

She could no longer run away. If the Raven Clan decided to kill her, Araba and Quaeto, then they would die fighting. After her battle with Coyote, Li-tia felt sure that she could drive Matezi's blade into at least one more enemy.

"There is where the Raven Clan people live," she announced one afternoon after crossing a wide, shallow river.

Araba sat down on the riverbank with a weary sigh. There were many trees here and she saw signs of beaver and muskrat. Ducks and other good eating birds were everywhere, their calls filling the early autumn air. She held Quaeto suspended above the gentle current and he waved his feet; he made a small sound whenever they touched the water.

"Li-tia?"

"Yes?"

"Why can't we stay right here? There is food and wood for our winter fire. We can live here and not worry about the Raven Clan or any other people."

The same thought had already occurred to Li-tia and she had been grappling with it from the very first moment they had viewed this slow river.

"Because we would die here before the winter was past," she told her young friend. "All these fat birds will fly away. The fish will no longer be hungry. Beaver will crawl inside his hut and sleep all winter while Icy Wind comes down from the mountains to freeze our bones."

"But the wood will not go away! And . . ."

"*If* we survived until spring," Li-tia said, cutting the argument short, "then other people would appear at this river. When they find us, they will know we are Chacoans and they will also learn that you are the wife of the Matezi, next leader of the People."

"Who would tell them that?"

"Who has not seen you when visiting Matezi to ask for trade? Did he not always show you off like some worthy prize?"

"Yes," Araba admitted, "he did and I was always glad."

"He would have found an even prettier woman in a few more years, dear one. And then your heart would have turned as hard and black as flint. If we stay, we will be returned to Chaco Canyon and a very bad death."

Araba fixed her attention on the mesa high above. "So there is only *that* little hope?"

"Yes." The girl looked so saddened by this news that Li-tia felt compelled to add, "But at least we will not suffer a long death, if that is to be our fate."

"Is it?" Araba collected her baby. "Maybe they also will believe that Quaeto is cursed! Li-tia, I would die before I would step aside and let them kill him!"

"I know." Li-tia reached into her pack and found Matezi's sharp knife. "Araba, give me Quaeto."

The girl stared, face gradually twisting into an expression of dread. "*You* would kill him rather than let the Raven people do it!"

"Of course not, you fool! I have been thinking about this and have decided that it is Quaeto's hand that is so ugly. And it is the blue skin between the little fingers that gives him the look of Swimming Turtle."

"And also the arm. But that . . ."

"Give me Quaeto," Li-tia commanded in her sternest voice.

Araba inwardly struggled, then handed her the baby. Li-tia took a deep breath and said, "Hold the arm so that I can cut between the fingers."

"Li-tia!"

"Hold it or I might cut all the hand away and he will bleed to death! Is that what you want, stupid mother?"

"No!"

"Then do it! Do it now!"

Li-tia did not know if cutting away the ugly blue membrane would make any difference to the Raven People or not, but it was possible. Furthermore, if Quaeto survived these cuts, he might just be able to grip an axe or a skinning stone. The stunted arm was too short to be useful for throwing, but to give Quaeto even limited use of the hand was worth taking this chance.

"Please don't!" Araba begged as Quaeto began to squirm with anxiety and confusion.

Li-tia cut the membrane away in quick, slashing motions. Quaeto howled, face growing red, eyes wet and wide with pain. Li-tia dared not look at his face. Across the long miles of their journey, Quaeto had always allowed her to hold and comfort him when Araba's arms grew too weary. Now, Li-tia was certain that she had forever lost Quaeto's innocent trust.

It could not be helped. Gritting her teeth, not only did Li-tia separate the spiny little fingers but she also cut away all the ugly bluish-pink membrane. Sprinkling a piece of cloth with crushed sage, she bound up the infant's hand, securing her work with strips of rawhide.

"Will he live?" Araba asked, wiping tears first from Quaeto's face and then her own.

"He will *live.*"

Araba finally soothed her baby into silence. Night fell

softly on the river valley and the stars blossomed like desert
wildflowers after the rain, all bright and full of promise.

Li-tia knew that Araba was angry with her and so was
Quaeto, but she hoped that tomorrow—in the mountains and
before the fearsome Raven Clan—they both would understand and forgive.

Eleven

It was a very difficult climb toward the mesa. Li-tia was not sure that Araba, still weak from childbirth, would be able to make it. So, in midafternoon, they stopped under the shade of a large tree and rested for several hours.

Araba buried her face in her hands and cried while Li-tia rocked little Quaeto in her arms. To Li-tia's surprise and relief, the infant already had forgiven her and his hands were healing just fine.

"Araba, stop crying. What is the matter?" Li-tia finally asked with exasperation.

"I am so tired and afraid. We should have stayed at the river."

"I told you why that was impossible. And remember that big campfire? No, little mother, we would have been caught and taken back to Chaco Canyon."

"At least we would be killed by our *own* people."

Li-tia threw her head back and gazed at the mesa, still more than a thousand feet above.

"I have been thinking again," she said, more to herself than to Araba, "that your husband's bow and arrow, his knife and some of our things might be acceptable gifts to these people who are said to love warfare."

"They probably will *kill* us with Matezi's weapons. Cut us up into little pieces and . . ."

"Stop it!"

Araba's head rocked back as if she had been slapped. She

used the back of her arm to wipe away tears, then raised her chin and reached out, commanding, "Give me Quaeto!"

"Why? I will not let you take him and go back down to the river."

"You would kill me first?" Araba said, dark eyes growing wider.

"Yes," Li-tia decided out loud. "And then I would take Quaeto up to the mesa. If need be, I would offer myself as a sacrifice and give them your husband's prized weapons asking only that your son be raised better than a slave."

"But we agreed that we would fight to the death."

"I will," Li-tia said, reaching for Matezi's best knife. "And, if it must be, starting now."

Araba blinked, then turned her moist eyes back to the mesa. "If we stop talking and start moving," she said, "we will be up there before dark. Maybe they won't discover and kill us until tomorrow."

"Maybe they won't kill us at all," Li-tia said, handing Quaeto back to his mother and taking up her gathering basket.

Without another word, she attacked the steep mountain-side, following a well-worn trail.

Sun was slipping being the jagged western peaks when they finally staggered over the rim. Now Li-tia saw that it was very lush with piñon and juniper pines and there were many varieties of grasses and even some oak. She took a deep breath and inhaled the sweetness of pines and felt the cool breezes play with strands of her long black hair.

"This is a good place to live—or even to die," she told her friend. "We will make a camp and rest tonight."

"But no fire."

Li-tia agreed. "It is better that we first see the Raven Clan people in daylight. Perhaps they will not appear as ugly and bad as we have been told."

Araba managed to nod but it was clear from her expression that she didn't believe those words.

They found a sheltered place at the edge of the forest,

where they listened for the sounds of people but heard none. Li-tia knew that Araba was afraid, but she also knew that she would overcome her fear; the girl-mother had already more than proven she was a fighter and had an indomitable will to live and protect her child. Still, Li-tia knew that everything could go wrong and that they might soon be discovered, taken captive and cruelly tortured to death. Araba was so young and beautiful that she might be spared but Li-tia had no such illusions about herself—or Quaeto.

Once, she had been considered a great prize and many young men had courted her, but Li-tia had chosen a solitary life with all the rewards and deferences given to a medicine woman but at the price of loneliness. Now, her span of life had left Li-tia's hair streaked with gray and she had wrinkles in her still handsome face. The remarkable thing was that Li-tia didn't feel old. Instead, she felt strong and very much alive. The terrible events of these last few days had given her an enormous and unshakable confidence. And, as for the loneliness and lack of a husband, Li-tia was not complaining. After all, men always fussed over a beautiful girl like Araba, but when she grew older and heavier . . . well, then she became nothing but a man's slave working for an indifferent husband who now coveted someone young and slender.

Li-tia did not intend to tell Araba all of this. What good would that do? Her husband, Matezi, had had a number of wives and they had all been cast aside like worn-out sandals. And that large house that Araba was so proud of? It would have been given to a younger wife by next year. And the promise that little Quaeto would one day become his father's favored son and therefore his successor? Bah! That too was what Matezi said to all of his youngest and most favored wives. It was better, Li-tia thought, if Araba became a medicine woman, perhaps even the most important of all Raven Clan medicine women—provided that the Raven Clan people were wise enough to respect their powers. Li-tia would teach Araba all her secrets of healing and prayer, but the girl would have to be willing to learn well. Everyone knew that a bad medicine woman was a curse on her people.

Araba and Quaeto fell asleep under the glowing eye of Moon but Li-tia could not. Instead, she took her gathering basket and stretched out upon a large flat rock in order to have a clear view of the night sky. There were so many big stars up here! Even Moon seemed far brighter. Sun was, of course, sleeping and although it was not the custom to pray to Sun while he slept, Li-tia prayed to Sun anyway, and to Moon and to all the stars. She prayed that the Raven Clan people would allow her the chance to plead that she and Araba had important gifts. Surely these people had nothing so fine as Matezi's handsome bow and arrows. Or the knives or the precious corn, bean and squash seeds that were the secret to the famed Chaco Canyon harvests.

But even more than that, Li-tia thought, was the secret knowledge that she held for the Raven Clan inside her head. She and Araba could teach them many important things . . . if only they would listen!

"Make them listen, Sun, Moon and stars," Li-tia chanted over and over again. "Make them stop and listen before they shed my blood. And, if it must be shed, have them spare Araba and little Quaeto, both frail but strong inside."

Li-tia fell asleep on the rock, bathed in moonlight, her lined face softening in repose and her silver-streaked hair catching the glimmer of mountain moonbeams.

When she awoke, Sun was well up on the horizon and the heavy mesa forest rang with the songs of birds. A noisy blue jay seemed particularly excited by her presence. Li-tia sat up and saw a pair of curious ground squirrels dive into the rocks. Moments later, they both reappeared, hesitant, but with little tails wagging as they reared up on their hind feet and stared.

She took a deep breath, savoring the sweetness of the forest air, and spent a few lazy moments gazing up at the huge, billowing clouds. They were still high above. Li-tia wondered if they would come down to rest on this mesa as the Chacoan wise men claimed. She hoped so, for that would be a very fine sight. What would it feel like to be wrapped in the cool mist of a cloud? The very thought of it gave her a pleasurable shiver.

"Li-tia!"

She grabbed her basket and climbed down from her perch, then hurried over to Araba and Quaeto expecting something terrible. Instead, Araba was smiling.

"This tree is filled with ripe pine nuts! And so are many others. There is food everywhere for the taking. We should fill your basket and *then* go back down to the river and . . ."

Li-tia shook her head. "We must find the Raven Clan people and ask that they give us a home and protection. That cannot change just because we have found piñon nuts."

Araba didn't agree but they did collect several handfuls of the nuts and then risked a small fire so that they could boil and mash them with Li-tia's metate. The piñon nuts were delicious, and on full bellies both women then felt their strength and spirits restored.

"What do we do now?" Araba asked, licking the residue of the nuts from her lips.

"We find the Raven Clan people and watch them," Li-tia replied. "Then we decide how best to approach them."

Li-tia had no idea where to find these people. This was a huge mesa and, when Li-tia stood on the cliffs and gazed both west and east, she was quite sure there were many other mesas almost as large, all fingering south and divided by deep, silent canyons.

"Come," Li-tia said, "we will look."

Hiking uphill, they walked for miles searching for tracks, campfires or any other evidence of the Raven Clan. Sometimes, they found old campfires and charred bones indicating where Raven Clan hunters had feasted. Certainly there was no shortage of wild game. Mule deer were everywhere but Li-tia also saw evidence of black bear, cougar and coyotes. Both ground and tree squirrels were abundant, as were chipmunks and rabbits. Once, Li-tia saw a band of bighorn sheep standing on what appeared to be a sheer cliff. The animals gazed at them across a mile of open air, then returned to browsing. Li-tia heard the call of wild turkeys and quarrelsome blue jays followed them, darting from tree to tree while decrying them as unwelcome invaders.

By late afternoon of that first day, it was clear that they were nearing the home of the Raven Clan. She saw no planted fields such as would surround the villages in Chaco Canyon, but there were many more campfire rings and everywhere she looked, Li-tia saw the stumps of trees cut for firewood. There were also open meadows with withering brown grass surrounded by a dense forest which was penetrated by a maze of well-worn trails. It was while on one of these narrow, winding forest trails that Araba first heard the sound of human voices.

"Li-tia!" she hissed, dropping to her knees. "Listen!"

Li-tia did not at first hear the voices, but after a few moments, they came to her and she motioned for Araba to follow. As they crept forward, Li-tia heard the songs of women and children. This was a stroke of good fortune because, if they had come upon a hunting party . . . well, it was not difficult to imagine what might have been their sad fate.

"Look," Li-tia whispered, kneeling down behind some brush. "They are harvesting pine nuts!"

Araba clutched Quaeto to her bare breast and they watched as about ten women and twice that many children, some barely old enough to walk, gathered piñon nuts from the trees and dropped them into woven baskets. The women were singing songs unlike any that Li-tia had ever heard before, but she could understand every word.

"They wear almost nothing in this cold," Araba whispered.

"Shhh!"

Li-tia, too, was surprised at how scantily these people dressed. The children were completely naked while the women wore only short leather skirts and woven sandals despite the early morning chill.

"They must have thick skin or they would be cold," Araba said, as they watched a mother playfully chase her giggling child, then scoop him up and drop him in her basket and whirl him around and around.

Li-tia's hopes soared. These people were acting like her own people. Only, instead of working in fields, they worked in cool, blue-green forests. And, as for the songs, Li-tia herself had always sung during the autumn harvests and enjoyed the children who played near their mothers' sides as they harvested the crops.

"I am going to speak with them now," Li-tia said, steeling herself. She wore a full buckskin blouse and skirt and slipped Matezi's best knife into her pocket . . . just in case. "You stay hidden here."

"No!" Araba hissed, grabbing her arm in near panic.

Li-tia pried loose the girl's fingers. "These women do not look bad to me, but . . . if there is a fight . . . then you *must* run."

"But . . . but where? Where could I run without you?"

Li-tia had no answer. She jumped up and started out into the meadow, wanting to get far away from Araba.

The Raven Clan people did not notice her until she was almost among them. Then, a girl of about ten saw her, and frantically tugged on her mother's skirt and whispered something. The mother turned and, when she saw Li-tia approaching, she dropped her basket of nuts and screamed.

Li-tia froze with indecision. *Speak to them, you fool! Say something friendly!*

"I am Li-tia," she began, trying to smile. "I come from far away." *Better not to tell them that she was a Chacoan.* "I come in peace seeking the protection of the great Raven Clan."

The nervous women glanced furtively at each other. Finally, an old one came forward. "Are you friend, or enemy?"

"I come seeking help. I have gifts to give in return."

"What gifts?"

At that moment, Araba decided to stand and make her presence known. This too caused quite a stir among the Raven Clan women and children.

"Who is *she?*"

"Her name is Araba and her baby is Quaeto."

"Where are your husbands?"

"We have none."

The old woman's brows knitted in disapproval. "Why?"

"We have been . . . banished."

"Li-tia! Don't . . ."

"Show them Quaeto's hands and his withered arm."

Araba was pale and shaky but she came forward with her chin up, making Li-tia very proud.

"My name is Tumsea," the old woman announced. "What is wrong with her child?"

"You will see." Li-tia turned her back on them and walked over to Araba. "These women will not harm us. There is no hatred in their eyes—only worry."

"Why should *they* worry?"

"Because they do not yet understand us," Li-tia said, reaching for Quaeto. When Araba resisted handing over her child, Li-tia said, "Don't fight me!"

Araba let go and Li-tia presented Quaeto to Tumsea who stared at the child, now wrapped in rabbit skin. Li-tia saw kindness in the old woman's eyes and even a hint of a smile when Quaeto cooed and gurgled happily.

"He is a fine son but his father was evil and that is why we ran away to find you," Li-tia offered.

"What did his father do?"

"He put a curse on Quaeto but only a little of the curse had power."

"Why would he do such a thing?"

"Who knows?" Li-tia said, shrugging her shoulders and noting that a lone raven now sailed over the mesa which gave her the inspiration to add. "This curse was twisting little Quaeto's body until Araba called out to Raven."

Li-tia lifted her eyes toward the sky and the other women followed her gaze. "*That* very same Raven then swooped down to grab Quaeto and carry him away to this mesa where we found him only yesterday."

"Li-tia!" Araba cried, staggering backward with Quaeto clutched in her arms.

Li-tia ignored her friend. "And so, we are here with Quaeto on whose body the dark curse has left its mark."

"In what way?" another woman asked, pushing forward to stare at Araba's infant with fascination.

"Quaeto's arm and hand are twisted and bloodied because he was carried so far by Raven. Would you like to see the proof?"

Tumsea nodded eagerly.

"Araba, show them."

When Araba hesitated, Li-tia tore the leather covering from Quaeto so that all the Raven Clan people could see the stunted arm and blood-crusted hand. But now the ugly webbed membrane between the fingers was gone, and Quaeto's hand no longer appeared like the foot of Swimming Turtle.

All of the Raven Clan women and children stared at Quaeto's withered arm and hand. Li-tia observed their reactions very closely. She detected shock and sadness rather than revulsion. One little girl's eyes turned misty with tears and Li-tia marked this child as one who would receive her special attention should she ever fall to illness or injury.

It was Tumsea who broke the spell of silence when she handed both Araba and Li-tia gathering baskets and resumed the important gathering of piñon nuts. Soon, all the other women and children had forgotten Quaeto and were busy with the harvest.

Araba began to cry. Not with sound, but deep in the stillness of her grateful heart. Li-tia noted her tears and how her

head was bent protectively over Quaeto, her chin covering
his face.

"Come," she said, touching Araba's cheek and offering her
a woven basket. "We must help our people."

"But can their men be as kind and understanding?"

Li-tia shrugged her shoulders. "I no longer think that these
people are bad or like killing. They are only different from
our people in Chaco Canyon. As for their men, I cannot say,
but I think they will allow us to join them."

"Even Quaeto?"

"Yes." Li-tia smiled. "Don't you understand what I have
done, little fool? I have made them believe that Quaeto is a
special gift of Raven. I have made him the friend of their
god."

"This is so!"

"Of course. You saw their faces."

"But it was a lie!"

"Not all a lie," Li-tia argued. "Who is to say that Raven
did not save and then deliver us to these women and children
instead of their hunters? Who is to say that Raven who
watches even now from above is not happy to see us joined
so that his people can become wise in the Chacoan ways we
will teach?"

"Yes," Araba said, looking up to Raven still in the sky. "I
believe this is true."

"Then *act* as if it is true," Li-tia told her pretty friend.
"From this moment to the last moment of your life, act as if
you and Quaeto are gifts to these people."

"I will! And you, too, because *you* are the most important
gift of all to Raven Clan."

Li-tia laughed for the first time in many years. She did not
even recognize her own laughter. It was rough and as cracked
as rocks, but it felt good.

"I also will try to remember this. Now come, let us gather
the harvest. It is not corn, but almost as sweet."

That afternoon was one of the happiest that Li-tia had ever

spent—happy because these people were filled with songs and laughter. Happy because Araba glowed as she gathered piñon nuts beside other young women and their children. Li-tia often gazed up at the sky, seeking Raven to offer him thanks but not finding him again. No matter. He was close and, when the daylight began to fade and these people returned to their homes and to their men, Raven would watch and protect.

Li-tia felt no shame for the inspiration of her lie about Quaeto. She believed that her words were created by Raven who never would do anything bad for his own clan. So, all was well.

As the sun began to slide into the western horizon, Tumsea called out to her people and they left the trees and began to walk across the mesa.

"We may be gifts to these people," Araba confided as they fell in behind the procession, "but I am still afraid."

"Do not be, or their men will know that I have lied. Everything depends upon us being brave and acting as if we are very special. And we are, you know."

"How?"

Li-tia thought about this a moment as they walked along. "If we were *not* special, surely we would be dead long before now."

"This is so."

"You are very brave, Araba. I see this in you now."

"You are much braver than I."

"Because I have so much less to lose."

"But what . . . ?"

"They are singing that song again," Li-tia interrupted as the sun melted into the canyon rock, turning them lavender and crimson. "Do you remember the words?"

"Yes."

"Then we should be happy and sing, too."

Li-tia raised her chin and joined her voice with these people. She would not admit to Araba that she was still afraid of what was to come when they faced the men of the tribe. After all, women were of one spirit and mind. They were gentler and more forgiving. Especially these women whose openness and trust were almost childlike. But the men, the hunters, might be very different.

Soon they would know.

TWELVE

Twelve

At the most brilliant moment of sundown, the Raven Clan women and their children arrived at the edge of a great canyon and then disappeared over its rim as if falling into the center of earth. When Araba and Li-tia came to the edge and peered down the steep, narrow trail, they froze.

"I *cannot* carry Quaeto down that!" Araba cried.

Hearing her, one of the young women climbed back up to the rim and reached out for the baby. "I will carry him. Follow us, it is nothing."

Araba resisted for only a moment, then relinquished her child. Smiling, the young woman tucked Quaeto under one arm and started back down as if she were taking a leisurely walk in the woods.

"We have to do this," Li-tia said, feeling her throat go dry with fear. It was not as if she and Araba were completely unfamiliar with heights or difficult trails. As children and even adults, they had climbed the walls of Chaco Canyon hundreds of times and considered themselves brave and sure-footed. But *never* had they faced anything to match this.

Araba took a deep breath and let it out slowly. "I would throw myself over the side of this cliff before I will lose Quaeto," she vowed, starting downward.

Li-tia found herself standing alone. Knowing that she had no choice but to attempt the descent, she made sure that her large and heavy gathering basket was securely tied to her back, then followed, worried that she might slip and fall. Even more terrifying was the possibility that her plummeting body might strike Araba and others so that they would all tumble to their deaths.

But, after a few minutes, Li-tia could see that the foot and handholds were chopped deeply into the rocks and that they were solid. If you didn't look down, it wasn't so bad. She kept moving, hurrying to reach whatever waited below before being caught in darkness. Li-tia's concentration was so intense that she forgot time until she entered a huge cavern and pivoted about to face Araba and several hundred Raven Clan people. Li-tia had never felt so alone and unsure of herself. The scene had an unreal quality and she wondered if she had awakened inside a vision. The immense cavern walls glowed warmly and fire shadows danced on the ceiling above. Li-tia could see past the people to pit houses, very much like the ones she had known in Chaco Canyon. *So this is what middle earth looks like,* she thought.

A tall man of her own years came forward to regard Li-tia and then Araba and finally the baby. His face was inscrutable, but not unkind, and Li-tia thought she saw more warmth than suspicion in his dark eyes.

"My name is Kenta," he said to them. "I have been told that Raven carried the boy to us so that you would follow."

"This is true," Li-tia heard herself reply.

"I am leader of this Raven Clan. What people are you?"

From the day that they had fled Chaco Canyon, Li-tia had anticipated this vital question but, until this exact moment, she had not known her response. The last thing she wanted to admit was that she and Araba were Chacoans, legendary enemies of the Raven Clan. And yet, to lie about this now might arouse suspicions because these people were intelligent and curious. They would examine her belongings and discover the truth. Then, her story about Quaeto would be judged a lie. Li-tia did not know the custom among these people, but to lie to a Chacoan leader was to invite death.

"We *are* Chacoans," Li-tia declared, raising her chin. "But we were sent by Raven to save this boy for your people."

"What can *he* do for us?"

"Ward off evil spirits. And someday he will become a very wise leader among your good people."

Kenta considered this for several long moments before he asked, "And you?"

"I am the Chacoans' *most favored* medicine woman and my healing powers are great. My friend will learn my secrets so that the Raven Clan will long be blessed. They will live in good health and be favored by all the spirits."

The leader turned to regard his peers and gauge their re-action to this bold statement. Their reactions seemed to range from awe to anger. Kenta then turned back to Li-tia. "And how do I know this to be true?" he asked

"I have fought wild dogs and killed them. Would this not require the help of great spirits?"

"And how do we know this to be true?" he repeated.

In answer, Li-tia passed by these people and strode to their nearest blazing fire. Without a word, she let her clothing fall to her ankles. With the firelight gleaming against her body, Li-tia displayed the angry red scabs and proud flesh ravaged by the fangs of the wild dogs she had fought and killed near the place of death and abandonment.

Kenta came to her and leaned close. His fingers touched her arm, then her bare calf. The leader of the Raven Clan did not seem to notice how Li-tia shivered at his gentle touch.

"Let me see your weapons," he said, looking back into her eyes.

Li-tia bent and lifted her buckskins to cover herself again. She still carried Matezi's finest knife in her pocket and now she gave it to Kenta who turned the blade one way and then another with growing admiration.

"This is truly a fine weapon," he pronounced loud enough to be heard by all the Raven Clan.

"It is my *gift* for your kindness."

Kenta's eyes widened with pleasure. Li-tia knew that their future was assured when he announced, "You are welcome to stay for as long as the sun rises to greet our people. A house will be prepared for you and Araba. Husbands will soon be found and . . ."

"No."

Kenta blinked.

"No husbands," Li-tia said, locking with his eyes. "Leader of the Raven Clan, we are *medicine women.*"

"Why both?"

"There are evil spirits that require our powers."

"And these powers," Kenta said, pulling his eyes from the knife. "They will not work if you have husbands?"

"No."

"But . . ."

Li-tia dared to interrupt. "Kenta, please know that we ask nothing—not even a house—yet we are willing to give much. Look."

She reached into her big gathering basket and extracted Matezi's best bow and arrows.

"It is clearly a weapon. How is it used?"

"I will show you this secret," Li-tia promised. "But first we are weak from travel and hunger."

"My son," Tumsea scolded, "you ask too many questions. Let them be cared for by the women!"

Kenta nodded, then made a sweeping motion with his hand and the clan dispersed. The men and older boys went back to their fires and Li-tia could well imagine they would have much to talk about this night.

"Come," Tumsea said, motioning for Araba and Li-tia to follow.

Araba had her baby back safely in her arms when she took her place beside a fire ring. Quaeto began to cry until she gave him her breast and gazed into the fire looking very sleepy but also content. As for Li-tia, she was so weary and limp with relief that she could hardly keep her eyes open.

And when her chin began to tap heavily on her chest, Li-tia curled up, hearing the Raven Clan women talk. She was filled with happiness to know that she, Araba and baby Quaeto were safe and that they would have a position of great respect among these mountain people protected by Raven.

Li-tia awoke at dawn the next morning, shivering. She hunted sunlight and warmth, creeping past sleeping figures until she arrived at the lip of the cave. The sky was turning pink, the canyon below was rose colored, filled with trees and decorated by a thin ribbon of shining water. The air sparkled and the azure mesa sky was pale and cloudless. Despite all this beauty, this cave dominated everything. Last night she and Araba had been so exhausted that she had not fully appreciated its size until now, with her neck bent and her eyes drinking in the high domed ceiling spotted by campfire smoke. Li-tia had to struggle to grasp the size of this cave. It was so large it could have hidden every Chacoan who had ever lived! She sat on a rock, drew her knees up to her chin, and closed her eyes, wanting to subordinate sight to sound and smell. Now she could hear the clucking of turkeys. She recalled being told that a large flock was kept in the back of the cave, mostly for the gift of their feathers. Li-tia not only could hear, but she could smell the turkeys and expected to see them foraging among these people.

The aroma of turkeys and canyon forest could not begin to mask the powerful stench of rotting garbage and human waste. Opening her eyes for a moment, Li-tia gazed downward to realize that the Raven people simply dumped their offal and waste over the lip of this cave. Now, as the air warmed and lifted, it was pungent with the reek of decay.

Li-tia's nose wrinkled with displeasure. In Chaco Canyon, there had been special places where refuse and human waste collected, but always downwind and away from the villages.

Perhaps, Li-tia thought, in time I will be able to convince Kenta and the other leaders that there is a better way.

There were no dogs among these people, perhaps because warning barks were unnecessary in a cave which was impossible to surprise and attack. Li-tia felt a sharp peck and turned, causing a turkey to suddenly retreat. They were all about now, vigorously pecking and scratching around last night's campfire. Li-tia wondered how they could stay healthy without ever having the gifts of sunlight and fresh air.

Soon, the Raven people awakened and began their morning prayers and preparations. Li-tia remained at the rim of their world, wondering how she and Araba would fit into this very odd cavern society and if they could ever hope to achieve happiness and acceptance. The key, she decided, was to make herself and Araba indispensable.

And so, when Kenta and the men came to see her use the Matezi's bow and arrows, she was nervous because her skills were so poor with this weapon. As she stood at the edge of the cavern and prepared to launch an arrow into the canyon below, she had no intention of selecting a target.

"Wait," Kenta ordered. "What are you shooting at?"

"The canyon."

He did not appreciate Li-tia's attempt at humor. "That tree," he said, pointing, "hit the one with the white bark."

Li-tia knew that she could not, but she tried anyway. Drawing the bowstring back as far as she could, she shot an arrow down into the canyon. It sailed completely over the tree and vanished into the heavy brush on the far side of the canyon.

The Raven Clan people were dumbfounded. They could not believe their eyes.

"I'm sorry," Li-tia said. "I'm not a hunter."

"What is this called!" Kenta exclaimed, tearing the bow from her hands.

Li-tia explained as she handed an arrow to Kenta.

He studied it very carefully. "It is a little spear that travels fast and far. It flies like the bird, going nowhere and every-where."

"If you practice, you will find them to be very accurate," Li-tia promised. "Chacoan hunters could easily put their arrows into that tree from here."

Kenta looked closely at Li-tia as if she were crazy. When he saw that she was serious, he shook his head and picked up his own atlatl. Without a word, those around them stepped back to give their leader throwing room. Kenta drew back the throwing stick and launched it toward the abyss with all his considerable strength. The detached spear quivered in flight, reaching out over the canyon, then succumbing to gravity, only to plummet downward and impale its stone point into the earth at least fifty yards short of the target tree.

"Kenta?"

A younger man, strong and in his prime, approached his leader, who nodded in consent. This man made a show of setting his spear tip on the atlatl and then positioning himself at the very edge of Great Cave. With a tremendous heave and grunt of exertion, he launched his spear into the canyon. It seemed to Li-tia to hang like a hunting bird, then dip and dive toward the white-barked tree. But it too fell short. Li-tia heard a few snickers from the older boys and the hunter's face darkened with embarrassment as others among his people began to giggle.

"It was a *great* throw," Li-tia said. "Both of them. But your spear is too heavy and the arrow is very light."

"Why the feathers?"

"To give it the lift of Raven or Eagle."

They nodded with understanding.

"Do it again," Kenta ordered.

Li-tia made a second attempt, now more relaxed because she realized that these people were intelligent enough to see the obvious advantage of the bow and arrow over the atlatl. Her second arrow sailed through the bright autumn leaves of the target tree and elicited cries of admiration from the women and children and grunts of approval from the men and older boys.

"These weapons are easy enough to make," Li-tia said. "The points are like those on your spears. The bowstring is the gut of deer or the fibers of yucca. The arrows are the most difficult."

"Can you make them?"

"Yes," she said. "But not ones as good as these."

Kenta examined another arrow. "I can do this well," he said.

"Of course you can! You *all* can. After you straighten the arrows, Araba and I will show you how to attach the feathers."

"These are *not* the feathers of Raven," Kenta said.

"No, they are not. Other feathers will do. This morning, I heard the sound of turkeys penned in the back of Great Cave. I saw many blankets woven with rabbit skin and turkey feathers. Those feathers will do."

Kenta nodded with relief and before Li-tia knew it, the young men were jumping over the edge and scrambling down into the canyon to retrieve the spears and her arrows. Li-tia had no doubt that they would become skilled arrow and bow makers during the long winter ahead. By spring they would be well practiced in the art of shooting.

When they were alone, Kenta said, "These gifts are great. You and Araba will be respected in Great Cave."

"And Quaeto. Him, too."

"Yes," Kenta promised. "I had a vision just before dawn. It said that you were sent by Raven to help and protect our people."

Before Li-tia could say anything more, Kenta turned and walked away.

In the days that followed, Li-tia and Araba came to realize that these people were not as simple as Li-tia had first supposed. Li-tia learned that their pit houses were to be found both in Great Cave and in the mesa, where they were used by the hunters in bad weather. These comfortable houses consisted of a large living room and a smaller antechamber. They were almost identical to those in Chaco Canyon, indicating that these people had, at some time or other, spied upon the Chacoans.

Each pit house was constructed by first digging a shallow pit and placing four strong roof-supporting timbers in each corner. These timbers held a thick latticework of roof over which were spread juniper bark and then several layers of mud. On top of the mesa, the Raven Clan people built the roofs very thick, but down in the caves, they were only strong enough to support the weight of a few men.

Inside, there were two rooms, just as she had known in Chaco Canyon, and the larger room was used as a sleeping quarters and work area while the antechamber was for storage. As in Chaco Canyon, entry to the pit houses was by a ladder through the roof. The cooking fire was ventilated by a small opening in the adjoining antechamber. A stone slab set in the passageway between the two rooms served to deflect heat and also channel fresh air around the hearth.

"They live almost exactly as we did," Araba confided. "This is not so different than being home."

"This *is* our home now," Li-tia replied. "And yes, they do live very much like the Chacoans except for their food. These people have better land and are hunters, not planters."

"Do you miss . . . ?"

"No," Li-tia said shortly. "I never allow myself to think of it."

"I wish I could do the same," Araba admitted.

"You must remember that we are Raven Clan people now and until we die."

A week after their arrival, Kenta came and inquired if Li-tia had any more Chacoan knives. "No, but I do have other gifts that will please you and your people."

"If you took husbands, you would have no need of gifts,"

Kenta said, not meeting her eye. "They would belong to your husband and your family."

It was all that Li-tia could do not to laugh outright and inform the leader of the Raven Clan that *other,* far more demanding things, would be expected by husbands. No, she thought, independence was worth everything.

"I have seen you practicing with the bow and arrows," Li-tia said.

"It is not easy to learn. Especially when I am so good with the atlatl. My wives and children are not pleased to chase the arrows so far."

Li-tia almost suggested to Kenta that he should sometimes chase his own arrows, but she held her tongue. Kenta had two wives, one young and the other her older sister. She had joined his household after the death of her husband. Together, the wives had five children and all of them bore a strong resemblance to their father. Despite her station and beliefs, Li-tia felt an undeniable attraction to this man. Kenta was handsome and never loud or angry. He could be stern, but there was a willingness to listen to opposing arguments. These were rare qualities in a clan leader, qualities that Li-tia never had witnessed and which would have been considered by Chacoan men as an indication of weakness.

"The young men," Kenta was saying, "can do little except make bows and arrows although we must hunt and prepare as much food as we can for winter."

Li-tia gazed out of Great Cave. "Are the cold and the snows long and deep here?" she asked, knowing they would be.

"Yes, and some will weaken and die."

The way Kenta said this caused Li-tia to wonder how many of his own family had been lost during the worst winters of his life due to cold and hunger. The unmistakable sadness in his eyes prompted her to say, "Next spring I will give the Raven Clan people even more important gifts than bow, arrow and a Chacoan knife."

He snapped out of his reverie and asked, "What gifts could be more important?"

"I will show you."

She hurried over to her things and brought out her little woven basket of Matezi's most prized corn, bean and squash seeds. Cupping them in her hands up before his eyes, Li-tia said, "Have you seen the fields of the Chacoans?"

"No," Kenta admitted, "but I have heard of them. I have heard that those desert people hunt very little and eat mostly what they grow. I have heard that they have green fields ringed by water. Is this true?"

"It is!" Li-tia could almost see the corn growing in Chaco Canyon and she remembered the joy of the fall harvest. "Kenta, next spring I will show your people how to plant these things so that you will never go hungry."

Kenta's eyes flashed with sudden and uncharacteristic anger. "My people do not go hungry now! And why should we grow such stupid things when we have all the food we need on the piñon trees and ready to shoot in the forests above?"

"Because some day the piñon trees will not bear a harvest and . . ."

Kenta grew even more furious. So furious that he grabbed Li-tia by the wrist and shook loose the prized Chacoan seeds, scattering them across the floor.

"Let them grow where they fall!"

Too late did Li-tia realize her mistake. It was the leader's responsibility to see that his people never went hungry. To even suggest that such a thing could happen was a grave insult that would not likely be forgotten. Had she insulted Matezi in such a manner, he might very well have drawn his knife and cut her throat.

"I am sorry!" Li-tia called. "I did not . . ."

He was already out of sight. Li-tia shook her head. What a fool she was! What had she been thinking?

Araba hurried over and began to help her collect the seeds. "What happened?"

"I insulted Kenta."

"I have never seen him look so angry."

"He is not as smart as I thought," Li-tia said as she hurriedly collected the seeds and stuffed them into her pockets. "And I am also not as smart as I thought."

Li-tia told Araba what had happened. She finished by saying, "Kenta does not want us to plant seeds."

"Then we should not!"

But Li-tia was not so sure. She had just put herself in a bad position. However, if she could plant a small and secret crop of corn, beans and squash next spring and bring it to harvest and *if* she could figure out a way to give the credit to Kenta, then all would be well between them again.

"Li-tia? Are you listening to me?" Araba demanded. "You must tell Kenta you are sorry and give him more of my husband's gifts."

"And what gifts would that be?" Li-tia asked. "I will not give up the last knife and he does not want the seeds. We have already given away our best knife. There is nothing left but what we have inside our heads."

"You mean, the knowledge of healing you will teach me."

"Yes, that and a better way of life by growing food." Li-tia shook her head. "We know that the piñons do not always yield a good harvest."

"But there are so many deer."

"And Kenta tells me they go down to the big river during the time of deep snows. Araba, we can do something very good for these people."

Araba hugged Quaeto tightly. "If you make Kenta angry, maybe he will tell us to go away or even have us killed."

"I will not make him angry again," Li-tia promised.

"And you must do something to make Kenta forgive you—and maybe me, too!"

"I know," Li-tia agreed. "But it will take almost a year."

Araba didn't understand that next spring, Li-tia was determined that they would build their own pit house up on the mesa near a small field where there was enough water to irrigate her prized Chacoan seeds. As soon as the planting was over, they would have to stay awake every hour of the night and day to scare away rabbits and the deer who would try to eat their tender crops. But come next autumn, when the piñon nuts were ready for harvest—Li-tia vowed to herself—these Raven Clan people would have a more varied and delicious feast than they ever could have imagined. And only then would that fool Kenta know how very important she and Araba were to the Raven Clan.

Thirteen

One cold afternoon, a powerful blast of winter wind from the north swept through their canyon, filling it with swirling rainbows of autumn leaves. Li-tia had never seen such a lovely sight. She braved the cold all day long to watch the spectacle. That night the temperature plunged below freezing and the Raven Clan people huddled close to their fires, listening to the icy wind shriek. The next morning their canyon was shrouded with a glistening mantle that smothered their world in frigid silence. Li-tia and Araba were enchanted by the glistening white beauty that surrounded them, but that sentiment was not shared in Cliff Palace.

"Now comes the time of sickness and death," Kenta grimly explained. "You should not look so happy."

Araba said, "Why is this so?"

"Look around you at the old people! Can you not see that their joints are stiff and that they are missing teeth? They will suffer the most but the weakest children also will die."

When a wounded Araba rushed off to find comfort with Quaeto and her new friends, Li-tia's eyes flashed with anger. "You should not have spoken so harshly."

"I have no patience for foolish questions."

"Araba's question was *not* foolish! We are from Chaco Canyon and never have known the teeth of your winters, or their beauty."

"Beauty?" Kenta almost laughed. "You will not think it

so beautiful when the People begin to suffer. When even the piñon nuts grow bitter on your sharp tongue."

"Then perhaps you should remember the Chacoan seeds that you scattered in childish anger!"

Kenta's hand lifted and he shook with rage. Li-tia expected him to strike . . . but he did not. Instead, his shoulders slumped and his expression reflected misery and remorse.

"You are wise in many ways, Li-tia, but you have never seen the white death of these mountains. It is hardest to watch the children grow sick and weak," he tried to explain. "I have lost a wife and two daughters to winter. It is always cold here in Great Cave. So cold that when the ground freezes outside, we must bury our dead with trash."

Kenta cast his eyes around Great Cave and there was fear in them when he added, "You soon will hear the old men and women moan with pain, then mothers and fathers wail with grief at the death of their weakest children. Some of my strongest hunters will fall screaming to their deaths because the foot and hand holds up to the mesa are slick with ice."

"Maybe you should move your people to the mesa," Li-tia suggested.

"I have thought much of this. But here, in Great Cave, at least we are out of the wind and snow. On the mesa we would suffer both."

"But you also would have more sunshine."

"Not on days such as this," he said, gazing back out at the leaden sky.

Li-tia felt Kenta's pain. She had not realized how much the Raven Clan people dreaded the sufferings of winter because they never spoke of this bad time. Li-tia had assumed that they would be warmed by fires and sheltered from the elements. Why had she conveniently overlooked the obvious fact that Great Cave faced west so that the sun could not enter and warm the People until late afternoon, and then only for a few short hours?

Kenta reached out his hand and his thick, callused fingers

were surprisingly gentle. "I am sorry. As this time comes upon my people, I grow sad and worried. Many die."

"But not from hunger."

"From the cold," he answered. "There will be enough food this winter because the piñon harvest was good. Our hunters have killed many deer and their meat has been smoked and saved. The women have collected seeds and the children have trapped squirrels and rabbits. We also have our turkeys."

"But I am told you do not eat them."

"Only those which sicken and die. Those that live we feed what we can so that they can provide us feathers for our robes." Kenta gazed deeply into her eyes. "Li-tia, is your medicine truly strong?"

"Yes, very strong."

"This is very good because my visions tell me that this will be a bad winter."

In the dark and suffering time that followed, Kenta's prophecy was fulfilled. The snows arrived early and often. In mid-November, a fierce, three-day blizzard battered the mesa and plastered their canyon walls with snow and ice. The Raven Clan people had worked hard through late autumn to stockpile mountains of dry firewood in order to feed the many campfires that burned day and night in Great Cave, but soon it became obvious to Li-tia that much more firewood was needed to keep the people warm. To make matters worse, Great Cave became thick with clouds of smoke. During the day and the night, when the canyon winds suddenly changed, Li-tia and the Raven Clan people were forced to rush outside to breathe. The old people, some of whom could barely move, would struggle and choke while the rest of them would be seized by violent coughing spells.

One bitterly cold night, when the air inside Great Cave was poisonous, everyone was forced to evacuate the cave and huddle at its entrance while being ripped by wind and snow.

Wet and shivering, Kenta chose those dark hours to join Li-tia and explain how, many generations ago when the legendary Echata had led his people to this mountain country, thick forests of piñon and juniper pine grew right up to the canyon rim just above Great Cave. But now, many generations later, the forest had been cleared of all trees for nearly a quarter of a mile back from the canyon's edge. The clan's woodcutters had to drag timber for a long distance through the snow, requiring much more effort than in generations past.

When the timber gatherers arrived at the rim directly above Great Cave, they shouted a warning and then pushed their logs and limbs over the edge. From deep inside the cave, it was frightening to witness the collision of rocks and logs whose impact was so great that the wood splintered and flew everywhere, causing great danger to the People and often spearing some of the frenzied turkeys. The good part was that the wood shattered so completely that it was easy to gather and store until it was needed for their smoky fires.

When the men were not cutting and gathering firewood, they practiced with their new bows and arrows and tried to hunt despite the freezing weather and icy winds that scoured the mesa tops. As the weather worsened, they took to their deep pit houses and kept warm, rarely being seen by their families, who lived above ground and were always preparing food and attempting to keep themselves healthy and well-fed.

"I am so worried about Quaeto dying," Araba fretted over and over. "He is Chacoan, after all, and therefore it is not in his blood to survive this terrible cold."

"Nonsense!" Li-tia countered with exasperation. "He is fat and healthy. *You* are the one who is much too thin."

"I eat as much as the other women," Araba said in her own defense. "How is it that you do not grow thin, too?"

"I don't know," Li-tia replied. "Maybe it is because I do not feed the men or any children. Quaeto is so greedy. He is always suckling at your breast."

"Because he is not getting enough of my milk."

Li-tia disagreed. She wanted Araba to give *less* milk and more piñon nut soup and porridge to Quaeto. However, Araba was staunch in her determination that Quaeto not only would survive this bad winter, but would even stay fat.

"I can see now that, in the season of deep snows, the Raven Clan men live much better than their women," Araba complained one gloomy afternoon as she and Quaeto huddled beside a fire that did little to warm their shivering bodies. "They hide down in their pit houses while we work."

Li-tia drew her turkey feather and buckskin robes close. "You have finally noticed this?"

"Mata-ki says that this is only right. That, without the hunting and wood gathering of the men, all of us would die."

"And without the food we prepare, the piñon nut harvest we collect, and without the warm winter robes that we weave, the men would freeze."

"Mata-ki says that her husband would like me to become his wife," Araba said without lifting her eyes from the struggling flames.

"Her husband already has three wives and many children!" Li-tia snapped. "Besides, one day you will be this clan's medicine woman."

"You have not been teaching me."

"I will." Li-tia was stung by this truth. "When winter deepens and the Raven Clan people begin to weaken, then I will teach you everything."

"You have great powers."

Li-tia hoped that this was yet true. Out of necessity, she had left many of her prized amulets and medicines in Chaco Canyon. Yes, she had brought some of her best medicines and her considerable knowledge, but that probably was not enough to ward off this winter's sickness and death.

"Li-tia?"

"Yes?"

"Your powers *will* be strong here, won't they?"

Li-tia heard Araba's need for reassurance but she was

plagued by her own doubts. Much of her healing power relied on ancient medicines made from seeds, roots and even ground hair, flowers and feathers. But none of that was enough in times of great sickness or injury. Then, Li-tia knew she must offer specific prayers and rituals. It was only when the physical gifts of earth and her spiritual offerings were in balance that real healing took place.

Li-tia had always prayed mostly to Sun for her powers, but now she felt that the spirit of Raven was the stronger medicine. She had collected three of Raven's feathers one autumn afternoon and kept them in a secret leather pouch under her blouse and near her breast. Every night she brought out the feathers and waved them through her sacred medicine smoke, chanting ancient prayers.

Despite all her preparations, Li-tia constantly worried that her powers would prove ineffective against winter's death. And so she almost felt relieved when, on a bitterly cold morning, as pellets of ice lanced through a gray, forbidding sky, she heard a terrifying shriek. Everyone rushed out to the edge of Great Cave to see the bodies of Ta-te and Su-mat lying motionless on the snow-covered rocks far below. The two young men had lost their footing on the icy cliff above. Now, women and children began to wail with grief as the two figures finally came to rest at the bottom of the canyon.

Kenta and his men began to shout and, when Li-tia looked up, she saw them making a furious descent. Even at a distance and through the blowing snow and ice, she could see that their faces were stricken with dread as they hurried down to retrieve the bodies of their companions.

"We need to go down and try to help!" Li-tia cried. "Hurry, Araba!"

"They are dead!" a woman wailed. "It is too late, they are *both* dead!"

But Li-tia and Araba were already rushing into the depths of the canyon. When they reached bottom, the men were chanting death songs and the fresh snow was stained with blood. Li-tia pushed past them and dropped to her knees beside Ta-te. The man *was* dead; his skull had cracked open and his brains were sprayed across the nearest rocks.

Li-tia hurried over to the second victim. Su-mat must have struggled very hard to slow his fall down the canyon side; his finger- and toenails were ripped away and his hands were bloody from trying to grasp cliff-side protrusions. He was bleeding from the ears, nose and mouth and his right leg was twisted at a queer angle, but the young man was alive. There was a pulse throbbing in his neck and blood flowed from a deep wound in his shoulder. Li-tia glanced up at the others, but they were blind with grief.

"Su-mat lives!" she cried. "Araba, he *lives!*"

Now the men gaped down at Su-mat who was covered with dirt and blood and half-skinned from the rocks and brush that he had slid across. When they appeared not to believe her, Li-tia grabbed the twisted and broken leg to straighten it, and yanked hard. Su-mat's body convulsed and a strangled cry was torn from his throat.

"See!" Li-tia shouted. "Kenta, cut away his clothes so that I can see his leg!"

Kenta did as he was instructed while Li-tia held her breath. If the leg bones had broken through Su-mat's flesh, the young hunter was lost, for his body soon would be poisoned and he would die. A moment later, Li-tia almost wept with relief at the absence of splintered bones.

"He has a chance," Li-tia told the gathering of Raven Clan hunters. "We must get him back to Great Cave and to a warm house. Hurry!"

Kenta's followers stared with disbelief. Several glanced upward to the high climbing place from which the two men had fallen, I-so-te, the former medicine man, voiced what everyone yet believed. "Su-mat is dying. We must not cause him more suffering."

Li-tia glared at I-so-te who had made it clear from the

beginning that he resented her powers and status. "I-so-te, this man can be saved!"

"No! Already, his skin turns dark with death. He will die."

Li-tia was afraid the old man was correct but his death sentence made her all the more determined to prove him wrong. I-so-te had never stopped trying to undermine Li-tia's status, especially with Kenta. Right from the beginning this jealous old man had plotted and spread rumors against her. And now . . . now this was the chance to fight back and prove whose medicine was strongest. If Li-tia could save Su-mat from death, she would forever insure her reputation among these people. But would that be possible, given Su-mat's precarious hold on life? Wouldn't there be a better time to prove herself? If she failed, she would not have a second chance to make her reputation. But, if Su-mat was saved, her standing would become so great that her wisdom and powers would never again be questioned.

All of this Li-tia debated in less than a pair of heartbeats, aware that every eye was fixed to her. And just at that moment, Su-mat's bloody fingertips bit hard into Li-tia's forearm, telling her she must choose to save his life.

"Kenta, I will make strong medicine. Araba will help and so will Raven."

"Can he *really* live?"

"Yes!"

Kenta saw how Su-mat's fingernails dug into Li-tia's arm. He called for his strongest young men to lift and carry Su-mat up to Great Cave. When raised, the young man screamed in agony, causing Araba to leap forward and shout in anger, "Be careful you fools!"

As they started up to Great Cave, I-so-te placed a bad curse on Li-tia who quickly returned the ill favor. The wind began to howl and the snow blew straight into their faces. By the time they reached Great Cave, everyone was shivering like leaves in wind, and Li-tia was afraid that poor Su-mat might already have entered the Spirit World. But the fallen hunter's pulse was still beating and, when Su-mat was lowered into a pit house and placed beside a hot fire, his eyelids quivered and his discolored lips trembled in an effort to speak.

"Be still," Li-tia pleaded, aware that even the effort of speech required strength. "Kenta, Araba and I must work our medicine alone now. You and your people must leave at once."

"He will *die!*" I-so-te crowed loud enough that everyone in Great Cave was sure to hear. "Su-mat's spirit is already cursed by this Chacoan witch! Leave Su-mat to me! I alone have Raven's powers to heal!"

Li-tia would have attacked the old man if Kenta hadn't thrown himself in her path. Li-tia struggled only a moment, then gathered her wits. "If Su-mat dies, it will be because that old fool has cursed his spirit! I will *kill* him if he does not leave at once!"

I-so-te hurried up the ladder, hissing and spitting vile obscenities until he was safely beyond Li-tia's reach. "That woman is *evil!* She is a witch sent by our enemies! They are *Chacoans!*"

Kenta spun away and went up the ladder, almost shoving the old medicine man through the roof. The moment they were gone, Li-tia knelt beside Su-mat and whispered, "You *will* live. Do you believe me?"

"Yes," came the faint reply barely heard over the crackle of their glowing fire.

Li-tia began to issue orders to Araba. First, they would clean and bandage Su-mat's many flesh wounds. Next, Araba needed to boil sage and add to the most powerful Chacoan medicines. Perhaps it would be best to cover part of the smoke and ladder hole in the roof so that Su-mat would be forced to breathe deeply of her medicine smoke. This might also help to drive evil spirits from his battered body.

"Li-tia?"

Araba had retreated to the wall of the pit house. Even in the poor light, Li-tia could see that she was shaking with fear. "Yes?"

"I am afraid that I-so-te was right and that Su-mat will die. He looks so bad!"

Li-tia's eyes became slits and she studied her friend for a long moment. "You have no faith and never will be a medicine woman," she said.

"I know," Araba whispered. "I was . . . afraid that if I told you the truth, you would be angry with me."

"I am not angry. What do you want?"

"More . . . more children."

"But not by Mata-ki's husband."

"He wants me very much. He has already touched me like a husband."

Li-tia drew in a sharp breath, angry that Araba had chosen this moment to divide her thoughts. "I do not like that man. *This* man is much better for you!"

"Su-mat?" Araba stared down at the half-dead hunter.

"Yes. He has great strength and spirit. If he lives, you can marry him."

Araba opened her mouth to speak, then closed it.

"What is it," Li-tia said, beginning to undress Su-mat so that she could cleanse and then bandage all of his wounds.

"He has not even said that he wants me for his wife."

"He will," Li-tia promised. "By the time that we have healed him . . . he will."

Araba might have blushed, but it was too dim in the pit house for Li-tia to be sure.

Because the ground was frozen and the weather was bad outside, they buried Ta-te in the trash heap at the very back of the cave. Li-tia observed with interest that the Raven Clan's burial preparations were very much like the ones in Chaco Canyon. First, Ta-te's body was bathed and his hair washed and combed. Next, his arms were folded across his chest and tied together at the wrists and his knees drawn up to his chest. In this position, Ta-te's body was wrapped in his best turkey feather blanket. Prayers were sung and Ta-te was buried with respect.

Li-tia learned that the Raven Clan believed that Ta-te's spirit could not depart his body until four days had passed. During that time, Ta-te's grieving family placed food and water on the trash heap until, on the morning of the fourth day, everyone in Great Cave rejoiced. Little children gathered in the pit houses and sat staring with wide-eyed anticipation at the sipapu holes that led down into Mother Earth, hoping to catch a glimpse of Ta-te's departing spirit. Afterward, his name would never again be mentioned.

Ta-te had left behind a wife and two small sons. They would be taken into his brother's family, just as they would have been in Chaco Canyon. Watching the burial ceremony reminded Li-tia how similar these people were to those in Chaco Canyon and that realization conjured up the ancient legend of Echata, the founder of this small but valiant mesa clan. Small wonder that these two enemies shared a common language, beliefs, burial practices and important traditions.

In the frigid months of December and January, six members of the clan died, including Kenta's younger wife. All were buried either in the back trash heap or in the larger one that fell away from the mouth of Great Cave. The People meant no disrespect by this and knew that the spirits of the dead would understand.

Only two of the six that died that winter were children. Everyone agreed that Li-tia and Araba were responsible for saving children. Li-tia watched them as a hawk watches for its prey and, at the first indication of a fever or illness, she took the child down into the pit house and made strong medicine.

Araba was always present to help and Su-mat was never far from her or little Quaeto. Su-mat's broken leg pained him in the cold and he could not walk without a pronounced limp, but soon he demonstrated a gift for making fine bows and arrows. Li-tia knew that this good-natured but lame hunter would gain a place of considerable respect among the Raven Clan. Most importantly, Su-mat had announced his desire to marry Araba and treat her and Quaeto with love and kindness.

As for Li-tia, she felt quite satisfied. No longer did anyone listen to the warnings of old I-so-te, who now spent his waking hours among the women and the children, tending the winter fires. The women of the clan, mindful that they or a member of their family might one day fall to sickness or injury which they believed was caused by evil witches, faithfully provided Li-tia with their best food, fed her fire and made sure that her pots were always filled with water.

"Your medicine is great," Kenta told Li-tia one mild afternoon as a chinook caused the mesa snow to melt and cascade down their cliff like a waterfall.

Li-tia sat on a rock just inside Great Cave, admiring the watery veil that sparkled in the welcome sunlight. She had been remembering spring in Chaco Canyon and knew that, very soon, the Chacoan men and women would be preparing their fields for the planting of corn, bean and squash seeds. That had always been an especially happy and a hopeful time of the year in Chaco Canyon.

"Will you pull old Tumsea's tooth today?" Kenta asked. "She is in great pain."

"I will," Li-tia replied, knowing that she would place a dagger-shaped stone against the infected tooth, then tap it out with a rock.

"Do not wait too long," Kenta advised before turning to rejoin the men.

"I won't," Li-tia promised, admiring how the sun created shimmering rainbows as it lanced through the watery veil.

Tooth extractions were commonplace among the People. Next to stiff and painful joints and aching backs, rotting teeth were a great curse upon the elders and there was little that Li-tia could do to relieve this pain. Also, many of the People had suffered severe injuries to their bones and had never fully recovered. Some walked bent over, while others slowly shuffled about and were unable to work or even care for themselves. No one in the Raven Clan complained of those unable to tend even their basic needs or do their share of the communal labor.

During one particularly cold spell in January, almost half of the clan's turkeys died. Too many of their feathers had been plucked for new robes. The surviving turkeys were miserable creatures. Li-tia thought that the turkeys had been much happier in Chaco Canyon where they could enjoy the sunny winter days and take shelter during bad weather. But here, the poor birds never left Great Cave and Li-tia believed that many died not only of cold due to lack of enough feathers, but also of sadness and too much smoke.

In March, Great Cave lost all of its charm as the weather turned warm and everything became very damp. Melting snow filled the canyon with the roar of rushing water and even in Great Cave, springs gushed through ceiling fissures and dripped down on the People both day and night. Li-tia became almost frantic with worry that her precious Chacoan seeds might get wet and rot. She constantly moved them from one dry hiding place to another, never confident of their safety. To make matters worse, the strong scent of decaying trash was pervasive in Great Cave.

When she complained of this to Kenta, he explained that during the summer, the air was so dry that nothing rotted. In the wintertime, everything was frozen. But now, with all the water and dampness, everything decayed, causing a stench that Li-tia found nauseating.

"I am moving up onto the mesa," she informed Kenta one beautiful spring morning.

Kenta was not pleased. "And why do you wish to leave the People?"

"To plant the seeds that will make living here in Great Cave next winter much easier," Li-tia explained, aware that this was a delicate and, in Kenta's mind, an unwelcome subject.

"Only the piñon and wildflowers and grass grow on the mesa and they are all eaten by the wild animals. Your seeds will not live to push their sprouts through the earth. If the mice, rabbits and other small animals do not eat them, then the hungry birds will."

"I can protect them," Li-tia vowed. "Night . . . and day."

"And when will you sleep?"

Li-tia had no good answer. She had already considered every way possible to protect her plants while she slept, even to weaving some kind of thick fencing with the boughs and branches of the piñon. This, however, would only be a waste of time and effort. Small animals would be able to penetrate her fence and nibble away at her young and tender crop long before it ever had a chance to bear a harvest.

"Li-tia?"

"I will find a way," she said, turning to leave.

But Kenta caught and held her by the arm. "The Raven Clan is a *hunting* and a *gathering* clan. I have heard of how they grow things in Chaco Canyon and other places."

"Then you must know that . . ."

"Those places are all in the desert! They have long, hot summers. Here, the summers are not so long or hot. And our earth has been made only for the wild plants and animals."

"If it will grow grasses, flowers, bushes and trees, it can also grow my corn, beans and squash."

Kenta's eyes hardened. "Chacoan Medicine Woman, what if I forbid you to do this?"

So, Li-tia thought as despair flooded her heart, *here it is at last. I have dreaded this moment since autumn when this proud leader mocked my precious seeds. Now, he is about to forbid me to plant . . . even though it might save his clan some terrible winter.*

"Then I would ask your permission to leave the clan. If it were given, I would plant my seeds upon the mesa far enough away so that you were not offended by my crops."

Kenta's expression grew harder but Li-tia pushed on recklessly. "Next fall, I would beg your permission to bring my harvest to Great Cave so that all the Raven people never would know winter hunger again."

"With your Chacoan bow and arrows, we have no more worries. Isn't that enough?"

"No, it is not," Li-tia replied. "It is important always to try and do things better for your people."

"Our ways are *good.*"

"Yes, they are. But, sometimes, among every people, there are better ways. The bow and arrow I gave you is superior to the atlatl and my medicine is stronger than that of I-so-te. As this is truth, so it is that my seeds will be your lasting gift to the Raven Clan, making your name as great as that of your legendary Echata."

Kenta had been about to argue but now his jaw dropped with surprise. "You have heard of Echata?"

"Of course. Surely you recall how he killed his own brother in Chaco Canyon."

Kenta's face made it clear that he *hadn't* heard this part of the legend and he appeared so disturbed that Li-tia almost felt sorry for him.

"Please," she said, "you are a wise leader. If I go from your sight so that my crops do not offend your eyes or in any way affect your hunting, why would you not allow me to do this thing with seeds? Have I not done everything I have promised and saved many of your people this winter? And has not my heart been generous giving you everything I have prized?"

His shoulders slumped and he was forced to nod with agreement. "This is true. You have been good for the Raven Clan. Araba is good too."

"She will make Su-mat a good wife and bring into this clan many fine children along with Quaeto."

"I believe this," Kenta conceded.

"Then believe me and let me plant my seeds in the mesa

earth. If I fail, I will never ask such a favor again for your clan."

"If you fail," Kenta said, "I will take you for my wife."

His words caught Li-tia completely by surprise, and she took a faltering step backward. Kenta caught and drew her close. "I have only one wife," he explained, "and she cannot please me as you do."

For the first time, Li-tia heard a yearning, no, a *pleading* in Kenta's strong voice. Without conscious thought, she realized that she was eagerly dipping her chin with complete agreement.

"Then it will come to pass," Kenta said, breaking into a wide smile. "A harvest . . . or a new husband."

"Yes," Li-tia replied, straightening and gazing into his eyes. "Or both."

It was Kenta's turn to be caught by surprise. Before he could recover, Li-tia pulled from his grasp and hurried away, her mind filled with a strange mixture of joy and confusion.

Fourteen

Li-tia was ready to leave Great Cave and journey to the mesa top, but on the morning of her departure, she realized how much she was going to miss Araba and little Quaeto, as well as old Tumsea and the other women of the Raven Clan.

"I do not understand this," the nearly toothless old Tumsea complained, clucking her tongue against her gums. "With these bows and arrows, we never again will have to worry about winter hunger. Why then must you put seeds in the ground? And why risk death up there all alone?"

Li-tia sometimes asked herself the same questions. Here in Great Cave, she felt safe and protected. On the mesa, there were cougars, coyotes, even bears, although most of those had been hunted out years ago. It was a harsh, unforgiving land where even a single mistake could result in death.

"We have just decided to come with you," Araba announced, taking Su-mat's hand and almost dragging him forward.

"No," Li-tia said in a firm voice that brooked no argument. "You are with child, is this not so?"

Araba's cheeks flushed. "Only you could tell so early."

"You have a strong, eager husband," Li-tia replied.

Su-mat's chest swelled as all eyes turned to him, some very envious, because the young woman from Chaco Canyon was beautiful and desirable. This would be Su-mat's first child and he was full of his new responsibilities. Studying him,

Li-tia could not help but whisper a little prayer that Su-mat never would grow tired of Araba.

"I will come visit you," Tumsea announced loud enough for everyone to hear. "I walk slow, but I will find you."

"And I will come with her," another woman said as others began to make the same heart-warming pledge.

Li-tia suddenly felt much better about leaving. These warm and loving people were so good that she was all the more determined that her mesa top harvest should be a success.

"Good-bye," she said, gathering her belongings and glancing about for Kenta who was nowhere to be found.

Some of the clan followed her to the mesa top. It was funny, Li-tia thought, how this steep, treacherous path was no longer even of slight concern. During her time at Great Cave, she had gone up and down this trail hundreds of times. In good weather, such as this, it was nothing.

Once on the rim, Li-tia gazed with fondness back down into Cliff Canyon. She had studied it so often during the bitterness of winter that she believed she knew every tree, every rock, every line and color, and how they would all change throughout the day as Sun traveled overhead.

Araba had left Quaeto behind and she was the last to say good-bye. "I am sorry that I did not become a medicine woman. I didn't even try very hard."

"It is not your way. It never was."

"What *is* my way?"

"To be a mother and a wife."

"And that is all?"

"There is no need for more. But, like me, you always will be Chacoan and so you need to help the Raven Clan people."

"After my child is born, I will join you with the harvest. And I will try to bring many others."

"Good. But never go against Kenta or your husband's wishes."

"I will if I must—to help you."

These bold but perhaps unrealistic words meant much to

Li-tia. Araba always seemed too compliant, but Li-tia alone knew that her friend's real strength and courage was masked by her rare beauty. Araba would be a true friend forever.

"Good-bye," Li-tia said, turning to walk into the forest and disappear until next autumn.

The moment she was out of sight, Li-tia felt very sad and alone. It was all she could do not to turn back to her friends or at least to cry like an abandoned child as she threaded her way through the piñon and juniper forest walking northwest. After a time, she reached the head of Cliff Canyon above the spring where the women collected water during the dry time of the year. Gazing back into the canyon, she could see Great Cave; and the sight was so painful that she quickly turned and hurried north into higher and unfamiliar country. She was so wrapped in her misery that she did not see Kenta as he stepped directly into her path.

"You would leave without telling the leader of your clan good-bye?" he asked, raising his eyebrows in question.

"I saw your family and told them good-bye. But I did not see you."

"I am hunting alone," he explained. "I forgot that this was the day you were leaving until just now. I saw a movement and thought you were Deer and almost put an arrow in your side."

"Oh," Li-tia said, not sure what to say.

"But then I saw you and remembered."

"I am glad you did not kill me, Kenta."

"That gathering basket looks very heavy just to hold a few seeds."

"It holds everything that I own," Li-tia explained, regaining her composure. "So it is heavy."

"I will carry it a ways for you."

Kenta removed the basket from Li-tia's shoulder, then slipped it over his own. This was a kind and remarkable gesture because the gathering basket belonged only to woman and never was worn by a man, much less the clan leader. But

Kenta did not seem to mind. Li-tia thought she must be dreaming.

"Do you know where you are going?" he asked as they walked side by side.

"No."

"Exactly what is it that you seek?"

"A meadow where the sun warms the earth and the grass grows tall."

"And your seeds will be planted in this grass?"

"No, I will dig all the grass away. My seeds must have their own sunlight."

"I see."

Kenta skirted Cliff Canyon, turning south again along the rim opposite Great Cave. Finally he said, "I know of such a place as you seek. Would you like me to take you there?"

"I would!"

"It is a good place and one from which you can always see Great Cave. If you are in trouble, you can make a smoke signal, or climb down into Cliff Canyon and seek our help."

"That is a good idea."

"Then," he was saying, more to himself now than to Li-tia, "you should light your night fires beside this meadow. And, every day at sunrise and sunset, you must stand and be seen by . . . the women."

Li-tia felt emboldened enough to take her leader's hand and squeeze it tightly. She knew that Kenta was trying to say that it also was important for *him* to see her silhouetted twice each day, at sunrise and sunset, and to watch the yellow glow of her campfire every night. It meant that he loved her. Li-tia found it difficult to keep her cheeks dry of foolish tears.

"Do you hunt often this far from Great Cave?" she managed to ask.

"I think I will do so more often. Deer are larger here and still unafraid."

"And is there good water?"

"Oh, yes! And tall grass for you to scrape away."

She glanced sideways at him, detecting a hint of amusement in his voice. "Kenta, I am eager to see this place."

"You will soon."

Kenta said no more but led her to a beautiful canyon-side meadow fed by a small, cold spring. The grass was indeed lush, as he had promised. They surprised a band of unwary deer, one of which Kenta shot with Matezi's bow and arrow.

"You will need meat to keep you strong for this work," he said, after offering a prayer over the fallen animal to thank it for the gift of its life. "I will shoot one for you each full moon."

"You should not have to go to such trouble."

He shrugged. "It is no trouble. Besides, I will kill another for the People."

"And how will you carry it so far back to Great Cave?"

"I will pitch it into Cliff Canyon, as we do winter wood."

She gazed across the canyon feeling so much better that Great Cave and her people would always be visible except perhaps during a bad storm or when clouds filled their canyon.

"You look happier now," he said, slipping his arm around her waist and drawing Li-tia close.

"I *am* happier."

"Do not be too happy alone," he warned, only half jesting, "because, when the leaves turn colors, you will be done here and become my wife."

"What about your other wife? Have you spoken of this to her?"

"She knows. Everyone knows," Kenta confessed, appearing embarrassed.

Li-tia would have liked him to stay the night but Kenta soon left. She watched him stride across her new meadow and when he reached its far side, he turned and waved. Li-tia felt so joyful it was all she could do not to run like a young girl to his side and pull him down into the grass so that they would make love. But now she was spring planter, so she just waved back before he vanished into the trees. It was more than enough to know that Kenta would provide meat and reappear every sunrise and sunset to wave at her across Cliff Canyon until her crops ripened . . . or withered and died.

Kenta had urged her to build a shelter as soon as possible because often there were fierce summer lightning and rain storms. With this in mind, Li-tia spent her first full day using her Chacoan knife to cut thick roof branches which she weaved tightly together with the strands of yucca fiber. Mindful of a sanctuary she had used to fight off wild dogs near Chaco Canyon, Li-tia used a crevasse to support her roof, and rocks to form a narrow, easily defensible entrance.

After taking care of her shelter needs, she studied her meadow for hours before deciding how and where she would construct a series of three dams. The dams would be porous and would not impede the gentle flow of spring water but, instead, would create three moist reservoirs where Li-tia intended to plant her Chacoan seeds. She decided to place her corn nearest to the source of the water and behind her first dam. Perhaps twenty feet farther into the meadow, she would sow beans and, nearest the rim, her squash, which needed more space and was a favorite of foxes, rabbits and other hungry varmints.

Planting was a joy to Li-tia, satisfying and familiar work that she had done since childhood. She soon lost track of time as she cleared her plots of grass and prepared the soil for her seeds. She arose early each morning, napped for a few hours during the warmest part of the day, and resumed her labors until sunset. Li-tia's mind was kept occupied by questions such as whether to prepare and plant her cornfield first, or to wait until all three fields were ready and then plant everything at the same time. She finally decided to plant each field as soon as it was ready. By the end of the first week, she began to plant corn seeds. With each seed, she offered a prayer to Sun and Rain and also to Raven that this seed would become a sweet and rich winter food for the Raven Clan.

As Li-tia worked on her hands and knees, she used a digging stick and offered her prayers as she sang happy songs, some belonging to the Raven Clan, but some that she remembered from planting with the Chacoan women and children at this same time of year.

One day Li-tia became especially dirty and the air was so warm that she had removed all her clothing as she planted, prayed and sang her happy songs. The hot sun felt good on her skin and a breeze riffled her long hair and cooled her brow. She was smeared with mud from head to toe but simply felt blessed to be alive and able to do such important work.

"You are still *very* beautiful," Kenta quietly remarked when Li-tia stopped working for a moment to lean back and press her hands to the small of her aching back.

She twisted around to see him standing beside a freshly killed deer, bow in his right hand, a pair of arrows in his left. Like herself, Kenta was no longer young; streaks of gray ran through his raven-colored hair. His hard but no longer supple body was scarred and his face was chiseled by the sun and years. Even so, Li-tia thought him almost beautiful, realizing that she had never wanted a man as much as Kenta. Dropping her digging stick, Li-tia raised her mud-smeared arms without words.

Kenta understood. He dropped his weapons, then stripped away his breech clout and hurried to join her. Soon, Li-tia felt as if this high mesa world was spinning and the sun was exploding before her eyes as their bodies locked in a passionate embrace. Later, when the world became still and their hearts slowed, they playfully rolled back and forth over the planted earth as if their grimy bodies, flushed and wet from lovemaking, were capable of nourishing the seeds resting inches below.

Kenta stayed with her that night and he would have remained longer if Li-tia had not indicated that he needed to return to his clan.

"As their leader, you are expected to be among them always," she said, as they stood together beside the rim so that anyone watching from Great Cave could witness their union.

"My heart is here with you," he said. "Besides, there are many younger and stronger men at Great Cave to protect our clan."

"But none so wise, Kenta."

"I am not so wise," he told her. "In anger, I once scattered your seeds."

"That has long since been forgiven."

"I will never do that again."

"I know. You acted so stupidly."

"Maybe not stupidly but . . ."

"Stupidly," she repeated, hugging him tight. "And now you must not be stupid again and must leave this old medicine woman. But first, tell me of Araba, Quaeto and her husband, Su-mat."

"Their voices sing like yours," Kenta told her. "Araba and Su-mat are very happy. Quaeto is everywhere. Strong and smart, that one."

"I believe that he will one day be very important to the Raven Clan."

"Have you seen this in a vision?"

"Yes."

"Do you have a vision that we also could have a son?"

"No," Li-tia confessed, knowing that Kenta would be disappointed. "I am too old."

"I am older than you."

"We are different."

"I do not understand."

"That is because you are a man."

Kenta did not pursue the inquiry but instead made preparations to leave. First, however, he asked, "Any sign of danger from wild animals?"

"None."

"If there was a danger . . ."

"I have already found a path into Cliff Canyon that would lead me home to Great Cave. A path very near to where I will plant my squash."

"Good," he said, not even attempting to hide his relief before he hugged Li-tia and then said good-bye.

Several weeks later, shoots of corn appeared almost as quickly as they would have in the lower, warmer Chaco Canyon. Soon after the corn came the delicate bean sprouts, then the curling squash plants, exactly in the order that they had been planted. Li-tia was delighted, but not surprised. The grass around her fields was lush, so why would she ever doubt that her carefully tended, weeded and watered crops would not also flourish?

But soon after the new plants appeared, hungry varmints began to converge on her meadow. First came the chipmunks, squirrels and rabbits, all determined to nibble away Li-tia's tender young crop. They were bold and quick but Li-tia was a deadly rock thrower. The moment she saw one of these furry thieves slipping forward in the grass, she would shout a warning. If the thief didn't scurry away, she snatched up a rock and let it fly, often to supplement her diet of stale piñon nuts and Kenta's gift of venison.

At night Li-tia tended a big campfire. The fire kept the critters at a distance but, when Li-tia nodded off to sleep and the firelight dimmed, the varmints dashed forward to have their meal. Sometimes they were successful, sometimes not. They preferred the corn and beans over squash, so that is where Li-tia waged most of her nightly battles.

"You look very tired," Kenta would say whenever he arrived with fresh meat. "Tonight, you sleep and I will watch over the crop."

At first, Li-tia tried to keep up a brave front and refuse his help, but, after a month she knew that she could not allow herself that luxury. "All right. But only tonight."

As often as not, Kenta would stay two nights. It was the second night that Li-tia most anticipated. Refreshed from sleep and frequent napping, they would make love with one eye on the starry heavens and the other on the fields. Kenta told her about his boyhood but was eager to learn about the life she and Araba had known in Chaco Canyon.

"There are many people living in Chaco Canyon," she told him.

"More than at Great Cave?"

"Far more."

"But they are not good hunters."

"They are *very* good hunters with the bow and arrow."

Seeing concern deepen in his face, Li-tia added, "But they are not nearly so strong or handsome as your Raven Clan men."

Kenta relaxed. "Did they ever talk about coming here to make war?"

"No. They believe that there are many Raven Clan people and that you are very, very fierce."

"We are!"

"Of course you are. That is why they are afraid of the Raven Clan and have no wish to enter these mountains."

"Then why did you and Araba come?"

"Because I knew that, if we went to anyone but an enemy people, we would be returned to the Chacoans where Araba's husband would kill us."

"And all because of Quaeto?"

"And because Matezi is rotten with foolish pride."

"Someday Quaeto will want to know of his father."

"Araba will have to decide about that."

"Were you happy in Chaco Canyon?"

"Not as happy as I am here with you."

These words pleased Kenta very much and this conversation was repeated many times that summer on the rim across

from Great Cave. There was really only one concern that
Kenta had which Li-tia could not dispel and that was about
her powers as a medicine woman.

"You said that you could not have these powers and be
married," he would remark, usually after a long silence had
stretched between them.

"I was wrong, Kenta. You will see. Next winter I will prove
my medicine is still strong even after becoming your second
wife."

"If it is not, then I have done a terrible thing to my people."

"You have not. You will see. My medicine grows stronger
each year. And now, with happiness in me, it will be stronger
than ever."

"I hope so. Even with corn, beans and squash, there always
will be sickness and death in winter."

"Less and less, my husband."

"You are a good rock thrower, Li-tia. I think that you have
killed all the rabbits and squirrels on this side of the canyon."

"No, there always will be more."

"I should stay and hunt here."

"You should go back to Great Cave because you are leader
of the Raven Clan."

Kenta went back but returned to Li-tia with increasing fre-
quency. She would often see him silhouetted on the far canyon and they would wave to each other like excited children.
This always gave Li-tia a sense of peace and protection, even
when she saw the yellow night eyes of Coyote and once of
Cougar peering at her from the forest.

Li-tia saw no signs whatsoever of the feared grizzly bear.
She did see a few black bears along with bighorn sheep, por-
cupines and raccoons. And although she would not have admitted it to Kenta, Crow, Raven and many other birds were
a constant threat to her growing fields, especially after the
emergence of the young ears of corn, bean pods and tiny
orange and yellow squash. To fend off these feathered thieves,

Li-tia had to spend long hours in her fields throwing rocks that never struck these squawking, elusive marauders.

As the summer days lengthened and grew warmer, growling storms often appeared late in the afternoon. Their approach worried Li-tia because she knew that, at this elevation, a violent hailstorm could easily destroy her entire crop. Fortunately, rain fell, but rain falling too hard was more threat than blessing.

Still, it seemed to Li-tia that, with Kenta's help and her own diligence, she was going to prove to all that there would be a fine harvest to feed the People next winter. This thought was more than enough to sustain her through the hot days and the long, moonlit nights when her mind and weary body begged for sleep . . . and for Kenta.

By mid-September, the rain stopped falling and the meadow grass withered and died. In the afternoon, the wind picked up dust and grit, scouring the mesa. It was then that many hungry critters wanted to feast on Li-tia's almost ripened crops. She fought them, throwing rocks until her arm was sore and her aim ragged. At such times, she would rush back and forth, scattering the little thieves and yelling like an avenging witch. Her weight dropped fast until she was quite thin but Li-tia didn't mind because her corn was beautiful and her squash of extraordinary size. Thick tangles of beans were supported by sticks that Li-tia had pressed deep into the mud. Just watching such a promising bounty was a joy and worth every ounce of her fading energy.

"I will bring the women over to help harvest these crops," Kenta announced as they weeded between the stalks of tall corn.

"Just a little longer," Li-tia told him. "Another week."

"Are you sure?"

Li-tia nodded, knowing that Kenta was almost as excited about this harvest as she was.

"Yes. The corn still has a few more days to ripen and sweeten; the beans, too."

He nodded, not able to hide his disappointment.

"All good things take time," she said, reaching over to squeeze his hand.

Kenta understood her real meaning. "Yes. This is true."

Nothing had ever given Li-tia so much satisfaction as raising this crop. Not even her medicine. And now, it was clear that she had been right in predicting that the sun and high mesa soil were perfect for growing.

After Kenta left, Li-tia diverted a steady trickle of the spring water to form a shallow pond for the thirsty deer and varmints who were suffering from the late summer drought.

"You can drink your fill, but you must not eat my corn, beans or squash," she would remind them with a rock clenched in each fist in case they mistook her kindness for weakness. "Next week, the crop will be harvested and then you can finally eat the leaves and stalks."

Four days later, on a particularly hot and humid afternoon, ominous thunder clouds rolled over the mesa. Li-tia could hear their growling and see spears of lightning lance into the mesa. A tree exploded like a torch and Li-tia tasted smoke on the hot, gusting wind. Moments later, three terrified does exploded out of the brush to race across her fields and then vanish back into the forest, running south toward the end of this mesa. When more deer followed with their eyes rolling in panic, Li-tia shivered with fear. She hurried to a big rock and scrambled to its pinnacle to stare horrified at the approaching firestorm now destroying everything in its path as hot winds sent it racing toward her crops.

Li-tia jumped off the rock and sprinted to the rim of the canyon. She began to wave her arms, jump up and down and shout. She had no idea what Kenta or his men could do to help but it seemed vital that they know of this unexpected calamity.

Li-tia watched the Raven Clan men begin to hurry to the top of the mesa. She thought that she recognized Kenta, but could not be sure. Didn't they realize that it would be impossible for them to round the mesa and come to save her and the crop? It was already far too late!

Kenta must have realized this as soon as he and his men were on the mesa because, after a few moments of apparent confusion, they scrambled back down into Cliff Canyon. Li-tia wondered if they might have decided that their only hope for survival was to retreat deep into the recesses of Great Cave.

Li-tia twisted around, needing to judge how much time she had left before the fire devoured her crop. Two hours? No, if the wind kept blowing, much less time than that. The wind pushing into her face already was carrying ash.

Jumping from rock to rock and waving her hands frantically, Li-tia suffered a mis-step and twisted her ankle. She cried out in pain and hobbled over to her camp, snatching up her gathering basket and then rushing to her beautiful field of corn. Fully ripened or not, her precious ears of corn must be harvested right now! Li-tia blocked out the pain of her ankle and began to tear the succulent ears of corn from the tall green stalks. She was soon coated with a thick mixture of sweat and ash but she didn't care. Dashing from stalk to stalk, Li-tia spent a frenzied hour stripping clean every last ear of corn and dragging basketful after basketful to dump into Cliff Canyon.

Never mind where it fell! Li-tia had no time to worry about that as she frantically began to strip the bean plants. This was much slower work and Li-tia could now feel the searing heat of the fire and see the plants wilting before her eyes. She began to cough and wheeze in the thickening smoke. Animals stampeded across her meadow, eyes glazed with fright. Trapped like herself at the end of the fingerling mesa, many flung themselves off the rim to crash to their deaths rather than face the advancing inferno, while a few retained enough presence to dash down a trail into Cliff Canyon at impossible speeds.

Li-tia only had time to fill one basket before the smoke

and heat became unbearable. When she twisted around and stared at the fire, she felt as if it were charring her flesh.

"Li-tia!"

She spun around to see Kenta leap out of Cliff Canyon. He was badly scratched and winded, as were the men close on his heels. Kenta shouted, "Drop the basket and run!"

"The squash!" she cried, hurrying over to grab one of the large melons. "We can still save the squash!"

Encouraged by her bold example, the men began to tear the heavy squash from their thick, twisting vines. Because they could not be pitched over the rim without being ruined, they had to be carried away. In a few moments, only Kenta and Li-tia remained on the blistering mesa and when Li-tia tried to stoop and grab one of the last of her squash, Kenta hooked his arm around her waist and practically dragged her toward the rim. Li-tia's gathering basket caught on the jagged stump of a rotting juniper and tore, spilling her precious beans. She tried to drop to her hands and knees so that she could collect at least a few but the heat was too intense. Her hair began to smoke and her eyes water so that she could not see.

Kenta dragged her over the rim. They began to roll through brush and might have tumbled to their deaths but Raven Clan men pounced on them, breaking their momentum before helping them to their feet.

Li-tia tried to run but was betrayed by her ankle and fell. Kenta and others pulled her erect while the other men collected ears of corn, her gathering basket of beans and all their ripe squash.

"Look!" one of the men shouted, pointing overhead.

They saw a hundred-foot wall of flame licking greedily at the sky.

"Run!" Kenta cried as he slipped his arm around Li-tia's waist and they scrambled the rest of the way down to the bottom of the canyon. Without daring to waste even a moment and look back, they fought their way up to Great Cave where the anxious women and children waited.

Li-tia collapsed into Araba's arms and they held each other tight, rocking back and forth while Kenta made preparations to save his people. However, it soon became apparent that the wind had not sent the maelstrom into Cliff Canyon; it had reached the tip of the far mesa and was dying.

By the next morning, the firestorm had consumed itself, but for days, smoke continued to drift up from the smoldering trees and brush. Unable to miss an opportunity, the People made countless trips to collect the bodies of charred animals which were then butchered and smoked.

"We have enough food for two winters," Kenta announced as he and Li-tia sat together watching a sunset made especially beautiful and interesting because of the lingering smoke clouds. "With all this meat and with your crops, we will grow fat and lazy."

Li-tia was not so pleased. "I have no bean seeds. They are all gone."

"Corn and squash is enough," he assured her. "We do not need beans."

Li-tia did not agree, knowing that beans were an important source of food to the Chacoans, almost as important as the corn.

"Li-tia," he was saying, "fat, maybe. Lazy, no. There is still wood to collect. Because of you, never again will the Raven Clan go hungry in winter. The time has come to become my wife."

Li-tia pushed the loss of her precious beans from her mind. Kenta was right. They had a harvest and, from this day to forever, life would be much better at Great Cave.

Moments later, when Kenta led her to a place where they could be alone, Li-tia also knew that whatever time she had left on earth would be a happy time.

Fifteen

How long, Araba wondered, *had Li-tia lived? Half a century?*

Araba could not say. Ages and dates meant little to the Anasazi people. Children usually could count how many winters they had survived; adults soon lost count or did not bother.

Li-tia had been very old. She had proven that she could remain a great medicine woman after her marriage, and then even long after the death of Kenta. One of his sons had been clan leader for only five years before he also died of a sickness. And now, because of Li-tia and her great wisdom and influence, Quaeto was being considered as a future clan leader despite his withered arm and hand. Quaeto alone had learned the ancient Chacoan secrets, rituals and medicines from Li-tia. And it would be Quaeto who would protect and lead the Raven People past her time.

"Mother," Quaeto said, "it was Li-tia's wish that I now make the long journey to Chaco Canyon."

Araba had always dreaded this day. "Why would Li-tia send you to your death? You were as much her son as mine."

Quaeto led Araba over to the mouth of Great Cave where they could speak alone. "Li-tia had sisters and brothers in Chaco Canyon, as you do."

"In my heart they are *dead!* When Matezi sent us out to the place of abandonment and death, my family of cowards was too afraid to step forward to save us!"

"You once told me they also would have been sacrificed had they spoken," Quaeto calmly reminded his mother. "And Li-tia told me many things about the Chacoans. Her last wish was that I visit and make peace with them, as well as trade for new bean seeds."

Araba's eyes flashed. "Those beans! Li-tia always talked about the beans. Why? We have meat, corn, and squash. But she never stopped remembering the stupid beans."

"I believed Li-tia when she said that they are very important and also that I should learn from the Chacoans. Li-tia described many Chacoan plants and medicines that are not found on the mesas but are strong against sickness and death."

Araba felt like weeping. Her beloved Su-mat was dead two years and, even though they had two now married daughters, it was Quaeto who had always had first claim on her heart.

"Mother," he said, "are you strong enough to come with me to Chaco Canyon?"

Araba gazed deeply into Quaeto's eyes, thinking she must have misunderstood . . . but she had not. He was serious. "My son, do you want us both to die?"

"I want us both to bring great prosperity, wisdom and health to the Raven Clan. You know that the harvest grows smaller every year. Li-tia said that it is because the corn and squash seeds are old and tired. We need fresh ones as well as the beans long ago lost in the fire."

"Have you forgotten what those people almost did to us! How many times have I told you the stories of the wild dogs and . . . ?"

"Yes, yes! But my father was much older than you. He must be long dead, but maybe not your brothers and sisters."

"I spit on them!" Araba spat onto the earth to emphasize her feelings.

"I am sorry," Quaeto told her. "For you should not always carry such hatred. I will start alone tomorrow for Chaco Canyon."

"No!"

"I must. It was Li-tia's only dying wish."

"She was crazy with pain . . . or . . . or we did not understand."

"Li-tia was not crazy and I understood her true wish. So, come with me! I will protect you. They will not even remember us."

"They might."

"Mother, you said that Li-tia made it look as if we were devoured by the wild dogs. If they remember that, they might think me a spirit . . . or a god. Then we will have everything our way."

Araba knew that her son was being ridiculous in order to hide his own fears but she laughed despite that. "All right, foolish son, I will go with you to Chaco Canyon—but you must travel slow."

"As Turtle," he promised. "Will you prepare the food?"

"As I always have."

"We will leave at dawn."

When the Raven Clan people heard this news, they were distressed. All the women came to Araba and begged her to stay at Great Cave.

"Everyone knows that the Chacoans are a very bad people," one woman said, her voice rising above the others. "They will not only kill, but *eat* you!"

"No," Araba said with firmness. "Remember, Li-tia and I were once Chacoans and I remember them well. They have rules and are quick to punish, but they also are quick to reward. My husband, Matezi, was the source of their evil. But by now, he will be dead."

"You cannot be sure! You cannot!"

"I can," Araba told the woman, "for he would have to be far beyond a man's years of life."

"Li-tia was also ancient!"

"Matezi is dead. I go with my son as Li-tia wished."

All the People looked to old Pi-mic, their temporary clan

leader, expecting him to forbid this journey. They were disappointed. Pi-mic said nothing and shuffled away to be alone.

After that, there was nothing left for the Raven Clan to
say, as Araba made preparations. She was soon joined by
many of her closest friends who brought food, weapons and
an extra turkey feather and rabbit-skin coat.

"We will not need the bow and arrow," Araba told its of-
ferer. "Neither Quaeto nor I can use that weapon. He has a
spear and it will be too warm in the low desert for a coat."

That night Quaeto said good-bye to the men and boys, then
went to be near his mother. He was surprised to find Araba
alone, sitting before her fire lost in a trance.

"Mother?"

She looked up.

"You do not *have* to make this journey."

"I want to," Araba replied. "For all of us, but especially
for Li-tia. Had it not been for her, we both would have died
long, long ago."

"Her spirit and that of Raven will protect us in Chaco
Canyon."

"I know," Araba said, uncrossing her legs and stretching
out on her robe. "Let us go to sleep now."

"Do you remember the way?" Quaeto asked with a yawn.

"I remember it like yesterday," Araba whispered as the
memories of wild dogs and flight carried her swiftly back in
time.

In the days that followed, Araba was reminded of how hot
it had been when she and Li-tia had carried little Quaeto
north searching for a new home in the high northern mountains. Fortunately, it was still spring and the yucca as well as
the cactus were in bloom, their flowers brightly colored yellow, white, pink and crimson. Along the great river that ran
to the south of the mesas, the cottonwood trees filled the air
with downy seeds and although Araba missed the perfume

of the mountain pines, the air was spiced with the bite of blooming sage.

"You do not look tired or afraid," Quaeto remarked as they trudged south.

"I had forgotten the beauty of the desert," Araba confessed. "I had remembered only the heat and bad things. If we are killed, then I am glad it will be in this sweet time of year."

Quaeto had brought a large deerskin bag stuffed with the beautifully tanned hides of cougar, badger and black bear . . . animals whose hides were not likely to be found in Chaco Canyon and, therefore, would be prized.

Their journey was uneventful until they topped a rise and witnessed hundreds of thin smoke ribbons drifting upward. "Do they come from Middle Earth?" Quaeto asked.

"No. From the Chacoans."

"How many are there?"

Araba shrugged. "How would I know? They were many when I was a girl and you were newborn. There must be far more now."

"How do they feed so many?"

"When you see their corn, bean and squash fields, you will understand. And remember, they have a river running through their canyon. This river is the source of their wealth and their life."

"While we have only a few springs, melting snow and sometimes summer rains."

"Yes, rains that may . . . or may not come to save our crops."

Quaeto glanced aside at his mother, wondering if he had been a complete fool to bring her back to this place of her childhood and to a people who thought them both long dead.

"Mother, what do you think will happen when they see us?"

Araba had thought about that question. "I do not believe it will be bad. I remember that these people always welcomed traders and that is what we are, Quaeto. Traders until we feel safe to tell them otherwise."

"And if we never feel safe?"

"Then we trade for the new seeds and leave in peace."

"Don't forget the Chacoan medicines," Quaeto added. "And anything else that looks interesting."

"You will find everything in Chaco Canyon interesting, my son. I have decided that it is very good we have come."

Quaeto was relieved to hear these words and was reasonably sure that he and his mother would be well received by the Chacoans. He was, after all, lively and skilled at conversation. He smiled often and, despite his deformity, was both tall and handsome. Quaeto also was strong, with good teeth and long legs that had earned him the reputation of being the fastest runner among the Raven Clan men. But despite all this, as they grew nearer to the home of his mother and father's people, Quaeto felt anxious. After all, what good would his foot speed be with his mother at his side?

None, he decided.

"There," Araba whispered when they halted to gaze down into Chaco Canyon, "is the place of our birth."

Quaeto collapsed on a rock in order to still his shaking knees. Araba sat down beside him as they surveyed the canyon, which was like a hidden valley surrounded by an endless plateau, barren of everything except sagebrush, sky and rock. Quaeto was stunned by the scope of this Anasazi civilization whose villages were scattered the entire length and width of the broad, shallow canyon. The Chacoan pit houses were much larger and more complex than those of his Raven Clan. Also, he saw many dome-shaped huts, both occupied and in various phases of construction. He could see that they were made of poles, covered with brush, then plastered with adobe.

And so many people! They wore almost no clothing and marched about the villages like a tribe of industrious wood ants. Hundreds labored in the extensive fields and gardens while the villages teemed with activity. Mingling with watchful children were large flocks of turkeys. Quaeto could hear their voices along with those of the shouting, laughing children. He also could see many small, noisy animals that looked very much like Coyote.

"What are those?" he asked.

"They are called dogs."

"They are not coyotes?"

"No. Dogs do not bite."

"What are they good for?"

"They are not very useful in themselves except that they protect the village turkeys. Some will hunt and kill Rabbit and all are very watchful at night."

"Can they be eaten?"

Araba shrugged but made a grimace of distaste. "I do not remember eating Dog."

"They are very noisy," Quaeto remarked. "Worse than Coyote at night."

"Some Chacoans like them very much. Matezi had many dogs and the men wagered much on them when they fought."

Quaeto turned his attention back to the fields and the Chacoan irrigation system that his mother said was the source of these people's wealth. It was clear that much depended upon the shallow stream that meandered down the center of the canyon. However, Quaeto also could see how these energetic people had built hundreds of canals in order to siphon rainwater off the surrounding plateau. Beneath these siphoning canals rested rock and earthen dams backed by glistening reservoirs which Quaeto was sure would be used to irrigate the crops in the hotter, drier time of late summer.

"Mother, I never dreamed there were so many of your people. And their fields are so large!"

"They make our mesa crops seem as nothing. See how tall their corn is?"

"It is hotter here with more sun."

"And water," Araba added. "And maybe better seeds."

"Which we shall have," Quaeto vowed, for he could finally

appreciate the great difference between the abundance these Chacoans enjoyed as compared to Raven Clan people.

"Look," Araba exclaimed, pointing to the south end of Chaco Canyon, "traders are coming!"

Quaeto could see perhaps thirty people descending a well-used trail. They were carrying heavy packs and their approach was well-announced by the barking dogs and then the happy greetings of children running to meet them.

Quaeto begin to fidget with excitement. "Maybe," he said, "we could hurry around and come in behind them so the Chacoans would think we were members of this trading party."

But Araba shook her head. "They would catch us in that lie and we would be punished. Better to state that we come from the north country to trade."

"And what if they ask us the name of our clan?"

"We tell them the truth and that we come in peace to trade your excellent furs."

"Can we go among them now?"

Araba had already decided it would be much better to enter Chaco Canyon early in the morning. "My son, we should wait. People are never warlike just after dawn."

Quaeto deferred to his mother's judgment since she alone among all the Raven Clan knew and understood the ways and temperament of her birth people. And maybe it was better this way because it would give him more time to become accustomed to the magnificence of Chaco Canyon and its thriving people. Why, dropped in among all these Chacoans, his Raven Clan would be like a few drops of blood lost in a river.

It was a sleepless night for both Araba and Quaeto. Arising well before dawn, they entered Chaco Canyon with the sunrise. They heard village criers calling out prayers for a new day and telling the villagers to eat well and then go about their work in peace and harmony.

So early was the hour that even the dogs were sleepy when

Araba and Quaeto entered the largest village. The Chacoans were finishing their prayers and hardly paid the visitors any attention, except for the children who stared at Quaeto's withered arm and the richly colored furs that protruded from his gathering basket.

"Who is the leader of this village?" Araba politely asked an old woman who gave them a toothless smile as she ladled a white, pasty meal into a beautiful bowl made of gray pottery.

The bowl was decorated with black zigzagging designs, a wonder to Araba because pottery had been very rare when she was a Chacoan child. Now, she suddenly was aware of pottery everywhere, some of it even ridged and formed in many interesting shapes and designs.

"Ge-taka is our leader," the old woman said, pointing to a nearby pit house.

However, when Quaeto approached it, a pair of sleeping dogs jumped up and almost charged him, barking furiously. Quaeto jerked his stone knife from its sheath, then braced himself for the expected attack. But the dogs sat down, tails thumping the earth. With large, soft eyes, they stared up and began to whine for attention.

Quaeto expelled a deep breath. He had never seen such friendly animals. The larger of the pair even jumped up on its hind legs, placed its huge paws on Quaeto's chest, and tried to lick his face.

The old woman began to laugh. For some reason, Quaeto began to laugh, too.

As was his privilege, Ge-taka had been sleeping late but was awakened by the ruckus outside his door. He was not pleased. Quaeto heard his angry shout and backed away. A few minutes later, scratching and yawning, Ge-taka himself appeared, very bowlegged, naked and perturbed. He was well beyond his prime with a pot belly, silver hair and a hook nose that was bent to the right. Despite his small stature and scrawny physique, Ge-taka somehow remained physically imposing.

"Who are you!" he demanded, eyes raking over Quaeto's poor sandals and dress before he regarded Araba with even more contempt.

"We come to trade," Quaeto said, managing a weak smile as he bowed politely.

"At this early hour! What kind of fools come at sunrise to trade?"

Araba handed her untouched bowl of food back to the old woman and marched up to Ge-taka. Since the moment of leaving Great Cave, she had prepared herself for death and realized that it held no threat. The only thing she really feared was that Quaeto would be tortured and killed.

"Ge-taka, we come with beautiful furs for trade." Araba pulled out of the basket an especially fine cougar skin that she had tanned. Draping part of the thick fur across her forearm, she asked, "Is it not very beautiful and rare?"

Ge-taka pursed his lips and his expression betrayed his sudden interest. "Woman, where did you get these?"

"From the mountains far to the north."

"And what is the name of your clan?"

Araba glanced sideways at her son, then turned back to the Chacoan leader to say, "The *Raven* Clan."

Ge-taka took a faltering step backward. "The *Raven* Clan?"

"It is so," Quaeto said in as firm a voice as he could summon. "We have come in peace to trade furs for food and other things of value."

"And to buy and learn to make pottery," Araba added.

"What about weapons?" Ge-taka demanded, his eyes trying to divine the hidden contents of their baskets.

"No weapons," Quaeto assured the Chacoan leader. "We only want peace and to trade."

Ge-taka recovered very fast. "How many of you live among the Raven Clan?"

"Many more than you," Quaeto said, waving his hand as if the matter were of little consequence.

Ge-taka glared, first at Quaeto and then his mother. When their eyes did not drop away in deference, he cleared his throat, motioned south and said, "We have many other peoples who live nearby. All good fighters and hunters."

"As we do, Ge-taka," Quaeto said. "But we want only to trade in peace."

"What happened to your arm and hand?"

"When my son was born," Araba explained, "Raven carried Quaeto up to meet Sun and to teach him many great secrets, but he bit off the middle of Quaeto's arm and then had to put it back together."

Ge-taka gaped, but quickly recovered. "You are friend of Raven and Sun? A god?"

"No," Quaeto admitted, already having decided that he might be asked to prove himself a deity which could only result in his disgrace. "Only a man. A hungry and weary trader. Nothing more."

"I thought as much," Ge-taka said, scratching his round belly. "We will eat now, trade later."

"As friends?"

"Yes," Ge-taka said. "For a gift of fur, you will have my friendship."

Quaeto glanced sideways at his mother. He had not expected to have to hand over a fur of great value just to be considered a friend. Confused as to what to do, he did nothing until Araba reached deep into his gathering basket and retrieved the skin of a red mountain fox. Very handsome, but not nearly as valuable as the cougar's thick, golden pelt.

"This is our gift for your help and friendship," she told the bowlegged little Chacoan leader.

Ge-taka hid his disappointment and ordered that they should enter his house. They climbed down a stairway through the ceiling and it became cool and dim. It took a few minutes for Quaeto's eyes to become adjusted to the sight of so much wealth. He also saw that there were two women present, one much younger than Ge-taka. They stared at their visitors, but not in an unfriendly way, as they prepared the morning's food.

Quaeto could not help but wonder if the young, pretty one was old Ge-taka's wife, or his daughter. She was younger than himself, every bit as shy and graceful as a young doe feeding in a meadow of spring flowers. Quaeto couldn't tear his eyes away from her despite the novelty of his surroundings.

"Quaeto?"

He abruptly turned to his mother who had an amused smile on her lips. "Isn't this a fine home?"

"Very fine," he said, remembering his manners. "Ge-taka, you are richly blessed to have so many good things, as well as two beautiful wives."

"One is my wife, the other is my daughter, Ja-cin," Ge-taka said, reaching for a bowl of food.

"Oh," Quaeto said, hoping his embarrassment did not show but then noticing Ja-cin trying not to laugh at him.

Quaeto knew he was making a fool of himself. He forced his eyes to drink in his surroundings which were indeed far nicer and more comfortable than any at Great Cave. Ge-taka's floors were covered with woven mats and the room was filled with pottery and baskets. Near a bed piled high with rabbit-skin blankets rested three pairs of new sandals, expertly woven with yucca fibers and leather strips. Drying squash, beans and corn dangled from cords tied to the roof poles.

Ge-taka allowed them plenty of time and his silence in order to appreciate his wealth before they were invited to take food.

"Eat and then rest well," Ge-taka said. "Tonight, we trade."

Quaeto was so impressed by the wealth he saw everywhere that he didn't even realize that Ja-cin was offering him a bowl until she grew impatient and gently bumped it against his chest.

He started, blushed and mumbled, "Thank you."

"You are welcome," she said in a voice like music.

Ge-taka tried not to pay any attention to the basket of rare furs. But after his guests had eaten and drunk cool water from a dipper resting in a large pot, he asked Quaeto to display the furs so that his wife and daughter could see their rare quality.

The bearskin especially excited the Chacoans and, that night when Araba and her son were introduced to the tribal council, their furs were displayed again causing much interest and excitement.

"What," Ge-taka finally asked, as the hour grew late and fire low, "would you want for the skins of these rare mountain animals?"

"A basketful of corn, beans and squash seeds and as much pottery as will fill my son's basket," Araba said without hesitation.

"This will be done."

"And a knife," Quaeto said, embarrassed by the crudeness of his own knife in comparison to those of his hosts. "And a pair of mated dogs . . . big ones that will fight off Coyote."

"You ask much," one of the Chacoans said, "for an enemy people."

"Trade with me and we are enemies no more," Quaeto informed his hosts. "Then we will return in the newness of each year to trade our furs for your prized goods."

"And how do we know that you will not return with warriors and attack our people?"

Quaeto did not have an answer, but Araba did. She told the ancient story of Echata, Matezi and Li-tia, then ended the account by admitting that she and Quaeto were once Chacoans.

It was a bold gamble but a good one. That night, tears were shed as they met relatives Araba had either long forgotten or never known.

* * *

By the end of summer, Quaeto was hopelessly in love with Ge-taka's daughter and asked for her hand in marriage. "If you give her to me, it will bind our clans together forever."

"And what do you give in return?"

"A fine fur every year for the rest of your days. And happiness for the rest of Ja-cin's life. Every year she will come back with me to present these gifts and we will have many grandchildren to make you proud."

"Then so be it," Ge-taka replied, looking very pleased with the arrangement.

With the cottonwood leaves turning yellow, red and gold, Quaeto, Ja-cin and Araba started north with two barking dogs as well as the knowledge of how to make pottery. Just as important, they carried the seeds of new corn, squash, beans and the powerful Chacoan medicines so long coveted by the great Li-tia.

At the last vista point before leaving Chaco Canyon, Ja-cin lingered. When Quaeto took her hand, he realized that the Chacoan girl's eyes sparkled with tears.

"If your heart is here, then you can stay," Quaeto gently told her.

"My heart is with you now," she said, turning to him.

"As mine is with you," Quaeto replied.

As they marched north, Quaeto began to describe to his wife all the beautiful things that she would come to see and love in the land of Raven.

Sixteen

Denver, Summer of 1890

Lisa Cannaday had spent almost the last of her money for Andrew's funeral. Mr. Oberlander, president of the Bank of Colorado, had sent a small donation and flowers, but had not bothered to attend. In the sad weeks that followed, Lisa tried to focus on the future and forget the past, but that had been impossible. Everywhere she looked, everything she touched, reminded her of Andrew. And while it would have been prudent to give up Andrew's little office in order to save rent money, Lisa simply could not. So she opened a bookkeeping service and visited the local merchants, to solicit business. Lisa was detail-minded and good with figures while most men were not.

Within a few months, Lisa had gained a steady clientele and enough money not only to keep paying office rent, but also enough to support her minimal needs. People seemed pleased with her work and everyone said that she would do fine. Lisa supposed that was true except that she yearned for something more fulfilling. And then Dr. Michael Turner from the Smithsonian Institution walked into her little accounting office.

Removing his expensive bowler, he said, "Lisa, I'm sorry that I couldn't be here for Andrew's funeral. But now I would like to visit his grave. Could you take me there, please?"

Lisa was so shocked by the man's appearance that she over-turned her inkwell, ruining a client's ledger. "Dr. Turner!"

"Yes," he said. "Better late than never."

Lisa wasn't so sure. She stared at the man, noting that his hair was starting to turn gray at the temples. This reminded her that Dr. Turner would be in his early forties, still hand-some, arrogant and insensitive. His cool, detached manner hadn't changed either and it rekindled Lisa's old dislike and anger.

"Well, well," she said, "the great Dr. Michael Turner has finally decided to pay his last respects."

"Please believe that I wanted to come sooner but it was impossible."

Lisa came out of her chair, oblivious to the ink that was soaking into the ledger destroying it completely. "Impossible? May I ask why? Did you have some important scientific paper to present in Washington? Or perhaps there was an administrative detail that simply took longer than expected? What was it, Dr. Turner, that kept you so occupied that you never responded to my request for reimbursement, much less to send your heartfelt condolences?"

Turner opened his mouth and his lips moved but there were no words. Visibly pale, he replaced his bowler, then reached into his coat pocket and retrieved a long envelope. "This is a bank draft which I hope will at least compensate for . . ."

"For Andrew's death!" Lisa stormed. *"Nothing* can repay me for my husband's loss. And don't you dare try to buy off your guilt."

He placed the envelope on the counter and retreated to the open door. "I'll find the cemetery on my own."

"Don't bother!"

Drawing himself up, the scientist replied in his most formal voice, "Mrs. Cannaday, please accept this donation from the Smithsonian in memory of Andrew. He was a fine scientist and . . ."

"Damn you, get out of here!"

Dr. Turner fled into the street while Lisa remained frozen by her desk, fists clenched tightly at her sides. Tears burned in her eyes. She glanced down at the ruined ledger and all she could think was that she was glad for the damage which would require hours of tedious entries and occupy her mind until it was time to close her office.

At five o'clock, the miniature grandfather clock Andrew had given her tolled. Lisa finished duplicating the ruined ledger, then prepared to lock up for the night, only then noticing Dr. Turner's envelope. If she could have afforded the luxury, Lisa would have torn it into a thousand pieces to demonstrate her contempt for both Michael and the Smithsonian. But she needed money, so she opened the envelope and grasped the countertop, staring at the bank draft with disbelief.

"Five *thousand* dollars!"

Lisa squeezed her eyes shut and reopened them. Yes, it *was* for five thousand! She had requested less than five *hundred* for their Mesa Verde expenses and Andrew's modest medical and funeral expenses. Why so much money? Perhaps there really was charity in Michael Turner's heart and compassion among the powers that ruled the famed Smithsonian.

With her hands shaking, Lisa placed the check in her purse, then locked the door and went searching for Michael Turner and an explanation. Her mind was in such turmoil that she walked an entire city block before realizing that she hadn't a clue as to where Turner was residing while visiting Denver. For lack of any better idea, Lisa decided to visit her husband's grave and that was where she found the prominent archaeologist.

The scientist had removed his coat and hat and lay sprawled across the grass beside Andrew's grave. As Lisa drew nearer, she could see that his lips were moving and she realized that Dr. Turner was speaking to her husband as if Andrew were still alive.

Lisa paused, unwilling to break this unexpected communion between Andrew's spirit and the man he had so admired. Could this really be the same man she always had thought so cool, ambitious and impersonal? And were those actually tears glistening in the setting sun? Impossible! But there he was, Dr. Michael Turner himself, conversing with Andrew's headstone.

Lisa leaned back against a tree, finding it impossible to believe that she had misjudged Dr. Turner; that Andrew had been right in saying there really was a good human being buried deep under the man's polished and erudite veneer. Besides, who was she to break such a deeply spiritual communion? Maybe Andrew was listening in heaven right now . . . and smiling.

The evening shadows lengthened. An owl hooted expectantly, then launched itself from the trees along Cherry Creek and sailed silently off to hunt. At last, Dr. Turner sat up, replaced his bowler, then gently pressed his fingers against Andrew's marble headstone. It was such a pure and tender gesture that Lisa had to bite her lip to keep from crying as Turner wearily pushed himself to his feet and bowed his head. Lisa could not hear his words but she knew they were a prayer being offered for Andrew's departed soul. At last, the archaeologist squared his broad shoulders and started back toward town.

"Dr. Turner?"

He turned to regard her a moment before saying, "Yes, Mrs. Cannaday?"

His cheeks were wet with tears and Lisa found herself at a loss for words until she remembered the need for an explanation about the money. "Dr. Turner, the bank draft you left me is for five *thousand* dollars."

"I know, and I'm sorry that the amount couldn't be much, much more. There's not enough money in the entire United States Treasury to replace a man like Andrew. I cared for him like a younger brother."

"And he also thought the world of you."

Lisa hadn't meant to give this man so much as a crumb of kindness so she compensated by adding, "Dr. Turner, I appreciate the money but still hold you responsible."

"I accept that."

He retrieved a monogrammed handkerchief from his pocket and made a pretense of blowing his nose while drying his eyes and cheeks. "Mrs. Cannaday, when I received your letter telling me of Andrew's death, I left my office and began walking. I had no clear destination but eventually ended up at my father's grave where I spent hours attempting to understand *why* these tragedies occur . . . especially to our best and kindest."

It took a few moments for Lisa to ask, "And did you arrive at any conclusions?"

"None at all."

He just stood there, head down, arms hanging limply at his side until Lisa said, "How old was your father when he died?"

"Forty-eight. Just forty-eight. Too young. But Andrew was . . ."

"Thirty-four. His death was a tragedy for which I will forever blame myself."

The man's voice was so tortured that Lisa stepped forward and touched his sleeve. "I'm sorry that I was rude and angry. Andrew's death wasn't your fault."

"Oh, I disagree."

"You see, the truth of it is that my husband was overjoyed to receive your offer to investigate the ruins at Mesa Verde. I'd never seen him so excited and happy as he was when we arrived on a mail coach in Mancos. Before your offer, Andrew was doing fine as a surveyor but it was archaeology and science that he loved. You always knew that."

"I'm going to Mesa Verde," Turner said. "I have to see it for myself."

"There's not much left," Lisa cautioned. "As I wrote in my letter, the Wetherills have excavated nearly all the cliff dwellings. They've unearthed and removed everything of scientific or monetary value."

"I find that hard to believe. Amateurs wouldn't know how to locate anything other than the obvious. And besides, I expect there to be archaeological sites scattered all across Mesa Verde, at sites the Wetherills could never imagine, much less uncover."

"So, that's why you really came to Colorado," Lisa said, her anger returning. "Not to pay your respects to Andrew, but just to visit Mesa Verde."

"I came here to present you with the money and extend my deepest sympathy, as well as to visit the site that your husband wrote of in such glowing terms."

Lisa expelled a deep breath. She was acting very foolish and unkind. This man's feelings for her husband were sincere and she felt ashamed and petty. "Where are you staying?"

"At the Fremont Hotel."

"Would you come by the office tomorrow morning? I'd like to show you a few artifacts that Andrew and I did manage to save."

"I'd like that very much," he said, managing the trace of a smile. "I'm stuck here in Denver because the next train to Trinidad won't leave for two days."

"I know."

Lisa studied Michael in the fading light. He was not as tall as she had thought and the crimson glow of sundown highlighted tiny wrinkles and creases in his handsome face, making him look vulnerable and far more human than she'd remembered from their Washington, D.C. days.

"If you're wondering," she said, as they strolled back toward town, "I'm surviving and even prospering, I suppose."

"That's wonderful news. I always judged you to be strong and very resilient."

"Oh really?"

"Yes, and I am an excellent judge of character, or lack of it."

Lisa glanced up at his face; he was sincere. "Well, Michael, I've even started a bookkeeping business that is growing so fast that I'm hiring an assistant in the next week or two."

"I never doubted that you'd mend and do well . . . or as well as anyone could, given such a tragedy. But what hurts is to remember just how much you and Andrew were in love. It was obvious in the way you looked at each other, even when separated by a crowd."

Lisa felt her cheeks warm by the compliment. "You actually noticed that?"

"Of course. We often notice things we lack and most long for. You see, I've never been lucky at love. The consolation is that I have been very fortunate in my profession. I've had the right people assisting me every step of the way and I've a . . . a gift for politics."

"You make your profession sound very calculating."

"Oh, it's not all that bad. Career success, in or out of government, is mostly a game and one that your Andrew was far too naive and honorable to play well."

"So what is left for someone like you, who has made it to the top? Where does Dr. Michael Turner go now?"

"I've chosen to change the game," he said without looking aside at her. "I've chosen to follow my heart, which brings me here to Colorado."

"You've resigned?"

"Yes, before I lost all my courage and professional curiosity. No matter what you might think of me, Lisa, I *am* a scientist, not an administrator or politician. That's also why I had no choice but to come here to reaffirm who I once was . . . and would like to become again."

They paused over a stone bridge spanning Cherry Creek and Michael continued. "I've no right to ask, but would you help me?"

"Help you do what?"

"Help me to complete the work that your husband died for."

"You're not serious!"

"I've never been more serious."

Michael bent and retrieved a pebble. "Less than three weeks ago, everyone thought I'd lost my mind when I tossed away my career as if it were this insignificant little rock."

Before Lisa could respond, Michael pitched the pebble into the creek. It made a little *plink* sound and they both watched a ring of ripples expand across the calm surface.

"Maybe," she heard him saying, "what I can accomplish at Mesa Verde will widen like those ripples into something much greater than I can imagine. Perhaps we'll discover truth and enlightenment there. Unearth secrets about how the Anasazi really lived day by day, season by season. And why they spent centuries building cities in caves like Cliff Palace and then abandoned them to go . . . only God knows where."

He smiled to himself but spoke to her. "Can you really bear the mystery of what the Mesa Verde Anasazi were like and what happened to them?"

"I'm not sure."

"Of course you cannot! Not after witnessing the majesty of Cliff Palace and holding a precious artifact that once meant everything to an ancient cliff dweller. Isn't that true, Lisa?"

She shivered because this man talked exactly like her Andrew, sharing the same vision and passion for archaeology and discovery. "My God, you really are a scientist, Michael! And I do believe that you *can* make new discoveries at Mesa Verde."

A bit of the old cockiness Lisa remembered and had so disliked crept into his voice. "With your help I'm sure that I can."

"I'm not a scientist."

"You're far more . . . at least to me. Lisa, in my eyes, you represent hope and atonement. Forgiveness, charity and goodness."

She was becoming rattled. What was he trying to do to her?

"Stop it!"

"I'm afraid that I can't. You're not meant to keep people's business accounts. You share our love of science."

"You don't know anything about me."

"Wrong," he said. "Or at least, I know more than you think. Andrew talked a lot about how much it meant when you went into these Rockies together hunting arrowheads or just looking for old Indian burial sites."

"Andrew told you about things like *that?*"

"Yes. And don't tell me they aren't true."

"All right, they are truth, but he was my *husband*. I can't go up there with you!"

"I'll hire a chaperon if that's your concern. You choose the person, I'll pay them. Choose someone you feel comfortable with and trust. We'll spend the rest of this summer and autumn season at Mesa Verde and return before the first snow."

"I can't believe that I'm even hearing this from you!"

"Believe it. And, if you won't do it for me, then do it for Andrew."

"Why!"

"Because, if you help me, then it will honor Andrew's memory in the best way. We both know that he died wanting to unlock the mysteries of Mesa Verde's past."

Michael started to reach out to touch her but Lisa jumped back with alarm.

"Lisa, don't you see how important this is to Andrew's memory? Don't you realize that if we leave Mesa Verde to plunderers and profiteers like the Wetherills, we've lost a piece of the puzzle of mankind that can never be replaced?"

Lisa found herself nodding. But before he could confuse her anymore with his lofty words and ideals, she hurried away shouting, "Tomorrow morning!"

"I'll be there!"

At the opposite end of the bridge, Lisa paused and gazed back. Michael was leaning over the side, dropping more pebbles into the moon-drenched water. From where she stood and from the way that she felt, Dr. Michael Turner seemed ethereal, perhaps an illusion. But he was not. Despite all that she felt and believed, Lisa knew that she would go with him to Mesa Verde.

Leaving for Mesa Verde with Dr. Michael Turner was insane! It was exciting and painful. Painful because the journey reminded Lisa of the time not so long ago when she and Andrew had ridden this exact same Denver and Rio Grande Railroad. Lisa hadn't even been able to bear looking at the quaint Victorian boarding house in Durango where they'd stayed for two days to go sightseeing and to make passionate love. She felt better when they climbed aboard the weekly mail coach for Cortez and then were finally left standing in Mancos beside a pile of supplies and provisions.

"I suppose we should rent a buggy or buckboard," Michael said, "but I've never learned to drive one."

"That doesn't matter," Lisa said, "because the only way to reach Mesa Verde is on a horse or mule."

"Oh, then we'll have to rent quite a few pack animals to carry all our supplies," he said.

"Yes, we will. I've done that often enough."

"And that," Michael said, "is very fortunate for me."

Lisa still could not quite believe where she was or what she was doing with a man she had always despised. But the truth was that Michael had so completely won her trust that she had not even considered his offer of a chaperon.

"Lisa, I'm glad that you are a real frontier woman! Can you also rope cattle and break wild bucking horses?"

"No. But I was raised on a ranch and I don't mind the work. In fact, I enjoy it."

"You never mentioned your ranching background when you lived in the capital."

"It would not have advanced Andrew's Washington career.

Later, it was my idea to return to the West, not his. And that's why I also take responsibility for his accidental death."

"You shouldn't." Michael gazed at the surrounding mountain ranges. "I'm sure that he fell in love with this country that you love so dearly."

"You can tell that I love this?"

"Of course!"

Lisa didn't think it a good idea to pursue the subject so she gestured down the street to the livery. "Out in the West, when you need a horse or buggy, that's the place to look."

Michael glanced at their provisions and some boxes of what Lisa supposed were valuable tools and instruments. "Can we just leave all this in the middle of the street?"

"Sure. Who would steal it?"

"I don't know. Come along. You do the dealing and I'll do the paying."

"That makes sense to me," she told him as they started for the livery.

They rented a pair of saddle horses and three burros to carry provisions and Michael's scientific equipment.

"I'm sorry about your husband," a tobacco-spitting liveryman named P. J. Boyd drawled as he gave Michael a suspicious and not too friendly eye. "I hear he was a real nice young fella."

"He was," Lisa replied, fighting back tears as she recalled how excited she and Andrew had been the first time they'd made this trip up to Mesa Verde. "Are the Wetherills working up on the mesa?"

"I expect so," Boyd answered. "Charlie Mason was on his way up there last week after delivering another load of old Injun stuff down to the Alamo Ranch. Those people sure are lucky! They're makin' a whole lot more money off that stuff than they are off ranchin', I can tell you!"

Michael's jaw muscles corded with disapproval and it was all he could do to keep quiet as the liveryman continued. "Yep, Charlie Mason told me that they found a whole bunch of mummies. Can't hardly wait to see 'em! Bunch of us are goin' over to take a look at 'em next Sunday."

"*Where* were they found and unearthed?" Michael asked through clenched teeth.

"Why, up in Johnson Canyon! Hell, there are cliff dwellings scattered all over that mesa and through them canyons. Charlie said they named the place where they found the mummies Fortified House. Don't mean nothin' to nobody what they name them ruins. But I sure am eager to see the mummies!"

When Lisa noticed the cold fury in Michael's eyes, she hurried over and grabbed his arm. "Well, Mr. Boyd," she said, trying to sound cheerful and happy, "we might as well get started."

"Good idea," Michael managed to say as they mounted their horses and were given the lead ropes to the pack animals. "Let's get out of here before I say something I'll regret."

As they rode out of Mancos, Lisa glanced frequently at the archaeologist, who was almost shaking with anger. "Michael," she said when they had traveled a few miles, "you're going to have to put a curb on your temper. Mr. Boyd had no idea how angry you were with him and he was not at fault."

"I know that."

"And neither are the Wetherills."

"Now *that* I do not know!"

"They're a nice family and, to their minds, this is no different than discovering a gold mine."

"A gold mine!" he exploded. "Lisa, they are digging up *bodies!* They are desecrating graves! Ruining a priceless archeological site!"

"You sound just like Andrew and I'll tell you exactly the same thing I told him. And that is—wrong though this may be—the Wetherills are within their legal rights to profit from their excavations. And at least they are trying to record and preserve their discoveries. Take it from me, many families would have rooted up everything without bothering to take notes or measurements—even if they could read and write."

"You're probably right," Michael admitted. "But it's going to be very, very difficult for me to be agreeable after the destruction I expect to observe at Mesa Verde."

"If you anger this prominent ranching family, they will run us off," Lisa promised. "These are strong men, individualists, not employees of the Smithsonian. Michael, you're going to have to understand that, or this trip will prove to be a waste of time, effort and expense."

"Very well. I'll . . . I'll try."

"You must do better than that."

"Okay."

Soon, they were following a well-worn trail into the hills and a short time later they met Charlie Mason returning to Mancos with three packhorses laden with pottery and other artifacts covered with a canvas tarp.

"Well, well!" Charlie called in greeting. "Mrs. Cannaday! Good to see you again!"

He reined his horse up and smiled at Lisa but just gave Michael a questioning glance.

"Charlie, this is my late husband's friend, Dr. Michael Turner, who has come all the way from Washington's Smithsonian Institution to see what you've found at Mesa Verde."

Now the Colorado cowboy gave Michael a broad smile. "You come to buy some of our collection?"

"Maybe."

"Mister, you're almost too late! We've sold most of the best of it, quite a lot to the Colorado State Historical Society, as Mrs. Cannaday has probably already told you."

"She has. What about those mummies you found at this place called Fortified House?"

"We already packed 'em up and shipped 'em out to an

Eastern buyer. We can sell mummies like hotcakes! No problem getting a couple of hundred dollars each for 'em."

Charlie glanced up at the sun. "You know, I missed breakfast and I'm awful hungry. Why don't we just build a cookin' fire and have some coffee and beans? We could visit and I'll tell you how we've been doing for the last few months."

Michael shook his head. "Thanks," he began, "but I don't think . . ."

Lisa interrupted Michael by saying, "That's a *good* idea. Dr. Turner, why don't you get out a couple cans of peaches and that pastry I bought in Durango?"

The archaeologist wasn't pleased, but he did as she asked. In no time at all, they had a fire and coffee simmering. It was a nice day with big puffy clouds sailing across a dark blue sky. A soft breeze carried the fragrance of pines.

Two mule deer watched them eating and Charlie winked. "Mrs. Cannaday, if I was so inclined, I could slip over to my horse, take out my rifle and get you some fresh venison."

"That's quite all right," Michael said.

"Fresh meat tastes mighty good when you're working real hard in them old Indian caves. It'll build up your appetite, I'll tell you for sure! Mummies or no mummies."

Lisa watched Michael struggle to be civil. She didn't think he was going to be able to pull this off but at least they would give it a try. "Charlie, why don't you tell us how you found those mummies?"

"Why sure! There was me, John and Richard all crawling around this new cave in a little side canyon we named after old Acowitz, the Ute who started this whole thing by telling us about these cliff dwellings. Anyway, just underneath the rimrock at the head of this box canyon is a building we named Fortified House 'cause some of the walls along the ledge where this place was built have to have been put there for defensive purposes."

"Were the mummies *inside* this house?" Michael asked with growing impatience.

"Not exactly. You see, we'd never have even found them except that John got to measuring things and we realized that there was a secret space in the middle of the building—one large enough for a room."

"Clever," Lisa said.

"Well, John Wetherill is no fool and we've been doing this for a couple of years now, and we have learned that these Indians have built plenty of secret compartments in the ruins."

Charlie poured them all mugs of steaming coffee and happily accepted Lisa's pastry before continuing. "Anyway, we *knew* that there was a hidden room in Fortified House and then John found a big rock that had been sealed over to hide the entrance. He pried it out clean but I was already usin' a pick to bust through the roof!"

Michael groaned with exasperation until Charlie looked at him with concern and asked, "You feelin' all right, Doc?"

"No, but it doesn't matter."

"Hope my coffee didn't burn a big hole through your soft city guts."

"I'll be fine, Mr. Mason!"

Charlie shrugged. "Anyway, like I started to tell you, when we busted into that secret compartment I never seen such a sight! Why, the room itself wasn't but five or six feet square, but in it were five skeletons, about a dozen pieces of pottery, some baskets—the finest any of us ever seen—and a big old bow and seventeen arrows, most of them layin' across the skeletons! Why, we couldn't crawl in there fast enough!"

Charlie stirred his pot of smoking beans before offering some to Lisa and Michael. When they declined, he continued spooning them into his mouth as he talked.

"That Indian bow was broken and lyin' beside a big skeleton—at least a six-foot Indian! That bow still had some gut string on it and was so stout you could see that it musta took that big Indian to draw it back all the way. The Indian was wearing buckskins—a cap, moccasins, everything—but the damned rats and mice had chewed most all of it away. I expect he was a chief because he had his own mug and even a turkey feather mat restin' under his head . . . as if it made any difference. John took a special medicine stick and . . ."

"Hold it!" Michael said. "What kind of medicine stick?"

"Oh, it was just a hollow stick with both ends wrapped in sinew. One end had a bone point tied to it so it might have just been a spear."

"How big was the stick?"

"About two feet long is all," Charlie answered. "Maybe it was more like a dagger. I dunno, but it was kind of neat. All five of the bodies were layin' on woven mats that had pretty much been eaten away, too. That matting was so chewed up and rotted that it wasn't worth savin' so we tossed it in the rubbish heaps along with the corncobs, ashes, some bones and other stuff no one would buy."

Michael shook his head, the picture of utter dejection. Charlie shook his head too, saying, "Best not drink any more of my coffee, Doc. I make it real strong and, if you ain't used to it, it'll give you the old green-apple-quick-step. Ain't that right, Mrs. Cannaday!"

"That's right," Lisa said, smothering a grin.

"We found four pottery bowls there, too, along with the bodies of three babies, two of 'em had been wrapped in buckskin. The other was bigger, probably a little girl. All three of the young ones were lying on the big fella with the buckskin jacket."

"Which direction were they pointed?" Michael asked.

Charlie frowned. "Let's see. The big Indian's head was pointed down canyon while the babies were facin' the opposite direction. That important, Doc?"

"Yes."

"Then you'd better tell Richard to write it down in the journal. We been tryin' to do this thing right, but we're not experts, you know."

"Have you noticed any differences in the skeletons that you've found, based on the depth of their burials?"

"What do you mean?"

"I mean, have you excavated very deep in some of the caves?"

"Sure! If we're findin' good stuff, we just keep diggin' until it's all gone. And yeah, we noticed that some of the deeper bodies have them flat heads in the back. Ones higher up don't, though. And we never found no arrowheads deeper than a couple of feet. Just spear heads."

"What about pottery?" Michael asked.

"Pottery is always on top. No deeper than the arrowheads. We have found woven sandals buried pretty deep. Most of 'em are in the trash pits where we're always finding things to sell. Sometimes we'll even find pots that ain't broken."

"Any evidence of war or conquest?"

"Some have had their skulls bashed in, but not very many. Down in them round pits where they seemed to have gathered, we found a few burned bodies."

"Burned?" Lisa asked with surprise.

"Yeah," Charlie said, "but Richard and the others don't think they were sacrificed or anything awful like that. Mostly, it looks like the roofs musta caught on fire sometimes. Maybe after years of fires down in them holes them roof timbers just got too damn dry and exploded in flames like tinder. Anyway, that's what we're thinking happened."

"I would tend to agree with that," Michael said, nodding vigorously. "What about seeds and evidence of what they ate?"

"We've found lots of deer, rabbit, bird and other small animal bones so they musta been good hunters."

"Corn?"

"Sure! Corn cobs everywhere. Some of 'em are preserved right well. Beans and squash, too."

"Yes," Michael said, digging out a small notebook and

scribbling furiously. "I should like to examine the pottery you've found."

"There's busted pieces of it everywhere on the mesa," Charlie said. "Can't hardly miss the stuff. Not too many pieces are still together, though."

They talked for another hour and then Charlie doused the fire, quickly packed his cooking utensils and headed on down to the Alamo Ranch.

"I just don't know how I can be civil to these looters and desecrators," Michael said as they prepared to ride on up to the mesa.

"You will for the same reasons that Andrew was civil—because you are both professional archaeologists who will sacrifice anything to preserve history and learn truth."

"You sound like me when I deliver a seminar to a class of young archaeology students," Michael commented, forcing a grin.

Lisa mounted her horse. "I'm as sorry as you are about what has been lost, but you told me that the entire mesa might have been inhabited. That means that there is much yet to find."

"I hope so. But if I could do things differently . . ."

"What?" Lisa challenged. "Would you really have quit your important job at the Smithsonian and raced out here to see Mesa Verde for yourself?"

"Yes, I would hope so."

"There's not much point in beating yourself up over what might have and should have been. Andrew is dead, the cliff caves have all been looted and we have left only what we can find on the mesa. We can still make some important discoveries before winter."

He studied her face. "You are an amazing woman, Lisa. Aren't you the least bit concerned about what people will say about us up here alone together?"

"No. I live in Denver and these people's approval means

nothing to me," she answered. "Besides, Dr. Turner, I *trust* you because Andrew trusted you."

Michael found that amusing but when she shot him a questioning glance, he quickly added, "As well you can, Mrs. Cannaday. As very well you can."

Seventeen

Lisa Cannaday felt the tension building between the Wetherills and Michael Turner. From the moment they met, it was clear that they weren't going to be able to work in harmony. When Michael first saw Cliff Palace and the other excavated cliff dwellings, he was stunned by their size and archaeological significance but appalled by the crude diggings undertaken by the Wetherills.

"You are destroying America's prehistoric heritage!" he'd shouted. "Looting it for profit!"

"We discovered it, we own it and we'll do what we want with it!" Richard had stormed back.

After that, Lisa quickly led Michael back up to the canyon rim.

"So what are we going to do now?" she asked when they stopped to make camp. "You've managed to destroy any hope of working in the Wetherill ruins."

" 'Wetherill Ruins'!"

Michael was so incensed that he grabbed a fallen tree limb and splintered it across the top of a large granite boulder. "These ruins *never* will belong to that family of desecrators! Mesa Verde is unique, a *sacred* Anasazi gift to every American, not just one greedy family who happened to discover it!"

"I'm going to tell you what I once told my husband," Lisa replied, curbing her anger. "In Colorado, the courts will favor the Wetherills' claim to this mesa and to the canyons and all the cliff dwellings they've found . . . and even might yet find. You or the Smithsonian Institution would have no choice but to file lawsuits that would probably go all the way to the United States Supreme Court. By then, it would be too late to save anything at Mesa Verde."

Michael paced back and forth in extreme agitation before he stopped, turned and said, "I'm staying here until the first snow and I'll work night and day doing everything in my power to make my own Mesa Verde discoveries. And when I'm not excavating, I'll sketch, map and take dozens of photographs. I'll convince not only the Smithsonian but also President Harrison and the United States Congress that Mesa Verde deserves the same national park status that Yellowstone has long enjoyed."

"Would that really be possible?" Lisa asked, hardly daring to imagine such a wonderful solution.

"Of course! But I'll have to go back to Washington this winter to lobby the President and Congress. That will take months, perhaps even years; I'll dedicate myself to the effort."

"How will you take photographs to show them?" Lisa asked. "I didn't see any photographic equipment on our pack animals."

"Oh, but there is," he said, calming down and then marching over to place his hand on one of their pack saddles. "I haven't mentioned it yet, but a brilliant inventor named George Eastman recently introduced a revolutionary box camera which he calls 'The Kodak' and which uses *roll* film."

"No glass plates?"

"Absolutely not! The Kodak is small and already loaded with film. All that's required is to follow simple instructions and take your pictures in good light before sending the entire camera back to Mr. Eastman's factory where the prints are developed and returned with your reloaded camera."

Lisa had a difficult time imagining such a simple method of photography. Like everyone else she was accustomed to seeing photographers lugging massive camera boxes and all sorts of cumbersome equipment. The idea that film could be easily produced from a small roll was amazing.

"I'd like to see this new invention."

"You'll not only see it, but you'll *use* it, Lisa. I've brought five and they are the current rage back east. I'm surprised that you haven't seen any yet but they soon will become commonplace, even in Colorado."

Talking about the Kodak had a calming effect on Michael. "I'm sorry about losing my temper back at Cliff Palace. I thought I'd prepared myself for the archaeological carnage, but I hadn't. Nothing could have prepared me for the scope and the degree of devastation that has been committed for profit."

"Don't you think you are exaggerating?" Lisa asked. "After all, the Wetherills are now using some basic scientific and excavation techniques."

"Well," Michael said grudgingly, "I suppose that's true. But the idea of selling Anasazi skeletons to the highest bidder makes my blood boil."

"What *should* be done with the Indian mummies?"

"They should be treated with the same respect we'd like our own bodies to be treated if we were disinterred by a future generation. I agree that we should examine them to learn about their health and way of life, but then return them to their burial places exactly as they were found."

"That sounds admirable but not realistic."

"And why is that?"

"Out West life is usually harder. People are more independent but often haven't the luxury of doing anything more than trying to survive."

"Oh, come now! Denver is booming."

"It's doing well," Lisa admitted, "but you won't see people strolling around in parks during the day or patronizing the arts as they do in Washington. It's too bad, but we don't have the time or money."

"Even with the five thousand dollars you've just received from the Smithsonian?"

"Well," Lisa replied, "I still have to pinch myself to believe that they really sent me that much money. I never thought of them as particularly generous. I put most of the funds in my savings account and I'm not going to touch them for at least a year, in case they have made an accounting error and added one too many zeros to the figure."

Michael chuckled. "Spend it! They didn't make a mistake."

"Time will tell."

"Will that much money change your life?"

"Of course. It already has enabled me to hire a very qualified assistant who is handling my accounts so that I could come here with you. If not for the money, I'd be slaving over some ledger right now."

"Then I'm glad that isn't necessary. It could be lonely up here."

"If you'd been more tactful with the Wetherills, loneliness would not have been an issue."

His smile faded. "Yes, I suppose that's true."

"Now why don't you go gather a bunch of firewood so that we can make supper and have a nice evening fire to enjoy?"

They didn't stop exploring for the entire first week. Lisa learned how to operate the wonderful new camera invented by George Eastman. They roamed the mesas, sometimes saddling their horses and riding, but often hiking through the pines. Lisa always had been a good walker; she had long legs and enjoyed setting a brisk pace. Michael wasn't accustomed to the altitude, but he was strong and too proud to lag behind. After the first couple of weeks, he was matching her, stride for stride, and looking fit.

"We're in the process of mapping and locating sites that

ought to yield the best archaeological information," he explained. "I expect that we'll see plenty of ruins, or least signs of them on these mesas. But there's also a knack that we have to develop in order to detect less obvious sites."

"What do you mean?"

"We need to study deviations in topography; hunt for depressions that give evidence that a subterranean kiva or pit house filled in over the centuries. Or, just the opposite, seek mounds that once were towers, walls or pueblos. We need to study the soil and try to determine where the Anasazi farmed, and if they used irrigation ditches to catch the spring snow melt. Watch for charred pieces of wood, bone and especially for pottery shards which last indefinitely."

This advice wasn't exactly news to Lisa because Andrew had always said the same kinds of things, but Michael was more knowledgeable and far more intense. He kept finding pottery and flint arrowheads even though they were almost completely buried.

"This whole mesa top is an archaeological gold mine," he announced one evening as they sat around their fire. "I have the feeling that I could dig anywhere and find buried pit houses, kivas and artifacts."

"Do you have any idea how many people might have lived on this mesa . . . or even when?"

"Lisa, at the height of this civilization, I'd imagine several thousand Anasazi lived at Mesa Verde. Anasazi culture was spread across much of the Southwest. We've discovered ruins not only in Colorado, but down in New Mexico, Arizona and even in Utah, where a geologist named William Jackson located the remains of a once thriving Anasazi civilization. He chose to name it Hovenweep, a Ute word that roughly translates into 'Deserted Valley.' Also, John Wesley Powell, on his epic journey through the Grand Canyon, mapped quite a few ruins. None of them as extensive as what we have here, but I'm sure that they were part of the same civilization."

"What do you think happened to the people of Mesa

Verde? If there was no great battle to drive them out why did they leave after going to so much effort to create their magnificent cliff dwellings?"

"There are several possible answers. Drought? In just one or two years, a drought would have forced an agrarian people . . ."

Lisa threw up her hands. "Wait a minute! Why is that so?"

"I've long felt that a nomadic society or civilization simply can't progress or improve its standard of living. They are too consumed by the day to day struggle for survival. They tend to follow migrating food sources or more benign seasons. And, because they are *continually* on the move, they never advance their technology or living standards."

"I never thought of it like that, but I guess it makes sense."

"It's not entirely an original thesis," Michael confessed. "But it's one that I support because stationary societies, like the one at Mesa Verde, *must* rely on agriculture in order to support an increasing population. Remember, populations *always* will increase to the level of their food supply, that being true not only among humans, but among all species. It is only when *overpopulation* results that they become susceptible to plagues and diseases, increased warfare and famines."

"Another original, Dr. Turner?"

"Hardly. But I've written papers that might have broken a little ground or shed some light. I'd be less than honest not to point out that scientists rarely break new ground solely on the basis of their own research. Rather, science is usually the result of thousands of small insights, discoveries, revelations or whatever you want to call them all fitting into a very complex puzzle."

"What pieces of the puzzle do you hope to find here?"

"The most I can hope for *us* is to learn something about the evolution of these people through their changing architecture and lifestyles. For instance, I would consider it very important simply to discover which came first, the cliff dwellings such as the ones the Wetherills are looting, or an agrarian civilization that once flourished atop these mesas."

"I don't see much evidence of a large mesa community."

"You will," he promised. "Soon, we'll choose an excavation site and set up a permanent summer camp. Are you any good with a rifle?"

"If you mean can I shoot a deer and keep us in meat, yes, I can. I'm not fond of hunting . . . even less of what must be done afterward, but, if you'll help . . . we'll do fine."

"Just show me how to cut up a deer or whatever you shoot and I'll do that part of it," he said, looking quite uncomfortable.

"I will."

Michael smiled with wry amusement across the fire. "You are quite a remarkable woman, Mrs. Cannaday. I had a very different opinion when you and Andrew lived in Washington."

"In what way?"

He pitched a branch on their fire. "I thought you were stand-offish and antagonistic."

"Me?"

"Sure. You were a Western woman and you made it quite clear that you thought Easterners were soft, pampered and overly concerned with trivia."

Lisa could hardly believe what she was hearing. "I never thought that!"

"Didn't you? On several occasions lately you've talked about Westerners being so self-reliant, independent and strong. Lisa, you've actually lectured me."

"I don't want to hear any more of that nonsense!"

He was maddeningly cool and unperturbed. "Then I'll never speak of it again."

"You're the one that was aloof and conceited!"

"All right," he said, "let's end this unpleasant conversation. Maybe we were *both* right . . . or wrong. However that might have been, it's changed now, hasn't it?"

"I suppose so," she managed to say.

"Of course it has or we wouldn't be together in this wilderness. You'd be in Denver, and I'd be . . . someplace else or perhaps up here alone. We've got to work together this summer, Lisa. And work *well* together."

"Fine!"

He started to say something, then changed his mind and went off to his bedroll. Lisa sat up another hour, watching the fire and the stars. She didn't know what she had gotten herself into by coming up here, but it had a lot to do with Andrew's death. After all, he'd given his life for Mesa Verde and that was sufficient reason for her to want to make sure that he remained a part of its discovery through her own small accomplishments. But now she was having conflicting thoughts about Michael Turner. Just when she thought she had him pegged, he suddenly metamorphosed into something new and unexpected. He was complex, and damned if he didn't exasperate her at times.

"Oh, hell," Lisa muttered to herself, "go to bed and get some sleep. Tomorrow, he'll be someone new to figure out all over again."

During a warm summer rain squall the next afternoon, they pushed out of the forest and came upon a significant ruin at the edge of a deep canyon, a pueblo-type village constructed in an L-shape which Michael said was very typical of the last Anasazi period. Although it was impossible to get an exact count, there were perhaps twenty rooms, mostly small, but there were a few larger compartments whose roofs had collapsed. Most interesting to Michael were six large kivas, each about thirty feet across. Centuries of neglect had caused them to be filled with brush, rocks and other debris, but it was obvious that they once had been quite deep.

"Look at this!" Michael shouted, hurrying along a low stone wall. "Lisa, what we have here is an early pueblo village that was replaced, modified or improved over many generations!"

Michael's excitement was contagious. To Lisa, the famed Dr. Michael Turner appeared exactly like a boy on Christmas morning.

"And just look at *this!*" he exclaimed, dropping to his knees. "See how this long wall's construction has evolved and been structurally improved?"

"No."

"Oh sure you do! To the south, the work is much more primitive. The walls are of single rock construction and, at the joints where rooms and perpendicular walls connect, the stones are *not* interlaced. That is a far more primitive form of masonry. All the joints have sagged apart due to the stresses of weather and the ages."

"Yes, but . . ."

"Now, Lisa, notice how, at the northern end of this wall we have a far superior workmanship and construction with *two* rows of stones filled in between with rubble and adobe. Also, the cornerstones are interlaced, which gives them more strength. And we can see clear evidence that the rocks on this later period of construction have been *shaped.*"

"By what?"

"Stone axes," he replied. "You can clearly see the old strike marks where these rocks were fitted and flattened to make a much more stable and appealing wall."

Michael removed his hat and ran his fingers through his thick shock of hair. "Lisa, these walls are the testimony of important improvements in masonry evolving over many centuries. This is an important find. And this type of wall construction is still being used by the Pueblo Indians."

Lisa felt her own heart beating faster. "How do you know all this?"

"Good question! You see, when I first wrote Andrew asking him to visit Mesa Verde, I began to study everything I could about the Anasazi and the Pueblo civilizations. There's more information on them than you might think. In addition to the discoveries and writings of William Jackson and Major Powell, a scientist named Adolph Bandelier, who works for the Archaeological Institute of America, has spent more than a decade studying the modern pueblos of the Rio Grande region, uncovering new archaeological sites and writing reports."

"Andrew often mentioned his name."

"He's a fine scientist," Michael said. "There is also an ethnologist named Frank Cushing who is gaining considerable respect and interest for his work on the Zuni people of Arizona's Salt and Gila River Valleys. You can bet that I'll be interested in reading his reports and noting what parallels can be drawn with Mesa Verde."

"Do you really think these civilizations are related?"

"I'm sure of it. This pueblo, for example, is not as large or as sophisticated as some near old Santa Fe, but there are clear similarities. I would not be surprised if these Anasazi people were related to the Hopi, Zuni, or other puebloan peoples. But I can't say for sure."

"But you'd *like* to be able to say, wouldn't you. Then you'd write a paper and present it to the academic circles back East."

"Yes," he confessed, "I'll admit that is one reason why I'm here. But there are other, less selfish reasons, as I've told you."

Lisa believed him. "So, do we excavate here?"

Michael pivoted completely around, hands on hips, expression very intense. "Yes," he decided, "but first I want to survey and sketch this mesa and mark each ruin on a working map. How are you at drawing?"

"Awful."

"I'm not much better. We will just do the best that we can and take lots of good photographs. We'll make this our permanent camp and do some serious archaeology."

"And what will we do with our findings?"

"I'd like to donate them to the Smithsonian. If we discover important pieces, I'm hoping they will generate future expeditions to Mesa Verde. That will be high on my list of Washington, D.C. priorities."

"Right along with gaining national park status for Mesa Verde and putting a stop to the Wetherills, huh?"

"Absolutely," Michael declared, glancing up at the sky. "I expect that we're in for another downpour this evening. We'd better drag out the tarps or we'll soon be soaked. And perhaps you can start thinking about getting us some venison."

"I always believed the *man* was supposed to be the mighty hunter."

"Not," Michael replied with a chuckle, "if the woman is a superior rifle shot."

In truth, Lisa appreciated the fact that Michael was secure enough in himself to realize that there was no need to play roles on this lonely mesa. If she was the better shot, then she should do the shooting.

It took them a full week to survey the mesa and make detailed sketches. There were so many ruins that it was obvious that a huge population had once lived on this mesa top, perhaps, Michael estimated, as many as five thousand.

"You can see how the Anasazi once lined this depression with rocks," he said, sketching with far more skill than Lisa could have attempted as they stood at the south end of a circular and masonry-lined depression almost a hundred feet in diameter.

"What did they do here?"

"At first I thought it was probably a major ceremonial gathering place, like an amphitheater. But look to the north and you'll see that it is fed by a very impressive irrigation canal system that probably carried snow melt and rain water down from the higher, northern elevations to this reservoir each spring. I also have noticed the remains of more canals and ditches that crisscrossed this entire mesa which once would have been covered with fields of summer corn, beans and squash. Some of these canals run all the way down to the cliff dwellings."

Lisa blinked with astonishment. "That would be *miles!*"

"That's right. I'd say that we are talking about at least five or six miles of canals and ditches. But remember, these people farmed here for centuries and, as they became increasingly dependent upon their crops, they would have had to develop advanced irrigation systems."

Lisa stuffed her hands in her pockets and glanced at the approaching rain clouds. "We'd better make a shelter before the storm hits."

Michael was scribbling. "I know, but I'm so excited about the potential on this mesa top that I can hardly bear the idea of holing up to weather a squall."

"Better that than running the risk of catching pneumonia."

"Okay," he said, impatiently stuffing his sketch pad and pencil into his pocket and following her back to their camp.

The storm brought a downpour but they were able to get their supplies and equipment lashed down under the tarp and also make a crude shelter that kept them almost dry. While huddling under a square of flapping canvas as lightning crashed and the rain pelted the mesa, Lisa realized that she was happy.

Michael asked, "Are you smiling, Mrs. Cannaday?"

"I don't think so," she replied, clutching the canvas. "Why would I be smiling in this awful weather?"

"I don't know, but you are. You're happy to be up here with me, aren't you?"

"I . . ." Lisa was not about to encourage him, but neither was she willing to lie. "I am not *unhappy,* Dr. Turner."

"Good," he said, his expression turning somber, "because you know that we never can hope to be more than friends."

Lisa wasn't sure that she had heard him correctly. "What?"

"I meant because of Andrew. I *am* responsible for his death. On top of that, there is the difference in our ages."

"But I thought . . ."

"Lisa, someday you'll want children. I'm past that stage of life."

"Michael, you're not *that* old."

He was forced to shout over the boom of approaching thunder. "I'm almost old enough to have fathered you!"

Lisa very much doubted that was true and Michael had become anything but fatherly toward her since they'd left Denver together.

"Mrs. Cannaday, don't you dare let us fall in love," he yelled.

"I wouldn't dream of it, Dr. Turner!"

Michael nodded, peering into the driving rain.

Eighteen

Summer, 1891

Lisa Cannaday stood on the passenger platform, waiting for the incoming Denver Pacific Railroad and a long anticipated reunion with Dr. Michael Turner. After leaving her last October with several boxes filled with Anasazi artifacts, he had gone back to Washington, D.C. to petition Congress, as well as the Smithsonian Institution, to take immediate and forceful steps to get Mesa Verde under federal protection.

They had corresponded up until the holidays and then Michael's letters had become less frequent. Lisa had received four letters since January, all short and not revealing. Although she could not put her finger on the problem, she was afraid Michael had run into indifference or stiff opposition from lobbyists representing ranching and mining interests opposed to federal land ownership. Lisa was also certain that the Bureau of Indian Affairs would object to transferring Ute Indian Reservation land into a Mesa Verde National Park.

When the train finally appeared, it seemed to take forever for the conductor to open the gate. When Michael hurried to her side, Lisa hugged his neck, saying, "I've a buggy waiting."

"Where am I staying tonight?"

"At Mrs. Hunnicut's Boarding House." He was acting quite formal with her and Lisa decided to stick to business. "Your letters became infrequent."

"I . . . I was very busy."

"I'm sure you were," she replied. "What about Mesa Verde?"

He looked away before replying, "I'm afraid that I failed completely."

"But . . ."

"Lisa, I made the mistake of giving my bag with the Kodak cameras to a train porter in Cincinnati, Ohio, who promptly lost them."

"All our wonderful photographs?"

"Every last one," Michael grated. "I'm sure that the bag and cameras were stolen. Whatever the case, I had no photographs and, as you well know, my sketches and drawings of the cliff dwellings and our mesa top ruins were something less than inspiring. Strong opposing congressional lobbyists followed me from one office to another, always ready to counter my arguments for federal protection against looting of the Mesa Verde cliff dwelling sites."

Lisa heard the defeat in Michael's voice and it was so uncharacteristic that she asked, "Then what kind of response did you get at the Smithsonian?"

"Now there I had a bit of success. Dr. Jesse Fewkes is in New Mexico working on Anasazi ruins. He is definitely interested in coming to Mesa Verde after completing his New Mexico excavations."

"And how long might that be?"

"A couple of years, I'm afraid."

Lisa had rented a buggy and driver and when they had loaded Michael's bags and climbed aboard, Michael appeared dejected. She wanted to comfort him but knew that would be unwise. It would not have surprised her if he admitted having a sweetheart in Washington, D.C. who had occupied all his spare time.

"I did meet a woman named Mrs. Virginia McClurg," Michael said, as Lisa drove away from the train station.

Here it comes, she thought. *The confession.*

"Mrs. McClurg is an important Eastern journalist whose passion is the preservation of ancient ruins."

Lisa turned to read his expression but came up blank. "Really?"

"Yes, and we had a long, fruitful discussion about Mesa Verde. Virginia wants to visit Mesa Verde and, I'm sure when she sees what is taking place at Cliff Palace and the other dwellings, she will become very active in their preservation."

"What can she do?"

"Plenty," Michael admitted. "The woman is respected and knows almost everyone important on Capitol Hill. She has access to the White House! Mark my words, Mrs. McClurg will become a very powerful voice in this fight and we must do everything we can to help her. For example, I promised to retake a lot of film and send it to her directly. Armed with good photographs, I expect that she will go to work even before she comes here to visit."

"That's wonderful," Lisa said with a decided lack of enthusiasm.

"*And*," Michael was saying, "Virginia introduced me to a Mrs. Lucy Peabody, a Washington socialite operating in the highest circles. She and Virginia nearly went wild over our Mesa Verde artifacts. They had me making presentations all over the capital."

"How nice. I trust that the attention didn't make you lose your senses and *give* our artifacts to them."

"What's the matter with you!" he snapped. "Of course I didn't give them our artifacts. But they did *buy* quite a few."

Lisa was appalled. "You sold our artifacts to private collectors? Michael, why!"

"Because I needed the money to outfit this year's exploration. Lisa, their purchases were a godsend."

"But I thought that you were going to donate everything to the Smithsonian Institution! You've been so hard on the Wetherills, now you've gone and done the same thing that they've been doing—"

"Dammit, Lisa, this is altogether different! Every dime that I received will go to the work we are doing to save Mesa Verde. That's hardly the same thing as buying more ranchland or cattle, is it?"

"No, but . . ."

He also was angry. "Thank you for seeing the difference! I thought that you'd be pleased, not critical."

Lisa reached into her purse and withdrew an envelope. "Here," she said, "I want you to read this letter before we reach your boarding house."

"What's in it?"

"I received this from the Smithsonian last December with a check for five hundred dollars for my husband's medical and funeral expenses."

Michael returned the envelope without bothering to read the enclosed letter.

"When I received this money," Lisa continued, "I knew at once that the five-thousand-dollar check you gave me last spring had come out of *your* pocket."

She waited for his denial but it didn't come so she asked, "Why did you do that for me?"

When Michael didn't answer, she pressed him. "Michael, you are very generous, but you're not rich enough to be giving anyone five thousand dollars."

"I'll do fine."

"Oh, really? Well, I wrote a few letters of inquiry to Washington, D.C. and learned that you sold your house last fall. Is that where the five thousand came from?"

"Lisa, could we please just forget about the damned money?"

"Not until I give it back to you and tell you how very much I appreciate the gesture. I was . . . I am, deeply touched."

"Don't be," he snapped. "Five thousand dollars is small recompense for Andrew's life."

"I can't keep your money," she told him flatly.

"Then . . . then give it to some charity because I won't take it back!"

After that, not much was said and Lisa felt miserable. She hadn't realized until the last few days how much she'd missed Michael. She'd even managed to forget that he had said that they could never be husband and wife. Now, it all came crashing down on her.

"Here we are," she said, pulling the team up before Michael's boarding house.

"I'll just go on in."

"Would you like to come over for dinner tonight?"

"Actually," he said, "I'm so travel weary that I'd prefer to do that some other time. I'll be turning in very early."

"Then I'll see you in the morning?"

"Yes. At your office."

"Very well," Lisa said as he tipped his hat and gathered his bags. "It was good to see you again."

"Same here," he said before hurrying away.

They left for Mesa Verde two days later, the tensions still heavy between them. Lisa could not imagine how they would be able to live and work together on the mesa if things did not change, and it was all that she could do not to scream whenever he spoke in glowing terms of Virginia McClurg or Lucy Peabody. For all that Lisa could tell, both women were about Michael's age, intelligent, attractive socialites with wealth and influence. If they even had husbands, they might as well have been ghosts for all the interest that Michael had in them.

It was quite a relief to see the smiling face of liveryman P. J. Boyd again when they finally stepped off the mail coach at Mancos.

"Good thing you sent along that letter and deposit for horses and pack animals," he boomed. "Because there's this foreign fella, a baron or duke or some such thing and he's caused quite a stir up at Mesa Verde. Wanted to rent your horses and burros but I told him I'd already reserved 'em for you."

Boyd shook his head. "He even offered me double your money."

"Then you, Mr. Boyd, have proven yourself an honorable man," Michael said, "and one who should be rewarded."

"You mean that *you'll* pay me double?"

"No," Michael replied, "but I *will* make sure that, when the Smithsonian Institution or any of my other eastern contacts arrive to see Mesa Verde, they know exactly whom to rent horses and pack animals from."

"Me, right?"

"Right! And I promise you that these people are always big tippers who appreciate the loyalty of honorable businessmen. With that in mind, Mr. Boyd, I think you may conclude that your decision not to rent our horses to this European nobleman was very wise."

"Well, gosh!" Boyd exclaimed, now looking quite pleased with himself. "I sure am glad to hear you say all them things! I was feeling a little cheated on the deal and not lookin' ahead at the bigger picture. But then, that's always been my problem. If I'd had some vision, I wouldn't be eking out a livin' here in Mancos, now would I?"

"Nothing wrong with Mancos," Michael said. "Now who *is* this European fella?"

"Beats me. He's a young fella. He comes from . . . let's see. Sweden! There's a country like that, ain't there?"

"Of course. I've never been there, but I understand it is quite beautiful. What does this Swedish nobleman hope to find at Mesa Verde?"

"Oh, he's real interested in our old Indian stuff! I showed him some of the things I bought from the Wetherills before they raised their prices so damned high. He rushed right down to the Alamo Ranch and the next thing I knew, he and Richard Wetherill is thicker'n thieves and they're off to Mesa Verde. Been up there about two weeks now."

"Is this Swedish nobleman *buying* Anasazi artifacts to take back to Europe?" Lisa asked.

"Yep! Some folks around here aren't real happy about it, but the guy is rich and so I guess he can buy anything he wants and do with it exactly as he pleases."

Lisa glanced at Michael whose expression reflected her own feelings of outrage. "That's not right, Mr. Boyd. And why would people in Sweden have any interest in American Indians?"

"Well," the liveryman said, "I asked him that very same question, and he says that Europeans are real interested in our cowboys and Indians. I guess a lot of 'em had come to the American West to hunt buffalo before they were mostly all shot out on the plains."

"He's right," Michael agreed. "Lisa, there's a tremendous amount of European interest in our vanishing Wild West. The Europeans read everything they can get their hands on, mostly dime novels and other sensationalist drivel. Haven't you ever heard of the adventures of Deadwood Dick, Hurricane Nell and Calamity Jane?"

"I've heard of Calamity Jane, but not the others."

"Those fictional characters bear no resemblance to reality. My feeling is that it all started with James Fenimore Cooper's Leatherstocking Tales—*The Last of the Mohicans* and *The Deerslayer.* I guess they were as popular in Europe as they were in this country."

P. J. Boyd scratched his whiskery cheek. "I sure don't see why them European folks would want to read about Indians. Most of 'em I've met are a damn sorry bunch. Hell, the Utes in this country will steal you blind and then try to sell whatever they stole right back to you!"

"Do you happen to recall this European's name?" Michael asked.

"Goosed-off something, I think."

"You mean, Gustaf?" Michael asked, trying not to smile.

"Yeah, that's what I said, Goosed-off. He wears them little round glasses on a gold chain."

"They're called monocles."

"Sure. And now that I think about it, I believe he's a baron. Is that a big deal? He didn't put on any airs or nuthin'. Acted just like a regular fella, polite and mannerly. Said he'd come out to see the American West partly for his health and that this Colorado country was a real tonic . . . whatever that means."

"Did he seem to be in poor health?" Lisa asked.

Boyd frowned. "Well, he coughs some and is pretty thin, but otherwise he acts okay."

"I'm sure that we'll be meeting him soon enough," Michael said.

"From what I hear," the liveryman went on, "Goosed-off hasn't found much yet and he's hired three or four men to help out. I guess that he got discouraged because him and Al Wetherill left to see the Hopi pueblos to the south."

"How interesting," Michael commented as he fidgeted, anxious to get their horses, pack animals and supplies lined up and ready to leave in the morning.

"Yeah, but he'll be back," the liveryman promised. "And he's still got men digging at Cliff Palace and some of the other places, hopin' to find new stuff to ship back to Sweden."

Lisa and Michael exchanged silent, disapproving glances, neither one of them was willing to get started on that sore subject. They started into the barn, making it clear that this conversation was over and it was time to prepare for their own departure.

"You'll like the baron," Boyd said to Michael. "He seems like a real smart fella and he don't mind throwin' a little extra money around to the common man like myself."

Michael figured that the liveryman was fishing for extra compensation but he wasn't about to get it.

* * *

Nearly a month passed on the mesa without a visit from anyone and Lisa didn't mind at all. She and Michael were up early every morning sharing coffee at daybreak and then hurrying to begin the day's excavations at their little pueblo. Michael had wanted to begin by digging out the kivas—they remained the most intriguing of all the Anasazi structures. By working hard from morning until night, it took them less than a week to excavate the first one. It was worth the effort and they found a great deal of broken pottery as well as many flawed stone points used for arrowheads and axes.

The last kiva was nearly twenty-five feet in diameter and ten feet deep. It had six evenly spaced masonry pilasters rising from a low, circular bench to support the roof—long ago fallen.

"Look," Michael said, "here is the sipapu, or entrance to the underworld and there is the rock deflector and shaft, just like we saw in Cliff Palace." Michael carefully excavated a highly unusual double mug whose graceful connecting arm was broken but which was otherwise in remarkably good shape. The mug had been resting far back under a section of rotting roof timbers.

"Now *this* is a find!" Michael announced, proudly hoisting aloft the double mug. "Have you seen anything like this before?"

"Actually, I have," Lisa said, "but none in such good condition."

"It's a remarkable specimen," Michael said, turning the mugs back and forth while he examined their black markings and excellent workmanship.

While his attention was fixed on his discovery, Lisa's eyes happened to shift to another cranny among the timbers and that was when she saw the big ornamental pot.

"Michael!" she cried. "Look at this!"

The pot was spilling over with turquoise stones and seashells, all hand-drilled and strung together on a number of magnificent necklaces.

"Oh, my!" Lisa whispered, easing the jug out between them. "And look at these beautiful feathers! Turquoise isn't found in these parts and God only knows where the seashells came from."

"Yes, but the feathers offer us the most profound insight! Don't you realize where they are from?"

Lisa shook her head. "No, I don't. I've never seen anything quite so colorful."

"That's because they are from the South and Central American macaws! Lisa, you have just found evidence that these Mesa Verde Anasazi were engaged in trade that originated into Mexico and beyond!"

Lisa's hand shook a little at this news. There were at least fifty of the mostly red, yellow, blue and gold feathers which had been resting in the pot as if they were flowers in a vase. "What about the seashells? Could they be from Mexico, too?"

"Of course! But they might also be from the Sea of Cortes or even the Pacific Ocean. There are scientists who specialize in these things at the Smithsonian and they will be able to determine the origin of these shells."

Michael hugged her. "This is an *amazing* discovery! Until now, Bandelier and others have theorized that the Anasazi probably evolved using a sophisticated trade system with other cultures. But most of these theories concerned themselves with trade between the Anasazi and northern plains tribes. But this . . . well, this sheds a new light on the subject. You can be sure it will cause quite a stir in academic circles."

"Then you will write about it?"

"Of course! And you'll be named as the discoverer!"

Lisa didn't attempt to hide her delight at this news and little else was accomplished that day as they spent hours examining and admiring their new discoveries.

* * *

During the weeks and months that followed, Lisa and Michael found many other artifacts and even some skeletons, but nothing matched the treasure jar and its priceless contents. To Lisa, time passed far too quickly, one day whistling into the next. Other than occasionally having to shoot deer and other wild game, she was in a constant state of joy and love for Michael.

They had their first frost in September and a week later, their first hard freeze. The canyon oaks took on their autumn colors and while out hiking one day they finally met the young Swedish nobleman whose full name was Baron Gustaf Eric Adolf Nordenskiold, scholarly son of a famous European arctic explorer and scientist.

"Hello!" Nordenskiold cried out when he first saw them walking hand in hand on the mesa top. "Are you Dr. and Mrs. Turner, from the great Smithsonian Institution!"

The Swede was wearing baggy Western garb including a large droopy hat and high-heeled boots. His clothes were so ill-fitting that he appeared comical but there was no doubting his warmth and enthusiasm.

"I am so glad to *finally* introduce myself to you, Dr. and Mrs. Turner," he said, pumping first one of their hands and then the other. "I have heard much about you!—All wonderful! So what have you found that I can buy for my collection?"

"Nothing," Michael said too abruptly. "What brings you up here when you have so much yet to dig in the cliff dwellings?"

Nordenskiold gave no indication that he detected Michael's disapproval. "We have found many things, especially after I left for the Hopi pueblos and did not get in the way of the *real* workers."

"Who probably ruined more artifacts than they salvaged."

"Michael!" Lisa snapped. "Don't be rude!" Then, turning back to Baron Nordenskiold, she added, "Baron Nordenskiold, it's a real pleasure finally to meet you."

"Gustaf! Please call me Gustaf! In America, we do not need to be so formal, eh?"

"Right," Michael heard himself say. "So what *has* been found by your workers?"

"Many skeletons and much pottery," Gustaf assured him with his engaging smile. "Come back to Cliff Palace tomorrow and you will see!"

"I'm afraid that we have too much work to do right here and it's late in the season. I'm sure you've noticed the bite in the air and the leaves changing colors."

"Ba! This is nothing!" Gustaf raised his skinny arms overhead and threw back his head. "Compared to my Swedish winters, it is *always* summer in Colorado!"

Lisa immediately took a strong liking to the young Swedish baron and, as they began to discuss their findings and theories about the Anasazi, she suspected that Michael did too. It was impossible not to like Gustaf but his racking chest cough did indicate that he had some serious respiratory problems. Lisa wondered if he, like many other wealthy Europeans, had come to the American Southwest in search of relief in the drier air.

The moment Baron Nordenskiold saw the double mug and Lisa's jar of feathers, seashells and turquoise all drilled and strung on necklaces, he wanted them.

"You have only to name your price!" he exclaimed.

"I'm sorry," Michael said, actually making it sound as if he *was* sorry, "but these items have a profound scientific value."

"Yes, yes, then just sell me half of the collection. I will pay you . . . five hundred dollars . . . if you will also throw in the double mug."

"Not a chance," Lisa said.

The baron was not discouraged easily. "Then *one thousand* dollars."

"Sold," Michael said, grabbing the baron's hand and pumping it hard.

Lisa was astounded. "Michael, no!"

"I promise we'll find more. And this extra money will allow me to go back to Washington, D.C. and carry on my lobbying."

Lisa knew that Michael was running very low on funds and she had not figured out a way to make him take back the five thousand dollars.

"All right?" Nordenskiold asked, looking at her with concern. "I would not want to cause any anger between you and . . ."

"It's all right," she assured the baron. "We'll take the thousand dollars."

"Excellent!" he cried. "It will make a grand addition to my collection which, after I show it on a grand tour of Europe, will someday be donated to our National Museum in Stockholm. I promise you that it will not be buried in someone's private collection."

"Not even your own?" Michael asked.

"Not even my own," the Swede vowed. "You have my word on that, Dr. Turner! And I promise you that I will write a wonderful report on my findings here, telling all the world of the importance of Mesa Verde."

Lisa believed him and Michael must have believed him too because they never worried about it for even a moment, not even after Baron Nordenskiold departed later that month with a large pack train of Anasazi artifacts.

When Lisa and Michael were struck by a snowstorm several weeks after the baron's departure, they learned that Nordenskiold's archaeologic collection had been seized by the authorities under pressure by an angry Durango citizenry very unhappy that the artifacts were bound for a foreign country. But, after a court session and the determination that there were no laws on the books prohibiting such exports, Nordenskiold and his collection were released and allowed to sail for Sweden.

When Michael departed Denver for Washington in Novem-

ber, he was talking again of the two Washington, D.C. socialites and the important role they could play in saving Mesa
Verde. Lisa was jealous. It was all she could do to keep from
shouting at Michael, who was again—thanks to their hard
work this year and a new portfolio of photographs to be developed—in very high spirits.

"Just don't sell any more macaw feathers or the remainder
of those beautiful Anasazi necklaces," she told him as he
prepared to board the train and return east. "Not to either
one of those women or anyone else."

"I promise I won't," he assured her. "Besides, I want you
to have one of the necklaces for your own."

"Oh, I couldn't!"

"Of course you could," he said, removing the prettiest
necklace of all with its polished turquoise stones and tiny
seashells. "You've *earned* this and I can't think of anyone
that it would look more beautiful on than you."

Lisa blushed and allowed him to fasten it around her neck.

"See!" he exclaimed. "You're a perfect match! And here,
take three feathers. There's plenty left for me to show off in
Washington."

Lisa chose one yellow, one red and one aqua-blue.
"They're beautiful," she said. "They must have been considered a great prize."

"I'm sure they were," he agreed, reaching down to pick
up his bags and board the waiting train.

"Michael?"

"Yes?" He paused, one foot on the train's platform.

"Give my regards to Mrs. McClurg and Mrs. Peabody."

"I will," he promised. "And I hope to bring them back
with me next spring. You'll like them, Lisa."

"I'm sure I will," she replied as he vanished from her life,
leaving her with nothing but priceless memories and the
Anasazi mementos—loving gifts from someone to someone
long, long ago.

Nineteen

THE WEDDING GIFTS

circa 900 A.D.
Mesa Verde Pueblo

Seventeen-year-old Itac lifted a wedge of rock and leaned back to admire the irrigation water rush down his ditches on its way into the family's tall cornfields. He enjoyed moving the water from one field to another and didn't mind the hard repair work needed each spring after the thaw. As he gazed at the lush fields of corn, beans and squash, Itac remembered hearing that long ago, when the People had first arrived on this mesa among the clouds, all this farmland had been covered by heavy forest. Itac found that almost impossible to believe because now the mesa was crisscrossed by dozens of irrigation canals feeding their ripening crops. These fields were owned in common by all the Raven Clan, but were tended by families and whose stewardship was passed by the woman from generation to generation. In this way, a man always farmed the lands belonging to his wife's family.

Itac's mother had brought his father to some of the mesa's best fields and, unless there was a shortage of late summer water, his family was assured of a good autumn harvest. Itac, his father, and younger brothers prided themselves on being exceptionally hard workers. Only Dasiu, Itac's older brother, was allowed to spend his summer days hunting and offering prayers because he was favored by true visions.

As the light faded, Itac saw his father motion him to hurry along the ditch, checking for leaks. Just then, Itac caught a glimpse of Dasiu sneaking out of the pueblo with Tasca. Tasca not only was beautiful, she also was the daughter of Ho-ai-m, the richest man on this mesa. It was a great mystery why Ho-ai-m had resisted giving his most desirable daughter in marriage to Dasiu, who one day would become Clan Leader.

Itac saw his brother and Tasca entering the chest-high cornfields. They stopped and embraced, a single silhouette against an ocean of sun-dappled corn. It was fortunate that Ho-ai-m was nearly blind because his favored daughter soon would be bearing Dasiu's child, and then he would have to let them marry and receive nothing for her.

Itac sighed. If he were handsome like Dasiu, tonight he also would be lying with a girl in these sweet cornfields. The very thought of coupling with someone like Tasca made Itac's pulse quicken, and before he gave evidence of his desires, he squatted down in the cool irrigation water. The day had been hot and the water was refreshing. Itac lay back against the wall of the muddy ditch and watched the sun fire the western sky with changing colors.

It was not Itac's fault that his ears were too large and had been a source of ridicule since his earliest memories. Or that the back of his head had not been flattened enough by the cradleboard and so was considered unattractive. In contrast, Dasiu was so physically gifted that at fifteen he had been able to outrun any man in the village, and then won the honor of being the clan's best marksman only two years later. He was also humble and popular. Everyone loved Dasiu . . . everyone that is except that rich and greedy old fool, Ho-ai-m.

Someday Itac would find a girl that would look past his large ears and poor looks. Until then, he was content, because this had been another fine year for the crops, thanks to an abundance of water. Their huge reservoir had been full all spring and even now remained several feet deep so that the children could still splash about and play.

Itac rolled his head sideways and gazed off toward the many pueblos scattered across the mesa. They were all filled with life and laughter, each with at least a dozen families, each separate yet one as members of the mighty Raven Clan. Yes, Itac thought, his people would live and prosper here forever.

Even their desert enemies posed no serious threat to Raven Clan, who had as many bows and arrows as the sweet kernels on a tall stalk of corn. They never could be conquered by siege, either, because they had a permanent source of water and enough grain stored in the cliff caves to last for months. There also were sentinel towers located among the pueblos where vigilant eyes watched for the enemy Desert People who sometimes tried to steal food and their young women. Twice in the past three years, the Desert People had even attempted to burn their crops on hot, windy nights. The second time they tried to do this, Dasiu with his great swiftness had overtaken the fleeing enemies and killed three of them with a war axe. For this, he was given great honors. One day, Itac hoped to be able also to kill his peoples' enemies and thus gain his own honors for he was nearly as strong and as fast afoot.

"Itac!"

Itac jumped up and scrambled out of the irrigation ditch to signal to his father that all was well and that water now flowed to their fields. Then, he hurried along the smooth, centuries-old footpath running beside the irrigation ditch as Sun melted softly into Earth. It was all he could do to resist a powerful urge to sneak past near the hidden spot where his brother and Tasca were making love, but he continued to his mother's pueblo, eager to enjoy the evening meal.

"Itac, what took you so long?" his father asked after prayers and as their meal of corn, beans and wild berries was being served. "And why did you sit down in the water?"

"I was very hot."

Vatika turned his attention back to his hungry family and was soon engaged in other conversation.

Late that night, when the moon was high and the stars as thick as berries on the bush, Itac went outside to enjoy a little silence because with so many children it was very noisy in his pueblo. He sat down beside a wall and gazed at the heavens, wondering if he would ever have a beautiful woman of his own.

He must have dozed off for he was awakened very late by his brother. "Itac, why are you sleeping here?"

Itac knuckled the sleep from his eyes. "I was tired."

"We work too hard," Dasiu said, squatting beside him. "There are easier ways to live."

"There is only one way for us to live, and that is what we are doing," Itac replied, a little defensively.

"Have you ever left this mesa?"

"You know that I have not."

"I have," Dasiu said, sweeping a hand across the entire starry sky. "I have gone far away on hunting trips and have met many traders."

"Traders?"

Dasiu nodded. "I have learned much about trade and not all from the Chacoans, either. Itac, I have heard of this other place where many people live. It is only seven days' walk following Sun and I am told that it is a great clan with more people than at Chaco."

"Are they enemies?"

"I am sure they are not Desert People."

"And what is the name of this place?"

"It is called Hovenwa and people there are said to be fat and rich. I would like to go to this place and I want you to come with me."

Itac's jaw sagged with surprise because Dasiu had never before asked him to go anywhere. They got along, but they never had been close.

"I am honored that you ask for my company, but am needed to work here."

"The harvest is almost ready and the women and children can do that work. You should come with me!"

"Father would not permit it."

"He would if I told him that I had a vision that we were to go together."

"You had this vision?"

"No," Dasiu admitted, "but I expect it tonight."

Itac could not decide if his older brother was teasing him or not. This entire conversation seemed unreal. Why would Dasiu take him and not one of his own friends?

As if reading Itac's mind, Dasiu said, "I have decided to take you to Hovenwa because I have seen you watching when Tasca and I slip into the cornfields."

"I have not!" Itac protested, grateful for the darkness because his cheeks felt hot. "Why would I do that?"

"Because you are old enough to have a woman. And this place that I have heard of has many women needing strong men. You see, my brother, their people are round-heads so you would be handsome among them and could pick a woman for your own to bring back here and bear you children."

Itac was wide awake now. He scraped his forearm across his eyes to make sure this conversation was not a dream. "Why do you want to go to this place?"

Dasiu's expression hardened. "I need special gifts for old Ho-ai-m so that I can take Tasca for my wife. I love only her. She is with my child!"

"Then Ho-ai-m cannot keep her from becoming your woman."

"But then she would he shamed!"

Itac could see that his brother was serious. More serious than he had ever been before. "Instead of me, you should speak to our Father."

"We have spoken and he has no answer. Ho-ai-m has listened to other marriage offers for Tasca. But she loves me."

Itac understood. This was not the first time that greed had come between a young man and the woman he loved, although such matters usually were settled amicably and in private. This was especially true among young people who had lain together often.

"I can trade for special gifts," Dasiu was saying. "We have the finest seeds, better even than those of Chaco Canyon."

"Do you know if these people are farmers?"

"They farm but mostly trade."

"Maybe they do not have enough water to farm well."

"Maybe," Dasiu conceded. "But maybe they have not yet figured out the irrigation secrets we have learned."

"What else do you have to trade?"

"Arrowheads. Sandals. Bows and baskets. Turkey feathers and the horns of Sheep and the teeth of Bear. They will not have these things and so will prize them."

"And what does old Ho-ai-m ask in exchange for his most beautiful daughter?"

"Seashells, turquoise and bright feathers."

"From what bird?"

"From birds that live far, far away. They are found in Chaco Canyon, or so I am told."

Itac also thought this quite likely. "Why do you want me to go?"

"I told you! There are said to be many handsome women in this place. Maybe they will even think *you* handsome. And I need someone to help me carry trade goods to Hovenwa."

"I don't know," Itac hedged. "Father would . . ."

"Would be proud of us both when we return!" Dasiu slapped Itac on the shoulder. "I will tell Father that we must leave tonight!"

"Tonight? But . . ."

Dasiu jumped up, threw his hands over his eyes and began to sway rapidly, bare feet shuffling. "Itac!" he cried, "I am having my vision!"

Like everyone else in the Raven Clan, Itac had seen these

powerful visions come upon Dasiu before, but none had been so dramatic. Dasiu's entire body began to shake and his eyes bulged. Waving his arms and shouting in a strange language, Dasiu suddenly began to spin around and around, arms extended. He spun faster and faster until he collapsed, heels and hands slapping at Earth, lips pulled back in a grimace and eyes staring up at the stars.

"Dasiu!" Itac cried, placing his hand on Dasiu's chest. He could feel his brother's heart pounding and was about to jump up and run for help when Dasiu regained consciousness and grabbed his arm.

"The vision was clear, my brother! We must go tonight and we will return with a wife for you and gifts for Ho-ai-m. Then we will build our own pueblo and Ho-ai-m must give me his favored daughter and his best fields so that we always can live easy and well."

Midmorning found Itac and Dasiu miles from Mesa Verde. Dasiu seemed to have recovered completely from his vision and now led the way carrying little more than his bow and arrows as Itac plodded along hauling their trade goods. At noon, Dasiu raised his hand and then turned to signal his brother that he should stop and remain silent. That was fine with Itac for his shoulders already were chafed and he was growing footsore because his sandals were too old and thin. He untied his packs and rested while Dasiu disappeared into the trees and brush, stalking game. In only a few minutes, his brother reappeared.

"We will eat well on this journey!" Dasiu proudly announced. "Come! It is much too early to rest!"

Itac thought differently. Unlike his brother, Itac had worked very hard the day before and had had almost no sleep the previous night. He was tired and hungry but at least now he would have meat to give him enough strength to pass through this hard day.

Dasiu led him to the kill and they butchered a fine young stag, eating its liver and heart raw. They skinned the deer and used its hide to fashion two slings in which they could carry all the venison they would need until they reached Hovenwa.

That night while Itac collected wood and made a cooking fire, Dasiu went off to be alone with his visions. He did not return until dawn, when he awakened Itac saying, "I saw Coyote chasing Rabbit across the sky until he disappeared behind Moon. Then Coyote howled in the dark and Raven appeared, wings as wide as the Earth."

Itac nodded, wide awake now. "Did Raven kill Coyote?"

"No," Dasiu said, shaking his head. "But he used his great wings to drive Coyote into Middle Earth. Then Rabbit came out from hiding with *two* heads!"

"What does that mean?"

"I am not sure," Dasiu admitted. He sighed and there were dark circles under his eyes so that he looked very tired. "I must sleep now. Maybe in my dreams the vision will reappear and I will understand its meaning. Sometimes this happens, but not always."

"Coyote will not stay in Middle Earth," Itac said. "And he always will hunt Rabbit."

"But not catch him, for the night sky is too big and black."

"But cannot Coyote see well in the dark?"

"Yes, but not well enough to see black Raven whose talons are as sharp as Coyote's own teeth and whose eyes are even keener. Once I saw Raven sweep down and lift Coyote from Earth and carry him up almost to Sun. He dropped Coyote, who howled as he fell back to Earth and that is why to this very day all coyotes howl at night."

"I see," Itac said in wonder. "But why is it that you have never told the wise men of our clan this great story?"

"Because," Dasiu said with an indifferent wave of his hand. "Until I am Leader, they would not believe that vision. They think Coyote howls at night only because he is hungry and jealous of Dog."

Itac would like to have asked more questions but his brother yawned and laid his head down upon their bag of seeds, falling asleep almost instantly. Having nothing better to do, Itac cooked some venison and then he too fell asleep, dreaming of Coyote, Rabbit and Raven chasing each other around the stars.

The journey to Hovenwa was hard, hot and dry. They might have missed the villages altogether had they not chanced upon a fine stream flowing through a wide, sage-covered valley. There were many tracks along the river and some of them belonged to people.

By now Itac was nearly lame, for his sandals had disintegrated and this land they crossed was filled with sharp rocks and thorns. He pleaded with his brother to allow him to wear a pair of their trade sandals, but Dasiu refused saying, "Wrap strips of Deer's hide around your feet. We only have three pairs of sandals to trade and they are of the finest quality. I expect to get much value for them. Besides, I am sure that we are almost to Hovenwa."

Itac understood his brother's reasoning, but he did not appreciate having to walk in stiff, blood-caked hide which chafed his feet. Also, he had wanted to look good when he entered this village of prosperous traders. With his feet wrapped in bloody skins, he was sure to be scorned, even among a people with heads as round as his own.

Their first impression of Hovenwa was disappointing. Unlike Raven Clan, these people were still living in the old-style pit houses and their crops were stunted and thirsty-looking despite the stream that flowed the entire length of their valley.

"No pueblos or towers," Dasiu said, crouching behind some rocks where they could see without being seen themselves. "These people are either very lazy, or backward."

The first thing that Itac noted was that these were round-headed people. Rather than strapping their infants in cradleboards, they allowed children to crawl everywhere, while older children made little effort to keep them from danger.

"These people are not fat *or* rich!" Dasiu said with displeasure. "They are only round-headed and ugly."

"Not so ugly," Itac dared to say. "But, if this is how they live, maybe you should not become a trader."

"Look!" Dasiu cried. "See the bright bird on the pole! It is as I was told! Such a bird is a great prize and would please Tasca's father."

But Itac was far more interested in the women, who were uniformly handsome. They were short of stature, but comely. Itac could see that they used both baskets and pots. Most wore turquoise and shell jewelry in the form of necklaces and pendants. Itac wondered how a people who appeared to be such poor farmers could have such precious jewelry and birds.

"What shall we do now?" Itac asked.

"You stay here," Dasiu ordered. "I will go and make sure they are friendly and can be understood before I signal you to come and join us."

"No," Itac said, surprising even himself. "I am coming, too."

Dasiu started to argue, but changed his mind. "Then come. I see they have many dogs, so we will not get close before we are seen."

"What if they are not a friendly people?"

Itac nocked an arrow on his bowstring without even looking down at his weapon. "Then," he answered, "the fastest among them will be the first to die before we run."

That was a good enough answer for Itac. Being fast afoot himself and taller than these people, he was sure he could outrun them even wearing a crude pair of deerhide moccasins.

"Hello!" Dasiu called as a pack of barking dogs surged out to either attack or greet them. "Steady, Itac!"

The dogs soon were yipping and wagging their tails which was a relief. One, however, kept worrying at Itac's feet, liking the smell of blood. He had to kick it in the side to keep it away before they proceeded into the village whose people gathered to meet them.

As always, Dasiu took control and began to speak but these people used a language that was not difficult to understand. Using sign as well as speech, Dasiu indicated that he had many prized goods to trade, and in return he expected jewelry and the feathers of the noisy macaw.

"They also have very good pottery," Itac said, admiring a fine water jar that was cradled in a pretty girl's arms. "And baskets. We could have some of them for Mother and . . ."

"No," Dasiu snapped. "Ho-ai-m cares nothing for those things! Itac, why are they looking at me like this?"

"Maybe they think you look funny with the back of your head so flat," Itac replied, grinning at a girl with a water jug and receiving a radiant smile in return.

Dasiu muttered something under his breath and when one of the village elders stepped forward and took hold of his bow and nocked arrow, Dasiu made the mistake of pulling away.

Almost instantly, he was surrounded by men with weapons while Itac stood frozen with indecision, whispering, "What shall we do, Brother!"

"Do nothing except to smile!"

Itac smiled and did not resist when his packs of trade goods were taken and opened. The sandals disappeared as did Dasiu's best arrowheads. Only the bags of corn, beans and squash seeds remained untouched.

"This is *not* going well," Dasiu gritted between his frozen smile as his bow and arrows were torn from his grasp. "These people are *not* friendly."

They acted as if they understood. Itac and his brother were rudely shoved forward and then herded to a ladder leading down into a pit house that they were motioned to enter.

"What do you think might await us down there?" Itac hissed.

"Maybe death, Brother. I will go first."

Dasiu took hold of the ladder and descended into the pit house through a hole centered in its roof. Itac was right behind him and the light was so poor that he nearly stepped on Dasiu's shoulders causing them both to tumble to the hard dirt floor.

They both heard the cackle of laughter and, to Itac's way of thinking, it was not a nice or welcoming sound. He drew himself up into a ball and tensed, expecting to be struck dead by an axe or club. The blow never came. After several minutes, his eyes became adjusted to the poor light and he saw the forms of several men who were sitting on a low, circling bench. He knew at once these men were Hovenwa's leaders.

"Where are you from?" an old man with a quavering voice asked in a slow, measured tone. "What people are you?"

"We are Raven Clan people," Dasiu said with remarkable calm. "We have come to trade and be friends."

"You have never come here before."

"This is true."

"Why do you have a flat head and he has a round head?"

"I do not know, for we are brothers."

"Round head," the voice said, "your brother is ugly. I will speak to you alone."

Something very close to panic swept over Itac. "But . . . my brother has visions and is leader."

"That's right!" Dasiu exclaimed. "And I . . ."

Itac didn't see the blow struck from behind them in the semidarkness but he did hear its impact against Dasiu's skull and then saw his brother slump forward into unconsciousness.

Before Itac could think of how to react, the old man with the quavering voice continued, "Round Head, what besides arrowheads and a few pairs of sandals did you bring to trade?"

Itac had a feeling that, if he answered badly, he also would be stoned. Sweat burst from every pore in his body and he reached out to touch his brother's head, feeling blood. A rush of anger overwhelmed his fear and he cried, "Is this how you treat those who come to trade in peace?"

"We are Desert People!"

Itac wondered if these enemies smelled his fear and sensed his utter confusion. "We . . . we also wish to be friends with the Desert People," he said, knowing how lame he sounded.

"You live very well," another voice said with an unmistakable hint of envy. "Your corn is tall, your squash heavy and your beans thick on the vine."

"We have learned from the Chacoans. We have brought their seeds which will make your harvests great." Itac dared to add, "And I am wise in the ways of bringing water to every field."

"And what does your foolish brother have besides sandals and arrowheads of which we have no need?" the quavery-voiced old man asked.

"My brother is a great hunter! He is quick and strong."

"Then he is dangerous and cannot be trusted. Are you also quick and strong?"

"No," Itac said, wagging his head.

"And will you show us these seeds and the ways that you bring water to all the fields?"

"I will!"

"And what can he show us?"

"How to hunt. He . . . he also has true visions. He is a friend of Raven and can sometimes foretell the future."

"I wonder," another voice said, "if he can foretell his own bad future."

Itac felt a chill pass down his spine. "Someday my brother will be leader of Raven Clan. This I know."

"So you also can see into the future."

"No, but . . ."

"Then how do you know what you have just said will come to pass?"

Itac was trapped. It would be a terrible mistake to tell these men that Dasiu had once killed three of the Desert People who had tried to steal their corn and fire their crops.

"How do you know!"

Itac drew a forearm across his leaking brow. "Dasiu has visions. He has great honor among my Raven Clan people."

"Because he can foretell the future?"

"And because he is . . . gifted by the spirit of Raven."

"As a hunter?"

"Yes," Itac whispered.

The elders began to speak in a different tongue. Their speaking continued for a long time and Itac's eyes grew accustomed enough to the dimness to see that his brother's chest was rising and falling and to use his fingertips to make sure that his skull was not crushed.

After what seemed like forever, Itac and Dasiu were left alone in the pit house. A short time later, food and water were brought down to them and then they were left in darkness and bewilderment for the rest of the night.

Dasiu was awake in the morning, but dazed and listless. Dragging Dasiu over to the shaft of light streaming down into the pit house, Itac examined his brother's head and discovered a deep scalp wound, with swelling, and Dasiu had bled from the ears.

"Brother!" he urgently whispered. "Can you hear or understand me?"

Dasiu opened his eyes and the pupils were large, shiny and unfocused. Itac shuddered when Dasiu began to babble like a baby and salivate like a hungry dog.

Trembling with dread, Itac decided he had little choice but to climb up the ladder and confront the village elders. He would ask to leave with nothing more than his life and that of his brother. They could even have Dasiu's bow, arrows and their clothing. Itac was sure that he could find the way back to Mesa Verde and that the only real question was if Dasiu would ever recover.

But when he climbed out into the sunlight, he found the

people of Hovenwa waiting. Itac stepped away from the ladder and swallowed hard. He had rehearsed a speech but now it was suddenly forgotten and his mouth was very dry.

"You will show us how to move water from the stream to our fields," one of the elders who wore three turquoise and shell necklaces announced. "And how to plant your special seeds next spring."

"Next spring?" Itac shook his head. "But we must go back to our own people now!"

"No," the man said. "You can never go back. Our peoples are enemies."

Itac wanted to object, but something deep inside made him nod in mute and humble agreement.

They were prisoners. Itac knew that his brother's head had been cracked and Dasiu might never regain his senses, much less his gift of prophecy.

Twenty

Itac had fallen in love the moment he'd first seen Zema holding her water jug as he and Dasiu were herded through the village and ordered down into the tribal elder's spacious pit house.

Zema was not high born, probably not even considered especially beautiful by her own people, but the girl had eyes that mirrored great intelligence, wisdom and inner peace. When she looked at Itac, those eyes read his thoughts and felt his sadness. Sadness because he missed Mesa Verde and his family, but most of all, because his brother had not regained his senses. Dasiu did walk about the village each day, but he was unable to respond to questions and showed no interest in his surroundings. His gait was unsteady, his hands shook, and his eyes were as empty as the evening sky just after sundown.

Only Zema was good. She dared to bring Itac and Dasiu special foods and, just lately, her hand had lingered on Itac's arm for a few precious moments. Itac knew nothing about her except that she worked with the other women in the fields and also in the village cooking and preparing meals. She was quite young, more girl than woman, Itac supposed, but her bearing reflected a woman's strong spirit. This spirit was being tested by some of the Hovenwa boys angry at her decision to befriend their captives.

Itac tried hard to win the village's trust and favor. Each morning he arose at dawn and said prayers that he and Dasiu would soon be able to return to Mesa Verde and that his brother's mind and extraordinary good health would be restored. After prayers, Itac worked every day demonstrating to the Hovenwa people exactly how and where to place irrigation ditches.

Itac drew pictures in dirt and then made careful lines slanting away from the year-round stream directly into each planted field. But the actual work of digging the irrigation ditches was slow and it was clear to Itac that these people were not accustomed to hard work. They preferred to sit around gambling and talking, although they did enjoy hunting and were usually successful in bringing back wild game.

In a very short time, Itac learned that these people had a secret place where they mined turquoise which they traded for food and other valuable goods. Itac realized that turquoise was Hovenwa's real treasure. However, he also reasoned that, in times of drought, turquoise would not save these people from famine, so it was vital that they improve the yield of their harvest. The trouble was that these people did not seem to worry about anything in the future.

"We need more workers to dig," Itac complained one blustery winter afternoon as he tried using a stout pole to pry a large rock out of his ditch. "We need many workers or we will not have the ditches ready by spring."

The elder who oversaw the fields just shrugged with indifference while the others watched and waited to see if Itac could dislodge the boulder or if they would need to widen the ditch all around it. Itac struggled mightily with the pole but the rock would not budge even though the muscles of his arms and back knotted with his considerable power.

"Ahhh!" he grunted angrily, hurling the pole aside and jumping out of the irrigation ditch. "You people are worthless! Even if we were able to move this rock and build an irrigation system so that you could increase the yields of your crops many times over, I do not believe it would be kept in good repair. Because of neglect, the system soon would fill with mud and become riddled with leaks!"

The elder replied, "Itac, this is hard work. We were not put on Earth to work so hard."

"But you have to work hard!"

"Why?"

"So that you can live better and have surplus grain so that you never starve."

"Too much grain will only go to rot."

Itac was finished trying to help these lazy fools. "I will not do this for you anymore!"

"Then you and Dasiu will be killed," the elder said as matter-of-factly as if he were speaking about the weather. "You will be sacrificed at sunrise."

Itac had been about to stomp away in protest but now he froze in his tracks. "You really would kill us?"

"Of course. If you will not help, then what good would you be to my people?"

"I am a great harvester of the soil and builder of irrigation systems. I can show you how to build pueblos and . . ."

"What are these pueblos?"

"They are houses where we live above ground."

"Oh, yes," the elder said, not at all impressed, "we have seen these. They look to be very difficult to build. They are said to be cold in the winter and hot in the summer. We do not want your pueblos at Hovenwa. Too much work . . . and for what!"

"They are hard to build," Itac agreed, "but they are better places to live than your pit houses. During the heat of the summer, they catch the cool evening breezes."

"Under the ground, it is always cool."

"Yes, but in the winter you have to breathe so much smoke!" Itac argued. "And sometimes, the roofs catch on fire and people are burned and die. Is this not true?"

"It is true, but our pit houses are also warm and untouched by the cold winter winds."

"But pit houses become wet inside during the heavy rains!"

"It does not rain so much here."

"If you lived in pueblos, you would never worry about everything being soaked. Also, you can store your food more safely in a pueblo."

The old man made an unflattering sound and indicated that he was wearying of this discussion. "Itac, did you mean it when you said that you would work no more?"

"No," Itac quickly answered. "I will work. But I need help with this rock."

The elder motioned forward his younger charges who climbed to their feet and then, with Itac's directions, put their muscles to the boulder, finally pushing it out of the ditch.

"See!" Itac said, chest heaving with exertion. "If we all work together, we can have this system in place by spring when it is time to plant the new seeds that I have brought you from Mesa Verde."

"We shall see," the man replied, looking skeptical.

"And then perhaps you will reconsider and allow my brother and me to leave as friends."

"We shall see."

Itac did not think these people had any intention of allowing him to return to Mesa Verde. If it had not been for Dasiu's broken health and—yes, for his growing interest in Zema— Itac already would have escaped. But he could never leave Dasiu among these enemy people and no girl at Mesa Verde had ever looked at him as Zema did.

The next day, when Itac managed to steal a few minutes alone with Zema, he dared to ask her a question that had long been burning in his mind.

"Zema," he said, walking beside her and pretending to inspect the pitiful irrigation ditches that he had managed to dig without much help, "would you leave this place and come with me to live with my Raven Clan people?"

"I have thought you might ask this of me some day," Zema

finally replied, brushing her long black hair back over her shoulders. "At first, I thought to say no, that I never could be treated as you are treated here."

"But you would not be!" Itac exclaimed. "You would be my wife and therefore respected."

"The Raven Clan people have flat heads, I have round."

"As I do."

"But you have told me that you were considered unattractive in your own villages. I do not want to be . . . unattractive."

"You wouldn't be," he promised. "Not to me, at least."

"And what of our children? Would I be expected to strap their heads tight to a cradleboard?"

"You are asking too many questions," he said, pausing to gaze back at Hovenwa in order to see if they were being watched.

"But you ask the most important question."

"Yes," he confessed, "I do. I love you, Zema. But I would not take you with me if I believed you would not be happier at Mesa Verde than at Hovenwa. It is a better place to live. Cooler and fragrant with the scent of pines. Our pueblos are superior to your pit houses and our fields are so big we will never again know starvation."

"Do all your people speak as highly of your home in the sky?"

"I cannot say," Itac admitted. "If Dasiu could speak, he would tell you about the beauty of our nights and of how the seasons change and, of the Great Cave, where we store our winter grain."

"What of Dasiu? How would we take him away?"

"I don't know," Itac replied with a feeling of hopelessness. "I would never leave him."

"No," Zema agreed, "for my people would kill Dasiu if we escaped."

"Perhaps we can help him grow stronger," Itac suggested.

"Each day, we could take him for longer walks until his strength has returned."

"Do you think that is possible?"

"Why not?"

But Zema looked doubtful. "I think you should ask my father if we can become husband and wife. In time, we will have children and you will become one of our clan."

But Itac shook his head. "I must take Dasiu back to my family who will always care for him."

"We would care for him here!"

"This low desert place is wrong for Dasiu and for me. I want to live and work on the high mesas again."

"Maybe for you. Maybe not for me," Zema said before leaving him.

Itac was very depressed that night. It was clear that Zema had chosen Hovenwa and her own people over him and his beloved Mesa Verde. And what if Zema revealed his plan to strengthen Dasiu's body in readiness for escape? Itac did not believe Zema would do this, but he could not be certain, and since his life and that of Dasiu depended upon this secret, he was beside himself with anxiety.

But the next morning as Itac wearily trudged off to work on the irrigation system, his heart was filled with joy to see Zema leading Dasiu out of the Hovenwa village.

She is going to help us! Zema has decided to go away with me and become my wife!

Suddenly, Itac's world turned brighter and his step became much lighter. He began to whistle until he realized that this caused the others in his work party to regard him strangely. So he forced himself to appear glum even as he glanced back over his shoulder until he could no longer see Zema walking poor Dasiu.

The days of winter grew shorter and the winds bit into Dasiu and Itac like icy fangs. Zema pleaded to her clan elders to give their Raven Clan captives robes so that they would not chill and die. Finally, Dasiu and Itac were given rabbit-skin robes, but ones so old and shabby that they offered little protection.

Food grew scarce at Hovenwa and the hunters often returned empty-handed. A heavy, wet snowstorm lasting almost five days was followed by warm weather and a thaw which ruined much of these peoples' winter food supply which they kept stored in rocky alcoves located above their stream. On days when the weather was not too bitter, Itac took Dasiu out to the irrigation ditches for his exercise because Zema had been forbidden to walk with him anymore.

Despite the trials of winter, Itac was encouraged. His brother was growing stronger. Dasiu's eyes were still vacant, but sometimes Itac thought he understood what was being said to him when they were alone together. And then one afternoon, as Itac struggled to dislodge another large rock, Dasiu said, "Brother, why do you work so hard for our enemies?"

Itac nearly fainted. He gaped at Dasiu who was regarding him with obvious amusement.

"Brother!" Itac cried, crushing Dasiu in his arms. "You understand again!"

"Shhhh!" Dasiu warned. "I have understood for several weeks now. And let go of me before someone from the village sees us like this!"

"Why didn't you tell me you were better?" Itac asked as confusion replaced shock.

"Because I was afraid that you would tell Zema and that she would tell someone in her family. If these people knew I was of sound mind and body again, I would be made to work like you and be watched very closely."

Itac had so much to tell his brother! "Do you know that I asked Zema to leave with us for Mesa Verde and become my wife?"

"That was foolish," Dasiu told him. "Zema is ugly."

Itac reacted exactly as if he had been struck hard between the eyes. "You are wrong! Zema is beautiful!"

"I was wrong to bring you to Hovenwa," Dasiu told him. "You have become a slave to these people and . . . to Zema."

"Dasiu, you still are not thinking well! Zema has helped you at great risk. She is *good*. I think that she has decided to come with us and become one of our people."

"Better that you stay here and remain a slave. But, if you value your honor, then we can still return to Mesa Verde with many fine wedding gifts for Ho-ai-m."

"You mean we should *steal* them?"

"They stole everything from us!" Dasiu argued with vehemence. "We walked into Hovenwa as friends and one of them almost bashed in my skull!"

"I know who it was," Itac said. "He is far worse than the others. I have been told that he was only supposed to strike just hard enough to silence your voice. Instead, he tried to kill you."

"What is his name?"

"That is not important."

"Who *is* he!"

"Kincha," Itac blurted. "He is the best hunter among these people. Dasiu, listen to me! I will talk to Zema and tell her that we must leave at night during the very next storm."

"Why?"

"Because then we could not be tracked."

"Zema cannot go with us. She would be slow and the cause of our deaths."

"I am not leaving her behind," Itac insisted. "Not if she has decided to come with me!"

Dasiu's voice changed, becoming reasonable again. "All right, Brother. We will leave Hovenwa tonight because the moon is thin, the sky dark and the weather good for travel. Tell Zema to meet us here with everything of value that she can steal from her family."

"She would never do that!"

"Itac, she must understand that, from this day on, you are her family," Dasiu told him. "At Mesa Verde, Zema will have nothing but you."

"I will tell her."

"And make Zema swear not to tell anyone of our plan. And do not tell her that I am again strong."

"Of course, Dasiu."

Itac watched his brother return to the appearance of looking broken and mindless. He watched with fascination as Dasiu's body contracted as if gripped by pain. Dasiu's head tipped forward on his chest and his eyes grew dull with incomprehension. In a matter of moments, Dasiu somehow made himself appear to be ancient and weak. Soon, his hands began to tremble as they had for months.

"Dasiu!" Itac cried, grabbing his brother and shaking him. "Dasiu, how can you be like this again!"

But Dasiu did not respond except that his trembling intensified and . . . he began to drool.

Itac returned early to the village and was fortunate to be able to tell Zema that they were leaving this very night.

"But Dasiu is not strong enough to escape!"

"He is stronger than I thought," Itac said, purposefully vague. "Anyway, we must go tonight while Moon is weak. Bring whatever you can of value."

"I have nothing of value, Itac, except three turquoise and seashell necklaces and some bright red feathers."

"Bring them," Itac said.

"Itac," the girl cautioned, "if we are caught, we will die badly. All of us."

"Then maybe you should stay here and marry one of your own."

"I would rather die with you."

Itac was so overcome by these words that it was all he

could do to say, "When the stars appear, come out to the place I have last been working."

"I will come," she told him in a firm voice. "But so will my people when they learn we have run away."

"Let them," Itac said, suddenly feeling heady with confidence. "Many will die if they are foolish enough to catch us. Wear your best sandals. Bring food and water."

Zema nodded with understanding and left him to return to her family. Only after she had disappeared into her pit house did Itac experience the full depth of her courage and love. She was willing to risk everything, even though she probably believed they had no chance of escaping torture and death at the hands of her own Hovenwa people.

It was dark when Itac returned to the small house where he and Dasiu lived apart from the villagers. But Dasiu was gone. Itac scrambled back up the ladder. Where was Dasiu? What was he doing?

Dasiu huddled in the darkness near Kincha's pit house and waited for the dangerous and powerful hunter to emerge. Kincha had two wives and three children and Dasiu did not wish to kill them to satisfy his need for revenge. So he waited. An hour passed and then another and the sky began to fill with stars until Dasiu knew that he could wait no longer. Slipping a knife from his robe, he walked up to Kincha's ladder, gripped it hard and called down to the family.

"Kincha! Kincha, come up and speak with me!"

A groggy voice finally replied. "Who comes at this late hour? Go away!"

Dasiu knew that his voice never had been heard in Hovenwa so he spoke loudly. "An old trader and friend. Come up! I have a gift for you!"

Long moments passed before Dasiu smiled as he felt his enemy climbing the ladder. He turned away so that his enemy could not see his face but only his silhouette draped in his thin, miserable rabbit-skin robe.

"Who are you and what is this gift?" Kincha demanded to know as he came around to peer into Dasiu's smiling face and then recoil with fear. "You!"

Dasiu jumped forward and drove his blade deep into Kincha's flat belly. He laughed when Kincha choked and quivered. "This is for striking me a death blow while I spoke as a friend!"

Kincha tried to grab the knife and tear it from his belly but when Dasiu began to rip it upward, the Hovenwa hunter suddenly cried out and then bit Dasiu like a rabid dog. His teeth fastened on Dasiu's nose, causing him to scream with agony. Kincha severed the nose and spat it back into Dasiu's bloody face.

Dasiu tried to pull free from the dying man, but Kincha would not let him go. He bit again, this time taking a mouthful of Dasiu's cheek as they toppled to the ground.

Wild to get away, Dasiu kept stabbing Kincha until the man quit struggling. Climbing unsteadily to his feet, Dasiu staggered, then collapsed back to his knees, hands frantically brushing the earth until he touched what had been his nose. He snatched the grisly object up and then swore as he hurled it at Kincha's body.

A woman's voice called from Kincha's house. Dasiu managed to regain enough of his senses to drag Kincha's body away behind a low wall. Just then, one of Kincha's wives appeared, calling anxiously for her husband. Dasiu crouched with one hand trying to plug the bloody holes in his own face and the other choking his knife. He would kill this woman if she seemed intent on waking the entire village. The anxious woman called out several times more for her husband, but then went back down into her house.

Dasiu was so consumed by the disfiguring Kincha had inflicted that he actually considered slaughtering the man's entire family. He could do it as if they were a flock of turkeys.

It even made sense. After killing the family, he could pitch Kincha's body down the ladder. He could loot the family's treasures adding to treasures he already had taken this day and then torch the household. The fire would conceal the murders and occupy these enemy people the rest of this night. They would be so grief-stricken that they might not even notice that their Raven Clan slaves had disappeared.

But Dasiu could not bring himself to murder innocent women and children. He had enough bounty to buy Tasca from her father, so he gathered the bow and many arrows he had stolen only a short time earlier and hurried to meet Itac and Zema. Although the moonlight was faint, a few minutes later when they saw the mutilation of Dasiu's once handsome face, they both recoiled with shock and horror.

"Dasiu!" Itac whispered. "What happened!"

"Kincha!"

Dasiu forced himself to place his hand over his bloody face. He could feel a sharp stub of bone where his nose had been and, when he extended his examination, he realized that he could probe a hole in his cheek and touch his tongue.

Dasiu sobbed and choked. He spat blood and then he drew in a deep breath. "Come," he ordered, "we must go as far as we can before daylight. We must be swift."

When the young couple did not move, Dasiu began to shake. "There is no turning back now! We must run!"

Zema recovered before Itac. She yanked on his arm and followed Dasiu who had turned and begun to trot eastward where the sun would rise.

Dasiu did not waste time or energy trying to hide their tracks. The Hovenwa men would know their path would lead directly to Mesa Verde and, although they would be six or seven hours behind, they also would be better outfitted with a good supply of food and water. Furthermore, Kincha's assassination would fire in them the need for vengeance.

When the sun finally warmed their faces, Dasiu was the one who most suffered. His village walks had been no prepa-

ration for the ordeal they now faced in trying to reach Mesa
Verde, and his strength had finally been broken. But his suffering was as nothing compared to that of Itac, who could
hardly bear to look at his brother's ruined face. Only Dasiu's
black eyes bore testament to a man once so admired. They
were eyes that burned . . . but now only in pain.

The first full day they rarely stopped for food, drink or rest
even though Dasiu was staggering by sunset. It was then that
Itac knew *he* was leader and that their fates depended on his
wisdom and clear thinking.

"We will sleep now," he announced when they discovered
a clear desert spring bubbling out of a red-rock wall. "I will
stay awake at first on guard."

"My people will not sleep this night," Zema warned him
as she glanced at their back trail.

"Then we must hide so they will pass us in the darkness,"
Itac decided, looking to his brother to see if he approved. But
Dasiu appeared not to hear or care. Soon, he was fast asleep.

"Even if we do escape, what will happen to him?" Zema
asked.

Itac was not sure. "My brother will be given great honors!
He has killed another enemy and is the finest hunter among
all the Raven Clan people. Dasiu also has gifts for Ho-ai-m
so that he can marry the beautiful Tasca."

"Oh, yes," Zema said. "She is the reason you came to
Hovenwa. Zema was quiet for a moment, then said, "What
if Tasca no longer wants to marry your brother?"

"You should sleep now," Itac snapped. "We will have another long night."

"Itac, kill me if we are caught."

"What?"

"I would want you to take my life rather than face my
family and be made to suffer before we are put to death."

Itac turned away, not wanting her to see how sick and afraid
he was without having Dasiu to rely upon. Feeling Zema's

hand touch his shoulder, he turned and managed to say, "Zema, I do not think I could do that."

"Dasiu then," she said, glancing over at him. "I know that *he* would not mind killing me."

"Why do you say that?"

"He has often told me that I am ugly and will be laughed at among your clan at Mesa Verde."

"Dasiu said that!"

"He did not want me to come. That is why he spoke so cruelly."

"Whatever his reason, he lied," Itac assured her. "We will return with rare gifts for old Ho-ai-m in trade for his daughter. Dasiu will marry Tasca, become leader of Raven Clan and all in our family . . . including you, Zema . . . will be treated with great kindness and respect."

"I believe you, not Dasiu," she whispered.

Zema rested her head in his lap and her trust was all the stimulus Itac needed to stay awake and on guard. The Hovenwa girl fell asleep very quickly and there was just enough starlight to see her lovely face. Itac stared at Zema for long, silent hours finding it impossible to believe that such a brave and beautiful creature as this would sacrifice everything to become his wife.

How could Dasiu say this girl was ugly? How could he! And now, look at Dasiu himself. What would the women of the Raven Clan think of him? Would they still think him such a prize? Itac very much doubted it. Fair or not, vanity demanded vanity and life never would be the same for Dasiu.

Or for me, either, Itac thought as love for Zema overrode his sadness and even sympathy for Dasiu.

Itac fell asleep just before dawn. The sun climbed high before Dasiu. His face, still caked with dried blood, shook him into wakefulness.

"Itac, we must go!"

Itac looked down at Zema who still slept with her head in his lap. Remembering last night's conversation, his anger returned. "I don't care what you think, Brother. This woman is beautiful."

"Zema will die if we do not hurry!"

Itac doubted that this was true. He had realized last night that they never could hope to outrun their pursuers. Rather, they would have to trick them and hide during the day and travel only at night. And they also would have to use guile and not head directly for Mesa Verde but loop south into new territory. That would add a few precious days to their journey, but it seemed to Itac to be their only hope. Dasiu was too weak to run hard for five or six days and Zema would soon tire as well. Itac knew that he was the strongest of them, thanks to the hard labor of digging Hovenwa irrigation ditches.

But when he voiced his opinion to Dasiu, he was met with immediate opposition. Their disagreement did not end until Zema stepped between them, pleading for peace.

"We cannot fight among ourselves," she said, "for to do that surely will bring us death."

"She is right," Dasiu admitted.

"You should wash your face in the spring before we leave," Itac said, stung by the way his opinion had been rejected.

Dasiu said nothing, nor did he bother to wash the mask of dried blood that covered the lower part of his disfigured face. Instead, he gathered his stolen prizes and his weapons, then left without a backward glance.

"He is wrong," Zema said.

"He is very proud and a great warrior. Dasiu will get us meat and, if we are overtaken, he will kill many of your people."

Zema's eyes filled with tears but she said nothing. Soon, they were again walking east and did so until midmorning when they came upon the tracks of their pursuers. Dasiu studied them closely and for such a long time that Itac thought his brother might be having another vision.

"There are five," Dasiu finally announced. "They passed through here less than two hours ago."

"Then we should . . ."

"Follow them," Dasiu decided aloud. "That is the only place that they will not think to look for us."

"Yes," Zema agreed. "This is true."

"All right," Itac replied. "We can follow them all the way back to our mesa."

Dasiu began to follow the tracks just as Itac had seen him do so many times on the trail of Deer. In the days that followed, Dasiu grew stronger. He shot rabbits and even a small deer. Being afraid to use fire, they ate their flesh raw which was very difficult for Zema.

On the fifth day from Hovenwa, Dasiu, seemingly restored by a belly full of venison, slipped out of camp and went ahead to see if he could spot their hunters.

"Don't move from this place," he ordered.

Itac had no intention of moving. He had gorged himself with so much raw meat that he knew it would be very uncomfortable to travel for hours. He and Zema fell asleep in each other's arms and again they did not awaken until first light. When Itac realized his brother had not returned, he jumped up crying, "Zema! We must find Dasiu!"

Gathering their belongings, they found Dasiu—or rather, he found them. Dasiu carried several packs filled with Hovenwa belongings. When they met, he grinned and said, "We will not have to hurry now. There is nothing to fear. We will walk to the great river and then tomorrow climb up to our mesa from the south."

"You killed them all?" Itac asked, staring.

"They were tired from so much running and easy to stone in their sleep," Dasiu replied. He reached into a black pouch and emptied it, dropping five pieces of flesh on the ground.

Zema cried out in disgust and retreated so fast she tripped and fell hard. Itac's jaw dropped and his stomach rolled. "You cut off their noses!"

"And left them with cracked heads," Dasiu replied as he collected the grisly prizes and replaced them in his pouch before adding, "let us go now."

Itac and Zema said nothing all that day but their repugnance must have been evident because Dasiu grew increasingly angry and upset as they approached the great river. After selecting a camp, Dasiu said, "I am going off to have a true vision."

This pronouncement brought Itac comfort for it had been a long, long time since his brother had even spoken of visions. Perhaps he could have his visions only when he was near Mesa Verde.

"I will come back in the morning," Dasiu said, looking at them in the failing light.

The night passed well as Itac and Zema slept in each other's arms. When Dasiu did not return in the morning, they followed his tracks along the river side. They found Dasiu lying beside a clear lagoon, his face pressed deep into the river bank mud . . . his body impaled on his knife.

Itac wailed with grief and collapsed in the water, shaking his head back and forth while Zema tried to comfort him. After awhile, Itac dragged Dasiu's body deeper into the water and it floated away. Zema pulled him out of the river and held him close, her eyes fixed on the mesa.

"Itac," she finally whispered, "is that my new home? Is that where the wind tastes always of pines?"

"It is," Itac managed to reply, leading Zema up into the land of the mesas and the clouds.

Twenty-one

Denver, summer of 1900

Lisa Cannaday brushed her hair, frowning because a few strands were beginning to turn gray. But why should she be so concerned about that? She was, after all, approaching middle age. The many hot and dry Rocky Mountain summers had taken their toll on her appearance while she, Andrew, and then Dr. Turner had hunted for ancient Indian artifacts. Lisa told herself that graying hair did not matter and that she should be grateful for her excellent health and finances. Besides, Michael was the only man she wanted to marry and his hair had turned completely silver.

The renowned scientist had returned to Colorado each summer for the past ten years and, together, they had camped on Mesa Verde, exploring, mapping, and excavating many of the cliff dwellings as well as the pueblo ruins scattered across the mesa top. Lisa knew that the respectable women of Denver and Mancos gossiped about her and Michael staying together unchaperoned for long summers, but she did not care. In fact, it kept other men from courting her, and that was a blessing. She had no interest in any of the local bachelors, many of whom she suspected were gold-diggers.

Lisa lived comfortably in Denver for most of the year. She was not rich, but in spite of her long summer absences she had prospered thanks to her steadfast friend and business partner, Bruce Humphries. Bruce was a quiet, detail-minded accountant who kept excellent books for their growing list of clients, while Lisa was far more suited to generating new accounts and getting involved in civic projects. Their very different personalities and talents resulted in a near perfect business partnership, so successful that they had been considering adding another partner to their firm.

Lisa heard a knock on her door and placed a tortoiseshell comb on her vanity, calling out, "I'm coming!"

It would be Bruce arriving to drive her to the train station where she would meet Michael. As usual, her partner was early. They would spend an unnecessary hour waiting at the depot . . . just in case the train was on time, which it never was.

The idea of seeing Michael again generated a tremor of anticipation which explained the blush in Lisa's cheeks this morning. But Lisa reminded herself that it was time to finally settle some important personal issues with Michael. Ten years of waiting was long enough and, although she was happy, Lisa realized that she needed more than a series of wonderful summer explorations followed by eight or nine months of loneliness. After all, she already had resigned herself to the idea of never having children and that was a huge sacrifice.

Lisa gave herself one more quick appraisal and headed for the door deciding that she still was attractive despite the crow's feet at the corners of her eyes and the silver in her hair.

"Mrs. Cannaday?"

Lisa came to an abrupt halt inside her screen door. "Who are you?" she asked the tall, dark complected man nervously clutching his hat and a notebook.

"My name is David Quincy," he replied. "Would it be possible to have a few words with you?"

"Concerning?"

"Mesa Verde and Dr. Turner."

Lisa squinted through the screen that separated them. Was this stranger's long, black hair really braided? He was wearing a brown suit and was respectably dressed, but wasn't that a beautiful Hopi, Zuni or perhaps even Navajo silver and turquoise ring on his finger?

"What *exactly* do you want to know, Mr. Quincy?"

He shifted his feet, rolling the brim of his hat with his long, tapered fingers. "I'm going to start a newspaper . . . the *Denver Eagle*. It will begin as a weekly, but I'm hoping that it will gain enough of a readership to turn into a popular and unique daily."

"I wish you success, but I haven't much time to talk right now, Mr. Quincy. Perhaps later."

"Sure," he said. "I know that you are about to meet Dr. Turner at the train station and I was hoping that I could tag along so that you could introduce me to him. You see, I've been back East trying to get an interview with Dr. Turner but without success. He can't seem to find the time to fit me into his schedule."

"I'm sure he can spare a few minutes to talk to you before we leave for Mesa Verde."

"I hope so," Quincy replied. "I've been working on a story about the Mesa Verde Anasazi for years and his cooperation—as well as your own—is vital."

"Is this story for your new *Denver Eagle?*"

"Yes, but I've also been writing articles for national magazines. It pays the bills and will subsidize my newspaper until it catches on and becomes profitable."

"I see. So what kind of information do you need?"

Quincy glanced sideways at an overstuffed porch chair, then extracted a cheap brass pocket watch. "I'd like to discuss the Mesa Verde artifacts that you and Dr. Turner have been sending to the Smithsonian. Mrs. Cannaday, do you mind if I sit down? These cowboy boots are new and killing my feet. I'm much more comfortable in moccasins but I try to look properly white and professional on all my interviews."

"You must be at least part Indian."

"I am," he told her with obvious pride. "My father was

Irish, my mother Hopi. When she died, Father took my sister and me back to the East Coast for a superior education. Believe it or not, I was admitted to Columbia University and graduated with honors."

"Congratulations," Lisa said, "for taking advantage of such a fine opportunity."

"Thank you. But I'm not here to talk about myself. I want to know more about you and Dr. Turner."

Lisa could see no harm in waiting for Bruce right here on the porch while visiting with this intriguing journalist.

As soon as they were seated, Quincy said, "I'd like to begin by discussing the Mesa Verde artifacts that you and Dr. Turner have been excavating over the past decade."

"Have you ever seen any finer collection!"

"No," Quincy admitted, picking up his pen and setting it to his notepad. "But I'm afraid that's the problem. You see, there is a large . . . discrepancy."

Lisa stared at Quincy for a moment, then blurted, "What does that mean?"

"Mrs. Cannaday, please don't take offense, but I've interviewed the shipping companies and examined their invoices that list the artifacts you and Dr. Turner have been sending back East all these years."

"And?"

"And what was sent does not begin to equal what was received by the Smithsonian."

"What!"

"That's right," Quincy pressed. "At least ten percent—and some of the very best artifacts—are missing."

"That's impossible!"

"It's true," Quincy insisted, "and I can prove it by comparing what left Colorado to what the Smithsonian actually received."

Lisa was at a loss for words.

"Mrs. Cannaday," he was saying, "would you please explain your professional relationship with Dr. Turner?"

Lisa's impulse was to explode with anger but something told her that this would be exactly the wrong thing to do. She needed to retain her composure and try to get to the bottom of this.

"Well," she began, "my late husband, Andrew, was also a scientist who once worked for the Smithsonian. In 1889, Dr. Turner hired us to visit Mesa Verde and either confirm or deny the extravagant claims of the Wetherill family about some newly discovered cliff dwellings he said he had discovered. Andrew and I traveled to Mesa Verde and realized that Richard Wetherill was not exaggerating. The importance of Cliff Palace and the other dwellings could hardly be overstated. But, to my great sorrow, Andrew suffered a terrible fall at Mesa Verde and died. The following year, Dr. Turner came to offer his condolences and provide me with a modest compensation for my loss. He wished to visit Mesa Verde so I accompanied him. We've been working there ever since, as long as the summer weather holds."

"You're also a scientist?"

"Not formally," she admitted, "but my late husband instilled in me his love of archaeology. I believe that it is important work."

"So do I," Quincy replied. "Mrs. Cannaday, did you and Dr. Turner uncover Anasazi remains?"

"Of course, though not as many as the Wetherills did."

"How many Indian skeletons do you estimate sending back to the Smithsonian?"

"I have no idea." Lisa replied, hearing an edge creeping into her voice.

"More or fewer than ten?"

"Oh, many more, although they were often incomplete. Half the skeletons we found were disjointed and their bones scattered about either by rodents or animals. Mr. Quincy, what is the meaning of these questions?"

"But you found at least ten skulls?"

"Yes, definitely!"

He scribbled on his pad, leaving her to fume. When he looked up a moment later, Quincy said, "The Smithsonian has only received *five* complete skeletons and skulls."

"Sir," Lisa grated, "you are badly mistaken!"

"I wish that I were, I am sure your friend, Dr. Turner, has been selling Anasazi skeletons and other artifacts to an international black market for substantial amounts of cash. There is, as I'm sure you are aware, a great demand for American Indian artifacts—especially human remains."

Lisa came to her feet with fire in her eyes. "Mr. Quincy, you had better leave right now!"

"I am just trying to get the truth," he told her. "I'd be deeply saddened if I were to learn that you and Dr. Turner have *both* profited. Are you by any chance secretly married?"

"Absolutely not! And what kind of lying, muckraking journalism do you practice!"

He folded up his notepad and placed his pen in his shirt pocket. "I'm very sorry to have upset you but your reaction here tells me what I had expected—that you are entirely innocent in this sad affair."

"Mr. Quincy, I deeply resent your insinuation concerning Dr. Turner."

"Yes, of course you do. He is your friend. Ma'am, asking personal and uncomfortable questions is the only part of journalism that I detest, but to shy away from truth is to violate the public's trust."

Lisa wasn't listening anymore. "It is now quite clear to me why Michael denied you an interview."

"If it means anything to you, Mrs. Cannaday, my desire is to preserve your reputation. That is why I was hoping to clear your name before Dr. Turner's train arrived."

"My name needs no clearing, Mr. Quincy! Ask anyone in Denver and they'll tell you I am honest."

"I have asked," he said, looking downcast. "That's why I found it impossible from the start to believe that you could be involved in stealing ancient Indian artifacts and then also passing them through a wealthy intermediate named Garland Wingate."

"I've never even heard of Garland Wingate!"

"I assure you he exists and is notorious for illegally obtaining American Indian artifacts which he then sells on the world market for enormous profits to the highest bidders. If I were you I'd be asking Dr. Turner some very hard questions and I'd also distance myself from him just as fast as possible." He turned and left.

When Bruce Humphries arrived ten minutes later it was all that Lisa could do not to vent her outrage at David Quincy's ridiculous accusations. She was determined to keep her own counsel until she could speak with Michael and warn him of David Quincy's charges. She and Michael would find a way to stop this so-called journalist and haul him in to court if he persisted with his lies.

"You seem especially excited about Dr. Turner's arrival this year," Bruce said as he helped her into his carriage. "I expect that you will have a lot to talk about."

Lisa glanced sideways at her business partner. Bruce was fifty-three years old and married to a sweet lady who had given him three attractive daughters, now with children of their own. He was a devoted Methodist and a complete gentleman whose reputation for honesty was admired. Lisa had never burdened him with her personal problems and she was not about to start now.

"Yes," she said, forcing a smile, "I *am* excited. How is your wife feeling today?"

"Oh, much, much better! She has gotten over the stomachache and is her usual chipper self again."

"Good."

"And you?" Bruce asked, looking at her with concern. "Are you really feeling all right?"

"Never better."

"Good," he said, as they drove away. "I arrived a little early in case the train arrived ahead of schedule."

"Fine idea," Lisa assured him as she tried to compose herself and banish David Quincy from her troubled thoughts.

The train was early and when Lisa saw Michael and he waved, all her doubts and fears evaporated. She rushed to him and they embraced.

"God," he whispered, "I've missed you!"

"Me, too. It's good to hold you again."

He gently pushed her back to study her face. "You're always so beautiful. I can't imagine how I've managed to leave you for the past ten years. I really can't."

Lisa blushed. Despite all the local gossip, she and Michael had never been lovers. He was much too honorable to have taken advantage of her compromised position, and she was too Victorian to admit that she wished he *would*.

"I can't tell you how much I have missed you this time," Michael said as he slipped his arm around Lisa's waist and guided her through the other disembarking passengers. "We'll have a lot to talk about this summer."

"We always have had a lot to talk about."

"I mean besides the Anasazi," he explained in a low, confidential tone as they met Bruce. The men shook hands warmly and exchanged greetings.

Lisa tried to act jovial as Bruce drove them back to her house, but she was on the verge of tears.

"May I pour you a drink?" Lisa asked as soon as she and Michael were alone in her book-lined front parlor.

"I'd like that. The usual two fingers of brandy, please."

"I think I'll have the same," she told him. "Why don't you just relax and I'll be right back."

Michael removed his hat and coat. Lisa was disturbed to note that he was thin and had visibly aged this past year. She wondered if he had been ill and had not wanted to write and worry her.

When she rejoined him with their brandy, he raised his glass in salute and tossed the liquor down. He refilled his glass saying, "Well, darling, how have you fared this past nine months?"

"We had a mild winter and early spring," she told him, noting a slight tremor in his hand. "Michael, are you unwell?"

"I'm fine! But, to be honest, I have been under an unusual amount of pressure at the Smithsonian."

"What kind of pressure?"

"Oh, the usual. Administrative matters. Employee problems. Budgets and all of that dry business that you really don't want to hear about."

"You look exhausted. Was it a bad train trip?"

"Yes, and I haven't been sleeping at all well." He tried to brighten. "No matter. Once I see Cliff Palace again, I'll be fine. You know how Mesa Verde always rejuvenates my mind and spirit."

"I do."

"Lisa," he said after a long pause of conversation, "do you remember how I once said that I was too old to marry you?"

"Of course, but I never believed that."

"Good! We should be married before we leave for Mesa Verde."

Lisa was momentarily speechless.

"Marry me, Lisa! I've thought of nothing else since boarding that train and starting West. Marry me and I'll never go back to the Smithsonian."

"Michael," she said, searching for the right words, "I am . . . flattered but I really don't understand this sudden change of attitude."

"I was wrong! I've admitted it. There's nothing mysterious about this proposal. Just marry me and let's become life partners and lovers. You have wanted that for a long time, haven't you?"

"Yes, but . . ."

He jumped up with agitation and reached for the decanter of brandy. Pouring himself another glass, he gulped it down and then said, "Lisa I *have* been gravely ill. But, worse yet, it's only fair to tell you that my professional reputation is under attack."

"Attack?"

"Yes, I've been accused of selling our Anasazi artifacts on the black market for personal gain."

"I don't believe that."

"I'm afraid that it's true."

"No!"

"Allow me to explain," he said, suddenly looking old and vulnerable. "Lisa, you've often asked about my family and I've been evasive."

"I decided that you must have your reasons."

"You are correct," he said, taking his seat again. "My past has a very dark side that I have tried to hide, even from you."

"What are you talking about?"

"I've been married. Her name was Clara and she was buried so deep in my past that not even Andrew was aware of her."

Lisa took a deep breath and waited to hear the rest.

"Clara and I were married very young and she never was a healthy or robust girl. Clara was not at all like you. She had a delicate constitution. And I, being foolish and blinded by love, allowed her to accompany me in my postdoctoral work in Central America."

"What happened to Clara?" Lisa whispered, not really wanting to know.

"Exactly twenty-three years ago she became pregnant. Clara was thrilled, as I was. However, she died soon after Angie was born in Honduras. Clara was the victim of yellow fever."

Michael's voice began to crack. "You see, there were no medical doctors in our part of the jungle. It was a nightmare then and remains so to this very day. I still awaken at night hearing her cries for help and the sobbing of a mind being consumed by fever."

"Oh, Michael, it wasn't your fault!" Lisa exclaimed, hugging him.

"I disagree. I put Clara at risk and I take the responsibility for her tragic death."

Michael's hand shook as he raised his glass to his lips, eyes distant as if he were traveling back to the fetid, feverish jungles of Honduras. "Clara's father, Mr. Garland Wingate, is a very wealthy and prominent businessman who has international connections. He had financed my graduate studies and I owed him far more than money. Clara was his only daughter, and when he found out we buried her in the jungle, the man went insane with anger. He took Angie and demanded that she be raised on his estate and that I never contact her again."

"And you agreed?"

"I had no choice! I was indebted to them. And I knew that Angie would be raised in circumstances far superior to what I ever could provide."

"I don't understand how you could do that!"

"I made a mistake. In those days I was consumed by ambition. I thought I was doing the right thing, that I was giving Angie the best chance for an easy and happy life."

"One without ever knowing her real father?"

"The Wingates were already acting like Angie's parents. They adored her. Lisa, I know it was wrong, but I was devastated by Clara's death so I relinquished my daughter to help clear my conscience. After that, I plunged into my work, determined to become famous. The truth of the matter is that my professional accomplishments now seem trivial in comparison to the price I paid."

"You must reestablish ties with your daughter," Lisa said.

Gary McCarthy

"And you've been much too hard on yourself for all these years. What has all this to do with the charges that you have sold Anasazi objects for personal gain?"

"I'm coming to that. Wingate approached me nine years ago and offered to buy some of our first Anasazi artifacts. He has many wealthy friends and had kept up on my professional career. I had just sold my house to . . ."

". . . give me the proceeds because of Andrew's death."

"Yes," Michael admitted, "and I was in severe financial difficulties. So . . . I sold a few artifacts. Duplicate pieces, just a few pieces of unremarkable pottery."

"I see nothing so terrible about that. After all, Richard Wetherill and his family have done very well selling Mesa Verde artifacts of every size and description."

"Yes, but the Smithsonian—which financed my Mesa Verde field work—has me under a contract that prohibits me from receiving personal gain."

Now Lisa was beginning to understand. "And Mr. Wingate must have discovered this."

"Certainly! But he never mentioned it until years later when I sold him some better pieces."

"Human remains from Mesa Verde?"

Michael sighed. "Yes. I was such a fool! Wingate next convinced me to invest the proceeds of my sales in the silver market."

"But why did you take such risks!"

"Because I wanted to repay the Smithsonian and make things right. And also so that I'd have something to offer you and Angie. Lisa, I've never made that much money and I'm a poor financial manager. I wanted to generate some wealth and security. I was too proud to ask you to marry me when you were so much better off. And I wanted Angie to believe that I had succeeded."

"In the silver market?" Lisa couldn't mask her disbelief.

"Yes! But that damned, scheming Wingate had obtained insider knowledge that Congress would pass a currency act

establishing gold as our country's new monetary standard.
When the legislation passed in March and it was signed into
law by that idiot, President McKinley, I lost everything."

"And now you are being blackmailed by your former father-in-law as well as by David Quincy?"

Michael paled. "How did you know about him?"

"He paid me a visit just a few hours ago."

"Then I'm finished!"

"So, Mr. Quincy *is* blackmailing you."

"I'm not sure. But David Quincy realizes I sold Anasazi
artifacts for personal gain. He has an important story which
will ruin me."

Lisa went to stand at her window and gaze out at her roses.
Flowers had always given her hope. "Michael, what do you
propose to do now?"

"What *can* I do?"

"Tell the truth to my friend and one of the best local edi-
tors! His name is Pierce Hannibal and I promise you that he
will tell the story honestly, with no axe to grind."

Michael was appalled. "Lisa, I'll be destroyed!"

"No you won't! We are human and we all make mistakes.
You are a wonderful scientist and a fine man. Admit your
errors and let's move on with our lives."

"I could be sent to prison!"

"I doubt that." Lisa took his trembling hands in her own.
"We have given a great deal of ourselves to Mesa Verde. Year
after year, we're the ones that have been down on our knees
every summer doing the hard, necessary scientific work. That
ought to be worth something!"

"But it won't be," he said. "I'll be banished from my work.
But at least I can clear your name. If nothing else, that is
important."

"How much do you owe for the objects you've sold?"

He shrugged as though it no longer mattered; the amount
was too great to repay.

"Michael! How much!"

"About six thousand, give or take a few hundred dollars. Mr. Wingate paid me just well enough so I'd never be able to repair the damage."

"Maybe I can come up with it," Lisa heard herself say.

"No!"

"My half of the accounting partnership is worth at least that much. And this house is paid off."

"Do you think I have no pride left? That I could ruin you, too?"

"Michael, listen to me! After I sell everything and pay off the Smithsonian, we'll still have enough left to go back East and meet your daughter. She deserves to know her real father! It's important. After that, we could move to some other place in the West—perhaps Santa Fe or Albuquerque. Those areas have Anasazi dwellings yet to be discovered, mapped and excavated."

"But even if your assets would settle the debt, I'd still be a pariah in my field. I'd be discredited and ruined."

"Then we'd just have to work for ourselves and find a way also to benefit science," Lisa said. "We'd make a pact never to sell to private collectors, no matter what they offered, but only to museums and historical societies."

Michael stared at her with disbelief. "And that's it? I take my chances on not going to prison, you ruin yourself financially, and then we hope to ride off into the sunset to dig up northern New Mexico?"

"That's it."

He slumped forward, head hanging low, then ran his fingers through his hair, Finally, he looked up and said, "All right, let's do it. But I won't marry you until this trouble passes. I won't compromise whatever shred of honor I have remaining."

"I'm not worried. I'll always be proud of you, Michael."

His voice thickened with emotion. "You really mean that, don't you?"

"With all my heart."

"All right," he said, voice husky with emotion. "Let's strike a compromise. I'll confess everything to your city editor friend and then we'll hurry off to Mesa Verde. If they don't come and put me in irons or there isn't a marshal waiting to arrest me this fall when we return to Denver, we'll be married."

"And we'll honeymoon back East to reunite you with your daughter."

"I love you so much," he choked as he gathered her in his arms.

"I love you too, Michael," Lisa answered, knowing that he really needed her now and that she had never loved him more.

Twenty-two

Mr. Pierce Hannibal, long-time editor and publisher of the *Denver Daily News,* listened to Lisa and Dr. Turner for nearly twenty minutes before he squinted over his expensive cigar and declared, "It would seem, Dr. Turner, that you have committed a professional breach of contract and a very serious error in judgment."

"I'm afraid so," Michael agreed. "And I deserve punishment. It's just that I want to make sure Mrs. Cannaday is in no way connected to my mistakes. She neither knew nor received any financial gain from the sale of the Mesa Verde artifacts."

"Of course she didn't," the editor said, glancing at Lisa. "I've known Mrs. Cannaday for a good many years now and I am totally confident that she has gained nothing and has sacrificed much in the name of archaeological science. And, as for yourself, I am sure that some way can be found to . . . well, mitigate the damage."

Michael leaned forward. "How? I'm guilty."

"Oh yes," Hannibal replied. "Not only of a breach of contract . . . but of violation of professional standards. And believe me, Dr. Turner, I neither condone nor forgive you that latter transgression. In every profession, we are held to certain standards that we must never consciously violate."

The editor studied Michael and then added, "However, the greatest attribute of mankind is forgiveness. You were under duress and you erred. Now, you repent and seek only to absolve Lisa from all complicity and to make the necessary reparations . . . six thousand dollars worth."

"Which I don't have," Michael admitted. "In fact, I expect to be dismissed from my position the moment the Smithsonian learns of my professional and contractual violations."

"I see."

"Pierce," Lisa began, "I can balance the books in this matter."

The editor's bushy eyebrows lifted. "Oh?"

"I won't allow her to do that," Michael quickly interjected.

Lisa folded her arms across her chest and spoke directly to the editor. "Dr. Turner has asked me to marry him when we return from Mesa Verde this fall and I have accepted. So you see, we are in this together."

The editor leaned forward and extended his hand. "Allow me to offer you congratulations!"

"Thank you," Lisa said. "But please don't announce our engagement now. And, as for Michael's situation, is there some way to . . ."

"No," the editor said, "I'm afraid that it must be publicized."

"He's right," Michael said. "If this newspaper doesn't break the story, David Quincy will publish it himself or give it to another paper. God only knows what they will print."

"Exactly so," Hannibal said, tapping his cigar along the rim of a silver ash tray. "And this newspaper will publish the story without either sensationalizing or minimizing the facts. When are you leaving for Mesa Verde?"

Lisa and Michael exchanged glances. With so much facing Michael, they hadn't even talked about their departure.

"Well?" the editor persisted.

"Mr. Hannibal, do you think it wise to leave, given the mess that I'm in?"

"I believe you must. The sooner the better. Tomorrow, if possible."

"But why?"

Pierce Hannibal came to his feet and began to pace back and forth. He was past his prime, and overweight, but he possessed restless energy and did his best thinking on his feet. "Dr. Turner, the way I see this," he began, "is that this David Quincy has enough evidence to destroy you professionally right now. He no doubt will put the facts in the most disagreeable light in order to sensationalize his story. His angle will be that Mesa Verde has been plundered and exploited yet again."

"You're probably right," Michael said, looking desolate.

"Of course I am! If he's any journalist at all, that's the angle that will create the most outrage and interest in Denver. Given that fact, I believe that the wisest action we can take is to break the story first in the *Denver Daily News*. We won't alter the truth, but we'll soften the story by revealing the motives that drove you to your mistakes."

"I see."

"And," Hannibal added, "by printing the story first, we'll take the wind right out of Mr. Quincy's sails."

Lisa agreed. "Pierce is right, Michael. Let him break the story."

"Whatever you both say. But I still question whether or not we should run off to Mesa Verde. I'm not afraid to face the public and take my medicine."

"Nonsense!" Hannibal boomed. "The public is quick to anger but also quick to forgive. By the time you and Lisa return this fall, they'll be stirred up about other matters. There is one thing that I would strongly suggest."

"And that is?"

Hannibal's eyes narrowed and he leaned forward. "Work like beavers all summer! Take pictures, write articles, create a major discovery. Do something spectacular."

"That's not very likely," Michael confessed. "We've about exhausted any chance of a major find. But . . ."

"Bring me back some very important story when you return this fall," Hannibal urged, stabbing the air with his smoking cigar. "I want photographs and a tale of the ancient Indians so gripping that my readers wouldn't give a damn even if you put a ton of dynamite in Cliff Palace and blew it to smithereens!"

"Are you serious?" Lisa asked, trying not to smile.

"Of course I am!" the editor exclaimed. "The public loves to tear people down and then build them up again, bigger and better than ever."

"Pierce, what exactly will you print about Michael in tomorrow's news?"

"Just the bare facts and quite a bit about his accomplishments and the sorrow of never knowing his own child. Dr. Turner, I'll put you in a very sympathetic light. Believe me, this is a human interest story with the spicy ingredients of money, pride, corruption and family blackmail. I have no intention of whitewashing your sins but, at the same time, you deserve a good measure of sympathy."

"What about Lisa?"

"When I finish this story, she will be hailed as a courageous widow willing to sacrifice everything for love . . . and science."

Lisa knew better than to object, even though she wanted to. Instead, she asked, "Pierce, does that mean my accounting firm will retain your business?"

"Certainly! That is, assuming Bruce Humphries will continue to give us his personal attention."

"I intend to sell my share of the business to him."

The editor scowled. "That would be a real pity. And, as for you, Dr. Turner, I predict you will survive this crisis. But it would make things ever so much easier if you and Lisa could generate a major archaeological discovery on Mesa Verde this summer, something more newsworthy than pottery and bones. Something my readers will relate to deep in their guts and in their hearts."

"That's a tall order, Mr. Hannibal."

"Perhaps, but you are exceptional people," the editor replied. "Think about what we've discussed. Bring this newspaper back a scientific sensation!"

"We'll try," Lisa promised when Michael offered no response. "We'll try harder than we've ever tried before."

"I know you will," Hannibal said, "and that's all any of us can ever really do."

Lisa's jaw was set with determination when she left the editor. She would set steps in motion to generate money to repay the Smithsonian, and do so without regret. After all, the archaeological work she and Michael shared made all else seem trivial.

Their trip to Mesa Verde was unlike any they'd taken in the past. Michael was completely preoccupied with his dark thoughts.

"I'd just like to know what you are thinking," Lisa said as they led their pack animals up the long, familiar trail onto the high mesa.

It was a sunwashed afternoon but, thankfully, there was a refreshing breeze rolling down from the higher elevations. Michael removed his hat, wiped perspiration from his forehead, and replied, "I just keep thinking that there ought to be some way to avoid your having to sell your accounting practice in order to keep me from going to jail."

"There isn't," Lisa told him as they dismounted in the shade of a pine and let the horses rest. "All we can do is put the past behind us and try to make this the most important summer of our lives."

Sarcasm edged into his voice, "Yes, I almost forgot, we need a scientific sensation. Isn't that what Mr. Hannibal asked for?"

"Michael, stop it," Lisa snapped. "Pierce just wants an exciting story. Something that will grab his readers and deflect the disapproval we're going to face when we return to Denver."

"Maybe we'll even stumble upon a perfectly preserved mummy with a note telling us his or her life story."

"I don't want to hear any more of this," Lisa clipped. "I know it's a tall order but I was thinking we could retake some pictures of Cliff Palace, then . . ."

"That's not what Pierce has in mind and you know it. He's asking us to do the impossible."

Lisa sympathized with Michael's frustration but she had her own idea. "Michael, I don't believe that we need to make any *new* discovery but instead we need to interpret what we've already found."

"Meaning?"

"We have to do more than find new artifacts. We must reveal the mystery of those vanished people. We need to uncover evidence about why the cliff dwellers vanished from Mesa Verde."

"They probably were under siege," Michael said. "And yet, we've found almost no evidence of violence."

"Then they must have been decimated by famine or disease. Perhaps they eventually surrendered or even joined with a larger, fiercer people. You're the scientist. You tell me and then we write a story for the *Denver Daily News* that is based on scientific evidence."

"Dammit, Lisa, I'm not a dime novelist spinning fanciful tales set in the American West! I can't create characters and situations that are not supported by scientific evidence."

"But you can speculate based on our findings and . . ."

"I can't! I'd be ridiculed by my colleagues."

"Damn your colleagues!"

Lisa was so angry she cut their rest stop short and remounted. "Michael, I'm not suggesting that you fabricate anything. But the truth is that no one is better qualified to write about these mysterious people than you. Pierce was trying to say that it's story time."

"Story time is for children."

Lisa bit back a reply as she gathered the lead ropes and

forced her saddle horse up the steep trail. She was just as troubled as Michael but at least she and her editor friend understood what they had to do this summer in order to redeem Michael's professional reputation.

July was hot on Mesa Verde and August brought thunderstorms and soaring humidity. Lisa worked hard, but her heart wasn't in the effort and she kept expecting to see a local marshal appear with a warrant for Michael's arrest. But the days passed uneventfully as they struggled to excavate a large, two-story pueblo that had collapsed on itself centuries earlier. Lisa kept praying that they would uncover a skeleton with a stone axe or knife buried in its chest or something . . . anything . . . to fire Michael's imagination and enthusiasm.

By early September and, with only a few weeks left before they would have to return to Denver, Michael lost all interest in their pueblo excavations. Hollow-eyed and haggard from poor sleep and chronic depression, he had taken to wandering off to explore the dozens of small canyons and arroyos that channeled snow and rain off the mesa. When Lisa questioned him about his long absences, he avoided her eyes and muttered, "I need to search where no one has before."

"I thought that was what we were doing."

"No," he replied in a vague, disquieting manner. "That's not what I mean."

"Then what do you mean?"

"I'm not sure," he admitted, wagging his head back and forth with dejection. "But, if I am to find something dramatic, it's not going to be at this pueblo. We're almost out of time. I'm desperate and need a miracle."

Lisa tried to cheer him up but failed. Michael seemed to have lost all interest in the mesa top and spent every daylight hour in his lonely explorations of side canyons. Lisa grew anxious from the moment he left until the time he returned; if he twisted a knee or ankle, or fell and injured himself, he might never be found. Even so, she knew better than to object to his long absences. The best she could do to keep her own spirits up was to work hard on their latest pueblo excavation, probing for the unusual or dramatic artifact that might shed fresh light upon the mystery of the Anasazi people.

During the first two weeks of September, Lisa discovered bone awls and needles, as well as three metates and several fire drills. But the prize discovery was a set of bone gaming pieces with unusual markings. "It's clear they loved to gamble," she said.

But Michael showed no interest. "They won't help us," he said. "No miracle there."

Lisa stomped away, feeling hurt and betrayed. For the next week, they hardly spoke, and each morning they awoke to see the mesa glittering with frost as the nights grew cold. Their supplies ran low and Lisa spent more time hunting for fresh meat. Sometimes, she felt so discouraged that she would gaze off at clouds and wonder what would happen next. She loved Michael and she really didn't mind selling her share of the accounting business, but Michael seemed broken and she worried that he would never recover.

And then, one gray and overcast day in early October, she heard Michael shouting again and again as he burst out of the forest, waving his arms as though he had gone berserk.

Lisa's first thought was that he was being chased by a bear or cougar. Or that he was fleeing arrest. Then she realized that Michael was laughing.

"Lisa!"

She jumped out of an excavated depression, spilling tools. Her face was streaked with sweat.

"Lisa, I found an *entire wall* of petroglyphs. They're incredible! Just amazing!"

"Where!"

"About three miles from here down in a canyon that I doubt anyone has ever explored." He grabbed her hands, squeezing them so hard they hurt. "Lisa, this wall is coated with a layer of mud and overgrown with brush but I think it tells the entire story of Mesa Verde's lost people!"

"Can you interpret it?"

"I think so." He bent over to catch his breath. "I didn't even take the time to clear away all the brush but I can tell you that we finally have a story."

"Take me there!"

"Sure, but let's just slow down. And . . . and we had better bring some tools and some gunny sacks to clean the wall's surface."

"How big is the petroglyph?"

"Ten or fifteen feet square. It has to be the history of these people. I've interpreted petroglyphs, both on this continent as well as in the jungles of Central America, and I'm certain that we finally have made a breakthrough!"

Tears of joy clouded Lisa's eyes. She hugged Michael with all her strength and then practically dragged him back toward the canyon's rim in her excitement to witness this great new discovery.

It took them almost two hours to descend into the little canyon and locate the petroglyph wall. When Lisa first saw it, she was amazed that Michael had found this astounding treasure. It was camouflaged with mud, gravel and vegetation that had taken root wherever there was even a tiny fracture in the mostly smooth wall face. But despite all of that, Lisa could immediately detect the precisely chiseled figures and symbols which some ancient stoneworker and storyteller had pecked into the hard rock surface. Crude but striking images of human hands, birds, animals and Anasazi hunters were displayed among long concentric grooves that Michael said represented the paths of Anasazi life as it had been experienced more than six centuries ago.

"You've done it!" Lisa cried, overcome with emotion. "This is a miracle! But will you have time to decipher it before we must return to Denver?"

"I will even if I have to chip away ice and snow all winter," he vowed. "Right now, with most of the petroglyph covered by dirt and brush, I'm not sure what we'll learn but I expect this could be the most significant Southwestern archaeological discovery since Richard Wetherill and Charlie Mason first stumbled upon Cliff Palace."

"Can you tell anything about it yet?"

Michael used his finger to trace a few symbols and lines in order to translate their meaning. "There is no doubt in my mind that this is the entire story of Mesa Verde. For example, note this circle and this groove that passes by Sun. And this huge bird hovering over everything is either an eagle or a raven."

"It looks more like a raven," Lisa decided, "you can tell that from the shape of its head and the absence of a hook in its beak. Also, it has no talons."

"I see what you mean," Michael agreed. "Then I expect these people called themselves Raven People—or People of the Raven Clan. Anyway, this petroglyph is like reading a history book. It will tell us how the Mesa Verde Anasazi hunted, fished, farmed and created the elaborate pueblos and irrigation systems we've discovered and mapped up above. Once it is all uncovered, we'll also find symbols relating to their religion, fertility and passage of life during the seasons."

"Do you see any evidence of enemies and war?" Lisa asked.

"Not yet," he said, fingers scraping away crusted mud, "but I expect to."

"Then we really have unlocked the puzzle," Lisa breathed.

"Yes," he agreed. "You can write a human interest story for the *Denver Daily News*."

"You want me to write it?"

"Absolutely! I can write scientific articles but that isn't what your editor friend wants."

"No," she said, "it isn't. But we don't want a complete fable."

"Don't worry," he assured her. "We'll not only use what

we read on this wall, but also incorporate everything we've learned this last decade during our research."

"Yes," she said, with growing excitement. "I've always been a good letter writer. Why, I've even tried my hand at poetry."

"You'll be perfect! My prose is so dry and lifeless that Mr. Hannibal would find it unprintable. But I know that you will do a wonderful job."

"As long as it is printed under your byline."

"Why not both our bylines?"

"Because you're the authority and it will be better received with your name alone. Besides, the entire point of this is to give your reputation a boost."

"I suppose. But I wish that . . ."

"It's your career that is in jeopardy," she reminded him. "The satisfaction I'll have from seeing Pierce's face when he reads the article will be enough reward."

"You're wonderful."

Lisa could not believe the change in Michael. It was as if a weight had suddenly been lifted from his shoulders making him appear ten years younger.

"Michael," she said, "in the morning, we can move our camp and horses as close as possible and then drag our tent, food and supplies right down into this canyon so that we won't lose a moment of working daylight."

He glanced up at the dark clouds building to the north. "It wouldn't hurt if we had a rain hard enough to wash some of this mud-coat away."

"I'm sure that would help."

"I think it would make a big difference if we ripped all the vegetation out by its roots and then painstakingly broke up every square inch of crusted surface on this wall," Michael told her.

Lisa searched for a hand-sized rock.

"We just have to be careful," Michael warned. "We don't

want to be inserting our own sentences into the pages of their history."

"Are you serious?"

"Yes! Even a few unintentional marks could give rise to misinterpretation or confusion."

Lisa hefted a stone and pressed it against the dirt-caked wall. "Gently," she reminded herself out loud as she began tapping at the crust very much as some long-forgotten Anasazi storyteller would have done. "Gently."

It stormed that night but neither Lisa nor Michael complained. Instead, they snuggled together in their blankets chewing venison and tending a small, sizzling campfire. Huge, brilliant bolts of lightning shafted across the indigo sky, momentarily exposing their mesa in an eerie white light. Thunder cannonaded up and down the canyons and they were forced to hobble their animals in addition to keeping them tethered among sheltering trees.

"In this downpour," Lisa said, her hair plastered to her face and her skin glowing in the firelight, "I think we're going to find your petroglyph wall washed as clean as glass."

"I trust you're right," he said, staring out at the pounding rain. "And I just hope that the story we have uncovered is exciting enough for the *Denver Daily News.*"

Neither slept that night. Although the rain was still falling at dawn, they couldn't wait to see their petroglyph.

"Oh, sweet Jesus thank you!" Michael cried, rushing up and placing both palms on the rain-washed wall. "Lisa, just look at what we have found!"

Lisa stared at the great rock tabloid, trying hard to imagine what Michael would learn when he finally translated the mystery of Mesa Verde. She would tell the story from the point of view of the artist, so long ago, who had spent years chipping away at this stone wall in order to pass on his life history across many, many Southwestern centuries.

* * *

THE MYSTERY OF MESA VERDE AND
CLIFF PALACE
exclusively written for
THE DENVER DAILY NEWS
*as interpreted from an
Ancient Anasazi Petroglyph
by*
Dr. Michael Turner

*My name is Storyteller and I am of the Raven Peoples. I
live in great cave where I was born. I am not a hunter or
leader but what I have to say will last forever.*

*My story begins with my ancestors who rest in all the
places I have ever walked. From childhood I learned about
great warriors that came from far away and hunted with
throwing sticks. These sticks threw stone-tipped spears into
animals that were once plentiful but my ancestors became so
skillful they killed everything on these mesas. Now our hunters must walk long distances and only Mother Earth gives
us good food.*

*My father was a storyteller as was his father back until
the first of our Raven Peoples fled from the low desert country. I do not know exactly when people first lived in cliff caves
but I have seen their bones and weapons. Now, we are the
last of the cave dwellers and there will be no more.*

*Many lifetimes ago my people lived on the mesa tops and
built homes under the ground. Later they only built round
ceremonial places underground and we have kept them always. Their homes on the mesa top were good and were put
wherever crops would not grow. My ancestors built many
canals and a great reservoir to catch and hold the melted
snow. They were always happy. The ancient Raven Peoples
never knew hunger until their enemies in the desert became
hungry and began to steal their crops and burn their cornfields. Legend tells me that one year Desert Enemies came
in the night and took precious seeds so that my ancestors*

had none for spring planting. Many then died of hunger and my ancestors were no longer strong enough to defeat the Desert Enemies.

Now I mark this story on rock for all to see the great sadness of the Raven Peoples. I tell you that many enemies have been killed but also many Raven People. Women and children were taken away and our dogs and turkeys all slaughtered. The leaders of our people prayed and danced seeking words from Raven and the great spirits. They were told to move back down into the cliffs like our first ancestors and then to build houses which we could forever defend.

My ancestors built a great city and multiplied until they were again strong. But the Desert Enemies still raided and burned our crops on the mesa so life became hard again. They could not burn our cliff houses or steal our corn seeds because we shot and speared them when they tried to climb.

Not all peoples are enemies. We trade with the Chacoans and sometimes they come here to live in the hot time of year along with peoples from other far away places who trade with us for turquoise, shells, feathers, arrow points and silver.

Many bad seasons of deep snow killed my people and they were buried in our waste. This has sickened our people so that more and more die. I tell you that we cannot fight the Desert Enemies any longer. Maybe soon, we will go away from here and find a better place with wood, more water and Deer as it was in the beginning. I do not know. I am only Storyteller and that is my story.

Now, I will cover this rock to hide it from our enemies if we are all killed. But maybe we will go away to join the Chacoans. I do not know for I am not a leader. Maybe in a better place the Raven Peoples will again multiply and then one of my sons or their sons will also become Storyteller.

At the editor's office of the *Denver Daily News*, Pierce Hannibal placed Lisa's article on his desk and closed his eyes for a few moments as if listening to the fading voice of Storyteller.

"Well?" Michael finally asked. "Is it all right?"

"It is excellent," the editor said with a broad smile as he opened his eyes and leaned back in his chair, beaming. "It's not nearly as long as I'd like, but we can expand it."

"Expand it?" Lisa asked.

"Yes!" Hannibal exclaimed, eyes bright with excitement. "And we need to develop Storyteller as a person, with a romantic name," Hannibal mused aloud. "How about Kokoman or . . ."

Michael groaned but Lisa giggled and said, "I see no harm, as long as everyone understands he's fiction."

"Exactly! Our readers aren't imbeciles. They understand that you have created a prehistoric character, setting and a situation. But so what? They'll love this guy and want to know everything about him and his wife and sons."

"Oh now wait a minute, Mr. Hannibal!" Michael cried, bouncing to his feet. "We got lucky but this literary nonsense you're suggesting is entirely out of line."

"Is it?"

Hannibal reached for one of his expensive cigars, myopic eyes squinting as he struck a match and inhaled. "Dr. Turner, may I suggest that anything that sells newspapers and is not false but clearly has to be fiction is neither out of line nor in any way unethical? After all, my assumption is that this article is based on years of your scientific research at Mesa Verde, and there must have been a Storyteller for he left you with the history of his people, is that not so?"

"Yes it is, but only in the nature of a very broad interpretation."

"How broad?"

"What do you mean?"

"I mean," the editor said, squinting through spectacles and smoke, "were they really called the Raven Peoples . . . or something of that nature? And did their earliest ancestors really use spear throwing sticks?"

"Yes, we call them atlatls."

"There! See my point? Fiction steeped in fact."

Michael brushed his hand across his eyes. "Mr. Hannibal, there is little doubt about those facts, but . . ."

"And, Dr. Turner, did these Anasazi first live in the cliffs as simple hunters and, across the centuries, evolve into an agrarian society which later constructed pueblos and these kivas? And did they not complete their societal evolution by constructing places like Cliff Palace and those other magnificent edifices of stone?"

"Of course!" Michael cried with mounting exasperation. "The evidence leaves no doubt about that. But I'm not entirely sure they were destroyed by desert enemies."

The editor scowled. "They couldn't have all gotten sick with some plague, could they?"

"Not likely."

"Then they had to either be destroyed by enemies or enslaved! Either way, you can write a splendid series, gripping human-interest stuff that will not only increase my readership but entertain and enlighten based on your best professional judgement."

Michael looked to Lisa for help.

"We're writing *pre*history, Michael," she said. "There can't be any question of that. What's the harm?"

"You'll become a celebrity!" Hannibal said. "Your sins will be completely forgiven. A few weeks after we ran your story, it was old news."

"What about David Quincy?" Lisa asked.

"He disappeared!" Hannibal laughed. "Right after we ran the story, he came in for a visit. I expected him to be upset but he wasn't. In fact, Mr. Quincy congratulated me on the story and then he said that the real story was yet to be told."

"What the hell did he mean by that?" Michael demanded.

"I thought you might know," Hannibal replied.

"Well, I don't."

"No matter. The important thing, Dr. Turner, is that you will be in immense demand as a public speaker. And I have no doubt that you can generate far more interest in Mesa Verde and the Anasazi with a sizzling series of Storyteller articles than you could ever hope to have done writing in some scientific journal. Hell, no one reads those things except academics hoping to discover some tiny flaw so that they can rip open a colleague's jugular."

For the first time since entering the editor's plush office, Michael actually grinned. "No offense, sir, but how would you know about that?"

"My father was a medical doctor. I've perused stacks of their publications and, believe it or not, I even subscribe to a few technical journals written for the publishing trade. Dry, pompous stuff."

"Lisa," Michael asked, "what do you say?"

"I agree with Hannibal. I'm sure we can come up with a series. We can even talk about it on our honeymoon."

"Honeymoon!" Hannibal exclaimed with alarm. "My dear Lisa, there is absolutely no time for that now. The moment our Storyteller series begins I'll be besieged for more articles."

Lisa almost burst into laughter. "Maybe," she said, "I have just found myself a new profession."

"*You* wrote all of this?" Hannibal asked with amazement.

"With Michael's help and direction."

"I'm a scientist," he said a little stiffly. "She's your storyteller."

"Remarkable, Lisa! And I thought you were a frustrated amateur archaeologist." Pierce Hannibal smacked his lips and blew a big smokering over their heads. "I predict that we are going to have a very, very good run with this series. Better, I suspect, than you might imagine."

"That would be nice," Lisa said.

"So when can I expect the second article of your new Storyteller series? A weekly would be perfect."

Lisa took a deep breath and expelled it slowly. Michael obviously wasn't thrilled by this new enterprise, but Lisa had a hunch she was going to enjoy it immensely.

Several minutes later, as Michael and Lisa were preparing to leave, Hannibal called out, "One last thing."

They paused in the doorway.

"Dr. Turner, do you think Storyteller died of natural causes, or was he killed by those Desert Enemies?"

Michael turned away but Lisa answered, "Pierce," she said with a wink, "I'm afraid you're just going to have to wait until the end of the series to find out."

When Lisa turned to follow Michael, Pierce Hannibal's laughter followed her through the busy newsroom and right out into the street.

Twenty-three

THE STORYTELLER

Spring, 1264 A.D.
Cliff Palace, Mesa Verde

Storyteller was old and his teeth were almost gone, causing his body to become very thin and weak each winter. Like all the old ones among the Raven People, he suffered terribly from rheumatism during the cold months. He had labored hard all his life helping to build a protected city in Great Cave where seventeen clans numbering almost four hundred Mesa Verde Anasazi lived. During his many years of faithful labor for the Raven People, every knuckle of Storyteller's hands had been smashed at least once against rock as had many of his other bones, some of which had never mended properly.

Despite these infirmities, he was happy. His position demanded high respect, earned after years of listening to the Raven People's earlier Storytellers and then remembering their words. Now, as the first of spring's chinook winds flowed up from the low desert country to thaw the deep snows, Storyteller pressed his withered flesh against the warming rocks fronting Great Cave. He had not expected to live through this past winter, so he was filled with prayers and gratitude as he watched his people prepare for a new cycle of seasons during which he would again be privileged to tell and retell the story of the Raven People, especially to those children already wise enough to listen.

Ten-year-old Xcinco was one of the older children who sat at the feet of Storyteller this first balmy day of spring. Xcinco, the precocious son of one of the Great Cave's architects, would have much preferred to have played on the rocks that tumbled down into the canyon or even, had the footholds leading up to the mesa top been cleaned, have gone with his father and brothers who were inspecting their fields and soon would be planting.

"Great Cave is the center of our people," Storyteller was saying as his clear brown eyes moved slowly about the great cavern, missing nothing that was taking place among the people who filled his world with talk and laughter. Storyteller's eyes noted the sly and admiring glances that flowed between the young men and women, but he also heard the deep, racking coughs of the old who were battling sickness and possible death.

But now Storyteller had an audience and, at this point in his life, storytelling was his purpose. "Great Cave," he began, "is the place where our first peoples came after they had escaped Middle Earth and then the deserts.

"This is the happiest time of the year. Spring is the season of new life, of prayers and planting. The time when all of Earth is glad as are the Raven People. Look at the trees and see the new buds and notice the flowers that poke their pretty laughing faces up to the warmth of Sun! Hear how sweetly the birds sing as Water tumbles down our canyon. Everything born in spring is especially blessed, but things born in winter will sicken and die."

"Was I born in spring?" Xcinco dared to ask Storyteller.

The old man gathered his bony chin in his swollen arthritic hands. He gave the matter serious thought and then, not wanting to disappoint, nodded his head saying, "Yes, Xcinco, you were blessed to be born in spring."

Never mind that, as the other children asked the same question, they were all given the same pleasing answer.

Emboldened by being so special, Xcinco rested his chin in the cradle of his hands and said, "Will you tell us the story of how the People came from Middle Earth to this world?"

"Of course." Storyteller yawned; the unaccustomed warmth of Sun made him sleepy. He decided that today's version of the creation story would be short.

"In the beginning," he began, "the People all lived in Middle Earth and were very happy. They lived peacefully and were governed by Great Chief and many priests who were wise and good. The People were never cold or hungry. But after a long time, the priests became too many and divided their favors so that some of the People found themselves more or less favored than others."

"Did the People fight each other?" Xcinco asked.

"In time, they did," Storyteller confessed, making a very sad face. "Some of the rich priests took the wives of the poorest men and soon everyone was fighting and no one listened to the Great Chief anymore. Great Chief, whose given name I have forgotten and which is not important today, called all the priests to a council and asked them for their advice on how to make the People equal and happy again. But the priests could not agree upon anything and soon, even they began to fight."

"Did they live in the ceremonial kivas where the men live today?" a girl asked.

"No," Storyteller told the girl, "because they already were living down in Middle Earth. But anyway, Great Chief grew even angrier and called upon Owl to give him advice. Owl is very wise, you know."

The children nodded and Storyteller's voice changed slightly so that they would know that he was speaking, not in his own voice, but that of Owl. " 'Great Chief, why do your people fight among themselves?'

" 'Because we have lost our vision and Middle Earth is growing too small.'

" 'This is true,' Owl said, turning his large eyes up to the top of Middle Earth. 'The People have become too many. Once, when you were few, there was no such thing as priests and poorer people. All were equal, or very nearly so.'

"But what can be done about this?' Great Chief asked.

" 'There is a bigger place called Upper Earth,' Owl answered. 'I have not seen it, but I know it exists.'

" 'Who told you about this?' "

Storyteller frowned in silence, then said, "Children, Owl is very wise but he could not remember. But then he said, 'I think maybe it was Eagle.'

" 'Call him,' Great Chief pleaded.

"When Owl called, Eagle swooped out of the Middle Sky and landed among the quarreling council. He did not know of Upper Earth, either, but said that he would fly up to see if it were really there."

Storyteller stopped speaking and asked for water, which was promptly given to him. He ladled it from a small water pot, spilling nearly as much on himself as he swallowed, but the children knew enough not to laugh.

Refreshed, Storyteller continued. "Eagle could not fly high enough to escape Middle Earth and he was almost dead when he came back down to the council where all the People were gathered anxiously to wait."

" 'Did you see it!' the priests cried, all speaking at once.

" 'Yes,' Eagle said, 'but it is too high for me to reach.'

" 'Then who can reach it?' Great Chief asked. He and all the priests tipped their heads far back and stared up at the top of Middle Earth but were unable to see the hole leading into Upper Earth.

" 'Raven,' Owl said. 'His wings are strong and he is very wise. Not that you, Eagle, are not also wise.'

" 'Raven is wiser and can fly higher to see all the world above,' Eagle replied, not really meaning it but still so weak that he did not want to be asked to try to find Upper World again.

"Owl then called Raven, who came swooping down high above the clouds where the sky was dark. As he came down to the People, they could see that Raven was very strong indeed and an even better flier than Eagle. When asked if he would try to find Upper Earth, Raven agreed. Prayers were made for him and all the People blew sacred smoke on his great wings and gave him their special blessings."

Storyteller paused and craned his own skinny neck up at the sky. He raised a bony, crooked finger and began to make a circular motion as he continued. "Raven did not start off so fast as Eagle, for he was much wiser. Instead, he slowly began to circle higher and higher until he looked like a fly and then . . . he was gone! The People waited almost until sundown, singing prayers and smoking their pipes. As darkness grew heavy and their hopes began to fail, Raven suddenly appeared!"

"Look!" little Xcinco cried, knowing Storyteller's words by heart. "It is Raven!"

Storyteller was not pleased to be upstaged. "Xcinco, you should not try to tell the story of your people! I alone am allowed to do that."

"I am sorry," Xcinco said, hating the snickers of the other children. "But isn't that exactly what the People cried when they saw Raven floating down from high above, no bigger than a fly?"

"Yes," Storyteller said, "it is. Black Raven and blackness came together so fires were lighted to guide Raven to the People and their anxious council of priests who cried, 'Raven, what did you see?'

"Raven did not immediately answer, for he was very tired. He asked for food and drink and when it was taken and he had regained his strength, he told the People that he had found Upper Earth and that it was so big that the People never would be able to fill it and would have so much food, water, shelter and good land that they all would become as wealthy as the priests and no one would ever need to fight again.

" 'But how will we reach Upper Earth?' one of the council priests asked.

"Everyone looked to Great Chief but when he shook his head, they then looked to Owl, who said that even he did not know.

" 'What about you, Raven?' Eagle asked.

"Raven was pleased to be asked such a hard question and although he did not want to show the People that he not only was stronger than Eagle but also wiser than Owl, he finally said, 'I saw tall trees in Upper World. Trees that touched the clouds and tickled the belly of that sky.'

" 'But what good would such trees do us?' Great Chief asked.

" 'Tomorrow, when I am well rested, I will fly back through the hole into Upper Earth and get the seed of this tree and bring it back for planting. If you pray and water this tree, it will grow so tall that you and the People can climb it into Upper Earth.'

"Owl nodded, for he knew this was true, and he told Raven that he was the wisest and strongest of all birds. Raven, being modest, protested but the People knew that Owl's words were truth, so they named themselves the Raven People."

"But Storyteller, how long did it take for the tree to grow into Upper Earth?" Tani asked.

"The seed that Raven brought down to Middle Earth was blessed by the Great Spirit who still watches over us all. The People watered and took good care of the tree and even placed prayer sticks on its lower branches. It became the center of their life and it began to grow faster than weeds or corn or anything you have ever seen. Faster and faster until it grew up through the hole in the sky so that all the People could climb into Upper Earth where we now live in harmony."

"Even the old ones, older than you, could climb it, Story-teller?" a little girl asked.

"Yes," Storyteller said, deciding that he could wait no
longer to take his first nap of spring on the flat rock where
he had napped for the past few years. It had been swept clean
and made ready by the old women for his pleasure. "Even
older ones than me climbed that tree to Upper Earth. They
are buried all around us, but we must never search for their
bones or even speak their names."

Storyteller pushed himself erect, swaying on his spindly
legs. Steadying himself, he yawned, then shuffled to his napping rock where a rabbit-skin robe awaited his pleasure.
Stretching out in the warm sun, he soon was dreaming of
Raven and the magic tree that reached all the way up into
this world.

In the days and weeks that followed, Xcinco heard many
stories but he also spent a good deal of his time playing, and
setting traps for squirrels and chipmunks which he would
skin and present to his mother.

"Why is it that you and the women are making water jars
and pottery?" he asked.

"Because this is the time for it," his mother replied. "The
ground is soft and we can easily dig out the best clay that is
found just under the mesa. Also, making pottery takes much
water and it is everywhere now because of the melting snow."

She patted Xcinco's head in a way that he hated. He would
be her last and favorite child and this he also hated for sometimes she treated him like a girl.

"Xcinco, today you can help me gather the clay and make
a big water jar."

"No, Mother!"

"Yes," she said sternly, "my hands and feet hurt. I need
your help so that my family will not go thirsty this summer
when the hot winds blow and the streams and springs go
dry."

Xcinco did not like to be with the women who were always

ordering him to fetch this thing and that. Instead, he yearned to disappear into the canyon to set his squirrel traps and to practice shooting his small, well-made bow and arrows. But his mother was leader of his clan; she owned their house and she owned the land that his father, older brothers and sisters and even their husbands farmed on the mesa. Besides, if he helped her make a water jar, she would secretly reward him, usually with a very tasty succulent morsel of meat or corn bread flavored with spring herbs or tangy red and blue berries. Xcinco especially loved to eat a bowlful of corn mush spiced with flavorful puffballs that sprouted each spring and then were mixed liberally with salt and wild onions.

"Are you going to make pottery again all spring with your mother?" Tani asked mockingly as she passed him, following her own mother up to the clay gathering place.

Xcinco snatched up a small rock and hit the girl in her skinny, wagging backside hard enough to make her yip. Before Tani could retaliate, Xcinco was bounding down the canyonside howling with laughter. Later, he would be punished by Tani's mother who was as stern and protective as his own. But for now, Xcinco did not care.

For three days Xcinco helped his mother dig up the wet, clinging blue-gray clay and then carried it back down to Great Cave so that they could make pottery. During that time, Xcinco was also forced momentarily to turn his own backside to Tani so that she could hit him with a rock. It was humiliating but did not hurt much because, like all girls, Tani could not throw well.

It seemed everyone who wasn't up in the fields, or recovering from the rigors of winter, was either making pottery or replastering their houses and building new ones for those who were soon to be married. There were a few boys his own age who also were being humiliated by woman's work, but that did not make it any easier for Xcinco. His only joy was in the times that he could sneak off and listen to Storyteller.

When he was with Storyteller, even his mother dared no
drag him back to the awful pottery making.

"Potsherds," his mother said as she began to mix wate
into the clay. "I need more potsherds! And this time, hurry
Xcinco!"

He hated to hurry. Even worse, he was afraid of meeting
Tani and some of her girlfriends in the trash heap where they
would dig for broken pottery. Xcinco did not know what good
it did to add the old pottery fragments to the new, but he did
know that it was essential or else the clay they used to make
new pots would shrink and crack when it was being fired
His mother often had told him that the new pottery was always
part of the ancient pottery so that, even in eating and drinking
they would be aided by the spirits of their ancestors. Xcinco
liked to believe that, but he still hated making pottery, one
part of the old with plenty of water and two parts of the new
clay.

When the mixture was firmed, he and his mother rolled it
into ropes no wider than their fingers but at least twice as
long. These ropes were then coiled, one on top of the other,
around and around until the jar or pot itself took form. Each
rope was pinched into the next so that all were closely joined.
The inside and outside of cooking vessels that would be tested
by fire were left rough and furrowed between the coils. There
was no point in decorating these vessels, for soon they would
be coated with soot.

Water jars, mugs and all other pottery was usually
smoothed both on the inside and the outside so that the potter
could add a thin glaze of white clay before it was left to bake
in the sun. After that, each piece would need to be polished
with a smooth stone. Paint made from the dark brown liquid
of boiled beeweed would mark each piece of pottery as to its
proud maker.

The first time Xcinco was allowed to use a yucca plant
brush and paint pottery, he had practiced by tracing various
designs in the dirt.

"You must never do that!" his mother had exclaimed in a sharp reprimand as she brushed away an hour of trial designs. "Xcinco, you must always pray for a design and let the spirits guide your hand. This is our way."

"But why?" Xcinco had demanded, feeling the accusing looks of the other pottery makers digging into his flesh as if he had committed some terrible betrayal.

"In all of life, we must give ourselves over to the spirits or else they will feel neglected and become angry. They could send witches to punish you with sickness or even death!"

Xcinco's defiance was instantly replaced by fear because everyone knew that the evil witches were everywhere, even hiding in some of the People. He did not question his mother or ever try to first draw designs after that. And it was then that he realized that this practice was also followed in the building of new living compartments, stairways, courtyards and kivas. Nothing was drawn, but all came from prayer and inspiration brought about by asking for help from the good spirits that fought to protect the People from the evil witches.

The final step in making of the pottery was to fire it in special pits. This process was as vital as any of those before it and, if the wood that was gathered from the canyon burned too intensely over the new pots, everything that was done before would be ruined. Xcinco's mother would not allow him to do anything but gather the firewood. After that, he was sent away while the most skilled potters laid the wood to be burned down in a prescribed fashion and then prayed and sang while the pottery baked, hardened and its brown paint turned black.

The cliff dwelling people were especially proud of their black on white pottery. It was of such high and consistent quality that, along with their coveted mesa deerskins tanned with brain, their pottery was traded for silver, salt from a lake ten days' walk to the south, seashells, cotton for soft, comfortable summer clothing, blue-green turquoise, and obsidian for arrowheads, none of which could be found at Mesa Verde and all of which were greatly prized by the Raven People.

"You have done enough," Xcinco's mother announced one fine morning in March when the men were almost ready to plant corn, squash and bean seeds after removing them from the protection of Great Cave.

Xcinco could not have been happier. Finally, he would be treated like a man and given a digging stick of his own. He would sing and pray because planting was a joy shared by all with a good heart, strong legs and back. Until now Xcinco had been forced to stay with women, while the men and older boys had been working to clear new fields which then required new irrigation canals. Big trees were burned and their roots laboriously chopped out with heavy stone axes. Smaller trees and brush were cut down or pulled free while the ground was still wet and yielding after the winter's snow.

Xcinco loved planting because it was a gathering of all clans from all the cliff dwellings. It was a time when he saw friends that he had not seen since the previous autumn's harvest. Planters met planters and tried to outdo each other with grim tales of winter hunger, sickness and death. Those missing among the old, weak and sickly were noted and offered prayers.

Planting was a time when everyone was thin but eager to begin a new season of hope which would be spawned by the rich, red soil.

Like most of the families, Xcinco's dared not rely on one field for its bounty but cleared and farmed small, narrow and irregular plots found in the low draws where the deepest snows had lain in shadow and which now held abundant winter moisture. By working these many difficult fields, they would be partially protected in case of drought. The People had suffered through droughts and knew they were worse than the coldest, harshest of winters. Because they were so afraid of drought, everyone built terraces to catch water.

Very early in his life, Xcinco learned that it was not un-

common for a hundred people to be used in a single draw
that might add up to less than half an acre. No effort was too
great, no precaution too difficult or time-consuming to protect the Raven People against drought. To avoid runoff of a
heavy but badly needed rain, all the early spring weeds were
uprooted, the red soil was then poked, prodded and loosened
to a foot's depth with heavy digging sticks. For the hardest
ground, obsidian stones were lashed to the digging sticks,
and all day long Xcinco could hear the sound of obsidian
striking and breaking softer stones buried in the waiting
fields.

"Brother," Xcinco panted one hot afternoon as they carried
even more rocks from their fields to make new water basins
and terraces, "when will the planting begin?"

His brother's name was Kowiki and he was in love with
Noita, a girl of the Red Corn Clan. Noita lived in a nearby
cliff dwelling not nearly so large as Great Cave but which
was warmer in winter and cooler in summer because of its
more favorable position to Sun. Xcinco could not imagine
how his brother could love someone that he saw only during
the planting and harvest season. Even then the pair hardly
would have crossed paths except that Noita's family farmed
land in adjoining fields. Xcinco found it embarrassing that
Kowiki and Noita stared so long at each other. Maybe one
of them had bad eye trouble.

It was pitiful to watch, but Xcinco loved his brother so he
wisely said nothing. He had no desire to further humiliate
poor Kowiki whose eyes always seemed fine whenever he
went hunting.

"Little Brother, you know that the planting cannot start
until Sun Watcher says it is time."

"But what is he waiting for?"

Kowiki stopped his digging. The back of his head was
flattened perfectly from the cradleboard, and he was so good-
natured that Xcinco could not understand why he wasted his

time staring at a half-blind girl from a modest little cliff dwelling and born of an undistinguished clan.

Kowiki wiped his brow with a forefinger and flicked the sweat to the earth, saying, "My brother, Sun Watcher is as important as Storyteller. Maybe even more important because he must watch for the return of birds from the south since they understand when good weather comes to this mesa. He must also study the growth of weeds and plants and how the clouds form in the sky and from which direction they come . . . that also tells Sun Watcher when we can expect rain. Sun Watcher becomes Moon Watcher at night for he knows that our planting must take place only when Moon is growing larger."

"Why?"

"Because," Kowiki said, "if we plant while Moon wanes, so too will our crops wither and die. Sun Watcher is praying every day and night so that the good spirits and not the witches will tell us when to plant. He offers prayer sticks, corn pollen and meal to Wind who carries it to the good spirits and away from the evil witches."

Xcinco listened intently, believing.

"And," Kowiki said, "the planting of our seed must soon be followed by Rain. Too much rain and the seed will be washed away—too little and it will not sprout through Earth. Everything, Xcinco, must be perfect and that is why Sun Watcher is even more important than Storyteller."

"Only," Xcinco had to argue, "for a few weeks."

"No," Kowiki countered. "Sun Watcher is important all the while our crops grow so that we will have a good harvest."

Kowiki started to say more but suddenly was afflicted with staring at Noita. The sight was so ridiculous to Xcinco that he left his brother and returned to his own digging.

Five days later, with dark storm clouds rumbling far off, Sun Watcher finally announced that it was time to plant the seeds. Everyone who could climb out of Great Cave rushed up to the fields and no time was wasted.

Unlike the people who lived in the orderly fields in faraway
Chaco Canyon, the Raven People of Mesa Verde did not plant
their seeds in neat rows, but instead adapted to the rugged
and uneven terrain by simply planting where it was suitable.
Men and boys grunted as they dug holes with their sticks.
Women and girls dropped the seeds into the holes and then
swiftly covered and tamped them down with the heels of their
bare feet. Corn was given the deepest holes while the seeds
of squash and beans needed less covering by earth. During
all this busy and exciting time, Sun Watcher and the priests
offered constant prayers for the harvest. Everyone's eyes re-
volved back and forth between the soil and the sky while
praying for a gentle, life-giving rain. The planting took less
than a week.

"Listen!" Kowiki whispered, shaking Xcinco into wakefulness just a few days after the last seeds were covered by
Earth. "Brother, can you hear Thunder! Rain is coming just
as Sun Watcher predicted!"

Xcinco would have preferred to go back to sleep but
Kowiki was too excited to sleep, and soon many others were
hurrying to the mouth of Great Cave feeling a brisk wind
heralded by a bold vanguard of thunder. The People stood
just under the lip of Great Cave. They clapped their hands
and danced with joy to see the first shimmering bolts of lightning. Soon, the wind grew strong in the canyon below and
then the rain began to soak all of Earth.

Just as Sun Watcher had asked in his prayers, Rain was
firm but gentle, and within a few hours, sheets of water began
to cascade down from the mesa top, passing close, so the
People in Great Cave could extend their hands and wash their
grinning faces.

"I told you his powers must be very strong!" Kowiki cried
with exultation. "Some day, I will become the next Sun
Watcher!"

Xcinco couldn't believe he had heard correctly, but when
a bolt of lightning illuminated Kowiki's face, Xcinco saw that

his brother was serious. This important and secret confession caused Xcinco to blurt, "And someday I will be Storyteller!"

"I fear that Storyteller has already picked one to take his place."

"Then I will be the one to take the *new* Storyteller's place," Xcinco declared.

"That is possible," Kowiki told his brother, placing his arm across Xcinco's skinny shoulders. "It would make our father proud."

"And our mother."

"*Your* mother," Kowiki reminded. "My mother is dead. We are only half brothers."

"More than half."

Kowiki laughed. "Yes! Much more than half!"

The rain lasted for days and the People feasted and celebrated inside all the cliff dwellings. This long but gentle rain meant that there would be no drought and the autumn harvest would be abundant.

Every morning Kowiki and his father, along with many others, braved the slippery trail up to the mesa to stand for hours in the rain and study their fields, noting how their canals fed into their large reservoir. Just before dark, they returned tired and wet but in high spirits and there was much laughter in Great Cave.

"I have spoken to Mother and Father," Kowiki told his little brother when the storm was finally blowing off to the south. "I have asked their permission to marry Noita."

"Then you will have to live with her and her poor people!" Xcinco cried.

"I love her, Brother. And although we have only spoken with our eyes, I know that Noita also loves me and that we will always be happy."

Xcinco was heartbroken. "Couldn't you find some other girl—one with good eyes who lives here?"

"I cannot."

Xcinco well knew that no one was permitted to marry another in their clan, the penalty for which was banishment . . . or death. "But there are many *other* clans also living in Great Cave!"

"I must follow my eyes and my heart," Kowiki said in a way that left little room for argument. "Tomorrow, your mother will speak to Noita's mother and the arrangements will be made."

Desolated by this news, Xcinco hurried away with tears in his eyes. However, the next evening, it was Kowiki who cried because his marriage proposal was refused.

"Noita's mother is greedy!" Xcinco's mother raged. "She demands too much of my family's harvest and even some of our best planted fields! I will never give up our land!"

Xcinco was happy again. Kowiki would find another girl to marry, one who lived in Great Cave and whose mother wasn't so foolish. He and his brother could always live close together.

But the next night, Kowiki and Noita vanished. Xcinco was nearly as anguished as his mother and father. How far would they get before they were caught by the Desert Enemies and killed?

In a rage, Xcinco's mother went to berate Noita's mother. Noita's mother said terrible things, and the two attacked each other and had to be pulled apart. Now there always would be bad blood between the two families, and between their clans.

"Given this bad trouble," Xcinco's father lamented, "it is best if Kowiki and Noita never return to Mesa Verde."

"No!" Xcinco cried. "It would not be better!"

"Yes it would," Father said in bitterness. "It would be better if they were now dead."

Xcinco hurried away, running to find Storyteller and to ask him if he could look into the future. But Storyteller was sleeping and even after he awakened, he would not look into the future, but only wanted to talk about the past.

"Xcinco, have you heard the story about how the People first came to kill Bear?" the old man asked, yawning.

"Yes, I have!" Xcinco shouted, not caring if he finally hurt old Storyteller's feelings. "And I don't need to hear it ever again!"

Xcinco then rushed up to the mesa top and began pulling weeds with a fury that he had never felt before.

Twenty-four

Summer, 1272 A.D.
Cliff Palace, Mesa Verde

Xcinco was beginning his eighteenth year of life and was considered by the Raven People to be a man. Four winters ago, Storyteller had perished and a new Storyteller had taken his place. Xcinco did not like the new Storyteller very much because this one had never worked as hard as Old Storyteller to build Great Cave or to help with the planting and the harvest. This Storyteller considered himself an artist and a craftsman. He fashioned jewelry and scribbled story pictures in the dirt, or else added them to the smooth outside plaster of their homes.

Xcinco had thought that every Storyteller must earn his way through life by doing all the things that every other man was expected to do, but this one had never married, fathered children, hunted, or even farmed. Rather, he seemed of quite a different world. New Storyteller was kind and gentle, his stories were very good, but often he seemed lost, as if his mind were clouded by troubling visions, especially after he drank a very dark and secret tea. Xcinco knew there was something mysterious and maybe even evil about New Storyteller. Perhaps he was possessed by witches.

Kowiki never had returned to the Raven People and Xcinco never had recovered from that loss—nor had his father, who had favored Kowiki over Xcinco. There had been no more trouble between Xcinco's clan and those of the Red Corn Seed, but there continued to be a distrust and dislike between them.

"I never will believe that Kowiki and Noita are dead," Xcinco told his father one summer morning as they weeded their fields. "I still believe that someday he will return."

"No, Xcinco. Your brother is dead."

"Maybe he lives with our ancestors in Chaco Canyon."

"If this were so, we would have heard of it from the Chacoans who come to trade with us."

Xcinco knew better than to argue with his father, who was bitter that his favorite son had abandoned him, their clan and their fields. Kowiki would have made life easier for everyone in the family.

After Spring, there had been no more rainfall and now their crops were suffering from thirst. Every field had to be protected both day and night from predators. Birds, especially crows, were so brazen and hungry for the ripening crops that they would swoop down and tear away both beans and corn. Even Raven tested the people, though no one dared do more than sail a rock in his direction. Every night the boys of the village were expected to build fires on the mesa tops and stay awake and vigilant until dawn. Last week, two coyotes had sneaked into the gardens and eaten four squash, then dashed away with two more in their jaws. The boys responsible for protecting that field were whipped and chastised before all the People. Guarding the village's winter food supply was the first obligation a boy faced before admission to the kivas.

"My son, there is something we must talk about," Xcinco's father said just before noon as they weeded the fields.

Xcinco stopped and gazed longingly off toward the shade of the nearest juniper trees. When it was this hot, afternoons were given to taking naps, gambling or talking. Most of the conversation was about the crops. Family men bragged good-naturedly about how high their corn was, or how large their squash in comparison to that of their neighbors. Older boys

were obsessed with talking about girls or about the hunting
of Deer.

"Xcinco, your mother and I think it is time that you took
a wife."

"Yes, Father." This news was not unexpected. Xcinco was,
after all, in his eighteenth year, as strong and as tall as most
men of his clan and every bit as good a hunter.

"Your mother is making arrangements for one now. This
is what we should talk about."

Xcinco dropped his weeding stick and followed his father
through the waist-high corn toward the nearest trees. This
would be a long conversation and it needed to take place in
shade where it was cool and private.

"You must have known that this is your year," his father
said when they came to rest, squatting on their naked
haunches.

"I have been very busy," Xcinco said, trying hard not to
sound too interested.

In truth, he was happy about the idea of taking a wife,
though the painful memory of Kowiki and Noita was still
sharp. Xcinco was afraid something bad could happen to him
concerning this difficult but important marriage business.

"You have a special gift for making arrowheads," Xcinco's
father said, momentarily circling the subject. "Other men
have told me so."

"I am better at making jewelry."

His father lapsed into a long silence, broken when he finally said, "Yes, you have the same gift as Storyteller."

Xcinco nodded. Although he didn't like Storyteller, the
man was an artist whose jewelry brought him much when
traded to other clans and cliff-dwelling peoples.

"Maybe, like Storyteller, that should be your trade when
you are not working in these fields."

Xcinco had given that idea considerable thought. Since
losing his brother and their secret, shared ambitions, he had
lost all interest in one day becoming Storyteller. Stories he

had memorized with ease now seemed irrelevant. The new Storyteller had once dared to ask Xcinco why he no longer listened. Xcinco had been unable to give the respected man a good answer.

"My son, you could do well making jewelry and painting pottery for those who lack your gift. I have heard women plead for you to decorate their best pottery."

"Pottery is a woman's work, but I do enjoy making shell and turquoise jewelry. It pleases me and I have traded well for what I make."

"I know! We have never had so much cotton or salt! Your mother is very happy. That is why she wants a special marriage for you. She has chosen Tani of the Moon Ring Clan."

Xcinco's eyes bulged. Tani? The loud-mouth girl he had teased and baited since childhood? "Father, no!" he pleaded. "Not that one."

"My son, Tani is a prize. As you know, her clan is held in high honor and you could remain in Great Cave to help me and your mother as we grow old."

"But I hate Tani!"

"You must not say this! Even now, your mother is speaking to Tani's family."

Xcinco jumped to his feet, striking his head against a low limb. "I will not take that girl for my wife!"

"You will not defy and shame us like Kowiki. Your mother and I have agreed that you should marry Tani. Great Chief and all our priests agree."

Xcinco collapsed to his knees. *So, this hated marriage is already made. Neither Tani nor I have any choice. We are both trapped, but I must go and live with her mean mother and awful family. I must become a member of their house!*

"My son, do not look so sad! Tani is a beautiful girl and skillful, too. She is a good cook and even though she is so young, her pottery is already of the highest quality. We will build you and Tani a fine house to sleep in at night and raise children."

"But I do not like Tani or her clan people!"

"Xcinco, you are a man so you must know that is not important. I did not choose to marry your mother but was ordered by Great Chief to do so after my first wife died. I knew that she was not a good cook and that her pottery was not the best. Even so, your mother has made me very happy. Tani will make you happy and bear you many strong children."

When Xcinco's expression remained stricken, his father asked, "Is there some other girl that we do not know about?"

"Would it matter?"

The reply was slow, but definite. "No."

Xcinco clenched his hands at his sides and pushed himself back to his feet. "I am going to Great Cave."

"To see Tani?"

"To speak to Mother. To tell her of my true feelings about Tani and her clan."

"You must not do that! Have you learned nothing from the lesson of Kowiki and Noita!"

Xcinco felt his father's hand clamp on his wrist and although he could easily have broken free, he did not. Instead bowed his head and felt tears on his cheeks. "I will do as I am told in this matter, Father. But you must not expect any grandchildren."

"What kind of a marriage would that be!"

"The kind that you and Mother should expect given that I hate Tani," he replied, removing his father's hand and walking away.

By evening the tongue-waggers had done their work. Everyone in Great Cave and even those in the nearby caves knew of the marriage that would take place at the end of summer between Xcinco and Tani. The families had reached a fair settlement. The price for Tani was extremely high: Xcinco's mother had paid it by giving half her harvest but without parting with any of her beloved farmland. That evening, as children tittered and pointed, as women discussed where the new couple's house should be placed and as the flocks of turkeys were driven far back under the cave to the protection of their rocky roosts, Xcinco and Tani sat glaring at each other across Great Cave.

"Go speak to her!" Xcinco's mother hissed. "Xcinco, what is wrong with you!"

"I hate her!"

"Act like a man, not a spoiled child! Xcinco, I have been waiting, watching and thinking about this for many years and Tani is best for you. She will work hard and bring you both wealth, many children and much happiness. Her pottery is beautiful and she already cooks nearly as well as I do! She never spills the water that she carries on her head from the far spring, and even you must have noticed the fine turkey blanket and sandals she made for her mother. I never have had such fine things."

"Mother, Tani has a sharp tongue. It cuts like a knife and she . . . she makes fun of me sometimes!"

"That is because she likes you, Xcinco!" His mother smiled wickedly and whispered, "Don't you know that is what girls do to the young men they most favor?"

"I make fun of Tani, but only because I hate her!"

The smile died. "Stop it!" his mother warned. "I will hear no more of such talk. Go speak to Tani now or your father and I will be even more ashamed than we were when Kowiki ran away with that ugly Red Corn Clan girl."

Xcinco had no choice because now everyone in Great Cave stopped talking in order to see if he would be an honorable son and soon an honorable husband.

Like a man about to die, Xcinco shuffled across the roof of a kiva, hearing the rising laughter of men engaged in happy conversation. He desperately wished to climb down into this kiva and lose himself in their company and conversation. Instead, he came to Tani and could not even bring himself to look down at her as she furiously began grinding corn meal.

"Sit down beside me and I will show you how well I can grind corn," Tani ordered without warmth.

"Must I?"

"Yes!"

Xcinco sat at a distance and he did not look at her corn grinding but instead folded his arms across his chest and stared at the canyon, waiting for sunset and a veil of darkness. Tani stopped grinding. Silence deepened in Great Cave until the girl said, "I am as unhappy about this as you are, Xcinco. I have never liked you."

"Then perhaps we should go up on the mesa and throw ourselves off Great Cliff to our deaths."

"You would kill yourself before you would marry me?" she asked, voice stretched into a thin whisper.

Xcinco was not quite ready to die so he said, "No."

Tani began to grind corn again, pressing down so hard on her flat mano stone that her larger metate screamed in protest. "Xcinco, what are we going to do?"

"I don't know."

It was a long time before Tani said, "There is no other way. We must be married."

"That I know. But I will always sleep in a kiva."

With a sob of anger, Tani smashed his kneecap with her mano stone and dashed into her mother's house.

"Owwweeeii!" Xcinco wailed, grabbing his knee and howling with pain.

A few moments later, Tani's family surrounded him with clenched fists and hard, unforgiving glares.

Xcinco was trapped and in danger of perhaps having his other knee broken. "Good corn meal," he moaned, wetting his forefinger and tasting it. "Tani makes *good* corn meal."

After what seemed like forever, Tani's family left him, still glassy-eyed with pain. Mustering all the dignity that he could, Xcinco somehow managed to push himself upright and hobble back to his mother's house where she greeted him with ice in her black eyes.

"Xcinco!" his father hissed. "Enough of this foolishness You will marry Tani!"

"Yes," he promised, realizing that it was the only thing let for him unless he wanted to leave Upper Earth and go searching for Kowiki's departed spirit.

By the middle of July, it still had not rained, and the People were deeply troubled. Their corn withered while their bean and squash remained small and hard. The water level of thei huge reservoir was dropping dangerously low and the women and children now spent all their time and strength carrying water jars up from the year-round spring far down in the canyon.

Everyone forgot about Xcinco and Tani in their struggle to preserve what little water remained in the reservoir. Instead of using their canals, they measured each drop and carried jars to the fields before pouring the contents to each thirsty plant. Men and boys who would have refused to carry water jars now helped the women and daughters so that a constant chain moved up and down the face of Great Cliff, even during the worst afternoon heat. Not a drop of water was wasted and the People drank none for themselves on the mesa but gave it all to their precious crops.

Sun Watcher, Great Chief, and all the priests prayed night and day and continually made offerings for Rain. If Rain did not come soon, the entire crop could be lost or, at the very least, be inadequate to winter the People. In their desperation, the men already began to speak of how far they would have to travel to hunt deer, bear, rabbits and squirrels. Later, dogs could be eaten, their flock of turkeys too. But then where would the warm turkey-feather blankets come from? And without the dogs, the People would be far more vulnerable to a surprise attack from the Desert Enemies.

This latter concern became even more acute one afternoon when three badly wounded Chacoans arrived. They had been a trading party of eight strong, well-armed men, but had been attacked by the Desert Enemies and had barely escaped with their lives, losing all their trade goods.

"The Desert Enemies are growing bolder each year," one of the wounded Chacoans warned, eyes haunted by the recent slaughter of his companions. "They raid villages, steal crops and burn houses. They take women and girls, but kill all the men and boys."

"How many enemies are there?" Great Chief asked.

"Who is to say? Each year, there are more and more. Even in Chaco, where our people number so many, we are now living in constant fear."

"Do you have good water and crops?"

"We will not grow hungry this winter, but the river that flows through Chaco Canyon grows weak. Our crops are poor, but enough. And what of the Raven People?"

"We will survive when Raven gives us Rain."

"Not if the Desert Enemies come to this place."

"They cannot reach us in these caves."

"They will not have to, after your food and water are all gone."

These words shocked the cliff-dwelling people because they were true. That night, everyone prayed harder than ever before asking for Raven to protect them and to bring Rain. For reasons even he could not understand, Xcinco went to visit Tani. They did not insult each other but instead sat in close, silent communion with their troubled thoughts.

It finally rained in mid-August. Violent storms clashed against the peaks of the distant Rocky Mountains and shattered on the western mesas. The People ran dancing to their fields, knowing but not caring that they could be killed by lightning. When the wind began to gust especially hard, some of them even tried to support the tall, drought-weakened stalks of corn with their bare hands and bodies. They watched the lightning anxiously, knowing it might set the forests and fields afire.

It had happened before.

The rains passed, after many days and nights, leaving the fields on Mesa Verde wet and steamy under the August sun. The People wept with happiness because the harvest was at last assured.

Xcinco and Tani were married before the harvest. There was no time or reason for ceremony. Now, every mind and body was focused on harvesting the crop and getting it safely stored in Great Cave before it could be lost to predators, the elements, or the Desert Enemies. After that, it was time for the fall hunting, the piñon harvesting and gathering of as much food as they could find in the canyon and on the mesa tops before the first snows of winter.

Tani's new house was built by her family and always would belong to her. Like all the other houses, it was small, only twice Xcinco's length in both directions. It had no window, and a key-shaped door. The house was for sleeping and coupling; all other things were done outside. It was Xcinco's avowed intention always to spend his nights in the kiva, but Tani had cried so hard over this that he remained with her until it seemed far too much trouble to move out. Besides, Tani made him a fine turkey-feather robe after spending long hours splitting each turkey feather down the middle, then wrapping them tightly around a cord made of yucca fiber forming a soft, fluffy cord which was then woven into the finished blanket. These blankets were as warm as a fur robe and much more valuable. The only trouble was, Tani insisted that the robe always remain in her new house at night.

Xcinco had never seen such a beautiful robe! Had the weather been colder, he would have paraded around Great Cave to show it off to everyone. Now, however, it was too warm so he had to content himself with sleeping on the robe beside Tani.

"Am I a good cook?" she asked him one night in the early darkness.

"Yes, a very good cook."

"You are not so thin as before, Xcinco."

"No?"

"No." Tani's bare thigh brushed his own.

"What are you doing?"

She giggled. "Nothing, my husband. After the harvest," Tani said, stroking him again, this time with the full length of her leg, "will you make me a beautiful shell necklace?"

"I have no money for shells," he said, scooting to the very edge of the fine turkey blanket. "Remember the price you cost my family?"

"I was worth it. You'll see."

"Go to sleep or I will move to the kiva."

Tani's hand brushed over his stomach and then came to rest on his stiff manhood. She sat bolt upright and cried, "Why Xcinco, your body wants to stay right here with me!"

Hot with humiliation, Xcinco would have carried out his kiva threat but, when Tani began to squeeze him, he realized how much he really wanted to stay.

Twenty-five

Autumn, 1287 A.D.
Cliff Palace, Mesa Verde

The drought lasted so many years that even Storyteller could not remember exactly when the harvest was abundant and the People happy. He was old now, old before his time, and ignored. No one wanted to hear stories of how things once had been good for the Raven People. How the deer had been plentiful, the wood for winter fuel easy to find and gather, the springs and the canyon creeks full and sweet.

What had the Raven People done to deserve such a long and punishing drought? Had the witches killed or chased away all the good spirits so that they could starve the People to death? Maybe the evil witches wanted everyone to die so that they could have Great Cave and all the other cliff dwellings for themselves. Yet, didn't they realize that if they did this, there would be no one left to torment which was their only purpose and delight? Surely they were smart enough to understand that this would bring them boredom and sadness.

Xcinco and the other leaders asked themselves these and a thousand more questions, over and over. Down in the kivas, debates on these vital issues lasted for weeks, but there never were any answers. Never any change from one bad year to the next. All that Xcinco knew for sure was that he had been more fortunate than most because of his talent for making jewelry, which was still in demand by traders who came to the mesa country with food and other goods, often with no purpose other than to see Xcinco and leave with his prized creations. Also, Tani's fields remained somewhat productive and they had saved dozens of the People by sharing everything they had in the worst of the famine winters. But even so, many had died of hunger and sickness. Xcinco's father had died eight years ago and now his mother, always so strong and happy, was gripped by such deep sadness Xcinco feared she would not last through the coming winter.

It was almost time to harvest the fields but there was no joy among the People because this had been another summer with precious little rain.

"We will do the best we can," Xcinco told his wife. "Maybe we will have a good hunting season."

"I hope so because there are very few piñon nuts to be harvested," Tani lamented.

"As soon as the harvest is over, we will hunt," Xcinco promised. "I think we will have a good hunt and bring back many deer. Enough so that, when all the harvest is shared this winter, no one will starve."

But Tani's expression hardened. "If the winter is long and the snows deep, there will be much more death because everyone is already thin. And we will *not* share my harvest!"

Xcinco found it difficult to believe what his wife was saying. Before he could protest, Tani added, "No more children will be sacrificed so that the old can live a few more years. The children must never go hungry again or we will no longer be the People."

Xcinco lost his anger. Tani was right. Starving children did not grow. Those children who had most suffered from previous winters already were stunted. Perhaps even more distressing, some of them were also listless, as if their minds had suffered even more than their little bodies.

"We should leave this accursed place!" Tani swore, casting her eyes toward the high, domed roof. "I am sure that Great

Cave and all the People's caves are now filled with witches and evil spirits!"

Xcinco could not help but look upward too, as if the evil witches would reveal themselves just to prove Tani's words. Realizing how absurd this was, Xcinco stared at his work-thickened hands and struggled to think of something encouraging to say to his wife.

"Tani," he began quietly, "we must remember that this is almost the green corn time. There is much work to be done with the harvest."

"We should take it and leave!"

"No. In Great Cave, we have homes and kivas, and there are many old and sick ones who need our care and feeding. Would you have us abandon them to starvation?"

"No," Tani whispered, eyes becoming wet with tears. "We never could do that."

"Of course not," Xcinco said, wanting to comfort her. "And besides, we are surrounded by Desert Enemies. To leave with the People so few and so weak would be to invite certain death—or slavery."

"I would choose death for us all!" Tani cried, throwing her arms around her husband. "Xcinco, please forgive me because I have spoken foolishly. Our children—all the children in Great Cave—will be fed again this winter because we will have good hunting but also because your jewelry is so prized by all the traders."

"As are your pottery and turkey-feather blankets."

"My husband, if everyone is close to starving, who will be left to buy anything but food?"

Xcinco had no answer. Until now, he had prospered because his and Tani's goods were so highly valued by traders who risked their lives to sneak past the Desert Enemies. But Tani was right; trade was dwindling as the stakes became higher and the difficulties greater during this endless drought.

"Xcinco, what is your answer?"

"It will be all right," he promised, realizing his words were

hollow unless the drought finally ended and the People multiplied and grew strong.

The time finally arrived when the village crier stood up
and announced that tomorrow would be the day of the Green
Corn Celebration when a small but very precious portion of
the harvest would be roasted. There would be feasting, laughter and dancing.

Some of the old ones objected, saying that this celebration
was foolish because it would cause even more starvation
when winter arrived. But Great Chief and most of the priests
prevailed, arguing that it would be an insult to Raven and to
the good spirits to ignore this important and traditional celebration. It also would be an admission to the witches that
they held dominion over the People; this would increase their
confidence to do even more evil work.

And so the Green Corn Celebration began as everyone
strong enough to climb up to the mesa fields gathered early
the following morning. The day before, Xcinco and all the
other men and boys had excavated a large roasting pit and
filled it with firewood. Throughout the night, the wood had
burned until it became a deep bed of coals. The coals were
scraped aside and the pit's walls lined with green corn stalks
and dampened leaves which smoked and sizzled. At last, each
person from all the cliff dwellings grabbed handfuls of green
corn and, after offering prayers, tossed them into the roasting
pit. When the pit was nearly full, a final layer of corn stalks
was placed over the corn and everything was covered with a
shallow layer of red earth.

No work of any sort was done all that day; everyone rested
and fasted, waiting for the first colors of sunset. The younger
children played while the older ones seemed transfixed by
the pit, each wanting to be the first to see another hissing
plume of steam break through Earth.

Just before sunset the priests lifted their arms and shouted thanksgiving to Raven and the good spirits. As soon as the prayers ended the young men scraped away the earth and uncovered the roasting corn. Jumping around and mindful that they could be scalded by the steam, they furiously began to uproot the roasting corn with their digging sticks, tossing it out to the excited people.

Soon, everyone was tossing the hot corn high into the air or back and forth between themselves, trying to make it cool. There was so much teasing and hilarity that even the specter of drought, sickness and the coming of another deadly winter were forgotten. The corn was plentiful and delicious this night. The People would eat, dance and laugh until they gave themselves over to exhaustion and sleep.

The harvest of the corn, squash and beans was taken very seriously during the following weeks. Fearing attack by the Desert People at this most vulnerable time of year, everyone strong enough to leave Great Cave worked swiftly and even by the light of Moon. Everything was gathered in large woven baskets and carried down to the cliff dwellings so there was a continuous stream of the People crawling up and down Great Cliff as busy and industrious as ants. The squash and beans were cut from their thick vines. The bean pods were then beaten by the women with long sticks until they shattered. Whenever there was a breeze, the pods were tossed into the air so that they blew, dropping the heavier beans to fall and be gathered. Most of the corn was taken down to the cliff dwellings still attached to the stalks. During the long winter they would be used for bedding, turkey feed and fuel.

Xcinco loved to admire the colorful corn decorating Great Cave. As the harvesting proceeded, Great Cave became even more beautiful than the canyon, filled to overflowing with its tapestry of stunning autumn colors. Curtains of drying red, black, blue, yellow and white speckled ears of corn were strung up or spread across every courtyard and roof, all mixed with hundreds of yellow and green squash and the impressive piles of dark brown beans. However, their large flock of turkeys was a constant problem as they tried to feed on the harvest and kept the children busy chasing them away.

After the harvest was safe inside the cliff dwellings, the People heaved a deep sigh of relief. The pace of the work slowed as the corn was shucked, the beans washed and collected in large, lidded storage pots and the squash cut into strips for drying. Deep into winter, the dried slices of squash could be soaked and seasoned, adding a welcome addition to the monotonous diet of piñon nuts, venison, corn and beans. In the good years, enough of the crop would be stored in rooms at the back of Great Cave to feed the People for a second winter, in case of some unforeseen calamity. Because of this terrible drought, however, there was only enough vital seed to plant next year's crops.

"If the fall hunting is successful, I think the People will not starve this winter," Xcinco decided aloud to his family one afternoon as he prepared to travel north with the Raven People's best hunters in order to kill deer migrating down from the higher elevations.

"And maybe we also can go onto the far mesas and find piñons to harvest," Tani said, wanting to sound hopeful.

"You must stay here where you are protected by our sons and those who are unable to travel so far," Xcinco told her. "After we return, then we will *all* go in search of piñon nuts."

Xcinco's oldest son, Patuwa, started to protest, but thought better of the idea when he read his father's eyes. Patuwa knew as well as anyone that the Desert Enemies were most likely to be climbing onto the mesas at this time of year, hoping to catch the People at harvest time, when they were most vulnerable to attack.

"Storyteller wishes to speak to you," Tani said as her nimble fingers worked to repair a sandal.

"Why?"

"He did not say."

Xcinco frowned. He had never felt either close or comfortable with Storyteller and the man's odd and solitary behavior had lessened his respect until the office of Storyteller meant very little in Great Cave. Storyteller was now someone to be tolerated and who required food even though he contributed nothing to the People except for an occasional story.

"You *have* to speak with him today," Tani informed her husband. "It would not be respectful to leave on the hunt without first doing that. Also, it could bring you and the other hunters bad luck."

Xcinco found Storyteller at the mouth of Great Cave, gazing down at the fall colors overflowing their canyon. His hair was long and almost pure white while his body was thin and bent. Studying him for a moment, Xcinco was reminded again of how fortunate he was that he had never become Storyteller. Far better to be a respected jeweler, father, farmer and excellent hunter. To have sons and daughters who would care for him when he became as old and weak as this poor man.

"Storyteller," Xcinco said, breaking into his reverie. "My wife says that you wish to speak."

Storyteller turned to regard Xcinco with the same steady, penetrating gaze that had always made him feel uncomfortable. When he finally spoke, his voice was soft and heavy with sadness.

"Winter comes soon and I am ready to die," Storyteller announced without emotion.

"You will not starve," Xcinco promised, now believing that Storyteller desired assurance that he would again share equally in the field harvest, as well as the food gathered from the trees and killed on the far mesas. "You have my word and that of the other elders."

"That is not what I want to talk about."

"Then what?"

"I have no successor," Storyteller began, eyes shuttering as he watched Xcinco with a self-deprecating smile. "Xcinco, I have no family, no friends and no one who has listened to me these many bad years. Not even you."

Xcinco felt ashamed. Gentle Storyteller always made him feel ashamed. "I am your friend."

"No," Storyteller said, "but you should have been."

"What do you want of me?"

"Be my friend. You have nothing to fear from me and much to gain."

Xcinco walked past the man to sit at the very edge of the cavern. "Just tell me what you want."

"Food."

"I told you that would be freely given."

"A new turkey-feather blanket made by your wife."

"I . . ."

"And a necklace made by you, Xcinco. A beautiful necklace of shells and turquoise . . . and silver."

Xcinco bounced to his feet in anger. "I am going on the hunt and do not have time to talk of these things."

"There is no time left."

"What do you mean?"

"I have visions," Storyteller confessed. "I have true visions that you alone must hear."

"Storyteller," Xcinco said, realizing that he did not want to hear this man's visions. He suspected they would be terrible. "I must go and prepare for the hunt."

"I see more death," Storyteller began. "Much more death this winter. I see my own death. And the death of many children."

"Enough!"

"And I see you covered with blood."

Xcinco's heart nearly stopped beating before he recovered to ask, "Am I . . . dying?"

"No," Storyteller replied, his voice never more gentle. "You will live to become Great Chief, if that is what you wish."

"Me?"

Storyteller dipped his pointed chin. "Yes."

"But I do not wish it!"

"There is only one way that you can change the vision."
Storyteller paused for a long time. "And that is by becoming
the next Storyteller."

"But I am unprepared!"

Storyteller laughed, but it was not a nice sound. "You are
better prepared than all others. And I will teach you what you
do not know . . . starting now."

"I must go hunting."

"If you are killed by the Desert Enemies, the story of the
People will be lost forever. There is no one left after me . . .
except you. Is this not far more important than another deer
killed?"

It was, but Xcinco could not bring himself to say so.

"Do you understand the difference?" Storyteller demanded with surprising vigor. "Look deep inside, then answer me!"

Xcinco began to tremble and grow angry. So angry that
he jabbed an accusing forefinger in Storyteller's face and
cried, "You are a witch!"

Storyteller paled, began to wag his head back and forth,
voice dry and rattling like the tail of Snake, "No. No. No!"

"You *are!*"

"Then kill me," Storyteller commanded, turning his palms
upward in a gesture of complete surrender. "Or, if you lack
the courage to do that, then tell the People of my death vision
and then say that I am witch so that they will kill me. It would
be easier to bear than these visions that have long poisoned
my spirit."

Xcinco did the only thing he could think to do and that
was to run. Although he was no longer young, his legs were
fed by fear as he sprinted across courtyards and through family gatherings. Xcinco ran until he was with Tani. Then, despite the questioning looks that his strange behavior caused
among everyone in Great Cave, he took his wife's hand and
dragged her into the house where they had lain together for
so many good and bad years. In a few rushed, nearly breath-

less sentences, Xcinco told Tani of Storyteller's shocking prophecy.

Tani listened in silence with her eyes closed and hands clasped together for so long that Xcinco grew even more upset. "Tani, speak to me!"

"You must not go on the hunt," she said, opening her eyes at last. "You must stay here and listen to Storyteller so that our past is not lost forever."

"Why me!"

"Because you are the chosen one."

Xcinco was not hearing what he wanted to hear. "But I do not want to tell stories of defeat at the hands of our enemies leading to death, suffering and slavery."

"Storyteller's vision did not speak of defeat or slavery. He is not a witch, Xcinco, but instead a gentle man who has always loved only you who have given him nothing but contempt."

Xcinco would have jumped up and run off again, but Tani grabbed his arm. "Listen to his vision and his stories! Storyteller is right. One more hunter will make no difference. Send our oldest son in your place. It is Patuwa's time."

He felt like pottery ready to crack. "Do you say that I am too old to hunt?"

"No. But Patuwa is now stronger. Become the *last* Storyteller, my husband. This is what is important."

Xcinco began to weep, grateful that he and Tani were alone so that no others could see his weakness. He did not understand any of this and, despite Tani's words, still feared that Storyteller was not a prophet but instead a very clever witch. But what if he were not . . . and if his vision was true?

"Stay to protect us in Great Cave this time," Tani pleaded. "And spend many hours listening to Storyteller."

"But, if he is a witch, I will be forever damned to darkness!"

"Storyteller is not a witch," Tani repeated, voice ringing with conviction. "He is just . . . different."

Despite his misgivings, Xcinco remained with his family and with Storyteller while the other men left to hunt. In earlier times, each clan would hunt separately because the deer were plentiful and the danger of being surprised and attacked by enemies was slight. Now, with so many Desert Enemies to fear, all of the mesa hunters went off together under one Hunt Chief. Forming a single long line across every mesa where it was expected they would find game, all living creatures would be flushed and driven to the end of the mesa. Unable to escape, the trapped animals would be forced to turn and try to break through the line of hunters. Very few ever escaped the hail of arrows, spears, rocks and whirling stone clubs. The ones that preferred to leap to their death soon were gathered and added to the kill.

Xcinco felt miserable and cheated to miss the autumn hunt which always had been a very special part of his life. His skill with a bow and arrow was well known and he always had killed at least one deer. Now, he was forced to spend every day listening to Storyteller. It was, however, a surprise to discover that he had completely forgotten many of the People's stories and that there were plenty of others that he had not even known.

As one week stretched into another, the People in Great Cave grew increasingly anxious for the safety of their hunters. There was an early snow and hard freeze. The colors of the autumn leaves finally dulled and then Wind swept them all away.

To relieve his anxiety, Xcinco spent many hours with his younger sons on the mesa during the best weather, collecting firewood which often had to be carried or tied and dragged for several miles before being tossed over Great Cliff where it would be collected by the people below. But sometimes they just poked around in the barren fields, reminiscing about all the good times they had shared here on the mesa, especially during the Green Corn Celebration.

One afternoon, when it was late and they were leaving the fields to return to Great Cave, his youngest son, Miska, froze, then pointed and cried, "Father, look!"

Xcinco spun around to see five Desert Enemies break from the trees and charge across the barren fields. His blood turned cold and he shouted for his children to race back to the cliff trail as hard as they could fly.

"Run!" he screamed over and over as his hands fitted an arrow to the sinewy string of his bow. "Faster!"

His first arrow flew swift with very little arc. The lead attacker must have only heard an ominous whirring an instant before the arrow bit into his throat. He threw up his hands and tried to curse Xcinco, but died choking in blood. Xcinco stood his ground and fired a second arrow that struck the next enemy in the leg, knocking him down but allowing him to rise and hobble forward.

Two more arrows and they kill me, Xcinco thought, hands steady but mind erratically darting through his lifetime like a bat feeding on twilight bugs.

Two more arrows and two more kills. Xcinco drew his knife, looked over his shoulder and was pleased to see his children vanish over the edge of Great Cliff, voices raised to warn the People. He turned and planted his feet, satisfied that it was Raven's gift that he should die so honorably now.

The next enemy closed fast, raising his stone axe to slash at Xcinco who was able to throw his arm up and deflect what would have been his death blow. Xcinco felt his left arm break as it was laid open. Blood poured like warm rain over his face as he crashed over backward, his knife splitting this enemy's stomach like the belly of Fish. The man was young, not much older than Patuwa. He screamed and tried to raise his axe again but lacked the will or the strength. Xcinco ripped his blade upward until the powerful enemy died.

For a moment, Xcinco lay shivering as if he also were

about to pass into the Spirit World. He would have closed his eyes and offered his last prayer to Raven except that he heard a strangled curse. Rolling out from under the dead, he saw the last enemy with an arrow still projecting from his leg rapidly hobbling toward him with a club raised.

Xcinco crawled to his feet and decided to run for the safety of Great Cave. Though old, in extreme pain and not fast anymore, Xcinco was sure he could outdistance his badly wounded enemy. He would have run except that Miska suddenly reappeared and came racing toward him waving his little bow and arrows.

"Go back!" Xcinco shouted.

But Miska had no intention of retreating. Perhaps it was because there was so much blood on Xcinco and the boy thought his father was dying. Whatever the reason, Miska had lost his senses and would not stop.

Xcinco tripped on corn stubble, fell and landed on his broken arm. He lost consciousness for several moments and when his red curtain of pain parted, Xcinco was appalled to see that his last enemy was almost upon him. Doubting he could escape, and certain that Miska would not choose to escape, Xcinco wobbled erect. He gripped his knife tightly and used his broken forearm to sweep the blood from his face. His vision cleared, he shouted a challenge at his attacker and staggered ahead to meet his honorable death. But the enemy's leg wound betrayed him and his knees buckled an instant before he would have swung his stone axe and killed Xcinco.

When the enemy tumbled, Xcinco took his unfortunate young life.

Twenty-six

Winter, 1299 A.D.
Cliff Palace, Mesa Verde

One frigid December afternoon Tani surprised her husband by announcing, "Storyteller, this is your forty-fifth winter."

Storyteller huddled close to her fire, grateful that his wife and daughters had made such fine turkey-feather blankets and buckskin robes. "How would you know my years on Middle Earth?"

"Because this is my forty-third winter and I have always marked them on a counting stick."

Tani did not look that old, although her hair was pure silver. Like Storyteller and nearly everyone beyond thirty years of age, most of her teeth were missing because of so many seasons of chewing corn imbedded with tiny particles of ground rock. "My husband, I think it is wise to remember that we have lived long and well."

"Long at least," he agreed, unable to ignore the moans of the old who suffered during the deep cold from the pains of arthritis. Half of the children were sick and coughing as they huddled next to their smoky fires seeking a little warmth. For a few brief hours in late afternoon, Sun would also warm Great Cave but then abandon them to another long night of shivering misery.

A healthy person could adapt to the worst of the cold, but Storyteller knew his people were far from healthy. Everyone

was thin and weakened by hunger because this had been another year of poor rain and stunted crops. The country was
locked in a terrible drought that had persisted for nearly
twenty-five years. There had been a few years when good
rains fell and produced an abundant harvest, but those years
were far between and famine had deepened its grip on the
mesa country until no one believed it would ever end. Deer
were gone, sheep were gone and the People had scoured the
mesas and nearby canyons for so long that firewood was extremely difficult to find and to bring back to Great Cave. So
many days were given to this work that the People had little
time or energy to go far away in search of better gathering
or hunting.

This winter was typical of all winters in recent memory—
extremely cold and dry. There was little snow to melt in spring
and fill their reservoir so that they could water their fields
in the searing heat of summer. Without this vital source of
moisture, the People knew that it would be another bad year
for the crops.

Storyteller remembered all the names of those once living
in Great Cave who had died of hunger caused by this drought,
or else had abandoned the Raven People, hoping to find better
farmland somewhere to the south and beyond the dominion
of their hated Desert Enemies. A few had returned to Great
Cave, wounded or resigned to starvation after reporting that
the Chacoans and many of the other peoples also had abandoned their pueblo villages in search of good land and water.

Tani had an abscessing tooth that was making her ill-
tempered. "Storyteller, I do not understand why the medicine men cannot help those of us who suffer from rotting
teeth. Look at that old woman who also sits rocking in
pain."

The woman was younger than Tani, but Storyteller saw no
reason to mention the fact. And he did not want to look at
the old woman because her constant moaning tore at his heart.
Like Tani, she had an abscessed tooth but hers was far worse.

The abscess had eaten away part of her jaw and left her mouth running with a constant and putrid infection.

"She should have had the medicine man remove her bad teeth," Storyteller opinioned.

"She is afraid—as I am! The last time that was done, a stupid medicine man broke Quuma's jaw by striking her tooth much too hard with a pointed rock. With her jaw broken, Quuma could not eat and starved to death even though she was still young! Is that what you want for *me?*"

"Of course not. Even medicine men are not perfect."

"They are worthless! Why, that girl who fell last week trying to climb when the footholds remained filled with ice is dying."

"Tani, what can even the most powerful medicine men or their societies do after a broken bone breaks the flesh and turns dark? You know that this always causes death. Remember that our son Patuwa fell and broke his leg. But, with the prayers and potions of our medicine society, Patuwa lived."

"Yes," Tani said with much resentment, "but he is lame and never again will be able to hunt. When he walks you know how much he suffers even though he never complains."

"You should be thankful that Patuwa has the gift of making jewelry. I am teaching him well."

"But no one has money to buy it anymore!"

Storyteller felt bitterness boiling up from his empty belly. He raised his left arm which gave him agony in this terrible cold and demanded, "What about my arm? Do you hear me complain!"

"No, but you should remember that I am the one who cleaned the wound and set the bone! Me, not the medicine men or anyone in their society. And did they even compliment or credit me for this? No!"

Storyteller had no more patience for his suffering wife and climbed to his feet. When Tani became upset like this, it was best to retreat to his kiva where he would be warmer and happy in the company of friends.

"So, are you leaving your family to freeze again this night?" Tani said without hiding her anger.

"My wife, you and our daughters have a fire and many blankets and robes."

"But you and our sons have kivas! Down there it is warm and comfortable while, up here, we freeze!"

Storyteller sat down again. "Then I'll stay and freeze too," he offered with exasperation. "Will that make you happier?"

"No because you do not freeze well or in silence," Tani said crossly. "Go to your warm kiva. But don't just sleep, gossip and gamble . . . offer prayers for more snow and not so much cold. You also should work to write more of the People's story on rock."

"It is too cold to do that now." He held his hands up, wiggling his stiff fingers in her face. "My hands become like ice and they hurt."

Tani acted as though she had not heard him. "Finish the story on rock this winter so that we can take what children and family we have left in Great Cave away to some better place."

"I think we should die here," Storyteller said foolishly.

"Our children and their children have had enough hunger, sickness and dying! They want to go where there is wood and water, where Sun shines warm even in winter. Where our Desert Enemies are few and weak."

"There is no such place!"

"Yes there is," Tani argued. "Remember that before he died, Old Storyteller told you he had visions of green fields of corn, a deep blue river and timber everywhere. Have you forgotten how Old Storyteller said that there were also Deer as thick as summer bugs and piñon nuts so delicious that Rabbit and Squirrel grew fat eating them every fall?"

"No, I have not forgotten."

"Storyteller, listen to me! We must find the place of those visions while we are still strong enough to walk! Do you want to get weak and die in this freezing cave?"

"I am not afraid of death," he said.

"Then think of our children, and their children. Think of what is left of the Raven People! We have no choice but to leave Great Cave and all the other caves. Even the soil on the mesa is dying because it has been used too long. Remember the year we had of good rain and even then how the corn would not grow much taller than your chest?"

"I remember."

"It would not grow because even the Earth of our mesa is tired and wants us to leave. That is how it is telling us to go away!"

"That may be true," Storyteller admitted, feeling unsteady because he was weak from lack of food like all the others. "I will go now to think and pray on this matter."

"The time has passed for thinking and prayer!"

But Storyteller emphatically shook his head. "You should not say that, Tani. Prayers will never stop being important."

"Prayers have done nothing for the People! But you go pray if you want. Smoke, and enjoy your warm kiva while your wife and family freeze!"

Storyteller felt angry and humiliated. He muttered, wishing he could think of a stinging response but knowing that he could not. Besides, he was cold and eager for the warmth and fellowship of his beloved kiva. Was there any evil in that? Of course not! What Tani did not choose to remember was how he had bravely left his own family when little more than a boy so that they could be married. From that day to this, he had lived with Tani's family, in *her* house working *her* fields in order to harvest *her* crops. In that respect, he had little and owned nothing except his clothing, weapons, jewelry and sandals. Only the kivas were owned by the men and each society used them at their pleasure.

During wintertime when it was too cold to hunt or to farm, the men spent most of their time enjoying the warm and secret sanctuary of their kivas. Storyteller was proud that he was the most popular and respected elder in his kiva. Unlike his predecessor, he was an excellent speaker with a good voice and a strong presence. As Cave's honored Enemy Killer who once had even been offered the position of Great Chief, he was considered a great man by his kiva brothers. Storyteller's words were always listened to with respect and serious consideration.

And besides, women and children were sometimes allowed to enter the kivas in order to bring food and water. During those times, they were allowed to linger and enjoy special dances, prayer offerings and sacred rituals. They could not remain or participate. Storyteller knew that rankled women like Tani and caused them to complain loudly each winter.

Without a backward glance and with as much dignity as he could summon, Storyteller strolled over to his kiva and climbed down the ladder. The kiva enveloped him like a warm, somewhat smoky cocoon and he heard the pleasant greetings of his lifelong friends. A gentle hand guided him to his privileged place near the fire but away from the rising smoke. Storyteller bowed his head as if praying until his eyes grew accustomed to the dimness.

The main purpose of his kiva society was religious, but it also focused on much prayer and ceremony against the evil witches. Other kiva societies prayed for rain and good weather, or the return of Deer to the mesas, or perhaps the general health and welfare of the People. At times, all these societies left their kivas to climb to the mesa and visit the still unfinished but very holy Sun Temple where everyone prayed, fasted and danced. In the old days this would happen as often as the full of Moon, but now it occurred far less frequently because most of the kivas had only a few members young or healthy enough to participate.

This was very sad. In Storyteller's kiva, nine men and five youths in training to become men could be found almost any time during the cold of winter. Married men spent at least as much time in the kivas as the bachelors did because they were understood to be a necessary sanctuary against wives who complained too much or too sharply. On any winter night, their floor was packed with snoring men and older boys sleeping warm in their blankets. Unlike the little houses and other above ground rooms owned by the women, kivas enjoyed fresh and smokeless air supplied by a well-placed ventilator shaft. A stone deflector sat between the fire and the ventilator hole so that the society's wood did not burn too fast or hot resulting in even more complaints from the women who collected most of the winter's firewood.

Now, after a suitable amount of prayer and meditation that no witches be present, Storyteller raised his head and favored the room with his gaze, accepting everyone's greetings. Being Storyteller and Great Cave's honored Enemy Killer, Storyteller accepted his role as the most renowned member of his society of Witch Watchers.

His brothers listened for him to speak. Storyteller wiggled his skinny haunches on the circular bench that ringed his kiva and considered what to say. While he was not expected to tell a story every day, he prided himself that he could. Now, his eyes happened to settle on the kiva's sipapu, their symbolic entrance to Middle Earth where many gods lived and through which the People's prayers and spirits always passed after death.

"As you know," he began in his fine and resonant voice, "all the People once lived in Middle Earth and grew in such numbers that they began to quarrel and to steal from each other. There was murder and even the priests began to take the wives of those who were considered less important than themselves. I have told you how Raven was finally able to reach this world and how he brought back a seed from Tree and how the People fed and watered this tree until it grew so tall it reached Upper Earth or what some clans wrongly call, Upper World."

Storyteller lapsed into a protracted silence, as if his mind were receding so far in time that he could visualize the two worlds connected by the Great Tree.

"What I have *not* often spoken of is how the light from the Middle Earth changed into the light of the Upper Earth. This is a very important thing and I can best explain it by telling you of Sun. Sun is our Father and which warms and gives life to our Mother, Earth. As the ancient ones climbed Tree toward the roof of the Middle Earth, Sun guided and protected them. At first, Sun gave them only a little light, as we see now with each dawn and dusk, but this light, though small and weak, seemed very bright and beautiful to the People who had lived in darkness. Sun knew that it could not shine too brightly or the People would be blinded and so created clouds to protect their eyes.

"Higher and higher the People climbed Tree until they began to wonder if Upper Earth was light . . . or dark. Hearing this argument, Sun made Rainbow. The People never had seen anything so beautiful and would have stopped right there on Tree because they were so excited, except Sun then created Thunder, then Lightning and finally Rain."

Storyteller looked around, expecting to see everyone perched with anticipation on their circular bench. He was not disappointed and continued his story. "During the storm, the People became fearful and did not know what to do but then Raven appeared and told them to hurry and climb higher until, finally, they reached Upper Earth."

"What about all the animals left behind in Middle Earth?" a boy nearing manhood asked.

"Many that were evil were left behind to roam in Middle Earth and some of them became witches. When that happened," Storyteller said, eyes touching each man in the kiva, "they were able to fly up to this Middle Earth where they took the form of animals and the People who already had died. That is why it is so hard now to recognize them."

"Can you recognize them?"

"No," Storyteller admitted, recalling how foolish he had been to label the last Storyteller a witch. Soon afterward, he had realized what Tani had long understood, that the man was simply different and afraid to reveal his true but tragic visions, all of which were coming to pass.

Storyteller still shivered whenever he thought about how close he had come to publicly branding that lonely visionary a witch and damning him to banishment or death. If it had not been for Tani's wisdom . . .

"What happened to those good but not strong enough to climb Tree to this world?" another young man asked.

"Raven flew down and carried them on his wings which were then much longer and more powerful. And, after everyone was in this world, he led them to these cliffs and mesas where it was cooler in summer and where there was more game and where the crops would grow whenever Rain fell generously."

Those in the kiva listened intently and considered these words. One of the elders surprised Storyteller by asking, "Why has Raven now forgotten to protect us?"

It was often asked in Great Cave and the question elicited many answers from the priests and from Storyteller. He had answered by saying that Raven was testing the People, making them strong through hardship and prolonged suffering. But on this afternoon, with Tani's words and Old Storyteller's grim prophecies burning in his mind, Storyteller said, "Raven has found a better place to live and wants the People to join him."

The soft crackle of burning wood was the only sound in the kiva for a very long time. Finally, an old friend of Storyteller asked, "Are you sure?"

"Yes. I have given the matter much thought and I believe that, whenever things are bad, Raven will guide us to a better place. He has taken away many already. There are few left now and those strong enough must find Raven again and rebuild our people."

"And what of our Desert Enemies?" another asked with deep concern. "Will Raven guide and protect us on this dangerous journey?"

"He will," Storyteller promised, swallowing hard.

"Are *you* leaving Great Cave?"

"I must," Storyteller decided. "This spring I will lead my family away."

"And leave us who are not strong enough to travel?"

Storyteller suddenly felt very bad, for he knew that he must do this or else his family would die of either hunger or at the hands of their enemies.

"Better some than all," he replied, forcing himself to look from one lifelong friend to another so that he would never forget this place and this moment in time.

After that the kiva was quiet. No one, not even the young, spoke until the next morning when Storyteller left to announce to Tani and his family that they were leaving Great Cave after the cold winter death and during the first warm days of the coming spring.

Twenty-seven

June 29, 1906
Denver, Colorado

"Lisa!" David Quincy shouted as he burst into the editorial offices of the *Denver Daily News*. "Lisa, he *did* it!"

"Did what?" Lisa asked, glancing up from an editorial she was writing about President Theodore Roosevelt being honored as the first American recipient of the Nobel Prize for his role in mediating an end to the Russo-Japanese War.

"Teddy Roosevelt just signed the bill that finally makes our Mesa Verde a National Park!"

"Hooray for Teddy!" Lisa cried, jumping up and allowing herself to be swung around in a full circle by the exuberant Mr. Quincy.

"You had a lot to do with putting the story in the public eye, Lisa. That long-running petroglyph series put Mesa Verde on the map. Why it even brought you recognition in Europe!"

"It was mostly fabrication."

"Almost entirely," David agreed, "but it sure made good copy."

Lisa extracted herself from David's arms, aware that the other employees were staring and would probably end up teasing her unmercifully. But that wasn't really important, compared to this wonderful news. Lisa had fallen in love with Mesa Verde exactly seventeen years ago when she and Andrew first saw Cliff Palace and that love affair had never ended.

"We should celebrate," David insisted. "It's almost quitting time. Come on and I'll buy us dinner and champagne!"

"Now wait a minute," Lisa mildly protested, needing time to adjust to this unexpected but flattering offer. "I'm not sure that Hannibal would approve of me consorting with the competition."

David scoffed. "I'm no competition to the *Denver Daily News!* Everyone in town knows that."

"Oh," Lisa said, raising her eyebrows in question. "How many subscribers do you have now?"

"Paying?"

"Of course."

"Well, only about eight hundred, but . . ."

"You're really growing!"

He blushed because he was proud. The *Denver Eagle* had earned a loyal readership because of its well-researched and written feature stories, like the one exposing Dr. Michael Turner for being a charlatan and a cheat.

Lisa had lost three thousand dollars and her heart to Michael, and her heart had taken a long time to mend. However, had it not been for David's investigation, she would have learned much too late that Michael was still married and had never fathered a daughter named Angie, except in his imagination. Other than the sad truth that he and his father-in-law had been partners participating in an international black market selling priceless Indian artifacts, his entire past had been a fabrication. Thanks to David Quincy, he finally had been caught.

"Lisa, I hope that you're not angry with me after all these years. After all, I did save you from making Dr. Turner a bigamist in addition to all his other sins."

"I was hurt, and always grateful. I just wish that you had worked faster."

"I tried," he said. "Now, how about dinner? We can celebrate Mesa Verde National Park together and I'll tell you what I think that petroglyph really says about those lost Anasazi people."

"And how would you know?" she asked with amusement.

"I'm part Indian, remember?" David winked. "Lisa, I know things about petroglyphs that a pure white-eyes could never understand."

"Is that a fact?"

"Yes, but I'll share my petroglyph secrets over a dinner and champagne."

Lisa didn't need to spend time considering the offer because she always had thought David Quincy bright, industrious and attractive. And who could say what might happen between them if she finally dropped her defenses and admitted that not all men were as devious and dishonorable as Dr. Michael Turner?

"All right," she agreed, rising from her desk, "this article on President Roosevelt's Nobel Prize can wait for tomorrow."

David extended Lisa the crook of his arm. He finally had abandoned his moccasins, but Hopi blood radiated in his beautiful eyes, his absolute fearlessness and his dry, but keen sense of humor.

"As I said, Lisa, I *know* things about petroglyphs."

"Then tell me your secrets," she replied with a half smile, "and we're almost sure to have ourselves a good time."

Quincy actually threw his head back and let out what sounded like a wild Indian war hoop. Lisa didn't know if it was or not, but at least David had captured the full attention of everyone at the *Denver Daily News* and started her laughing again.

Epilogue

The one named Miska, who would be the next Storyteller, was in his prime as he led his small band of Raven People up the great canyon of the caves. Each time they spied another cliff dwelling, they shouted to their lost people but there was never a response. The only sound was that of Raven mocking them from the top of a dead, lightning-burned pine.

"There it is!" Miska finally shouted, pointing upward at Great Cave.

The young men who had been sent from far away to find and reunite the last of the Raven People began to scramble up the familiar trail to Great Cave.

"Patuwa! Brother, answer me!" Miska cried, legs churning and chest heaving as he bounded up the steep canyon wall until he reached the yawning mouth of Great Cave.

The dust on the floor was two inches deep and the cavern was locked in a deathly silence. Miska and his companions clutched their weapons and trembled with fear.

"Miska, we must run from this place because now it belongs to witches!" one of Miska's friends cried. "All the People are dead!"

"Shhh!" Miska ordered, signaling the others to fan out and inspect the city.

Though the air was cool, Miska's skin was clammy. He saw no bodies or bones lying on the stairways or in the courtyards. No sign of a terrible battle and then the looting and slaughter of the old and the weak by their hated Desert Enemies. The pottery and baskets of the women had not been disturbed. Miska hurried to his mother's house and it was just as he remembered, only empty and eerily silent. Miska longed to hear the laughter of playing children, the happy chatter and songs of women as they reduced corn to meal. Even the incessant barking of dogs or the unceasing gobble of turkeys would have reduced him to tears of joy.

But he heard . . . nothing. Nothing but the moan of the canyon wind . . . or perhaps the excited whisperings of witches.

"Patuwa," he breathed, remembering the brother who had been physically unable to leave Great Cave and had volunteered to remain behind with the old, the sick and the dying. "Patuwa!"

Far away, somewhere out in the canyon, Miska heard Raven's raucous call again, and again. He weaved his way through the musty maze that was Great Cave, peering into each house, crossing every courtyard and climbing all the stairs. He desperately wanted to know what had happened to the last of these poor, abandoned Raven People.

Without conscious thought, Miska was drawn to his father's kiva where he stood shaking with dread.

"Miska, don't go down there!" one of Miska's friends pleaded.

"Why?"

"Because that is where the witches will be waiting!"

Miska understood what his friend meant. Storyteller had warned him that, whenever evil defeated good, it always wanted to live like maggots inside its most hated enemies. Kivas had been the religious heart of the People in Great Cave, and so that was where the witches would now live happiest. And *this* particular kiva, once home of the Society of Witch Watchers, would please the witches most of all. But Miska had promised his mother and father that he would find Patuwa, dead or alive. They had prayed for his return so long and they had so little time remaining on Upper Earth.

"I have to go down," Miska heard himself say in a voice he scarcely recognized. He gave up his weapons, knowing that they would be useless against witches.

"If you go down, you will become possessed!"

Miska began to tremble so violently he was no longer sure that he had the strength to descend.

"We should all run away now!" another begged. "We should run from this evil before it is too late!"

Miska locked his hands on the tops of the ladder poles, trying to absorb strength from the wood which had been polished by his father's hands and that of so many other brave members of the Society of Witch Watchers.

To boost his failing courage as he began to climb down, Miska tried to remember how proud he had been the first time he was allowed to enter this sacred kiva where Storyteller and the wise ones loved to pray, to sing and to tell stories.

Halfway down, Miska's hair stood on end. He sucked in his breath, sickened and dizzy with the stench of death burning his nostrils. He paused, gasping for air, feeling the witches swirl around his body. Certain that his legs were about to buckle, he dropped to the floor and then forced himself to release the ladder poles.

Witches screamed, torturing his mind. Miska strained to see but his eyes refused to adjust. And, when they finally did, he howled to see flesh-crusted bones. Shrunken eyes. Yellow and rotting teeth. Patches of hair. Half-eaten leather and turkey feathers. Droppings of ravenous rats and mice.

Miska would never have recognized his brother except for a familiar and distinctive piece of jewelry dangling loosely on wrist bones.

Miska clung to the ladder, fighting for his sanity. Each time he inhaled, he could feel the witches entering his lungs and poisoning his body.

Miska scrambled out of the kiva, taking the rungs two at

a time. When he reached the top, he crawled to the mouth of Great Cave, pale, dazed and shaking.

"We must go now!" he wheezed, trying to cough out the witches.

His friends grabbed his arms and, together, they fled without stopping until they had put Great Cave far behind.

"Look!" one of Miska's friends called, stopping to point at the sky. "See how Raven flies into Great Cave to join the witches!"

Miska saw black Raven disappear into the black maw of the great cavern. He placed his hands over his eyes and wept. A mile deeper in the canyon of the caves, Miska remembered a second promise he had made to his aged parents.

Using his father's well-worn stone chisel, Miska located Story Wall and he added the final entry:

All the mesa and pueblo people have gone southeast to a new land where the crops grow tall, Deer is everywhere and a river flows in every season under the Sun. Among us, only Raven survived, captured and possessed by witches.

We are gone forever from this evil place and we are Raven People no more.

Author's Note

Mesa Verde is one of the most mystical and magical of all our National Parks. I have tried to tell the story of her Anasazi people through the artifacts that would actually have been used during their society's long and successful evolution.

The first of these people arrived somewhere around A.D. 1 and we call them the Basket Makers. They were primarily hunters and gatherers of nuts, insects and seeds. They inhabited Cliff Palace and many other caves but did not build houses or kivas inside them. About A.D. 550, most of the cave dwellers relocated onto the mesa and began to make pottery and take shelter in pit houses. They had turkeys, were farmers of corn, beans and squash and quit hunting with the atlatl to use the far more accurate bow and arrow.

During the Pueblo Period from A.D. 750 to A.D. 1100, Mesa Verde's agriculture was both extensive and sophisticated, requiring vast irrigation systems and large reservoirs to insure that every drop of winter snow melt and summer rain reached the acres of thirsty summer crops. The pit houses were replaced by pueblos characterized by many small connecting rooms and flat roofs. "Kivas" became the heart of the religious community. Special places of worship like Sun Temple were extremely important ceremonial sites. During this time infant cradleboards became hard, and against them the heads of Anasazi babies were tightly bound so that the back of their skulls became flattened. This "beauty fad" did not last for more than a few centuries and is not found among the skeletal remains of latter-day cliff dwellers.

The People flourished during this mesa top period. Their "Desert Enemies" were few and conflict was rare. The traditional black-on-white painted Mesa Verde pottery became beautiful and the new corrugated or layered effect used for cooking pots was a definite improvement because it facilitated heat transfer. Prize macaws from Central America were brought north and their colorful feathers have been unearthed at Mesa Verde to offer indisputable evidence of the extremely active and extensive trade taking place. The Mesa Verde people would have swapped their handsome pottery, yucca baskets and soft deer hides for precious goods like silver, shells, turquoise, obsidian and cotton.

The years A.D. 1100 to 1300 were the zenith of Mesa Verde's long and vigorous habitation. During this time, Cliff Palace, Sun Temple, Long House and the four-story Square Tower House, as well as hundreds of other magnificent dwellings, were constructed. Over seven centuries later, they remain intact, not only because of the protection of their deep sandstone alcoves, but also because of their excellent engineering, knowledge gained by the repeated and hard lessons of trial and error. Their soaring towers, pinnacles, and graceful stairways and balconies still merit the envy of modern-day architects and bespeak a people who took immense pride in their buildings and beloved kivas.

Why, then, did the Mesa Verde peoples as well as so many other great Anasazi communities like those found at Chaco Canyon, Hovenweep, Canyon de Chelly, Salmon, Keet Seel and even the Grand Canyon abandon their homes after centuries of prodigious labor?

From this novelist's point of view, it would have been most dramatic to create a climactic battle pitting the Raven Peoples against a superior force of invading Desert Enemies. But archaeological facts refute this outcome. There is no evidence of the annihilation of an entire cliff-dwelling society. However, dendrology, which is the analysis of tree rings, suggests that the People suffered a devastating drought between the years A.D. 1275 and 1300. This severe and prolonged drought, coupled with the eventual depletion of the mesa soil, firewood and wild game combined to force the cliff dwellers south, probably into the Rio Grande Valley and even beyond. Their present descendants are thought to be the Zuni and the Hopi, whose religion and architecture may well have begun with the Anasazi.

Richard Wetherill and Charlie Mason were the first to discover Mesa Verde, just as in this novel. The entire Wetherill family became very active excavating and selling artifacts for profit, but did their best to minimize excavation damage and always preferred to sell to museums and historical societies rather than to private collectors. One notable exception was the sale of many artifacts to the Swedish nobleman, Gustaf Nordenskiold, who had them sent to Europe. Nordenskiold gave something in return, though. He wrote an excellent book, *The Cliff Dwellers of Mesa Verde* and took over 150 extraordinary photographs of the early Mesa Verde ruins. These photographs offer the best insight of how the cliff dwellings appeared soon after their discovery and before their excavation and later reconstruction.

In this work, Andrew and Lisa Cannaday, Dr. Michael Turner and David Quincy are, of course, fictional characters. However, Virginia McClurg and Lucy Peabody were very instrumental in the fight to preserve Mesa Verde. The later excavation and preservation efforts of Dr. Jesse Fewkes, an archaeologist from the Smithsonian Institution as well as Park Superintendent Jesse Nusbaum, were monumental and farsighted.

My "Cliff Wall" and the legacy of the last Storyteller are based on an exceptionally large and well-preserved petroglyph found within easy hiking distance from Spruce Tree House. During a research visit, I was informed by one of Mesa Verde National Park's rangers that no one can exactly decipher its bold message, but that the petroglyph depicts the Anasazi history of birth, hunting, gathering, farming and of dreams won . . . and lost. The petroglyph chronicles the history of a determined people who struggled out of the blistering lowland deserts to reach the high, cooler mesas and then to flourish for more than twelve centuries before being forced to abandon their beloved pueblos and soaring cliff palaces.